BLOOD
FEUD

BLOOD FEUD

THE DIVINE VAMPIRE HEIRS, BOOK FOUR

by

GINNA MORAN

SUNNY PALMS PRESS

ISBN 978-1-942073-35-2 (soft cover)

This is a work of fiction. All of the characters, organizations, and events portrayed in this novel are either products of the author's imagination or are used fictitiously.

Cover design by Silver Starlight Designs
Cover images copyright Depositphotos

For Inquiries Contact:
Sunny Palms Press
9663 Santa Monica Blvd Suite 1158
Beverly Hills, CA 90210, USA
www.sunnypalmspress.com
www.GinnaMoran.com

For those who fight for love.

MANIPULATED

"AGAIN, ORLANDO? YOU ASSHOLE!" SWINGING my arm out, I sucker punch Orlando in the nose. I don't know what he expected coming to Haven Springs again, but I thought I made it clear to him that I'm pissed the eff off. He betrayed me. He scared me. He ruined everything I had going for me with the guys I love and would do anything for.

Blood sprays across me, and I scramble away and hit my back on a tree. My mind spins with a million thoughts. I'm so confused. He's messing with my mind again, and there's nothing I can do about it.

He cups his nose. "Damn it, Jewel. I'm giving you another chance to see reason."

"Get away from me. You can't keep coming here. It's not going to change things." I grab a branch from the ground and swing it at him as he comes closer. "You can't mess with my head anymore. You know I hate that shit."

My mind feels like it's never going to recover. I'm still missing pieces, missing memories and information he stole from me. All I remember in this moment is that without him, I'll die. I don't even know why exactly. I've been changed, altered, long before Katherine Duchanne used her venom on me. Before I triggered Kingston's by accident. Before...my head throbs as I grasp to remember the last few days—a week? Two? I'm not even sure. All I know is that I'm trapped in a place I don't want to be without Austin, Diego, and Kingston. Donor Life Corp sentenced me to what feels like a life imprisonment in a community that I'm pretty friggin' sure hates my guts. But I don't know for sure. I can't remember leaving my room. I'm in a constant state of falling asleep and waking up here to find Orlando.

I cover my eyes with my hands. "Just leave."

Orlando ignores me and closes the space. He cups my face in his hands and leans into me so close that I feel his breath blowing the loose strands of hair hanging down my cheeks. "No, Jewel. You know I can't."

Tears burn my eyes. "Please, just don't mess with my mind."

"I do what I have to."

I try to knee him in the groin, but he jerks back. "Liar.

You didn't have to do any of this. I was fine. Happy. You ruined everything."

"You were in danger."

"The Divines love me."

He raises an eyebrow. "Do they? Then why aren't they here? It's been two weeks, and they have yet to show their faces."

My chest clenches. So it *has* been two weeks. Five visits so far from Orlando since and the same bullshit every time. And right now? I hate that he asks the question on my mind. Where are Kingston, Diego, and Austin? "They have shit to deal with. I know it." I hope that's it. A part of me fears something happened to them. They wouldn't let some stupid rule about vampires not being allowed in Haven Springs stop them from coming for me. I remember their promise not to abandon me.

"You hope."

I try so hard not to cry. It seems like that's all I've been doing since waking up in an unfamiliar room. The only time I've left my cousins'—my new home—in Haven Springs is because Orlando has had Hayden drag me out. Why they're working together? I don't know. If I did know, Orlando forces me to forget. It makes me hate him more by the second, though I know I haven't always. Small fragments of my memory break free again, and I can envision all the times I met him in the shadows, even times without my dad.

I ball my hands into fists and attempt to punch him away. "Just leave me alone. I don't want you coming here. I don't need you anymore. Don't you understand? Whatever friendship we had was destroyed the second you decided to play these games with the Divines."

"Friendship?" His eyes flash silver, and his lips twitch into a frown. Something familiar sneaks up on me—another memory—and I feel like I've had this conversation before. Actually, I know I have. Maybe last night. Maybe the night before. Maybe every night since I was forced here by Donor Life Corp.

Reaching out, he touches my cheek. "I understand that you've fallen in love with a life you think is better than the one you were born into. And I can't blame you for that. What Noah forced on you was unfair."

"My dad did the best he could."

"He could've—he should've—done better. All he had to do was stick to the agreement." Orlando's voice comes out barely a whisper, his eyes breaking from mine to stare off into the distance.

I flare my nostrils, fury pouring over me. "An agreement neither of you consulted me over."

"You don't understand what is best for you."

"Like you do?" I ask, peering around the dark grove. I don't know why I bother to look for a way to escape. I'm powerless to the vampire who thinks I belong to him. Who thinks I need him. "If you knew what was best, you'd have never taken my dad. You wouldn't have matched with my best friend and changed her. You wouldn't have let Brayla kill him."

"That was an unfortunate accident."

"Was it? You were quick to swoop in to try to take me from my home. You took my sister."

He releases me and turns away. "I won't lie to you. It was rather convenient. But I also underestimated Donor Life Corp. Mitchell's need for power. He hasn't changed his ways from the back-world, you know. The only reason you're here is because he sees the flaw he created by allowing his heirs to share you for far too long. They're as possessive as he is."

I groan. "You asshole."

Tipping his head back, Orlando stares at the sky through the trees. He doesn't meet my gaze, even though I try to vaporize him with my glower. "I'm only being honest. I hadn't expected the outcome, either. But at least I was right about them in the end. They're Divines. They don't see you as I do. They have no idea what an incredible being you've transformed into."

"Incredible? I'm—" I can't even manage to spit out the words.

"Dangerous. Lethal. The perfect companion to my coven like I've imagined since before The Divide. You know I've waited a long, long time for you, precious Jewel. Don't think I'll give up on our future so easily. I'm patient."

"Obsessive."

"We had an agreement."

"We had nothing. You messed it all up. I can barely stand to look at you, Orlando." Tears burn my eyes, another dozen memories breaking free in my mind. "I trusted you."

"I've done nothing but care for you. Assured that you'd survive. Guaranteed your freedom."

I close my eyes and turn away. "I don't need you anymore. You can't hold me to some agreement you had with my dad."

"It far exceeded your father."

Curiosity gets the best of me, and I stop struggling to break free. Instead, I resort to pressing my hands into his taut chest to get him to take a small step back. His closeness, his weird familiarity, digs into me in a way that leaves me feeling like my world is spinning out of control.

"Like I'm going to believe you," I manage to say. "Every time you tell me something, you just make me forget. Don't think I'm stupid and naïve. I'm not the sheltered girl my dad made me. I know better now. I know how vampires act. I've been in your world for months."

"You've only known the world from the edges, Jewel. Your matches assured to keep you as isolated as your father had. All you know is how the Divines act and what they want you to know. You have a lot to learn."

"So what? Maybe it's what I want because they'd never

hurt me like you have."

Orlando tightens his jaw, searching my face. "You're hurting now. I can see it in your eyes."

I try to turn expressionless, keeping my gaze trained on the rise and fall of his chest, as he plays on my insecurities. His heartbeat sounds fainter than what I'm used to, and it sparks worry inside me along with a whole bunch of other emotions that make my eyes stupidly water more. "My pain is from you."

A soft hand touches my shoulder, but I don't look up. I can't. Orlando might have broken into my mind and told me to remember him, but I can't forget everything else that he's done since he realized my dad was going to skip out on their deal.

My mind might be foggy, but the longer I stand here in this forest, the more I remember.

I can't stop hating myself for even thinking that my dad was going to trade me to Orlando to get my family out of Dark Terrace Ranch. But I still don't know exactly what he planned on the day he told me he was leaving the city. Had he told me, I could've better prepared. I could've done something more. At least I keep telling myself that.

Because now, along with the fact that I lost everything I had with Kingston, Austin, and Diego, I grieve for the man who did his best to raise me in this messed up world.

"Forgive me, Jewel," Orlando says, the softness of his voice only making things worse. "You must know that everything I do is in your best interest."

Yeah-friggin'-right. "Then why not let me remember permanently? This isn't enough time. What you're doing hurts me. I can't live like this."

He frowns for a split second before tightening his jaw. Giving me a long, intense look, he drinks in my face like he can read my thoughts if he stares at me long enough. "I'm sorry. I will not risk leaving your mind open."

I grip the front of his shirt, keeping space between us. If my hands weren't between us, he might try to cage my head in with his arms. "Why? You obviously think no one's coming for me."

His eyes flash silver. It's enough for me to know that he doesn't actually believe that. He knows my guys will come. "I'll do it, but you have to agree to come with me."

Like hell I will. "I told you I can't leave my cousins."

"They're not part of the deal. It's too risky." He obviously doesn't know me like he thinks he does. To even assume I'd be okay with leaving my cousins here if I'm going anywhere that isn't back with my guys is friggin' crazy. I don't care about the risk he claims I face by staying here. I have more than enough hope and faith to help me through this until I can go home to the Divinity Estate again.

I shake my head, my dark hair pelting my cheeks in the process. "Then that's a definite eff no. I'm staying here and waiting for the Divines to come for me."

Orlando blurs away from me and punches the trunk of

a nearby tree, splintering the wood. The loud crack resonates through the air, hurting my ears, and I use my hands to muffle the noise as my super hearing chooses now to work, triggered by my fear.

Silver blinks in his blue eyes, and he looks ready to throw me over his shoulder and take off with me. I don't know why he doesn't, but I don't question it. Instead, I inch away from my spot and look for an opening in the trees. I can't outrun him for long, but if I can get out in the open, he might not follow.

Silently counting to three, I dash away and run toward the glowing lights of the community a few hundred feet away. Branches snap behind me as Orlando moves at a human speed to follow. A figure blurs in front of me, and relief washes through me. I knew my guys would come for me.

"Jewel," Orlando calls from behind me. "Stop."

"No!" I yell.

"Jewel."

Strong hands grip my shoulder, spinning me around. I screech out and swing my fists, doing everything I can to stop Orlando from locking his hands on me.

"Help!" I know better than to scream out. The last thing I need is to send the community into a panic, but I know what Orlando wants to do now, and I'll fight as hard as I can to stop him from breaking into my mind.

"Diego," I call, seeing the blurring figure in front of me

again. "Austin, Kingston. Over here!"

Cool fingers cover my mouth, stopping my words from sounding out. I stomp my bare feet, striking Orlando's boots, but he doesn't let me go. I no longer see the blurring figure in the trees either. Maybe I never saw anything.

Tears burn my eyes. Brayla saunters through the trees from the direction I thought my guys were searching for me. It wasn't them after all. They're not here. It was Brayla.

"Lover, we have to go." Brayla's soft voice trickles to me. "We only have a couple of minutes. Hayden's been paid."

"I'll meet you at the wall. There's still one more thing I need to take care of with Jewel," Orlando says.

I thrash against his hold. "No, please," I mumble against his fingers.

Brayla steps a few feet closer. "Do you need help?"

Orlando adjusts me in his arms. "No, she's still rather upset. She thinks the Divines are coming for her."

Brayla hums sadly, the low pitch of her voice, the pity in it, annoying the hell out of me. "She's never going to agree to come if she believes they'll get her. You know that, right?"

"Even so." His breath tickles my ear.

"She thinks she loves them."

I elbow Orlando. "I don't think. I know. And they love me too. They promised me forever."

Orlando groans deep in his throat. "Those thoughts

will keep you miserable."

"I don't care," I snap, fighting against my body reacting to Orlando's closeness, trying to sink against him while my mind wants to fight.

He sighs. "They don't deserve your loyalty or love. They don't deserve you."

"They do." I don't know what else I can say. No one knows my guys like I do. No one understands our relationship. "They're my perfect matches. They'd do anything for me."

"You mean if Mitchell allows it."

I jerk in Orlando's arms again, and he finally lets me go. Brayla frowns at me, keeping her distance. I scramble to put space between me and them and trip over my own feet to land hard on my knees.

Pushing up, I manage to get back to my feet to face the two vampires. Unfamiliar emotions—something that looks like amusement on Orlando's and pity on Brayla's—cross their faces, pissing me off even more.

I swipe my hands across my cheeks, yanking the hair veiling my vision away. "You know nothing. It's me who keeps them following Mitchell's orders. They'd leave him for me. They'd face the shadows. They wanted to already."

"I don't believe you."

"Break into my mind and ask me."

Orlando stares at me, twisting his lips to the side, drinking me in like he can see the thoughts spinning in my mind. The fact that I gave him permission to ask me in the most invasive way possible proves that I'm not lying. He knows it. "If that's true, it changes everything."

I gasp in small breaths of air, my hands trembling. His words freak me out. "What's that supposed to mean?"

"Nothing for you to worry about just yet."

"Tell me," I say, pressing my lips together.

Orlando rushes me and lifts me off my feet. The world blurs as he carries me deeper into the orchard. I land on my back in the dirt, my breath heaving, fear pouring through me. Orlando flashes his fangs and bites his wrist.

"No, plea—"

Blood drips over my mouth, and my body reacts, tensing and buzzing with the rush of his annoyingly delicious blood. The sweet flavor, with hints of something spicy like cinnamon, coats my tongue and sends tingles through me. My mind screams at my body to quit licking my lips, but I can't. Orlando's blood triggers a hunger—a need inside me—that I can't ignore.

"You'll feel better the more you drink, precious Jewel," he whispers, holding my stare like all the other times I've drunk his blood, the taste of it stirring the memories. "You'll also forget that I've come here. Forget everything. You'll no longer feel the pain of missing the Divines. You won't remember anything that's happened to you since the day before your father left you."

"What?" I ask, trying to break his stare.

He leans in more to me, so close that all I can see is the silver flashing in his eyes. "Forget about the Divines. If they're deserving of you, then you'll remember."

Shadows edge my vision with his words. I try to open my mouth to beg him to stop, but my body lies placidly, unwilling to obey me while he captures me in his stare and opens my mind.

"You are Jewel Jordan from Dark Terrace Ranch. You're afraid of the shadows," he says. "Repeat it."

Pain explodes behind my eyes. "I'm Jewel Jordan of Dark Terrace Ranch, and I'm afraid of the shadows."

"If the Divines come for you, you will not know who they are. You will be afraid until they're worthy."

I silently stare, my head pounding.

"Orlando, what are you doing?" Brayla asks.

He growls without breaking my hold. "Helping her."

"By stealing all her memories?"

"She won't survive this place with her love of vampires."

"What about the Divines? What if they come?"

"I'm counting on it. They'll prove whether or not they're loyal to Jewel. If they deserve her, they'll get through to her."

"And if they don't?"

"Doesn't matter. She'll be mine either way."

TRUSTING A VAMPIRE

"OVER HERE, FALLON," A SOFT voice calls, dragging me from the dark recesses of my mind.

"Oh, God. Is she okay?" Dana asks.

I shift on the dirt and roll over, my body aching with a pain that radiates through me. Everywhere hurts. My head, my skin, my muscles, my limbs. Tears burn my eyes, and I blink them away, digging my hands into the ground to push up to my knees.

"Jewel, jeez. Let us help you." Gentle fingers lace around my arms, and Fallon pulls me to my feet. "What are you doing out here? Have you been here all day? You missed your meeting with the council."

I wobble, my body begging me to sit my ass back

down, but I stumble toward the nearest tree and lean on the rough bark for support. Squeezing my eyes shut, I take a few deep breaths, settling my nerves while trying to get my shit together. I'm so confused. Why am I outside?

I lick my dry lips. "Help me walk. We have to hurry."

"Hurry where?" Dana asks, joining Fallon at my side. They each wrap an arm around me, helping to support my weight.

I clear my throat, peering around the dark grove. "Home. You guys are crazy for even being out here. You could've been drained. Did Ramona send you? She's going to be in so much trouble."

"Drained? Ramona? What are you talking about?" Fallon stops in her tracks to swivel to face me.

"The shadow dwellers. They're coming. Come on. Let's go. Keep your heads down and maybe they'll leave us alone. You guys are young and off limits, but you know they don't really care." I jerk both my cousins forward and drag them along with me as I jet toward the concrete path.

Fear speeds up my heart, and I bow my head in an attempt not to look at the world around us. If I hunker down, I might still look under eighteen. They couldn't possibly know for sure. It might be my only saving grace.

Whispers trickle through the air, sending fear through me. Vampires are everywhere. Too many to distinguish from the hushed noises radiating around us. I can hear the sound of their feet, but I can't see them. They're hiding. I can feel it deep in my bones.

Dana pulls me to a stop. "Jewel, I think you're confused."

"I am," I say, rubbing my fingers into my temples. I've never been more confused. Something happened. I know it. But I can't remember what. I'd never willingly miss curfew. Maybe I stepped into a shadow and... I touch my hands to my neck, fear washing through me at the pain erupting under my fingers. I've been bitten. Shit. I've heard stories of it happening to curfew breakers—getting bitten and released—but it's rare. Dad said most die without a night pass.

Fallon squeezes my fingers. "Then take a breath and focus on me."

I can't. My eyes flick to gaze at the night around us. I got so friggin' lucky. I can't believe I've been bitten and released in a strange part of the city. I can't even remember how I got here. "Do you know what happened to me? I think I've been attacked. Can you check my neck? My dad's going to be so pissed." I bring my hands to my face and notice my missing donor bracelet. And then I notice more bite marks. "Fuck. They stole my bracelet. Do you know what that means?" I'm screwed. Dad's going to have to donate extra on my behalf to get me a new one because I can't give more blood yet, especially if I've been attacked.

Opening and closing her mouth, Dana gapes at me a moment, trailing her eyes over me. It's then that I notice something about her seems off. She looks different. Healthier. And wearing...makeup? What the hell?

"Jewel, you're confused," Dana repeats, frowning.

"Is that vampire blood on her shirt?" Fallon leans close to her sister and presses her lips to her ear.

I peer down and gasp. "Vampire blood? What the actual hell? How do you even know what that looks like? And why am I out here in my night clothes? If my dad sees me like this, I'm doomed. We're so getting in trouble for missing curfew. My dad's going to—"

Fallon grabs my cheeks and gets in my face, peering into my eyes. "Jewel, where do you think we are?"

I gawk at her. She looks so pretty too. Mrs. Peppers must've cut her hair like she wanted. Maybe that's where the two of them got the makeup from. Mrs. Peppers has been a bit nicer lately since...

"Jewel, focus. Tell me where you think we are." Fallon sucks her top lip between her teeth, her forehead wrinkling.

I swallow and peer past her. "Dark Terrace Ranch. Where else would we be? Where's Ramona, anyway? Is she okay? God, she wasn't with me, right?" I absently rub my arm, feeling the ache caused by the bite marks. "Why can't I remember what happened?"

"Shit," Dana whispers to Fallon. "Something's wrong with her. You don't think Donor Life Corp..."

"They promised her," Fallon replies, tugging on the ends of her dark hair.

"But look at her. Someone snuck in and messed with her head."

I frown and pull away from my cousins. "You guys suck at whispering, you know. What are you even talking about?"

My cousins look at each other, speaking without actually saying the words. I know that look anywhere. Me and Ramona do it all the time. And whatever it is they're silently conversing about involves me.

"Tell me what's going on right now," I say, crossing my arms. "You guys know what happened to me, don't you?"

Fallon grabs me by the arm and tugs me along with her. "Jewel, come on. Let's get you home, and we'll explain."

But I don't want to wait. I want to know why the hell I'm out here in an oversized T-shirt with supposedly vampire blood all over it. Or why... My stomach clenches and burns, the pain enough to send me clutching my middle. If Fallon wasn't gripping onto me, I'd fall to my knees.

"Shit, you need to back up," I say, yanking my hand back. "Something's wrong with me." If I was bit, what if I caught the plague? Donor Life Corp is strict for a reason. They say we've been vaccinated, but there's no possible way to know for sure. My dad said things could change just like they did before. We're never really safe.

"We know that, Jewel. That's why we're trying to get you home." Dana takes her place at my other side and locks her fingers to my arm.

"I need to go to the medical center," I argue.

Both my cousins pull me forward through the trees and toward an unfamiliar path. "Not yet. We need to make a call first."

"A call? How are you two so calm—" My eyes bulge. "What in the actual hell?" I freeze in my tracks, gawking at the row of identical houses stretching into a neighborhood straight from a friggin' classic movie with white fences and green grass. Flower bushes and trimmed hedges. Shutters.

"Ah, shit. Are we in a restricted zone?" I ask, searching our surroundings for the vampires I hear louder the closer we get to the houses. Their voices hum over the trickling of—what is that noise? Water? I lick my lips, suddenly dying of thirst.

"Jewel, it's going to be okay. We're going to go home and get this all sorted out," Dana says. "Just keep moving, and try not to freak out. You're safe."

"Safe? But the vampires. I hear them. And where the hell are we? Where is the city?" I yank away from my cousins and spin around.

"Jewel—"

"Why is there blood on my shirt?" I ask, my panic bringing my mind back to focus on my appearance. "And the dirt. Fuck. We don't get to bathe until next week."

My cousins don't respond, looking at me with their own panic crossing their faces. "Jewel, you—"

Pain explodes inside me again, and I clutch my knees. My stomach twists and turns, my head spinning. I can't catch my breath.

And then I throw up.

I stare at the dark liquid on the concrete in front of me. "Is that blood?"

"Oh, no," Fallon whispers.

"Shit balls." I turn my attention up to look at my cousins. They take an automatic step away, freaking me the hell out with the fear in their eyes.

Their hearts pick up pace in a race against each other, and pain burns through me again. No. No. No.

"Jewel—"

"I can hear your hearts," I whisper. "And the pain in my stomach...the blood."

Dana straightens her shoulders. "It's not what you think."

"I've caught the plague." I know it. This proves it. Dad was right about it not going away. "Shit. You guys need to run—"

Something grabs me from behind, yanking me off my feet. I screech out and flail, doing my best to fight off whoever holds me. A cool hand slides through my hair and presses my mouth into a muscular shoulder, suppressing my screams. The world blurs, spinning me around, making my head hurt worse.

One second I'm outside with my cousins, and in the

next, my back hits something soft and bouncy. I struggle to comb my messy hair from my face to glance around a large, luxurious room I've never seen before. I scramble back a few feet, gripping at the comforter and pillows, only to move too far that I fall back.

Strong arms catch me and cradle me, a strange, pleasant scent tickling my nose as...

"Holy shit balls!" I scream and ram my palms into the rock-hard chest of a friggin' scarily attractive vampire. And massive. Oh, God. I don't stand a chance. He's the one who attacked me. He had to have been. Now he's come back to finish me off.

"Jewel, beautiful. Hey, it's okay," the guy says, setting me back on the bed instead of tearing into my throat like I expect him to do with his fangs peeking from beneath his full lips. I can't stop staring at his mouth. Or him. What is wrong with me? He doesn't look like a normal shadow dweller, is what. It weirds me out how hot I think he is.

I suck in a few sharp breaths. "Where did you take me? Who are you? Please, don't bite me. I'm a registered donor...I think." Shit, I don't have my bracelet. But on my other wrist rests a pretty, sparkling sapphire and diamond bracelet. "Oh, God. What is this? I swear I don't know how I got it. Is this why I'm here? I didn't steal it. I—fuck me. Something's wrong. I caught the plague, didn't I? Please don't hurt me."

The vampire's brows furrow, his gray eyes glassing over

for a split second. "Why would I do that?" The pout crossing his face does something strange to my insides, and I nearly throw myself at him to hug him.

I clench my hands to my chest. "I don't know. You tell me. I obviously caught the plague. I think I'm turning. Did you do this to me?"

"You're not turning." The guy straightens his back, peering at me with his intimidating, friggin' ginormous height. Sheesh.

"I'm not?" I ask.

He shakes his head.

I've never seen anyone like him. He's so tall that if he raised his arms, he could touch the ceiling. And he does just that. Stretching up, he tilts his head back and blinks his eyes a few times while revealing his muscular stomach to me. I can't take my eyes away from him. He's nothing like the vampires I'm used to. He hasn't even flashed his fangs in a snarl at me yet.

I shift as my body starts to relax, the threat of being devoured seemingly gone. At least for now, according to my slowing heartbeat, though his picks up speed, out beating mine. Whoa. It's such a strange and almost comforting thing to hear.

The guy turns his attention back to me and links his fingers through his brown hair.

So much for my heart. It chooses now to thrash about once more, threatening to crash through my ribcage to drop on the mattress. But not out of fear. Friggin' A. My body does all sorts of weird things under the intensity of the vampire's gorgeous eyes. What am I even thinking?

I squirm, peering around the tidy room, my nerves shot. "Then what are we doing here? If you plan to kill me, can you just make it quick or whatever?"

The guy raises his eyebrows, his lips tightening into a line. He swallows and clears his throat. "Really, beautiful? Not even going to give a fight? I taught you better than that."

It's my turn to blink in confusion. "Um, I'm pretty damn sure I've never seen you in my life. I'd remember."

"Can I sit down?" he asks, inching closer.

"Do I have a choice?"

He nods. "Always with me."

"Then no."

I'd think I just slapped the guy with my response. Who knew vampires could be so pouty? His lips puff out, crinkling his chin, and he spins and faces the door to get me to stop looking at him.

I half expect him to leave, but all he does is reach into his pocket and pull out a small black device. The wall of the room lights up, and I take his sudden distraction as my chance to get the hell out of this place. I don't care how hot he is. He's a vampire. He will eventually get hungry and devour me.

"Where is she?" a smooth, deep voice echoes through

the room.

Two more vampires appear on the projection, and I scoot to the edge of the bed and plant my feet on the pristine white carpet.

"Someone got to her," the vampire says, making me look over my shoulder at him.

"What do you fucking mean someone got to her?" The abrupt, loud voice startles me, and I trip over a pair of tennis shoes and face plant on the floor. "Is she okay?"

Strong hands hook around my waist and pull me back up, and the guy sets me on the bed again. "Physically, yes. But she...doesn't remember me." The vampire gulps and clears his throat again.

I make a second attempt to creep to the window, this time carefully monitoring my feet to assure I don't stumble again.

"What do you mean, Diego?" the first voice I heard asks.

The vampire, Diego, groans. "Dana and Fallon found her unconscious in the grove outside their house. She was disoriented. Still is. They think she might have been gone all day. They thought she finally decided to meet the council."

Their house? My cousins have a house? And how the hell do these vampires know my cousins?

"Let me see her," the voice says.

I cringe and rush to the window. Kicking the screen, I

manage to get one leg out before a muscular arm blocks my way. Diego leans down, staring at me with his stormy eyes full of a bunch of unreadable emotions. His mouth refuses to do anything besides pout, and his eyes glass over again in concern.

"Kingston and Austin would like to speak to you, Jewel. If that's okay," Diego says, ignoring the fact that he interrupted my escape attempt.

"Do I have a choice?" It worked the last time I asked, so might as well try again.

"Come the fuck on, babe! You better talk to me," the louder of the two vampires says.

I twist my lips and glance from Diego and to the glowing screen on the wall. Holy friggin' hotness. Now that I have to look, I can't help studying how attractive the vampires on the screen are. Even scowling. Because the one on the left with a gaze darker than a night sky narrows his eyes at me.

"I mean it, babe," the guy says. He has the nerve to point at me.

I heave a breath. "Don't call me that, dude."

He makes a weird noise, his eyes softening. "Fuck, Diego. Fix her. And before I get there. We're heading out now."

"But the risk of you two coming here—"

"Is worth it," the other vampire says. His green eyes dart back and forth like he's searching for something. Maybe just me.

Midnight Eyes leans closer into the camera. "Yeah, we don't care if it's your night." He turns his attention to me. "Babe, when I get there, I'm going to ravish the hell out of you. You promised you'd never forget your first and true body match."

My mouth falls agape.

"Kingston, shut up," the blond says. "You're going to freak her out."

He flashes his fangs. "She loves when I talk to her like that."

"Fuck no, I don't. And no way in hell will you get anywhere near me," I snap, my cheeks warming. "I don't want any of your...ravishing." I frown as I repeat Kingston's words.

Shit, saying it out loud totally betrays the weird softness that overcomes my voice. Tingles prickle over my body at even the thought of being in the same room as the guy—and whoa. Something is seriously up with me.

Diego chuckles, flashing the most stunning smile ever. At least someone's amused by the asshole's suggestion that we do something I never even considered doing in my life. "Small miracles," Diego whispers under his breath. He looks at the projection again. "Just hurry up. I'll see what I can do before you get here, but I'm not accessing her mind unless she allows it. I won't force her into it."

"You better allow it, babe," Kingston says, pointing at

me again.

"Be brave, okay, Jewel? You can trust us. We're your perfect matches," the blond, who I think Diego called Austin, says. "We'll be there soon to sort this all out."

The line disconnects, and Diego slides the com device into his pocket and turns his attention to me. We stare at each other in silence, him standing still under my gaze, and me fidgeting as he drinks me in.

My poor body can barely control itself, and I squirm and shift, breaking his gaze. "Please stop."

"Stop what? I'm not doing anything," he says.

"Stop looking at me like that. Like you're hungry. I already donate the max amount of blood to Donor Life Corp." My voice comes out just as softly. "And you need to let me go. I need to find my cousins. They could be—"

A light tap on the door draws my attention from the serious vampire, and he glides across the room so quickly that I miss him moving. I startle and grab a pillow, holding it in front of me protectively, half expecting the two guys from the projection to come barging in.

But it's my cousins.

Dana slides past Diego, offering him a smile. "You didn't tell us you were coming."

"Tonight was the first time I could get away. I was visiting Midnight Valley and...it doesn't matter. I'm here now," Diego says, glancing at me. "How long was she missing?"

"I wasn't missing. You kidnapped me." I glower at him. "And possibly gave me the plague."

Diego sighs. "There is no such thing as the Blood Hunger Plague. You're not transitioning into a vampire."

Fallon gives me a once-over. "You sure, Diego? She's covered in blood, which might not be all vampire. Was freaking out about being hungry." God, I still want to know how she knows what vampire blood looks like.

He nods. "I'm positive. She's hungry because..." His voice trails off as he stops himself from speaking freely. I wonder if it's because of my cousins or because of me. "She's acting like this because someone manipulated her mind. Do you remember anything weird happening? When did you notice her gone?"

My cousins frown at each other, and then Dana says, "Not until near sundown. We didn't even know something had happened."

"She left a note on her bed that had said she was going for a morning walk. We had assumed she went straight to her meeting with the council, but Mr. Barton called and said she didn't show. We thought maybe you guys came for her, but we know you'd inform us." Fallon doesn't look at me while she says it, talking about me like I'm not even here.

"Then I thought maybe...she got tired of waiting and tried to climb the wall and got lost trying to run away," Dana adds. "I mean, we wouldn't blame her. She cries herself to sleep. Hasn't even left this room except for the few nights we've found her on the porch. She won't talk to us much."

What is she talking about? I scrunch my nose, peering around the room again. Nothing here belongs to me. I don't live here. They're messing with me. This guy must've gotten to my cousins. They're young. They don't know any better. "What the actual hell? I talk to you girls all the time. And I leave the apartment every day to assist my dad or hang out with Brayla."

Dana swivels to look at me. "She also thinks we are in Dark Terrace Ranch."

"We are," I say. "You know we can't leave the city without a permit and those are expensive. That's why my dad only got one for himself to leave tomorrow night."

All three of them shake their heads, and it's Diego who says, "No, beautiful. You haven't lived in Dark Terrace Ranch in months. This is Haven Springs. Your dad is...isn't here."

"Haven Springs? You're shitting me. That's impossible. Haven Springs doesn't allow vampires within the walls." I scramble to get to my feet, rushing toward the door. "If my dad isn't here, then where is he? Does he know about this? I mean, how the hell do you two even know this guy?" I stare expectantly at Dana and Fallon, who look at Diego for a second.

And then they both sniffle. The looks my cousins give me send my heart sliding into my stomach. Without them having to say anything, I know something is even more wrong than it already is. My breathing comes in pants, and I stumble back to the bed and cover my eyes with my hands.

"Jewel, we're sorry," Dana says, plopping down to hug me. "But something happened."

"He got caught, didn't he?" I ask, swallowing the burning in my throat. "They murdered him."

"I'm sorry," Fallon repeats, holding my hand.

I choke up, my chest hurting as much as it used to after my mom died. "Where's Ramona? I need to talk to her. I need to be with her."

Both my cousins start sobbing, setting me off. I'm so confused. I just saw my dad. I swear I did. He told me he wasn't leaving until tomorrow, and that he would come back for us once everything was settled. He—

"Jewel, can you look at me?" Diego's soft voice prods at something deep inside me, and I can't resist opening my eyes. Slowly lifting his hand, he grazes his fingers along my cheek, smearing the tears away. "I know you're scared and confused, but I want to help you. Will you let me?"

"Please, Jewel," Dana and Fallon say in unison. "Diego would never hurt you."

I rub my lips together. "I just—how are we here? Why are you here?"

Diego clears his throat and motions to my cousins to leave the room. I nearly shout for them not to abandon me, but one more look at Diego's gray eyes keeps me in place.

Moving slower than before, he strolls to the bed and pats the spot next to him. My good senses go out of whack, begging me to give in, and my body automatically scoots closer until I find myself next to him, my dirty, bare legs brushing against his pants. Then I shock the hell out of us both by sliding into his lap.

He chuckles. "Your mind might've been messed with, but your heart knows me."

He's right. My heart ricochets around in an attempt to throw itself from my body to crash into this sexy ass vampire. I squirm under the weight of his gaze and blush even harder because his junk obviously enjoys it, hardening under me.

He gently shifts me back next to him, resting his hands on my legs. "Beautiful—Jewel, I know you must be confused—"

"What happened to me?" I ask, leaning closer. Because it's obvious something happened. I mean, how the hell did I get into Haven Springs? Where are my dad and Ramona? What about the blood on me? "My dad and sister...are they dead?" I've heard of donors experiencing trauma so intense that their brains struggled to grasp with life after. Did that happen to me?

The second the words leave my lips, tears burst from my eyes. Something comes over me, and I throw my arms around Diego, burying my face into his hoodie. I expect him to stiffen or push me away, especially because I'm nastily snotting all over him, but all he does is bring his big hands up to my back to rub circles over my muscles.

"Jewel, can I help you try to remember?" Diego asks quietly. "I know you don't like people getting into your head but—"

I jerk away from him. "You can do that?"

He nods. "You've allowed me before."

I frown. "I don't know you."

"But you do. And it kills me that you don't remember. I..." His voice trails off, going soft. "I'm so sorry I couldn't get here sooner, but things outside are...complicated." He carefully chooses his words. I wonder what in the hell is happening in the world. What's happened to my life?

He leans more into me. "But I'm here now. And I'm not leaving. I don't care what Donor Life Corp does."

"Why don't you care?"

His face softens, and he takes my hand. "Because I love you."

My eyes widen, and I search his face, taking in the fullness of his lips, his strong jawline, the way his gray eyes flash silver.

I should panic at the way his fangs extend, peeking from his lips or how he reaches up to brush my hair back to draw his gaze across my shoulder peeking from the neckline of this oversized shirt. But I'm not afraid. I might actually believe him.

"Did I love you?" I ask, failing to remain expressionless.

"I hope you still do."

I shift away from him to look at the unfamiliar room. "Will it hurt? Getting into my head?"

"I'll be careful. Promise."

Something nagging inside me begs for me to agree. The thought consumes me, eating away at me worse than the burning in my stomach. I feel like if I agree, then things might be okay.

Because I hate this.

I hate feeling like I don't know the things I should. I don't like feeling out of control, or how my body reacts to Diego, but my mind doesn't want to listen to it. And the way his gray eyes hold mine, begging for me to trust him, sends my heart racing.

I don't think I've ever wanted to trust someone so badly, a vampire at that.

"Okay, do it," I murmur.

"Are you sure?"

I shrug. "No, so hurry before I change my mind. I just—I don't want to be confused anymore. I need help."

Touching my cheek, he nudges my face to bring my gaze back to his. He offers me a small smile and leans in, sending my heart racing. Just when I think he's about to kiss me, he stops short and says, "Don't look away from me."

My body slackens under his command.

"Jewel, tell me what happened to you."

"Orlando made me forget," my mouth says without my permission.

"Forget what?"

"You."

HUNGER

DIEGO STARES AT ME FOR an incredibly long moment, and I can't do anything other than let him. Leaning even closer, he gets into my face, so he's all I see. I should be panicking that my body refuses to listen to my mind, but my heartbeat remains even as Diego peers at me like he can see past my flesh into my blood, maybe my soul.

"Why did Orlando make you forget me?" Diego finally says, running his fingers across my damp cheeks.

"It was part of his deal." Deal? And Orlando...the name sits on the tip of my tongue, teasing me, but I draw a blank about what the name means to me. Who it belongs to.

"What deal?" Diego asks, his eyes flashing silver.

"I don't know," I say.

He sighs. "Jewel, I'm going to have to prod a little

harder. It might hurt. Can I continue?"

"Yes." The words come so softly that I don't even have a chance to think about what my agreement means.

Diego closes the space between our faces completely, touching his nose to mine. Our breaths mingle, but he doesn't brush his lips to mine as much as my body wants him to. It's the strangest thing. It's all I can focus on.

"Jewel, what is the last thing you remember?" Diego asks.

"My dad getting ready to leave."

"I need you to try harder. What else can you remember?"

"I applied to the Blood Match Program." What? No, I didn't. But I can't tell Diego otherwise no matter how much I try to push the words out to tell him that my rebel mouth is full of lies. He should know, though. If I'm in Haven Springs, there is no way I could've Blood Matched.

His jaw tightens, probably noticing the wildness in my gaze I can see reflecting back to me from the silver of his eyes like a mirror to my soul. "Who did you match with?"

Pain bursts behind my eyes and my vision blurs with tears. I wish with everything in me that I could blink to see him clearly. That I could stop the tears from falling. He looks ready to break his hypnotizing stare because of it.

"Answer my question." Diego's eyes flash silver again.

"I—"

His fingers press gently into my temples, easing some

of the pressure expanding in my skull. "Jewel, if you can't tell me what happened to you, I want you to tell me who you matched with."

My head throbs worse at the question the longer he stares with his glowing eyes. It's like the answer hangs just out of my reach. I hold Diego's gaze, thinking about the Blood Match application. Now I remember I did apply. Ramona lost her shit over it. But did I actually match with a vampire? *Yes.* The thought comes to me, speeding up my heart.

"I—" Shit balls. Every time I attempt to open my mouth to spit out the words, pain swells through me.

"Tell me who you matched with," Diego demands, putting more pressure on my head with his long fingers.

"I—" A groan escapes my mouth.

"Jewel. Think. Who are your perfect matches?"

Convulsions seize my muscles, and my stomach clenches and heaves. My eyes water so much so that I lose complete focus on Diego's eyes as hot tears drip down my face and soak the front of my shirt. All I can see is the blinking silver. All I can feel is the coolness of his breath, the soft pant of air against my lips.

"Jewel, tell me," he repeats.

I scream out, agony exploding through my head. My body jerks so hard away from Diego that I fall back onto the bed. He breaks his stare on me but doesn't allow any space between us as he gently turns me onto my side to let me curl in on myself. His muscular arms encircle my waist, and I groan as he holds me.

"Shit, that hurt," I whisper, trying to catch my breath.

He rests his chin on my shoulder. "I'm so sorry, beautiful. I failed you."

Shifting in his arms, I roll over to face him. He combs my messy hair from my face and rests his forehead to mine. My body inches closer, something familiar about Diego burrowing into me. He was right about my heart knowing him. All I want to do is return his embrace and tell him it's going to be okay. That even though Orlando tried to erase him from my life, I'll never forget one of the guys who promised me forever. I want to tell him Orlando was wrong about him.

I gasp as the thought swirls through my mind. *Diego Divine. My first personality match. My current nutrients match. Loves adrenaline, physical activities, driving, biting, me...*

"You didn't fail me, Diego," I say, freeing my hand from between us to touch his cheek. "It just took a second. And now I want nothing more than to murder Orlando...but not before kissing you. I've missed you so much."

He inhales a small breath, and I steal it right from his lips, crashing mine to his, tasting the salt of my tears mixing with the sweetness of his mouth. Diego reacts, scooping me closer to run his fingers through my hair, devouring all the affection I shower him with.

"Jewel, you remember me?" he asks, tilting back slightly to gaze into my eyes, needing confirmation. To hear the words out loud.

I brush my lips to his again. "I'm sorry I forgot you. But Orlando, he—" My head explodes with more pain as I try to recall the last time I saw him. Fog steals my memories. All I can think about is how everything is okay now because Diego's here and I remember. Something about remembering him is important.

Diego rests his head to mine. "Take a breath. I must not have broken through his block completely."

"Try again. I need to know what the hell is going on. Why am I in Haven Springs? You guys bit me with your venom." Everything comes back to me in a rush that sends me bowing forward to press my face into Diego's shoulder. "The bites still ache. The hunger inside me. Shit. It's intense."

He hugs me close, resting his chin in the crook of my neck. "It's not blood hunger, Jewel. It can't be. Our venom didn't work. When was the last time you've eaten?"

"But the blood on my shirt." I touch my stomach, the dull ache still biting at me. "Are you sure I didn't just lose control? Have you checked around Haven Springs to assure everyone is still alive?"

Diego raises his brows. "You're not a vampire. The blood on you belongs to Orlando, beautiful. It's dry. You've probably been out since last night. The hunger you feel is from you not eating all day." He hugs me closer. "I'm sorry it turned out like this and it took me so long to come. We didn't have a choice in the matter. The board made us release you here. They thought we bit you as a form of possession and to give us time to prevent this from happening. They don't know we did use our venom."

"Or that I'm immune," I whisper.

"Or that."

"Fuck," I whisper. "This can't be true. Our forever—"

"Don't worry. Austin's on it." He twines my fingers with his and holds our hands together against his chest so I can feel the thrum of his heart. "He snuck your blood and has been working on trying to figure out how to reverse it when we're not forced to deal with...stuff."

"Stuff? I think I deserve to know, Diego."

He licks his lips. "I'm sorry. You're right. Tension has grown on the board with the death of Pierce Monroe, the board member Mitchell killed."

I search his eyes, recalling the man's severed arm. I wish that nasty friggin' image remained locked up.

"Mitchell requires our services in dealing with the hostile region. We're his heirs. We must act on his behalf."

Fear clenches my heart. "Are you in danger?"

He doesn't react to my words, not giving anything away. "We're okay. Things have settled some. It's how I managed to get away."

I bob my head, twining our fingers together. "How

long have I been here anyway?" I need to take my mind off of my inability to transform. "Everything is foggy since...shit balls." I can't believe Donor Life Corp agreed to cancel my Blood Match contract. Or that Mitchell and Viorica saw to it that I was given the Divine name and exempted from paying the Jordan blood debt. This is unreal.

Diego shifts to swipe his hands over my cheeks again. "Take a breath. It's only been two weeks since Mitchell brought you here."

"This is all so messed up," I say. "What's going to happen now?"

"Nothing you need to worry about," he responds. "We gotta focus on you right now, okay?"

"I want to go home."

"I know, beautiful. We'll make it happen soon enough. I promise."

I groan.

"How about I help you get cleaned up to take your mind off things? Make sure you're really okay. Get you something to eat, too." Diego holds his hand out for me to take, and I let him guide me into the attached bathroom.

He turns the shower on, filling the room with steam. I stand in front of him and let him help me out of my dirty clothes. He strips out of his own and smirks at me as I take in the curves of his body, wanting nothing more than to touch his every muscle to assure myself that I'll never forget him again.

"You okay?" he asks, taking my hand to pull me into the warm steam that relaxes my aching body. "Does anything hurt? Our bites still look a bit sensitive. I don't see any new ones, thankfully."

I purse my lips. "They're okay. Only my head hurts. It's just...two weeks here? What have I been doing without you?" I close my eyes and try to think about what the heck happened. All I can remember is my cousins finding me. Before that? Blank.

"Getting your mind messed with, apparently. I'm going to kill him if I ever see him again." Diego growls as he says it, surprising me by swinging his arm out to punch the tiled wall.

I snatch his hand and bring it to my mouth to kiss his bleeding knuckles. A wave of warmth crashes over me the second his blood touches my lips. I can't stop myself from gliding my tongue over the drops. It's as good as, if not better than, I remember.

"You should wait for Austin," Diego whispers, his fangs peeking out from his lips. "He and Kingston will be here in a bit."

I moan softly, kissing his fingers once more. "It's hard to pull back. You taste so friggin' delicious." And I mean it. His blood satiates the burning inside me. His closeness makes the pain radiating over me disappear.

He grins, my words finally lighting the seriousness of his face. It's now that I realize I'm not the only one struggling with all this. Diego is too. He needs something to distract him as much as I do. "Please tell me you crave me."

I giggle, flush warming my skin. "I feel extra bitey."

Laughing, he snuggles against me. "Damn it. I can't make you wait. Have at it. Whatever you want. Everything sucked without you, and I want to make it better."

"I just want to—" I shut myself up by pulling him down close enough to kiss me. Sliding my tongue into his mouth, I caress it to his, pressing my boobs to his slippery chest in the process.

And now all I can think about is him and me together.

Diego awakens something inside me that longs for his touch, his kisses, his love. It's a hunger—a wild need—that can only be tamed by his closeness. The assurance that he's here with me, and we're safe together, and the mess that my life was today is over and Orlando failed.

Diego reacts to my touch, releasing his own moan while moving away from my mouth to kiss my neck. His fingers gently explore my skin. Diego pulls me closer, standing me up on the shower step to kiss my breasts, sucking the sensitive skin just hard enough to make me gasp.

"Is this okay?" he murmurs, twirling his tongue over my curves, grazing his teeth gently across the heated flesh of my boobs, my body yearning with the desire Diego elicits.

"Better than okay." I blindly map my fingers over his taut shoulders now warm with shower spray.

I nip his skin, teasing him without biting down as

much as I want to. He moans into my hair, sliding his hands to my ass to pick me up slightly. I arch my back, yearning for his touch, pleading with him to hurry up without actually saying the words.

The full extent of him rubs against me, testing me for a reaction. I gasp and reach down, feeling his excitement with my hand. He moans and touches me back, spinning me to press my body against the cool tiles.

He tilts his head to look at me, the weight of his fingers building pressure between my legs. I don't look away, sucking my bottom lip between my teeth, both our chests heaving as we familiarize ourselves with each other.

"I love you," he whispers before kissing me again. "You have no idea how much it killed me when I found you tonight."

"I'm sorry," I murmur. "Never again. Promise."

"No, I promise. I'm not going anywhere, okay?"

I release a moan. "You better not."

"God, I've missed you."

"And I want you. A lot."

Moaning deep in his throat, he hoists me up, spinning me so quickly that I barely release a screech before he sets me into the cutout in the shower wall. My body hums with desire. A dozen thoughts cross my mind as I drink in his glistening skin, the way his eyes capture mine in the best way, and how his body ripples with his movements, his own excitement prominent with lust and a need unlike anything

I've ever felt radiate from Diego.

He wants me as much as I want him.

Standing in front of me, he takes a minute to look over me, his smoldering gaze heating me up more than the shower spray dampening my hair. I shift under his gaze, rubbing my legs together for a moment. He watches me, inching closer, waiting for me to make the next move.

"I know you had this idea of the perfect moment..." I suck in my lip and gauge his reaction at my words.

His eyes narrow for a moment with his thoughts. "Beautiful, I thought I lost you. Any moment with you is perfect."

"Then come here. I don't want to wait any longer."

He inhales a soft breath and closes the space. Leaning down, he kisses me softly for a moment. "Are you sure you want to do this here?"

I give him a slow once-over. "I thought it was obvious."

He licks his lips. "I just know your opinion on sex in showers."

My cheeks flush. "I guess you've changed my mind. Just be careful with me."

"Always."

He smiles and meets his lips to mine for a whisper of a kiss that turns ravishing the second I open myself up completely and wrap my legs around his body. His hand draws goosebumps over my skin, trailing lower, and I release a loud ass moan as his fingers rub between my legs, setting me off in a way that has me reaching to lace my fingers around Diego's hips to bring him closer to feel his hardness press against me.

"I love you," he whispers into my damp hair, nudging it away with his nose to kiss my skin.

Leaning into me, he kisses me deeper. His hands slide to my lower back to shift me closer until we're perfectly aligned. I pant and hold his gaze, watching his eyes close as he adjusts my body to his. I gasp at the pressure that sends tingles all through my body. Curling around him, I brace against his fervent movements, running my nails across his back, just enjoying every hot and explosive sensation created from this indescribable moment with Diego. My fingers explore his taut muscles, glistening with steam. He moans, his voice vibrating over my lips as he works his way toward my jaw to kiss the tender skin of my neck.

"It's okay if you want to bite me," I say, grazing my teeth over his earlobe.

"You first," he whispers, his voice deepening.

I nearly knock him back as I slip forward, making him hold me instead of sitting propped up. I just want to give him what he wants—what I want—and I sink my teeth into his shoulder, biting hard enough to draw blood. My whole body buzzes with the sweet, syrupy taste coating my tongue. He releases a sexy noise along with my name, and I suck harder at the sudden rush coursing through me.

And then I pull away and bite him again.

Diego steps back with the shift of my weight, and he accidentally crashes us through the glass shower door in an attempt to blindly find the nearest wall. I screech and laugh as the world spins. My back hits my bed, our wet bodies soaking the blankets.

He pulls away and grins at me before our lips meet again, and I devour his kiss. His mouth wanders to my shoulder, his fangs grazing my skin. I arch up, letting him slide his hands under me to bring me so close that no space would dare get between us.

"Take a breath," he whispers.

The second I inhale, pressure pinches my shoulder and his fangs pierce my skin. His lips take over, and he sucks my blood, his body still moving in perfect sync with mine that it's all I feel as he drinks from me until he gasps and pulls away with his release. He licks his lips and smiles at me, sinking with me deeper into the bed while pulling the blankets around us.

"You should drink more," he says. "In case. I was starving, but let me help you."

I nod, rubbing my lips together. "Did I bite too hard?"

He chuckles and brushes my hair from my face. "Definitely not. But your teeth are for fun. My fangs happen to be more efficient."

Diego rolls off of me only to pull me with him, so I sit nestled against him, my legs slung over his thighs. He bites his arm and brings it to my mouth, his blood setting my body off again. I moan and wiggle, my face flushing as something deep-seated snaps inside me.

A hunger unlike anything I've felt ignites in my stomach, burning through the rest of me. I suck harder on Diego's arm and watch him watch me. His chest heaves, and he remains utterly still, not stopping me. He gets more into it, shifting me again to run his hands over my body just the way I like it until I screech a moan so embarrassingly loud that I'm certain all the nearby humans might have heard. It's the only reason I stop, my breath gasping.

Diego smiles and props up on his elbow. He peers at me, running his finger along my jaw, smiling wider as I shiver. "You're incredible, Jewel. Everything about you."

"And you're my perfect match." I trace my fingers over his bare chest. "Who I might still want to devour."

He grins at me, studying my face for a moment. "Is that so?"

"Most definitely."

Something dark shifts in his eyes the longer he stares, and his smile turns serious. "Shit, beautiful. Your eyes."

"Um, what?"

His words were the last thing I expected after our moment of passion. Quickly composing the worry lining his face, he scoops me up and carries me with him, covering us both in the blankets as he strolls across the room to the vanity mirror in the corner.

Setting me on my feet, we both face the mirror. His

gaze locks onto mine in my reflection, and I startle at the flash of silver in my eyes. It disappears as quickly as it came, and I lean in closer in an attempt to get my aqua eyes to flash again, but nothing happens.

I bare my teeth and poke at them. "That was weird."

"Kingston swore you were transitioning completely at the Blood Match Center even before we bit you, but it didn't take. You're resistant."

"Maybe I need more venom." I know I keep flip-flopping with doubt about turning into a vampire, and it scares the crap out of me that I might change for the worse, but the thought of it being impossible digs into me, stealing my breath. I was set on forever with my guys, and if it's not possible. Shit balls. It kills me to think about.

"Maybe so."

I spin in his arms and hold my wrist to his mouth. "Bite me again."

His brows pucker with a frown. "It's not so simple. You were out for days before we had no choice but to bring you here. You wouldn't wake up. Austin worries what will happen if we try again until he can run more tests."

"We don't have time for more tests. What if Orlando comes back? What if something goes wrong with me?"

Diego engulfs me in a hug. "We won't let him get close. I'm not leaving you. When my brothers arrive, they're staying too."

"How? Look at all the windows. No tinted glass."

"You have a closet."

I laugh, the noise coming out strangled and high-pitched. "Seriously?"

"It'll only be for a few more days while we better plan and negotiate with Mitchell. He'll influence the board to release you to us."

I puff air through my lips and rest my head on his still bleeding shoulder. "What if you're caught?"

He hugs me. "It's under control."

"Diego."

"Trust me."

"Of course I trust you, but it doesn't have to mean I like it." Because Haven Springs leaves me on edge since our last misadventure here. They shoot vampires on sight. Not only does that put Diego at risk, but it could also put my little cousins in danger. It could put me in harm's way. If I can't have forever, I hope I can at least have a long life. "I worry about you."

Diego twines his fingers through mine and tugs me back toward the bed. "Come on. I can change that."

"I'm not so sure."

"Will you let me prove it?"

I smirk. "How could I ever resist?"

TEASE

"THE SECOND THEY FIND OUT about you, your life is over. They will cage you. They won't have a choice." Orlando stands before me, crossing his arms over his chest.

Brayla materializes next to him. "They'll drain you over and over again all because they can."

Anger ignites inside me, heating my skin, combating the cool night air. "They won't. You don't know them like I do."

Orlando closes the space to me and snatches my hands to hold them between us. "I know Donor Life Corp. You're in danger the longer you're with the Divines. They'll learn the truth. They'll know you need blood to survive, but they'll also realize how you can give more."

"They already know."

His eyes flash silver. "What?"

"They've known I'm different since Katherine bit me. She used her venom."

Scowling, Orlando glances from me to Brayla. "We won't have much time. Her only saving grace has been that they're possessive and give her their blood to prevent each other from getting into her head."

"They do it to stop you," I argue.

"That makes sense." Brayla looks at Orlando like I'm not even here. "That's probably the one thing keeping them from killing each other."

"Once they know the truth—I can't let that happen. They can't find out." Orlando turns to me. "Jewel, you have to come with me. I will not lose you to them. You're mine. I made a deal with your father to take care of you. They can't protect you like I can. They're at the mercy of—"

"No," I say, cutting him off.

He steps closer. "I don't want to force you."

"She'll never forgive us if you do," Brayla says.

I inch my way back. "Damn straight. I hate you."

Orlando's jaw twitches. "You'll forgive me."

"I won't."

"You need me."

"I don't."

"We'll see."

Orlando flies at me and lifts me off my feet to hold me

against him. I don't even get the chance to scream before he bites his arm and places it over my mouth, coating my tongue with blood.

"Forget me, Jewel," Orlando whispers, capturing me in his gaze.

My body reacts to his blood, buzzing at the burst of energy. I use it to my advantage and swing my arm, smacking him in the side of the head. He drops me to the ground. I land on my back, the breath heaving from my chest. Straddling me, Orlando pushes my shoulders into the ground and leans into me, locking me in his gaze.

"Forget me, Jewel. When you wake up, you'll go home. Stay inside. Don't talk to anyone unless you have to."

The edges of my vision darken, and I moan, pain swallowing me.

"Holy fuck, babe." Kingston's loud voice tugs me from a crazy ass dream. "Does this mean you remember who we are?"

Slowly opening my eyes to Kingston's glare, I fake startle and cover my face with the comforter. I groan and curl my legs around Diego, who smiles at the teasing game I play on his brother.

"Don't bite me." I try my best to keep my voice even so that I don't laugh. It helps that my heart still races from my dream.

"Damn it," Kingston says, moving closer. His silhouette shades the light filtering in through the covers. "But

I'm starving."

Something thumps, and Kingston releases a growl.

Austin's form appears next to Kingston's. "Kingston, you asshat. You're going to scare her."

I peek at Austin and Kingston watching me. Kingston raises an eyebrow, searching my eyes to see if I'm joking or not. Austin twists his lips unsure of what to make of the whole situation. Neither of them wants to risk upsetting me because they can't tell I'm playing with them. I shouldn't, but it's too good to resist. I can already imagine their faces when I attack them with my lips.

I shake Diego, pretending he's asleep. "Wake up, Diego. There are vampires in my room."

Diego shifts next to me and grins at me from under the covers, loving that he gets to be in on my joke. "It's okay, beautiful. Those are only my brothers. You sort of like them."

That gets a deep ass growl out of Kingston. "Sort of? Are you kidding me?"

I ease the blanket from my face again, keeping my mouth hidden because my smile will betray the fact that we're totally messing with them. "I do? They are cute, aren't they?"

Austin smirks.

"Cute?" Kingston grimaces. "Just cute?"

I give Kingston a slow once-over. "Possibly delicious. I can't be sure."

"I bet if you asked nicely, they'd let you find out like I did," Diego says, propping himself up on his elbows. He looks from me to his brothers.

I hum under my breath. "You don't mind?"

He shrugs his shoulders. "Definitely not. I could use a break, to be honest."

Diego sits up completely, letting the blankets fall from his chest. I run my fingers over the bite marks I left on his skin, some already healed with light bruises left behind. He looks proud as all get-out.

"Shit," Kingston says, rubbing his hands down his face. "She's getting worse. What the hell, Diego? What does she remember? Was this like the savagery of last time? This shit is—"

Austin punches him. "Your next words better be that this is fine."

It takes everything in me not to react as he reminds me of how I had a weird moment with Diego where I could not control my damn need to bite him, and not in a sexy way...at least to me. Austin thought it could be sex-related, and Diego seems to love it. But man. Mortifying. Maybe because I'm human.

"But look at him!" Kingston's voice rises.

Diego stiffens next to me. "There isn't anything wrong. I asked for every single one of these marks. If you're going to make a big deal, then you need to get out and get yourself under control."

I blush.

Kingston looks at me straight on, though his attention remains with his brothers. "But did you not hear our girl? She said I looked delicious and not in that sexy ass way I like."

Diego touches my cheek, smirking enough to make me laugh. "I thought it was sexy."

Austin elbows Kingston in the ribs. "Shut up. You're going to embarrass her." Stepping toward us, Austin braves coming closer. He stops at the edge of the bed and searches my face. I squeeze Diego's leg under the covers in an attempt to keep from laughing.

"How much blood did she drink?" Austin asks, keeping his voice even.

"Not too much. She was only being playful. Our girl's mind might have forgotten us, but her beautiful heart and body didn't. She came onto me. You should've seen her. So hot."

I snap my teeth at him, making him chuckle. "Because you taste friggin' amazing. I couldn't help myself."

Kingston throws his hands up. "She came onto you, and you boned her? Fuck, Diego. What's wrong with you? Jewel might not have done that if she were herself."

"She does keep mentioning how you taste, and those bites seem a little more excessive than usual," Austin says quietly.

Oh, boy. They are totally serious.

"We were at it for a while." My cheeks burn so much as Diego's says the words. We smile at each other, the memory still fresh between us with our next level moment I'm still buzzing over. I didn't know I could love him even more, but I do. I love them all so much. Our world might be out of control right now, but they're here and that's all that matters.

"Diego, you're going to make them jealous," I say, nearly ruining our joke.

But Kingston and Austin's heads are somewhere else as they look at each other. Diego's enjoying this way too much. I'll let him have it since he did have to deal with me first.

Kingston fists his hands, nearly shaking. "Are you sure it was about you, Diego?" he finally asks. "Our girl is acting weird. If the asshole is nearby, maybe he—"

Scooting up higher, I let the blanket fall just enough to show off my cleavage. Teasing my guys was exactly what I needed. The opportunity was way too much fun to pass up, and Diego's set on seeing how this plays out.

"No, I'm sure it's because I crave his cute ass. Kind of like I want you. Why don't you come here and let me find out if I like you?" I tease. Turning to Diego, I add, "Are you okay with that? He looks so yummy too. Just a little bite."

Diego tips his head back and laughs. "See? Playful. Not manipulated." He eyes me. "And I think you're going to have to be the one to go to him, beautiful. Kingston's nervous. You might have to ease him into it if you want his blood."

"How did she act earlier?" Austin asks, totally clinging onto his role as my health keeper. "She hasn't had our blood in her system. Maybe we were wrong before."

"Still looks sexual to me," Kingston mutters.

I ignore him and glance at Austin as he talks to Diego. If they're going to talk about me like I'm not here, then I might as well do the same. "What about him? He's friggin' hot. Looks brave."

Diego shrugs. "Why don't you find out?"

Austin's frown turns serious as I narrow my gaze on him. He swallows and inhales a deep breath, his Adam's apple popping in the motion. Stepping closer, he studies my face again, still trying to assess the situation. He's always been more reserved and shyer, but if I show him affection, he will always be quick to return it. And right now, Austin looks so damn prepared to give into me that I can't stop the smile crossing my face. It makes him smile so brightly that my heart races.

"Jewel, do you really want to?" Austin asks. He nods at Diego. "I'm sure you're so confused. Did Diego tell you everything that's going on?"

I scoot to the edge of the bed and slide off, leaving the blankets with Diego. Austin's eyes dart from mine to the rest of me, taking a moment to drink me in as I stand before him in only my undergarments. Heat warms my skin under the intensity of his stare, and I shuffle a few steps forward, loving where this little joke heads.

"He did," I manage to say, stepping closer. I can't stop smiling at him as I stroll closer. "My cousins confirmed it. You're my body match, right?"

Kingston groans and punches the wall. "Damn it. I was your first."

I flick my attention to him. "I bet we had a lot of fun."

His brooding face perks up, and he gives into my smile. "I can't wait to remind you, babe."

"We'll see, dude," I say. He raises his eyebrows for a split second and glares at me. "But right now, I want to see if this sexy-as-hell guy will give me what I want." I smile at Austin. "Will you? Maybe I'll remember more."

His cheeks blush a rosy color I just want to kiss. "If you think this will help..."

"Most definitely."

Licking his lips, Austin keeps his hands at his sides and lets me close the space to him. Kingston releases his breath along with what sounds like a cross between a moan and a sigh, but he remains in his spot a few feet away.

I stand before Austin and trail my hands over his shoulders to hook them to his neck. "Are you nervous?"

"Never with you," he whispers, his breath quickening as I step into his arms for a hug.

Austin gently holds me by my waist without moving his hands. I sink against him, feeling his arms around me just the way I love them. I hadn't realized how much I needed to hug Austin until this moment, and now it's all I want to do.

"Never?" I ask, reaching up to touch his flushing cheek.

He places his hand over mine, pressing my fingers deeper into his skin. "Never."

"Good, because I've missed the hell out of you."

I surprise Austin by jumping into his arms and brushing my lips against his, kissing him with the affection I know he craves from me. He releases a relieved breath into my lips and slides his arms lower to hold me securely to him. I pull away, burying my face into his neck, just smelling the freshness of his skin until—

He grunts, and I jerk back, touching my fingers to my lips. "Oh, shit. Austin, I'm sorry."

Holding my gaze, he smiles. "What for?"

"I bit you."

"That was the plan."

"But I was only messing with you guys."

Kingston swears and releases a breath. One second he's behind us, and in the next, he traps Diego in a headlock. Austin twists to protect me as Kingston and Diego fly past me and skid across the floor to hit the wall with a thud.

I wiggle in Austin's arms, but he snuggles his face into my shoulder, breathing in the scent of my hair. I let him.

Rubbing my hands up and down his back, I savor how perfect it feels to be so close with him. "You guys stop. You might freak my cousins out," I say from his arms.

"They're fine. The TV's so loud that they're not going to hear anything," Diego says, laughing as Kingston tries to punch him in the stomach.

I close my eyes and listen for the noise. He's right. "Still." I point at Kingston. "I'm sorry I messed with you guys, dude. It was all me. I couldn't resist."

"Savage," Kingston says, making me laugh.

"This is what you get for all the bullshit games you like to play with Jewel. Also for all the times you've rubbed in your body match. You should've seen how scared she was when I found her. She needed to tease you because look around us. This is messed up, and I'll do anything to make sure she keeps smiling. So chill out." Diego punches Kingston in the arm. "And get used to her new form of affection. Our girl loves it."

"It's okay, Diego. I love how you stand up for me, but we might've taken it a little far."

Austin kisses my throat. "Kingston just needs to lighten up."

I smile and snap my teeth. "I love him in all his intensity. And you don't have to worry, dude. I enjoy what I do because Diego does. That's it."

Kingston's eyes suddenly widen. "Fuck. You sure? Look at her eyes," Kingston says to his brothers. He closes the space to us and narrows his gaze on me from over Austin's shoulder.

"They were changing earlier," Diego says.

"Might be another side effect," Austin muses.

Kingston doesn't seem so sure. "Show me your teeth. Now, babe. And you better not use them...without letting me use mine first."

I offer him a smile, licking my tongue over my teeth. "You know I won't ever bite you unless you asked. But I give you permission to bite me. You look starved for more than my affection."

Kingston raises his eyebrows at me. "Babe, you're so in trouble for messing with us, you know. Austin, give her here."

Austin spins me away. "No way. You weren't even going to let her bite you."

"But she said I could bite her."

The world zooms around me as Austin plays keep away with me from Kingston. He tosses me, and I screech out and land on the bed. Diego links his fingers to my waist and pulls me back under the covers with him, making Kingston hesitate in his attempt to grab me.

I smile at Kingston and hold my arms open for him. "Come here, dude. You look like you could use a hug."

Kingston eyes Diego again but braves closing the space to me and sits on the edge of the bed. I motion for Austin to join us, and I hug my arms around each of them. They finally settle down and sink into me, savoring my attention as much as I enjoy theirs. No one even mentions the fact that all Diego wears are his boxers and me in my bra and underwear, though I'm pretty friggin' sure my guys don't mind. Kingston even has the nerve to bury his face in my cleavage for a second. They're getting as comfortable as I am with the level of my relationships I now have with them.

"Better?" I ask, linking my fingers through Kingston's unkempt hair to pull him up to kiss my mouth.

He shakes his head. "Need more."

Austin brushes his lips to my shoulder. "Don't fall for it, Jewel. He deserved your teasing."

I shift and kiss Austin next. "Thanks for being cool about it. I'm sorry if I freaked you out. I just—"

"Our girl needed some playful entertainment after everything," Diego says, sliding his arms around me from behind. "I wasn't going to deny her the opportunity."

"Like you weren't going to deny her—fuck." Kingston groans and rubs the heels of his hands into his eyes. "I'm not jealous. I'm not jealous. Shit. I'm so damn jealous. And hungry. And horny. The last two weeks have felt longer than my entire life."

I link my fingers through his and turn to Austin. "Do you have your blood draw stuff? I can't believe how long it has been. Everything is kind of fuzzy." I turn to Kingston. "Glad to see you suffered through gen. pop. blood."

"It was torture."

Diego growls. "You ass. Imagine what our girl went through."

Kingston pouts. "I can't. I want to destroy the universe when I do. I'm so sorry, babe. We've really failed you."

"You didn't, though. I'm—I'm going to be fine." My voice cracks at the words. "We're going to be fine. I just—let me feed you. I need that normalcy."

Austin sucks in his bottom lip. "I didn't bring it in my kit. I wasn't sure what to expect with you, so I prepared for other things in our rush out here. You gave me a scare."

"All of us, babe," Kingston says. "So time to make up for it."

I roll my eyes and bat my hand at him. "You're lucky I've missed the hell out of you. And Austin, I'm okay without the kit. You have no idea how much I want to take care of you three right now. So let me feed you."

No one moves, all three of my guys' hearts picking up pace at my words. I shift on the bed, my body suddenly humming with anticipation as Kingston, Diego, and Austin all look at each other and then to me.

"What?" I ask, smirking.

"Who gets to go first?" Kingston asks.

My mouth forms an O. "I'm not picking. You guys work it out."

I expect the three of them to start fighting, but they all look at each other again, now making me squirm under the heaviness of their silent conversation. Inhaling a slow breath, I scoot farther back on the bed and into Diego's arms, using him as a backrest. Without them having to say anything, I can tell they all want to drink together to save themselves an argument. And shit, does it excite me more than I thought. They once teased me about this, but we weren't at a point of readiness then.

But now? They all bit me and released their venom. We were set on eternity together, even if it didn't work, and I'm still stuck in a weird state between human and vampire.

Slowly lifting my arms, I hold them up to Kingston and Austin's mouths. Diego breathes a soft breath on my neck, and I tilt it sideways to expose my shoulder to him. I hear the familiar clicks of their fangs extending, their hunger and desire for me so palpable that I can feel it like a burst of electricity zinging through me.

"Jewel, are you sure this is okay?" Austin asks, his voice soft. "Just tell us if it's not. I'll wait my turn."

"This is fine," I say. "I want to."

"You can bite me after," he says, grinning at me.

Kingston hums deep in his throat. "Ah hell, me too."

I giggle. "Then what are you waiting for?"

My breathless laugh morphs into a moan as all three of them sink their fangs into my skin. A dozen emotions explode through me under the comfort of their touches. Austin drinks with his eyes closed while Kingston watches my face, and I lick my lips, rubbing them together. He pulls away and kisses me, not even caring about his brothers' closeness. With my sudden exemption and entrance into Haven Springs, any sort of boundaries we had have temporarily disappeared.

Kingston eases away and holds his arm to my mouth. I thought he was kidding about me biting him, but he's currently all in. "Let's do this. I'm ready to be devoured by you."

I laugh and shake my head. "Why don't you make it easier for me?"

"Fuck, I love you," he says, biting his arm. "You don't even know how much. I still want to run away with you. Give up everything. All I need is you."

I smile and suck on Kingston's arm, making him tip his head back with his eyes closed. His warm blood tingles down my throat, and I slide my legs over his, enjoying what it does to me. Both Austin and Diego ease away and watch me in silence.

"I thought this would be fucking weird, but damn it if I'm good with this," Kingston says, easing his arm away from my mouth.

"How could you not be? Look how happy it makes our girl," Diego says.

I lick my lips and sit up. "If only you could take me ho—" Shadows crowd my vision, the motion getting the best of me. Dizziness spins through my head, and I slump back in Diego's arms.

Cool fingers touch my cheeks. "Jewel, here. Drink more. Kingston, go find something for her to eat."

Kingston slides out from under my legs and disappears.

Diego continues to hug me against him while Austin offers me his arm. The second his blood touches my lips, something awakens inside me, and I surprise him by pulling him onto me, knocking both me and Diego back.

"Whoa, slow down. You don't want to drink too much," Austin says.

But I do. Pain burns through my stomach. I feel like I'll die if I don't drink.

Locking my fingers to Austin's arms, I don't let him pull away. My sudden death grip makes his eyes widen, but he doesn't fight me. He studies my face for a long moment. Diego does too.

The door of the room flings open, hitting the wall. Kingston flies inside and slams it shut. "Someone's here for Jewel."

"What?" Austin and Diego ask in unison. Then Diego adds. "Who?"

"New council member. She's being summoned for a meeting. Apparently she missed the last ten requests."

Ah, hell.

"Have Dana and Fallon tell them Jewel's sick," Austin says, rubbing his fingers over my shoulders. I'm pretty friggin' sure he's going to let me drink until I can't anymore. It freaks me out a bit, but my body wars with my mind, not allowing me to pull away.

Kingston frowns. "They're sitting with him right now."

"Beautiful, you have to let go of Austin and go downstairs. Tell him you're sick and that you'll schedule something tomorrow."

But I seriously can't stop. I'm out of control.

And my guys realize it.

This is like the first time I tasted Diego's blood, but the need overwhelms me. My body, now stronger than ever, refuses to relent to my mind's plea to calm the hell down.

Austin continues to stroke my back, not helping the matter. It feels so good, so familiar and comforting, just to continue. "Jewel, please try for me. I promise you can have more once you send the council member away."

I squeeze my eyes shut, willing my body to pull itself together, but it wants none of it. Fear squeezes my chest, and a dozen panicked thoughts cross my mind. What if something changed inside of me? What if Orlando did something to my mind to make me this way?

"Just pull her back," Kingston says. "Look how crazy her eyes are. She's transitioning. She has to be."

"If that's the case, she'll need human blood," Austin says. "Jewel, if Kingston's right, you're not going to be satisfied until you do."

My body disagrees. I've never felt better.

A knock sounds on the door, drawing all our attentions to it. "Jewel, Mr. Barton from the council is here to see you," Dana says. "Can we come in?"

Kingston swears.

"Tell him no, beautiful," Diego says. "Come on. Just

pull away for a second."

"Ms. Divine, you can't keep avoiding me. Donor Life Corp warned us that you might struggle with adjusting to exemption life. Please, just give me a chance to talk to you."

I manage to drag myself an inch away from Austin's arm, but my mouth wants nothing of the sort, and I lean back in and sink my teeth into his flesh. He releases a moan, flashing his fangs at me in the process. Diego reaches for me, and Austin growls and punches him away.

"Fuck," Kingston says, grabbing onto my legs. "Come on, Austin. Get it together." I'm not the only one losing control.

I scream as Kingston rips me away, and Austin tries to snatch me back, releasing a scary ass growl at his brothers. It's enough to get me to shut up and hold my palms up. Austin freezes, coming to his senses. A look of surprise morphs his expression before he covers his face with his hands.

The door to my bedroom flies open, and a man yells out my name.

All three of my guys tense, and I startle in Kingston's arms. My good senses return to me completely as I realize what the hell's happening.

"Run!" the man yells at my cousins.

They stand frozen.

So do my guys.

Then the man yanks a gun from a holster on his hip

and aims it.

    He shoots.

~76~

INTRUDER

"GET HIM!" KINGSTON YELLS AT the same time he pushes me away so fast that I trip and nearly eat shit on the broken decorative chair that somehow managed to escape my vanity table.

Diego catches me and scoops me up, wrapping the blanket around my shoulders. Austin hooks his hands around the man and disarms him. Kingston flies toward them and clutches the man's face, staring at him with silver flashing eyes.

"Don't fight. Don't scream. Don't you even fucking move," Kingston demands, his chest heaving.

And then I realize he was shot.

Breaking away from Diego, I rush across the room. He

stays right behind me but lets me go. I slide up next to Kingston and glare at the old guy. His gray hair falls in his face, and he flares his nostrils without struggling.

"You shot my Blood Match, you asshole," I say, jabbing him in the chest.

The guy doesn't respond, trapped in Kingston's gaze.

"I'm fine, babe," Kingston says without looking at me.

I gently touch my fingers near the bullet hole in his side, seeping blood through his light blue dress shirt. "Why'd you let him? You could've moved."

"To hide the evidence. You can explain the damage caused by whatever freaky ass things you and Diego did, but it's safer not to have to explain a bullet hole in your wall. We're not supposed to be here, remember? We're lucky it's late, and we're far enough out that people won't know where the shot came from."

"I'd have come up with something. Better than you dealing with this. How bad does it hurt?" Tugging his shirt up, I assess the hole like I even know what to do.

"I think I'm dying," Kingston says, lowering his voice. "It's agonizing."

Austin shakes his head. "He'll be fine. Don't buy into it, Jewel."

I smirk. "Don't worry. I'm not."

Kingston sighs.

Touching his cheek, I say, "I still want to take care of you. I mean, ouch. Just don't hurt the guy."

"If you insist, babe."

Diego pulls me away from Kingston, Austin, and the guy and motions for me to look at the bedroom door. My heart sinks at the sight of my cousins huddled in the doorway, gaping at the whole scene in front of them.

"You will forget what you saw here. You never came to check on Jewel because she called you and told you she was sick," Kingston says to the man, drawing my attention away from my cousins for a second.

I straighten my shoulders and pull Diego with me to the hallway. My cousins back up and allow us out. Quietly shutting the door, I lean on it and force myself to get my shit together.

"Girls, I'm so sorry you had to see that," I say, shifting awkwardly on my feet. "It wasn't what it looked like."

Fallon breaks her surprised expression first and giggles. "You don't have to explain anything to us."

Dana covers her smile with her hand. "Yeah, please don't. We're perfectly okay with pretending we saw nothing."

Thank friggin' God. "It really was nothing." I try to keep my expression even.

"Except for the fact that you were pretty damn set on devouring the three of us, babe," Kingston murmurs from the room.

A thunk hits the wall, and he heaves a breath. Austin appears in the doorway, holding the man over his shoulder.

Kingston comes up behind them, rubbing his arm, and he has the nerve to wink at me.

"Is he okay?" Dana asks first, shifting on her feet. "We're sorry about the interruption. Mr. Barton barges in uninvited all the time. People around here don't knock."

"Maybe you should start locking the door," I say, frowning.

"No locks. Apparently there is no need for them," Dana says.

"What?" I ask. "Seriously?"

Diego nestles his chin on my shoulder from behind. "Don't worry, beautiful. We'll insist on locks for you."

"Damn straight," Kingston says. "Especially if we're moving in."

Dana and Fallon gape at him, the same worry lining their faces as it does mine. My guys can't just move in here. We're in Haven Springs, after all. Not to mention the fact that I'm dead-set on moving out and back home to the Divinity Estate.

I flick Kingston's shoulder. "You're not moving in."

"Temporarily," Diego says.

Austin shifts the man on his shoulder. "We can't leave you alone, Jewel. Not after what happened."

"What do you mean?" Fallon asks.

Diego hugs me close from behind. "I've confirmed that Orlando has been visiting Jewel. He was responsible for messing with her head and stealing her memories."

Fallon's mouth drops open. "Oh, crap."

I wring my hands together. "He's why I haven't left my room much too."

"What the heck? Donor Life Corp needs to get their stuff together," Dana says.

Kingston chuckles. "Never thought I'd agree with a fourteen-year-old human."

"Fifteen next month," she replies.

A chime sounds through the hallway, and I spin around and search to see where the hell the annoying noise comes from. My guys all look at each other, and Dana and Fallon peer at them.

"What now?" I ask, hugging myself. "I thought people slept at night around here."

"It's your private communications line, Jewel," Dana says.

I frown. "It is? Do you think it's the council?"

Kingston disappears for a moment and returns, holding the small tablet in his hands. "Of-fucking-course." He holds the phone to his brothers.

I shift and lock my hand around his wrist to glance at the screen. My body cools as I read the name Viorica Vaduva blink on the screen with a picture of her above it. I nearly throw the phone at the wall. I never want to see that vampire again, even if she made it so Orlando couldn't make me pay a blood debt. Obviously, he doesn't care about that if he's still messing with me. I'm now more vulnerable than ever.

"Ignore it," I say, releasing Kingston's wrist. "We have more important things to deal with."

Again, my guys look at each other in silence. None of them give much away, though Austin's eyes flash silver. He's less composed than usual, fighting with whatever emotions he tries to hide from me.

Kingston clears his throat. "Austin, can you return Mr. Barton to his home for us?" He must notice what I do to his brother.

Austin nods, managing to rub his worry and annoyance away with the heel of his hands. "I'll be fast." Austin kisses my cheek and vanishes, leaving the rest of us in the hallway.

I stare after him, already aching from his absence.

Diego motions to my cousins. "How about we go back downstairs? Maybe you can show me around your place."

The phone chimes again in Kingston's hand, and he links his fingers around my wrist and rubs his thumb over my skin until I uncurl my fingers. I turn my gaze to him after Diego and my cousins disappear down the stairs. He tries to give me the phone.

I shake my head, pelting him with my long hair because he stands so close. "No friggin' way. I don't want to talk to her."

"You have to answer it." Kingston uncurls my fingers again and sets the device on my palm.

"Why?" I ask, taking a few deep breaths so that I don't

chuck the black box at the wall.

Kingston places his hand on my shoulder and tilts his head down to me slightly, his mouth incredibly kissable and pouty. It's all I can look at as his presence captures my full attention. "I know this sucks, but you have to tell Viorica that Orlando came here and attacked you."

I frown and twist my lips to the side. "What will that accomplish? She doesn't care about me."

"This is a tricky situation, Jewel, and I want to explain everything to you, but there isn't a lot of time."

"Make time. I already feel like I know nothing."

He sighs. "Did Diego tell you about the tension within the board?"

I nod.

"It's what prevented us from coming to you. Some members blame you for Mitchell's actions. They most definitely blame you for ours, and the only reason the Monroe Region hasn't...retaliated is because Mitchell assured things between us were over. But if Orlando is infiltrating Haven Springs, we can use it as leverage. It'll force the board to give us permission to be here to investigate."

"They don't know you are with me?" I ask, my chest clenching from his revelation. Forever is looking less likely. Surviving another day seems impossible.

He shrugs. "I assume they do since we haven't checked in. And if they don't, they will now."

My brows furrow together, and I stick out my bottom

lip. The last thing I want from this night is a confrontation. I'd much prefer to just snuggle the hell out of my tense vampire matches. "Why don't we just run away? I know it's what you want. We're with my cousins now. We can take them."

He rocks on his feet. "We can't. Things have changed, not only at Donor Life Corp, but also because of you, Jewel."

"Me?"

"I'm not going to lie. I'm a little worried about what's happening to you. You've changed. Without access to Donor Life Corp and the Divine name, we can't figure out what's going on with you."

Tears burn my eyes. "I hate this. I still don't want to answer."

Pulling me into his arms, Kingston hugs me tightly, smoothing the trembles from my back. "I know, babe. I hate it too. This wasn't how our lives together were supposed to be like, and I swear we'll fix this. I'm not giving up on our forever."

I nod and kiss him. "Promise?"

"I promise. Now answer the phone. Viorica will be annoyed it's taken this long. It's obviously important to her if she keeps calling back."

Inhaling a deep breath, I press my finger to the device and activate access to my private line. Straightening my shoulders, I compose myself, hiding all my emotions by pressing my lips into a tight line. Viorica and Mitchell appear on screen without the rest of the board. She smirks while Mitchell frowns, and they both turn their attention to Kingston.

"We should've known," Viorica mutters. "I had expected only Diego since he left Midnight Valley."

I don't respond to her comment and turn to keep my gaze on Kingston.

"My son, you're supposed to be in Dark Terrace Ranch," Mitchell says.

Kingston hooks his hand around my waist. "Well, it's a good thing I'm not. We have a serious problem."

OBSESSED

"YOU'VE GOT TO BE FUCKING kidding me!" Kingston yells, picking up my broken vanity chair to throw at the wall. "Jewel is my match. You should've told us. We could've prepared. Do you even care what the hell you put us through these last two weeks?"

"Calm down, Kingston," Mitchell says. "We needed authenticity. I admit, I let Orlando get under my skin, which made things more complicated. I apologize for that and only that. As my heir, you should understand. We all have our places. I've allowed you to ignore your duties for far too long. You were losing sight."

"Jewel nearly died." Kingston flashes his fangs and disappears from my side only to reappear near the door. He vanishes again and shoves the dresser over, sending it crashing onto the carpet. "If you had just told us—"

"I know she's important to you but—"

Kingston snatches the phone from my fingers and turns away from me. "You better not say what I think you're going to say."

"Watch it, Kingston. Think before you say something you might regret," Mitchell says in a tone I shouldn't be able to hear. "Your obsession over Jewel has become rather worrisome. It puts our coven at risk, especially if she has history with Mr. Ortega. You were right about his connection to Blood Rebels, but I need absolute proof before something is done."

He stiffens, his muscles noticeably bunching through his bloody dress shirt. "Proof? To hell with proof."

"Careful, son."

"Why? You're not careful. You put us all in jeopardy by allowing this to go on without my knowledge. We were in this together."

Mitchell growls. "You've grown distant with your infatuation with a donor."

Kingston looks ready to crush the phone. "I love her. And so do Diego and Austin," he says, lowering his voice.

"That's the problem," Mitchell says. "Your loyalty—"

"Is with you," he says, cutting his dad off. "Don't question it. But I'm still pissed the fuck off that you purposely hacked the results of the re-test to match Jewel with Brayla.

I'm angry you didn't feel the need to consult us. Do you know what kind of stress you put us through? And now this bullshit?"

"We did what we had to. Jewel was in jeopardy. This was for the best, Kingston," Viorica says, speaking up.

"How so?"

"Because the board is fed up with you putting the Blood Match Program at risk." Viorica narrows her eyes, pursing her lips.

Mitchell clears his throat. "I know you well enough that it's obvious you are perfectly content sharing Jewel with your brothers."

I frown.

"It's also obvious that she is enthralled with all of you. And who can really blame her? A donor from the Central Plaza Tower, barely able to sustain living, matches with the Divine Heirs? Even if she didn't love all three of you, I can see how hard it would be to give up all the attention."

I glare. Luckily the screen isn't on me or else I would totally give away the fact that I can hear her.

Kingston's gaze flicks from the phone in his hand to me. "She does love us, and it's not about that."

"How can you be so sure?" Mitchell asks. "Orlando still has a hold on her mind. He's obviously worried enough about the information she possesses that he risked going into Haven Springs to assure we haven't just like I expected."

Kingston zooms from his spot and punches another wall. "Damn it. I knew you purposely kept us away. You knew exactly what you were doing when you killed Pierce. No better way than igniting region tension to keep us away. You almost had me fooled."

"Kingston," Mitchell snaps.

Viorica has the nerve to hum in amusement. "If you'd allow us to open her mind—"

"Not fucking happening, Viorica." Kingston's chest heaves. I'm nearly certain another wall will crumble under his fist. This room never stood a chance.

"Then she stays in Haven Springs until we have the proof we need to stop the rise in Blood Rebels and assure power remains as is. Jewel will be our point of contact and representative amid the council. She'll assure things continue to run smoothly at our discretion, and she will update us with any changes."

Kingston's jaw twitches. "That's a terrible idea. The community—"

"But what better person to assure everything remains in order?" Viorica asks. "Jewel can manage."

Kingston snarls at the phone, looking scary as hell. "This is unnecessary. Jewel has done enough. We're taking her home."

"You will not. It is necessary Jewel remain there, my son," Mitchell says. "We have the traitor staff member to prove Jewel is connected to all of this. We can use her to lure out any threats. To keep track of Mr. Ortega. He thinks we're busy dealing with the Monroe Region."

"It's perfect," Viorica adds.

"The hell it is," Kingston says.

"Jewel's relationship to Mr. Ortega will make this easy."

"Relationship? She hates him."

"But has she always?"

A dozen emotions rush through me at Mitchell's assessment of me. It doesn't matter if I was ever friendly with Orlando. I'm not now. I never want to be ever again.

Austin appears in the doorway to the room and rushes to me, gathering me into a silent hug. I break, my breath gasping. This is all too much to take in. I can barely process being in Haven Springs, but to know that the true reason I'm here is because Mitchell and Viorica used me to lure Orlando out enrages me. My surprise match to Brayla was a lie and a setup. It nearly ruined everything. There's no way in hell I'll ever help Donor Life Corp.

"That's enough speculation," Kingston finally says, pulling himself from his thoughts. "It helps no one."

"Fair enough," Mitchell says. "As long as you know."

"I don't care," Kingston says. "Things have changed. Jewel is a Divine. She will be our futures. Vowed to each of us the way we want. Do you understand?"

"We might be able to persuade the board," Viorica says, "if you cooperate."

"I still don't like it," Mitchell says. "If your loyalty—"

"Don't. I told you already. Our loyalty is with you. So is Jewel's." Kingston says the words at a pitch I'd be able to hear. "Right, babe?"

"Right," I say, swallowing the burning in my throat.

"Then you wouldn't mind representing Donor Life Corp, correct?" Viorica asks me.

I nearly lose my shit and start yelling, but one look at Kingston keeps my ass in control. "I'll do whatever you need me to." Ugh. I hate that I have to agree.

"Are you sure you can handle it?" Mitchell's doubt does nothing for my nerves. "After the incident with—"

I cross the room and take the phone from Kingston, looking at Mitchell and Viorica. "Yes. I won't let the Divine name down. I'm set on forever with your sons in your coven, and I won't let anyone stop me."

Kingston and Austin both smile at me, noticing the threat in my voice. Neither Mitchell nor Viorica catch it, or they just choose to ignore it—because seriously, I'm not really a match to their power. It's enough to get my wobbly legs to stop shaking.

"We trust the four of you will be discreet. No one must know of the arrangements. Am I clear?" Mitchell says.

Viorica tips her head, studying me. "You mustn't utter a word to anyone outside Mitchell and the Vaduva Coven."

"Got it," I say.

"Okay," both Austin and Kingston say in unison.

Diego materializes behind me and rests his big hands on my shoulders. "You have our word."

Viorica and Mitchell both nod. "We will call a meeting with the council at sunrise. Be prepared, Jewel."

"Sunrise?" Kingston complains. "That makes things difficult."

Mitchell's eyes flash silver. "Get used to it, son. Haven Springs belongs to the humans, and we must keep it that way."

Viorica smirks, enjoying this way too much. "This will be the perfect opportunity for Jewel to show her capabilities. Do not let us down."

The line clicks off before anyone else can argue, and I stare at the blank screen. I half expect Kingston to lose his shit and start tearing the walls down, but all he does is stroll to the bed and plop onto it. Resting his elbows on his knees, he stares at the floor without another word.

"Fucking Mitchell," he mutters. "Fucking Donor Life Corp."

"Fucking Orlando," I add, nestling down next to him.

Austin takes my other side, and Diego kneels in front of me to rest between my legs to hug me with Austin and Kingston. I know how I feel about the whole situation, and I'm sure they feel ten times worse. They trusted Mitchell. Viorica too. And look what they got for it.

"I can't believe you told your dad that we're all together," I say. "He took it rather well."

"He's seething, babe," Kingston says. "I'm sure he considered murdering us."

My eyes widen. "What? All because we love each other? Come on, the stupid one donor to one vampire thing is lame."

"It's not that, beautiful." Diego reaches up to brush my messy hair from my face. His fingers trail down to the blanket wrapped around my shoulders, and he nudges it lower, grazing his index finger over the healing bite mark he gave me.

I realize that both Kingston and Austin do the same to theirs. I know they joked before about me leaving my mark on them, but it certainly means something fierce to them with their marks on me and not because I sustain them with blood. It's so much more.

"Do I have to beg you to tell me what it is about then?" I shift under the heaviness of their silence. They're refraining from telling me what Kingston meant by Mitchell's supposed anger. "Don't think I won't get on my knees."

Kingston tips his head back and laughs, lightening his friggin' pouty as hell expression. "It won't work. There's only one reason I ever want you on your knees and—"

Austin reaches around me and shoves Kingston off the bed, but he's quick to latch his hand around my waist and pulls me with him. Kingston purrs deep in his throat when I land on him with my boobs smothering his face. He buries his face between them and blows a breath, making me screech and scramble up to swat his chest playfully.

"If I didn't love hearing our girl giggle like that, you'd be in serious pain, bro," Diego says.

Diego lifts me up, and I pull Kingston with me, and he leans in, pushing his weight on me, trying to get me to fall onto the bed.

I laugh again and spin from his reach, holding my palms up to stop my guys from turning this into a game. "Freeze right there. I will not let you distract me. You haven't answered my question yet."

"I think we can get her to change her mind," Kingston says to Diego and Austin.

They all smirk at me, drinking me in. I hold my finger up and cross the room to the closet and pull out a T-shirt. "Tell me, or the pants come on next."

"Not going to work, babe," Kingston says.

I tug a pair of pajama bottoms from the shelf and shimmy them on. "Are you sure?"

He play-growls. "No, so stop testing me. It's nothing we want you to worry about. We have more pressing matters anyway."

"It's about your loyalty, right?" I ask. Mitchell mentioned it several times.

Austin closes the space to me super fast and startles me with a hug. I immediately sink into him when my mind catches up and brush my lips to his neck.

"Don't, Austin," Kingston says.

Diego comes up behind me. "Our girl can handle it."

Austin meets me for a kiss. "Doesn't mean she has to."

"Fuck it, fine. Yes, it's about our loyalty. Mitchell thinks that he'll lose it if it goes to you." Kingston sneaks his way under one of my arms. "That's why he's been adamant about calling you his heir. It's a reminder that you might be our future, but all of our futures lie with Mitchell. But don't worry. We won't risk him seriously questioning our loyalty to you without one helluva foolproof plan."

I bob my head. "He's your dad. I wouldn't want you to. We can handle him."

"Yes, we can," Diego says.

Kingston hugs his arms around us, squishing me in the best vampire sandwich ever. "At least for now. I mean, if he continues doing this crazy shit, I—"

"Have faith in us, dude," I murmur, kissing him. "I mean it. The universe is obviously on our side."

He raises his brows. "Doubt it."

"If it wasn't, I wouldn't be able to sustain the three of you. Donor Life Corp wouldn't have released me from the Blood Match Program, and now no one can force me to choose or punish me if I don't."

Diego smiles at me. "Thanks for reminding us of the positives. So you know though, we'd have never allowed it."

I kiss him next. "Well, now you don't have to risk anything."

Austin snuggles against my throat. "But we would for

you."

"I know you would," I say, shifting to caress my lips to his. "And I would risk everything for you. I *will* risk it. You guys always told me that you'd take care of things, or you'd fight for me. This is my chance to show you I can do the same for you. Even if we have to stay here for a bit. I'll do what it takes to assure our vows. All of them. No matter what."

"I fucking love you, babe."

Diego chuckles. "Our badass."

"Our forever," Austin says.

"If she survives the day," Kingston murmurs. "So you better practice hitting Diego now."

Diego shoves him. "Don't scare her."

Austin gets between me and his brothers as they start to play fight. "Jewel's got this."

Kingston straightens his shoulders and looks around the disastrous room. "I know. We'll assure it."

And I know they will.

THE COUNCIL

PLACING MY HANDS ON MY hips, I block the door. "No."

"What do you me *no*?" Kingston tugs back the hood of his sweatshirt.

"I mean nu-uh. I don't think so. No way in hell am I letting you three follow me into the sun." I wag my finger for good measure.

"But, Jewel—"

"I'm sorry, Austin. No arguing."

"Beautiful, you—"

"Diego, I mean it." Damn it. So much brooding. And kissable pouts. They might not even have to say another word to convince me to let them venture with me to City

Hall in the morning sun. But I don't know Haven Springs well. The shadiest area that I could see from the second floor was the grove of fruit trees surrounding the property. "Your safety is my priority, and my cousins will be with me. You guys are staying here. Maybe put those sexy muscles to work and attempt to clean up our room. I triple checked and made sure the blanket would stay secure."

"That's all on Diego," Kingston mutters. "Your guys' room. Austin and you will take Dana's while she shares with Fallon, and we're..."

"Taking Ramona's?" I ask, trying not to give away how hard it is for me to hear her name. She betrayed me and was willing to sacrifice my freedom for her own.

He shrugs. "Well, it is the biggest."

I sigh. "Okay, if everyone agrees."

"We're good, Jewel," Dana says, jogging down the stairs with her sister.

Fallon nods. "We already share most nights unless—"

Dana elbows her. "We're perfectly fine sharing."

"And Kingston always gets first dibs," Diego says. "Being the oldest and all." He smirks at me.

"I'm not that much older than you, bro," Kingston mutters, eyeing me in his peripheral vision.

"Like a decade," Austin says, laughing. Man, I swear my guys never pass up an opportunity to tease each other.

I snicker into my hand. I can't help it. These are my favorite moments. "Be nice. Age doesn't matter when you—"

"Look as young and as sexy as I do," Kingston says, winking at me.

I laugh again. "I was going to say behave like a horny frat boy from one of the classics, but whatever makes you feel better, dude. I love you regardless."

Leaning down, Austin whispers to my cousins, "Kingston's sensitive about his age around Jewel because he turned not long after the start of The Divide."

"What? Oh my God. That's like super old," Fallon says, her eyes widening.

"Time feels differently to vampires. Slow. Decades feel like years. Years sometimes feel like months," Austin adds.

"Except with our girl." Diego grins at me. "My life feels like it just started."

Dana coos, holding her hand to her heart.

Heat warms my cheeks.

"You like his cheesiness way too much, babe," Kingston says.

I stick my tongue out at him.

"I still can't believe he's as old as The Divide," Fallon whispers. "That's like great-grandpa status."

"Kind of weird, huh?" Dana whispers back.

Kingston groans. "Thanks a lot. You make me sound ancient when you put it like that."

I step forward and hug him, wiggling my nose to his. "Experienced, not ancient. Nothing old about you apart from your back-world mouth when you mutter things I can't understand. So don't worry. You're still super hot to me." I squeeze his butt and hop back into a beam of sunlight before he can grab me.

He hums deep in his throat. "Tease."

I grin at him. "You bet. Now you guys behave. I swear if I find out you followed me, I'll room with my cousins."

"I highly doubt you will, but okay," Kingston says.

Austin motions for me to step closer to him, and I slide into his arms, knowing that unlike Kingston, he won't try to kidnap me or lock me up and persuade me to stay. "Stay alert and be safe. I don't trust anyone here. If you start feeling strange like earlier, get out as fast as you can."

I blink a few times. "You don't think..." I let my words trail off because my cousins currently hang onto every one of them.

"I don't know, Jewel. Just be cautious." He brings his lips to my ear. "If you bite someone, they will consider you a threat."

Eff. I better not. I didn't even think about the possibility of the weird craving returning. I feel fine now. "Don't worry, Austin. I feel normal. You...satisfied me."

His cheeks bloom with a pink tint, and he breaks his serious expression with a smirk I kiss off of him. "I hope that's always the case."

My body hums with his words. "I hope the same. And I'll be back in no time, and we can enjoy our day together. Promise." I kiss him sweetly again and turn to Diego to hug him. "I don't want you to worry either, Diego. You trained me well enough."

He engulfs me in his arms and lifts me off my feet to kiss me. Whispering against my mouth, he says, "Try not to let anyone's remarks get to you. If I know the exempt like I think I do, they'll surely say something that'll upset you. Just let it go, okay? It's not worth it." He knows me so well.

I bob my head. "Got it."

Dana and Fallon head out of our house first, and I follow behind them, looking back once before I close the door. Sunlight stings my eyes, and I stop at the edge of our new front yard and shade my vision to peer around. It feels like it's been forever since I just stood in the heat of the sun and let it soak into my skin.

"You okay, Jewel?" Fallon asks, linking her fingers around my arm.

I open my eyes and smile at her. "Yeah, better than I thought."

Dana takes my other arm. "You haven't been outside during the day in a while, huh?"

"Just once or twice. Not for very long." I hadn't realized I missed the feeling until this moment, and I can't help feeling bad about it. Giving up the sun in exchange for forever with my guys is worth it to me, but now I want to enjoy it as much as I can until I can't. If that ever happens.

"Must be hard. I couldn't imagine it." Fallon takes a few steps, tugging me with her until I start walking and keep her pace.

A calming silence fills the air as we stroll toward the main path that winds between two rows of identical houses—all in perfect condition. Haven Springs looks exactly like the small picture in the Blood Match Program brochure full of lush greenery, trees, and colorful flowers. Soft bells ring through the air, and I catch sight of a wind chime hanging from a beam on a covered porch. Everything is so different than in Dark Terrace Ranch. Too perfect. I half expect to hear the growls of shadow dwellers lurking in the shade created on the sides of the houses from the rising sun, but all remains peaceful.

"Kind of creepy, huh?" Dana asks, watching me in the corner of her eye.

Fallon giggles. "It took us a week to get over the feeling that something was going to jump out at us at any second."

"But you two do like it here, right?" I ask.

"Love it," they both say in unison. "Way better than The Boxes," Dana adds. "Thank you, Jewel. For everything. I know you're not exactly happy about being here, but we're glad for it. We've missed you."

"It's not that I'm unhappy. It's just—" I let my thought drop. The last thing I want to get into with my cousins are the details of a life I didn't necessarily want them to be a part of. They shouldn't have to worry about my future. "It's nothing. I am happy to be with you. I never thought we'd get a day like this."

They smile at me, and I hug my arms around them, matching their quick steps. Even in the all-human community, none of us have given up the brisk walking pace we're used to. It takes City Hall coming into view for me to slow down. A dozen emotions rise inside me, quickening my heartbeat at the memory of my last visit here. The blood might be gone from the steps of the building, but it's still fresh in my mind.

Two boys around my cousins' age sit on the top step to the building. Their faces brighten at the sight of us, and I can't stop my brows from shooting up on my forehead. I knew Dana and Fallon had friends here, but it looks like these boys might want more than friendship. And then Dana kisses the boy on the left, surprising the hell out of me.

Dana grins at me. "Jewel, this is Berto and Raul Suarez. Their brother Ricardo matched with Carolina Charleston. They arrived here the day before us."

Berto, the taller, darker skinned of the two boys drapes his arm over Dana's shoulder. "Do you know of him?"

Whoa. This place might look huge, but it is still small. And I do know of their brother. I saw him only a...a couple weeks ago? I'm pretty sure it's only been that long since the disastrous party Brayla and Orlando crashed. And Ricardo, who I couldn't remember his name at the time, was definitely there.

I bob my head. "I do. He looked good when I saw him."

"Told you he was still alive," Raul says, elbowing his brother. He rubs his hand over his short hair. "We haven't heard from him in a while," he adds, looking at me.

I try to remain expressionless. Austin told me that a lot of heirs stop contacting the family member who was matched with a vampire. It's part of the whole matching guilt. Some matched humans also do the same, because seeing a life they'll never have is too hard. As for Ricardo? I have no idea. I kind of wish I denied knowing him.

"Vampire schedules can be intense," I say, rocking on my heels. "The next time I see him..." I let my voice trail off. "Sorry, I guess I won't be seeing him." Because I'm a resident of Haven Springs. I'm not supposed to have any contact with vampires—I guess apart from Donor Life Corp.

"No worries," Berto says. "It's awesome that you got to come here. Everyone's talking about it. You're the first to have ever survived a breach in contract with a vampire."

Raul turns his attention to me. "Yeah, sucks for Mona, though. No one can believe she was taken for a blood debt and they let you—"

"Ms. Divine!" a masculine voice calls out, cutting off Raul's comment.

I've never been so glad for an interruption that wasn't a kiss from my guys in my life. I press my lips together, pushing away the wild emotions threatening to turn me into a hot mess. Because, what the actual fuck? Diego was right that people might have the nerve to say whatever is on their minds to me. Ramona was here for a month. She made connections. And here I am, some former Blood Match who will remind all the exempt of what their heirs will never get—a way out of the program. Not to mention they probably think the whole situation is messed up since I basically took Ramona's place here.

"It's so nice to finally meet you." Mr. Barton offers his hand out to me, dragging me from my thoughts. "Are you feeling any better?"

I hesitate for a second and shake the old man's hand, trying to stay in control of my rebel expression wanting nothing more than to frown at the guy who interrupted my night and shot Kingston. Sure, he doesn't remember, but I'll never forget.

I inhale a breath. "Getting there."

"Well, we shouldn't be here too long." He turns his attention to my cousins and the Suarez heirs. "Why don't you all run along to school? I'll see to it Jewel has everything she needs today."

I frown. "I want them to stay."

"Sorry, Ms. Divine. Rules are rules. It's important in maintaining order," he says, attempting to hold my gaze.

"We'll come straight home," Fallon says, hugging me. "You're going to do great. Everyone's really nice."

Dana hugs me next. "She's right. I don't want to fall behind anyway."

I can't believe I'm friggin' pouting at the fact that my cousins abandon me to go to school. I should get my shit together. I've faced a lot of angry vampires in the last few months. I shouldn't be so scared of a couple of humans.

"Great girls. Your father raised them well," Mr. Barton says, motioning me to climb the stairs to the double doors that lead inside.

His comment, while seemingly innocent, gets under my skin. My dad didn't raise them well. Aunt Dottie did. My mom. All my dad did was mess things up. He betrayed me and left me to clean up the disaster of a mess he left behind. And it irks me that I still care about him. How angry I am that I'll never get to confront him. All I want to really know is why. Why put me in this position with Orlando? Why risk everything we had?

"You knew my dad?" I ask, stepping into the cool lobby of City Hall.

He shakes his head, strolling next to me. "Only of his radical ideas. It's a shame what happened. He'd be devastated if he knew about Mona. She had a bright future here. I do hope you don't take what she gave up for you for granted."

Holy shit balls. Is he for real? Donor Life Corp supposedly handpicked the new council of Haven Springs, but this man reminds me a lot of Hayden—or of Blood Rebels. "She gave nothing up for me apart from our sisterly bond."

Mr. Barton raises an eyebrow and stops in his tracks

outside an arched doorway to a spacious room with a long, narrow table that reminds me of the feeding tables vampire's use. Luckily, the place is empty, and only Mr. Barton hears my comment, which I regret speaking the words out loud. "That's rather ungrateful, Ms. Divine. Your sister loved you and fought to get you here."

Diego's words swirl through my mind, reminding me to keep my shit together as much as I want to scream in this man's face. Instead of throwing out all the horrible stuff Ramona has done to me or tried to do, I say, "You're right. My apologies. The whole situation sucks. I want nothing more than for Ramona to be here instead of me."

Mr. Barton's stern mouth softens at my words. He totally misses the snark in my voice, but I won't point it out. Because I really want Ramona to be here instead of with Orlando, but not with me in her place. I just want to return to the Divinity Estate.

"I'm sure it's been quite the adjustment," he says, squeezing my shoulder.

I wince at the pain he sends through me, unintentionally digging his fingers into one of my healing bite marks. I automatically jerk back and cover my shoulder. Panic washes over me at the warm liquid seeping through the dark fabric of my hoodie. Mr. Barton studies me for a second, and I swivel away from him and ease my fingers up. Blood stains my hand. The sight sends panic shooting through my heart.

"Oh, Jewel." Mr. Barton says my name for the first

time as he moves to get a better view of me. "You're hurt."

I clench my jaw, trying to think of a million reasons as to why I'm bleeding, but I don't get the chance to use any of them. Mr. Barton grabs my arm and tugs my collar away without my permission. I swing out and punch him in the shoulder, knocking him back. He hits the wall and gasps, stunned by my sudden strength and reaction.

"Don't touch me!" I scream, hiding the bite mark again. Peering around, I look for the nearest exit. If he knows I've been bitten, he'll know that my guys are here. Things won't end well like the last time.

"What's going on?" A woman with silver hair appears in the hallway and rushes in my direction, cutting off my escape. She touches her hand to the visible gun holster on her hip. The gesture nearly has me screaming for my guys, but she stops herself and turns to Mr. Barton. "Are you hurt, Miles?"

Mr. Barton rubs his arm and rotates his shoulder. "I'm fine, Liz. It's Ms. Divine who's hurt. She seems to still be healing from her service in the Divine household. I must have accidentally re-opened a wound."

I blow out a breath at his comment. Thank friggin' God. Of course he'd think these were old bites. No one knows I heal quickly in my weird transitional state.

Taking a few steps away, I hit my back to the wall in an attempt to get more space between us. The two of them turn their attention to me and shuffle closer, treating me like a frightened animal.

I raise my palms up. "Stay back. Don't touch me again. I mean it." I want them nowhere near me, especially with the way they look at me. Pity crosses the woman's—Liz's—face, and she gives me a long look, taking me in. I'd think she could see past my hoodie to the bite mark. She focuses on the spot harder than any vampire would. Most would ignore such a sight.

Liz finally shifts her attention to Mr. Barton. "You should never touch someone who's been enslaved in a vampire household, Miles. Jewel's probably so traumatized from the experience."

I'm distressed and upset, all right. But not because of her reason. It takes everything in me not to yell that the only thing that has traumatized me was getting ripped away from the Divinity Estate and dropped among people who obviously don't understand me. People who I won't be explaining to that I get off on my guys biting me, something I had no idea I'd enjoy. And I really just don't want Mr. Barton touching me because...blah. The man feels like trouble. And judgey.

"I wasn't thinking," Mr. Barton says, frowning.

"Obviously," I mutter under my breath. "And thanks a lot for making my shoulder worse."

With the way they talk to each other in front of me, not really acknowledging that I'm standing right here, reminds me of vampires. It makes me wonder where they came from, how long they've been in Haven Springs, and if it's why they were chosen by the board to run the community.

Mr. Barton turns to me. "I'm sorry, Jewel. It won't happen again." His sincerity digs into me, loosening my bunching nerves. "I can't imagine what it's like to be you, but I firmly believe that every donor has a right to freedom. I want you to feel comfortable and safe here in Haven Springs no matter how you ended up here."

"Then maybe never mention my sister again." I can't stop the words from coming from my mouth. "Because whatever you think you know is wrong. You have no idea about anything."

"Oh, Miles. You mentioned Ramona? What is wrong with you?" Liz asks, her brows puckering. She surprises me by whacking him over the shoulder with the back of her hand. I purse my lips as to not react. I hate that I kind of like this woman, or maybe I just like the fact that she calls out Mr. Barton. Turning to me, she says, "Ms. Divine, please accept my sincerest apology on behalf of the council. You must excuse Mr. Barton. He's new to his position. Previously ran the school house."

That makes sense with his earlier action, sending my cousins to school. "It's fine," I murmur. "And I'm fine. Just want to get whatever this is about over with, so I can return home and sleep. I'm still on a night schedule."

Liz studies me, trailing her gaze up and down my body

like she could properly assess me through my clothes. I toe the ground with my tennis shoe, feeling all sorts of awkward. She looks at me like vampires do, and I'd prefer not to be analyzed or whatever.

"I'm sorry, Ms. Divine. You have a full day ahead of you. I'll make sure the medical staff includes an energy boost during your physical to help with the transition," she says, offering me a weak smile.

I gape at her. Eff that. "What? A physical? You don't already have all that information? My health keeper was vigilant in assuring I was properly taken care of."

"We do, but it looks like the details of the state of your health condition were falsified. Don't be nervous, though. I'm sure our practices are far less invasive than those of your health keeper. I'll oversee it myself, since I'm Haven Springs' lead medical practitioner. I'll assure you're on the mend and feel better quickly."

I place my hands on my hips. "I'm fine, though. I'll heal." I consider standing up for Austin for all of a second, but then Diego's reminder of keeping my shit together flits through my mind. Just because this woman doesn't believe Austin was the best doesn't mean anything. He's amazing to me, and that's all that matters.

"Rules are rules, Ms. Divine," Mr. Barton says. "You need to be in optimal health for your busy schedule. You've already fallen behind."

Stupid friggin' rules. "My schedule?"

Liz nods. "You have your official tour of Haven Springs and the assessment test to see where you'll be most suited in the community. I know you've inherited an incredibly large stipend as a new Divine Heir, but everyone must help out around here for our community to work. It'll be good for your re-immersion into human society. You will also be required to attend at least five group meet-ups for newcomers. It'll help you with the new social norms of exemption life."

Eff. All of that sounds terrible. She acts like I have no idea how to function. I'm probably more adjusted than anyone here.

"But that'll all come after this morning's introduction meeting. Unfortunately, Donor Life Corp insists on checking in on you due to the circumstances of your situation," Mr. Barton adds.

My head spins with their information. I mean, come on. Medical exams? Tests? Meetings? What the hell is a group meet-up? I don't want any part of all these Haven Springs' activities. And I hate that these two people are just going to pretend the community didn't turn against me on my last visit here. I don't care if the Blood Rebels left, some of the people who fought were just regular exempts.

I scrunch my nose. "I'll do the meeting, but no to everything else."

"Ms. Divine," they both say in unison.

I stroll past them and into the meeting room with the eerily familiar looking table. "No. Not today. My life has already been messed up enough as it is. You will let me do things in my own time."

"I'm sorry, that's not—"

"Ms. Matthias, Mr. Barton." A familiar, booming voice echoes through the room, making me jump. A screen lights up on the wall opposite the long table so that whoever sits at it can view the screen while the currently non-existent people in the audience look at those at the table. "You will refrain from enforcing anymore of your community instated rules on my adopted heir." Adopted? Seriously? It sounds weird as all get-out to hear Mitchell refer to me as such.

"But Mr. Divine," Liz says. "Jewel wants to turn down medical attention. You lied in her documents about her condition, and it's in everyone's best interest that she remains in good health, is it not?"

Whoa. Even Viorica doesn't talk to Mitchell in that tone. If he wasn't only on a projection screen, I might be afraid for the woman's life. I still kind of am.

Mitchell doesn't respond to her comment right away. I slowly turn my gaze from Liz to the image of him on the giant projection screen. He looks amused as hell, smirking at me, knowing well enough that he didn't lie about my health condition.

"I suppose a little medical treatment would be fine," he finally says without taking his eyes from mine.

"Mitchell," I complain, full-on whining.

"Jewel, just this once. Appease Ms. Matthias and make

sure things are taken care of." By things, he most likely means her. If she's a true medical professional, she might see through my lie of opening an old wound unless I can put things off for another few hours. "She is right about it being in our best interest to keep you healthy. You are our liaison and will be occasionally required to travel."

"What?" both Liz and Mr. Barton ask. "You can't do that. She's a resident."

"And all residents can decide for themselves if they have security clearance." Viorica's sharp voice cuts over any response Mitchell was about to give.

"But no one has ever been granted security clearance," Mr. Barton says. "You can't expect Jewel to travel alone. Allow us to recommend a security detail to assist in any traveling."

Mitchell flares his nostrils at the suggestion. "She will get one handpicked by me."

"But—"

"That's final. Now, see to it that Jewel is medically tended to and send her home. No tour. No immersion. And send someone to install locks on her house."

"Are you kidding—"

Mitchell disconnects the line before Liz can utter her argument. Mr. Barton huffs and laces his fingers on the back of his head. Another man strolls into the room and stops in his tracks upon seeing me smirking at the two council members.

He automatically touches the knife on his belt. "Is everything okay?"

I hug my arms over my chest and put more distance between me and the others. I really hate that everyone assumes I'm a threat. I'm barely half the size of Mr. Barton, and Liz has more muscles bulging through her long-sleeved shirt than I've ever seen on a woman—especially one her age.

"No," Mr. Barton says, spinning to look at me. "It's not okay."

Ah, hell.

The man slides out his knife.

Liz holds up her hands. "Put that thing away, Jeremy. Ms. Divine isn't a threat."

The man, Jeremy, shifts his gaze to give me a once-over. And boy, does he drink in every damn inch of me. Not in a good way, either. If looks could vaporize me, I'd be a pile of guts on the floor.

"Everyone who gives up their human name is a threat," he mutters. "This traitor to humanity shouldn't even be here. She's responsible for Miguel's death. She's the reason we nearly lost this place."

My eyes widen at his accusations. "Seriously?"

"She has to go. I'm sure the rest of the council will agree." He doesn't even look at me as he says the words. How very vampire-like of him. But worse, I'm nearly certain that he's a Blood Rebel. Why else would he act so hostile toward me?

Fear bunches in my stomach, and I inch farther away and toward the door. Three more guys enter the room, unintentionally blocking my way. They assess what's happening, all grabbing at their friggin' weapons too.

"Everyone calm down," Liz says. "All rash actions will have dire consequences. Jewel is a resident here. She might have been given a vampire's name, but she's still human. She is on our side. Her heirs are here."

"That's not what I heard," another man says. "Sounds like she's here to report our every move to Donor Life Corp."

I squeeze my eyes shut. "Are you kidding me? I hate Donor Life Corp! They ruined my life."

Silence falls on the room, and everyone turns their attention to me. My whole body trembles with anger. All I did was show up to this meeting because I was told to. I don't want to be here as much as everyone seems not to want me here. I hate to even think this, and I don't know for sure, but I think Orlando made me stay at home for this reason. His way of keeping me alive or whatever, I guess.

Straightening my shoulders and pushing the thought away, I strut toward the archway to leave the meeting. I can't be here. I can't risk facing these people alone like this. I don't care what Mitchell demanded of me. He clearly cares very little about my life and more about his power.

I brave my way past the three guys, my heart threatening to ram through my chest under their glares. Thankfully, no one grabs me or tries to get physical. The men let me go.

"Jewel, wait," Liz says, rushing up beside me. "Let me walk with you to the clinic."

I ignore her and quicken my pace. "I'm not going to the clinic, so just leave me alone."

"Jewel."

"I said leave me alone!"

Pushing past her, I rush toward the exit and into the bright sunlight. Liz calls my name from the top step of City Hall but thankfully doesn't run after me. Jogging down the path in the direction I came with Dana and Fallon, I hurry to get back to the house and my guys. It's the only place I want to be.

I'm so focused on rushing that I don't see the figure emerge from the trees. I hit the person straight on and lose my balance, falling back onto the pathway. My breath escapes my lungs in a burning gasp, and I struggle to scramble back to my feet.

"Damn it, Jewel. You should pay more attention. If I were anyone else, you'd be dead."

I freeze at the sound of Brayla's voice.

Peering around, I search for the nearest burst of sunlight. "Stay back."

Someone grabs me from behind and covers my mouth.

I can't even scream.

UNEXPECTED MOVE

"PRECIOUS JEWEL, CALM DOWN." ORLANDO'S breath tickles the hair around my ear, making me shiver. "I'm only helping you. I won't hurt you, and if I wanted to kidnap you, we'd already be gone."

"Why haven't you?" I ask, my voice squeaking as fear pounds through me. I have no idea how much I should or shouldn't say. I wasn't expecting Orlando to come after me during the day. I know he's always sent someone to get me after dark to drag me into the grove. Now, I'm freaking the hell out.

Orlando spins me around in his arms to meet my gaze. His eyes travel over my face as he drinks me in. "You remember."

I don't answer him.

"The Divines?"

Again, I don't respond. Unfortunately, my heart responds for me, beating faster.

He hums under his breath, his eyes blinking silver with his thoughts. "That makes things more interesting."

"How so?" I ask, my mouth speaking before my head has a chance to catch up.

Orlando smirks. "I'll tell you in time. It seems Donor Life Corp made a rather unexpected and smart move. I'd like to see it play out."

"What do they have to do with us?" I ask, annoyance lining my words. "I want you to just leave me alone. If you don't, you'll regret it. I know we have some messed up history or whatever—"

"The Divines messed it up. Not me. And Jewel, I do not need the reminder. You made your feelings quite clear about the Divines and the future of our relationship, but it doesn't mean I can't persuade you otherwise."

"I did?" Thank friggin' God. Ugh. I don't even like the way he says relationship. It skeeves me out.

"But even so, you'll eventually be responsible for paying your dues. Right now, I'll just use this situation to my advantage."

"I owe you nothing," I say, lowering my voice. "And I won't let you use me."

"Donor Life Corp is the one using you. But don't worry. I won't let them for long. And if your matches are worthy of you, they won't allow it either."

Setting me on my feet, Orlando releases me. I spin around, taking a moment to assess the quaint living room we stand in. Shiny silver paper lines the huge window, blocking not only the sunlight but also our location. All I know is that we're somewhere in Haven Springs and not far from the path that leads to my temporary home. Orlando only carried me at vampire speed for seconds.

Orlando steps forward, drawing my attention to him. I attempt to step away, but he's too quick to cup my face. His eyes search mine again, sending goosebumps over my skin. I can't help thinking about what Mitchell said about me not always hating Orlando. But my guys were right. Even if I didn't hate him before, I hate him now.

"Jewel, I know you're upset and pissed off, but it must be this way," he says, stroking his fingers along my cheek. It's like he read my mind. "You don't understand the importance."

"Then tell me."

"Not yet. Not until you're mine."

"I'll never be."

"In time. I'll assure it."

Rage steals my words away, and I lose my shit, anger tightening my features. "You won't."

"Don't you get it? You don't have a choice."

Something about his response burns through me, and I

can't help but believe him. Because he's right. I've never gotten a real choice. I was stupid to think I could ever have an ounce of control over my life. That I could have a future with Kingston, Diego, and Austin. If it's not Mitchell messing things up, it's Donor Life Corp. And if it's not Donor Life Corp, it's Orlando.

Orlando drops his hands from my face and steps back, surprised by my body choosing now to tremble and cry and snot uncontrollably in the grossest way possible.

"I hate you," I whisper. "How could you do this to me? How could you come here and try to steal everything from me?"

His serious expression softens. "Jewel, this is for the best."

"You keep messing with my head. I can't stand it. I don't know what's real or not. My memories—"

"Because they can't know!" His voice booms through the room, startling me. Flashing his fangs, he glides closer and picks me up off my feet. My back hits the wall with a thud, and he glares at me, erupting a burst of hot dread through me. "Don't you understand what's at risk? It's more than your life."

I don't answer him right away. Because I don't understand, and I won't. "I don't care. I want you to leave me alone," I say.

He sighs. "You'll change your mind."

"I won't."

"We'll see."

"Just go. Get out of here."

"Don't think this is over. I'll give you time to cool off, but I will not let this opportunity go to waste. Do you understand? Now, one more thing. Let me give you what you need."

Before I can ask him what, Orlando bites his arm and brings it up to my mouth too quickly to stop me from arguing. His blood coats my lips, and he watches me so intently it feels like I'll disintegrate under his vibrant blue eyes.

"Drink, Jewel," he whispers, his own chest heaving.

I purse my lips together, not allowing a drop into my mouth.

He presses his arm to my mouth harder. "Do it. You need it."

"Orlando, we have to hurry. The shade's shifting." Brayla's soft voice trickles to me from a doorway somewhere to my right. "I'm not getting burned again because Jewel won't do what's best for her."

Ignoring her, Orlando attempts to capture my gaze. "Jewel, listen to me."

I shake my head.

"Don't make me force you."

"You'll only make her hate you even more," Brayla says.

Orlando flashes his fangs and roars in my face, sending strands of hair blowing away. I stiffen and squeeze my eyes shut, half expecting him to bite me. He gasps a couple of angry breaths in my face, shoving his hand into my clavicle to keep me in place. Tears streak hot trails over my cheeks.

The pressure of his arm releases from my mouth, and I shudder, my whole body freaking the eff out.

And then I do the only thing I can think of. I swing my arm out and clock him in the side of the head, whipping his head sideways. He releases a scary ass growl and lets me go. I drop to my knees, my legs forgetting that their only job is to keep me upright in this moment.

I cry out at the burst of pain but don't get the chance to do anything else. Orlando pushes me onto my back and kneels over me, holding my face still.

"You're only going to get worse, Jewel. Be prepared."

"Tell me what's wrong with me," I whisper, my voice barely audible.

He twists his mouth in consideration but then shakes his head. "There is only one way I'll give you answers."

"I'm not going with you."

"Yet. You have my word that I'll return as soon as I can. Now, be smart with what you choose to do next. Donor Life Corp doesn't care about you like I do."

Orlando vanishes, leaving me frozen scared on the floor. I stare through my watering eyes at the light on the ceiling until my body finally listens to my screaming mind and gets up. I focus my attention on my surroundings, trying to listen for signs of people, but the place is empty. Orlando and Brayla are gone.

Pushing to my feet, I head straight for the window and rip at the paper blocking out the sun. My vision stings from the change in lighting. I clutch the windowsill, catching my breath. The front yard looks identical to all the other front yards in Haven Springs, the only difference being that this place lies vacant.

Using the sleeve of my hoodie, I swipe Orlando's blood from my chin. His words tumble through my mind over and over again. He asked me to let him feed me. He claims I'll get worse. The action reminds me of the strange dreams, possibly memories, I had of my dad. How he used to take me to Orlando. How I drank his blood...but why? I think Kingston might have been right. This is more than a side effect. This has nothing to do with sex. I think it has everything to do with my survival.

The thought scares the shit out of me.

Laughter draws my attention to the pathway outside the house, and I duck out of the way, spying on a couple strolling by only to enter the house next door. I count to sixty, waiting to make sure they don't come back out, and head to the front door left ajar.

Closing my eyes, I listen to the world for another moment, focusing on the muffled conversations from inside the houses. The humans of Haven Springs are much louder than any of the staff at the Divinity Estate. I guess it's a good thing, despite how distracting it is.

I suck in a breath and steel myself, cautiously stepping from the vacant house. I half expect a dozen exempt humans to come charging at me with their weapons drawn because I'm trespassing, but luckily, I make it to the path unnoticed.

The identical set up of the houses leaves me confused as to where I'm supposed to head to return home. I end up walking the path until it dead-ends at the perimeter wall. I follow it along the outskirts of the community, now tense with nerves.

I friggin' hate this place. I thought the Divinity Estate was confusing.

"Security clearance? Shit. It's worse than what we thought." The deep, familiar voice stops me in my tracks.

My heart reacts, racing in my tight chest. Footsteps shuffle closer, crunching over the dry terrain of the lemon grove. I scramble away and rush to hide between two trees.

"Are you sure it's a good idea? I can extract her tonight. Take her somewhere until the deal is finalized."

I knew I was the talk of the community, but the last thing I expected was to stumble upon the guy I want nothing more than to greet with a power kick to his groin. Because I friggin' hate him. Even the sound of Hayden's voice grates on my nerves.

"No. I don't care. I don't trust him to keep his word. He's already changed things by allowing her to stay here. What makes you think he'll give us Mona unless we have

Jewel? We can trade them."

Of course Hayden isn't working with Orlando out of the goodness of his heart. And friggin' A. Whatever Hayden plans will jeopardize everything. For a guy who wants to protect humanity, he sure likes to treat humans—me—as property.

The footsteps draw closer, and I peer around, looking for somewhere to hide. A long shadow moves across the ground a few feet away and stops. Carefully bending down, I crouch beneath the lush, leafy branches of a lemon tree. My hair gets caught on a branch, and I accidentally shake the thing a little too hard, sending a piece of fruit rolling.

Hayden's voice cuts off for a second before he says, "Hey, I gotta go. Call me with an update once you install the locks at the Jordan house, okay? You can drop the key off at number sixty-two."

The crunch of his boots resonates as Hayden steps closer in my direction. I claw at the tree branch, rushing to pull my hair free. A sharp branch scrapes over my palm, and burning pain erupts on my skin.

Sucking in a deep breath, I prepare to scream as loud as I can.

But then a chime rings through the air, and Hayden's footsteps stop again.

I take the moment to untangle my hair and bolt away. As much as I want to hang around and listen to him chat on the phone again, my body already wars with my mind and takes control to get me the hell away. If I can manage to make it home, I can tell my guys, and they can come out here and deal with him...maybe. The sun rises higher in the sky, shrinking the shadows around me.

I focus on listening to my surroundings and manage to make my way to a cement path. It takes me right back to City Hall, and I pick up my pace and jog around the building, hoping no one sees me.

I full-on sprint at the sight of the path I know leads directly back to my house. Sweat beads on my forehead, and I shield my eyes from the brightness of the sun's rays. The second I spot the two-story house, large in comparison to most of the other houses but only the size of one of the guest houses at the Divinity Estate, I slow down and take a few deep breaths.

"Ms. Divine."

I don't even get the chance to touch my fingers to the door when Liz calls my name. Shit. I was too concerned with getting inside that I didn't see her sitting on the bench on the porch. She picks up a black bag from the ground next to her and carries it as she closes the space to me.

"Is everything all right?" she asks, stepping closer to stop me from entering my house. "I've been waiting here a while. I thought you'd be home before now."

I release the doorknob and turn to face her. "I got lost." I regret the excuse immediately because amusement crosses her face and she smirks. I did reject the idea of a tour of

Haven Springs after all.

"Maybe I can set up a tour for you tomorrow," she says, adjusting the bag on her arm. Friggin' knew it. She's smugger than Kingston could ever be.

I shrug. "Yeah, maybe. I might feel better by then. Now, I just want to lie down. I wasn't joking about being off my schedule. I'm doubly exhausted."

She cuts me off with her arm, stopping me from going inside. "Let me give you a quick exam, please. You can lie down while I do it. I also have a couple of extra vitamins in my bag. You might be fatigued from an iron deficiency."

I open my mouth to decline, but Austin whispers, "Just let her, Jewel. She'll keep coming back if you don't."

"Our girl is covered in bite marks," Kingston whispers. "No thanks to you, Diego."

Diego growls. "You remember what Mitchell said. We'll take care of her if she gets suspicious."

Kingston hums. "Right, fine. Babe, let her in."

Liz looks at me expectantly, not hearing my guys' words, and I heave the loudest sigh in existence. Kingston's soft chuckle comes through the wood, and I catch sight of my guys disappearing as I slowly open the door.

"Promise to leave me alone after?" I ask Liz.

She nods. "At least for the day."

I grimace. "Just a day?"

She follows me inside and peers around the cozy living area. "The sooner you get used to the community, the easier it'll be."

I roll my eyes. "Yeah, sure."

"You'll see. Come on. Show me to your room. I'll be quick." Liz waves me toward the stairs, and I hesitate. The last thing I want to do is take her anywhere near the bedrooms. I don't even know what kind of condition the one I now share with Diego looks like.

"The couch is fine," I mutter, ignoring her hand to cross the room. I plop down on it and stare at the ceiling.

"Whatever makes you most comfortable." She glances around again. "Now, if you can please undress for me, I'd like to check on your bite marks to make sure they're healing properly and to make sure Mr. Barton's carelessness didn't cause any more damage."

A low growl sounds through the air, but Liz misses it, not hearing the deep pitch of Diego's voice. It was Kingston who I expected a reaction from, not Diego, and I wonder if I should just insist I'm fine and shove Liz out the door.

"Like I said earlier, I'm okay," I murmur, deciding not to risk Diego flying in here.

Liz sets her bag on the coffee table. "But the one on your shoulder bled again. You don't want it to get infected. Your sweet, beautiful cousins just got you back. Don't you want to take care of yourself for their sake?"

I glare at her. "Seriously?"

"Just let me look at the one on your shoulder then. I won't touch it unless you say it's okay."

I tip my head back and stare at the beam of light coming in from the crack in the curtain behind me. I make a mental note to do something about it later, so my guys don't have to worry about burning if they come downstairs.

"Please," Liz says. She takes a seat next to me on the couch.

Hooking my fingers to the hem of my hoodie, I relent to her request and pull it over my head, leaving on my long-sleeved shirt. I drag the collar down with my fingers, exposing Diego's bite mark to the medical practitioner.

She shoves her hand into her bag and pulls out a flashlight and turns it on. "I don't see any signs of infection." Reaching up her other hand, she hovers it over my skin. "May I?"

I swallow the lump in my throat and nod.

Liz presses her finger near the wound. "Not hot or anything. I think you'll be fine after a quick cleaning and bandaging. Do you have any more for me to look at?"

I stare at my hands.

"Babe, we need to work on your lying face," Kingston whispers.

"Ms. Divine?" Liz asks. "You do, don't you?"

I sigh. "Yes, but I'm fine. None of them hurt. The one on my shoulder only does because Mr. Barton squeezed the hell out of it."

The revelation elicits all sorts of scary noises from up the stairs. Liz must catch something, because she turns her gaze in the direction of the staircase. I clear my throat and then cough. She still doesn't look at me, so I roll my sleeve up and pinch one of the small circular wounds, breaking the healing skin.

"Ouch!" I say. "Shit. It caught on my shirt."

"Oh, Jewel. Let me help you." Liz rushes to tug out and pop the top off her medical kit. Her nose scrunches as she places a towel across my lap and squirts a cool liquid over my skin. Quickly, she pulls the sleeve up on my other arm, taking advantage of the situation. "You've been bitten a lot. Four times total on your arms. Two of those don't look so good. The skin's slightly discolored. Mind if I swab them to test?"

"Yeah, I mind," I say, pulling my arm from her.

"But—"

A knock on the door cuts off her argument, and we turn our attention to the shadow of a figure through the light curtain. I don't even have a second to get to my feet before the door swings open. I rush to tug my sleeves down, but from the obvious wide eyes of the hulking, muscular asshole, I wasn't quick enough.

His familiarity sends my whole body trembling. A memory comes crashing back to me, and I recognize the guy. He was...shit. He was here with Hayden. He's the one who helped him kidnap me from my room and take me to Orlando.

Pointing my finger at him, I yell, "Get the hell out of

my house! You can't just barge in here."

Liz hops up and steps in front of me. "Jewel, it's okay. Brody is here to put on your locks."

I blink a few times at Liz's words. "What did you say?"

She tilts her head. "That he was going to put on your locks."

I stiffen, panic exploding through me. I overheard Hayden talking to someone about installing locks. About delivering the key somewhere.

"Diego!" I yell without responding to her. "Kingston! Austin! Blood Rebels!"

The guy, Brody, drops his box of supplies on the ground and reaches for a gun on his belt. Liz shoves me back onto the couch, falling on top of me. I don't even get the chance to fight. Her weight presses down on me, and a gunshot pops louder than anything I've heard in a while.

My ears ring for a moment.

Liz shouts.

LOSE CONTROL

"GET HER OFF JEWEL, KINGSTON," Diego commands, his voice muted through my still ringing ears.

Kingston growls, and Liz's weight falls away. "The only reason I'm not ripping your throat out is because you protected our girl. Don't make me change my mind."

Cool hands slide under me, and Austin pulls me from the couch and into his arms. His vibrant green eyes search mine, and I blink, suppressing my urge to start bawling my eyes out. Because, hell.

"Are you hurt?" he asks, stroking his finger across my cheek.

I shake my head. "Startled is all."

Austin snuggles his face into my neck, breathing in the

scent of my hair like he needs a moment of my closeness to keep himself together. A groan from behind us makes him spin around, and he gently sets me on my feet but proceeds to step in front of me to block me from the view of Diego gripping Brody from behind and Kingston holding onto Liz.

"You fucking traitor," Brody snarls, bucking in Diego's arms. "You shot me."

I dig my fingers into Austin's shoulder to stand on my tiptoes.

"You were going to hurt Jewel. She's a resident and under the protection of the council," Liz says, remaining utterly still. "Now, please. If you'd release me, Mr. Divine, we can sort this out. I hope my actions prove to you that Jewel's accusations—at least in my case—are unfounded."

Kingston isn't quick to let Liz go. "Not until I hear what our girl has to say first."

All eyes turn toward me, and I peel myself away from Austin's back, though all I want to do is stay hidden behind him with the way Brody glowers at me like if he stares long enough, I'll explode.

I slide under Austin's arm and clench my teeth at both Liz and Brody's reactions. Brody's lips twist in disgust while Liz stares at me in shock. "The council hired this guy to install locks while also instructing him to give them a key."

"We did no such thing," Liz argues.

I train my gaze to the floor. "The council also still takes

orders from Hayden. I—I saw him again. He's been helping Orlando but plans to turn on him." Lifting my hand, I point at Brody. "He's supposed to give him a key. They want to kidnap me again but to trade."

"You b—" One second Brody struggles in Diego's arms, and in the next, Austin rams him into the wall, cracking the plaster. He flashes his fangs, releasing a throaty roar, making the man wince.

And then he bites him.

I stare in shock as Austin loses control right before my eyes. Brody hollers and flails, attempting to punch Austin, but he's too strong. Too determined. Too starved. He rips back from Brody's neck and yells out, his face distorted in anger, his eyes remaining silver like I've seen on some of the shadow dwelling vampires.

"Diego," I whisper, my throat burning as I try to push his name from my mouth. "Stop him."

Diego yanks Austin away, dragging him from Brody. The man falls to his knees, and he clutches his bloody neck with one hand while trying to grab something from his work belt. The silver of a sharp stake gleams in the overhead light, drawing my attention from Austin snapping his teeth, trying to break free from Diego.

And then Austin does.

He flies across the room in a blur. It takes him stopping in front of Liz for my eyes to finally focus on him. She releases a small cry from Kingston's arms. He spins with her, kicking his leg back to knock Austin away. But Austin doesn't stop.

Locking his fingers to Kingston's shirt, Austin drags him back and throws him into the opposite wall. Kingston drops to the ground, releasing his own terrifying noise. Diego charges Austin, and the two of them throw fists, flashing fangs, the whole scene unfolding before me completely batshit crazy.

Every time Diego gets a hold on Austin, he manages to rip free. Brody doesn't even get a chance to defend himself as Austin rushes him again. The two of them collide right into the front door, splintering it. A streak of sunlight beams through a crack, cutting across Austin's face. He flies back out of the way, and Brody falls to the ground.

Austin stalks Brody inhumanly fast, reaching to grab him again, but the guy manages to rip part of the broken door free, sending more sunlight cascading across the living room. He takes advantage of my guys' sensitivity to sunlight and crawls on his hands and knees out of the broken door.

Austin doesn't let a little sunlight stop him from attempting to grab at Brody one more time.

"Austin, stop!" I yell, pleading with my voice for him to get his shit together. "Please, you have to stop. This isn't you. He's not worth it. You're going to burn."

Austin jerks his attention to me, his eyes still flashing crazy silver. Blood coats his chin, and he narrows his eyes, setting off my whole body in a bad way. Fear pours through me, and I take an automatic step backward. I can't help it. It's my body's way of telling me that Austin's a fierce predator and I better watch myself.

Diego takes the distraction and wraps his arms around Austin to pull him far from the sun shining in. Austin jerks back and forth in his hold, nearly making Diego lose his grip. The two of them start fighting again. Kingston abandons Liz, joining Diego, not even caring that the woman rushes to escape.

"Chill the fuck out, Austin," Kingston says, punching Austin in the stomach. "You're scaring our girl."

"What's wrong with him?" I ask, keeping my distance. This is far from a brotherly fight, and I know better than to try to get in the middle.

"It's going to be fine, beautiful. Just go upstairs, okay?" Diego says, spinning and shoving Austin into the wall.

"We'll be right up, babe," Kingston adds.

"But the Blood Rebels," I say, motioning to the door.

Kingston scrunches his nose. "Let them go. We'll deal with them later."

"Just go upstairs, Jewel," Diego says again, using my name this time. "Please."

I suck in a breath, finding my nerve to deny his request. As much as my body screams for me to obey him and get as far away as possible, I can't abandon Austin. Not like this. I know he's always struggled with his control. I know he's always taken pride in keeping his cool and keeping his act together. And while I'm sure Diego's right about Austin not wanting me to see him like this, I'm not going to let them shield me from each other.

"You better hold him tighter, Diego," Kingston growls. "Our girl's not leaving."

I place my hands on my hips. "And don't you dare try to make me. We're in this together. You can't just pick and choose the parts of your lives to include me in."

"But Austin—"

"Needs me. Just hold him still, okay?"

"Fucking stubborn. She's lucky I'm madly in love with her," Kingston mutters under his breath to Diego.

I smirk, taking a step closer to the three of them. "Love you too, dude."

Kingston glowers and grabs Austin by the neck. "Austin, I swear. If you don't get yourself together in the next ten seconds and then accidentally hurt Jewel, you'll be in so much trouble."

"Kingston," I say.

"Oh, no you fucking don't. You're going to be in trouble too, babe."

I roll my eyes.

"I mean it. No dates with Austin for a week."

"No cuddling with him," Diego adds. "And Kingston will be the one in charge of feeding you."

"It's a good thing I have access to a kitchen or else I'd starve," I murmur, braving to step closer to my guys.

Austin stops struggling in their arms, his silver eyes following my every move. He flares his nostrils the closer I get, standing utterly still. My heart races like crazy, threatening to spill out across the floor. I inhale a few slow, deep breaths, getting my own shit together. Because my friggin' humanity is afraid of the danger that comes with facing Austin like this. But the more dominant part of me, the part that knows it's going to be okay, gives me the nerve to continue to close the space.

"Austin," I say, standing right in front of him. He could grab me if Diego wasn't restraining him.

"Careful, babe," Kingston warns.

"Shut up and pretend to give us some privacy," I say.

Kingston's damn pout. He relents and closes his eyes, still obviously focused on us but now trying his best to keep his comments to himself. Diego averts his eyes as well, though his grip tightens even more. Austin jerks his head to glower.

Bringing my hands up, I scare the hell out of Kingston and Diego by cupping Austin's face. His attention returns to me, and I stand up on my tip-toes so that I can directly look at him. His fangs peek from his lips, his jaw tight, but he remains utterly still.

"Jewel," he whispers, his voice nearly inaudible, even to my super hearing. "Please, listen to—"

"I'm not going anywhere, Austin," I say, cutting him off. "I know you feel out of control, and you're struggling with your nature. You're afraid of hurting me, I get it. But I won't let you, okay."

"We sure as hell won't," Diego adds.

Kingston pinches Austin's shoulder. "Now get it the fuck together."

I flick Kingston in the chest, and he narrows his eyes at me, but I keep my eyes on Austin. It takes a good few minutes of gazing into my eyes for Austin's expression to finally soften. He relaxes, his clenched teeth releasing to smooth out the tightness of his jaw. Ever so slowly, I bring my face to his despite another warning from Kingston and brush my lips against Austin's, feeling the slight poke of his fangs.

"Can you control yourself if I let you bite me?" I ask him, my voice soft, nearly a whisper. "I know you're hungry."

"Jewel, I don't think—"

Austin suddenly stiffens and growls. I take a step back but realize his reaction isn't because of me. Kingston abandons Austin to rush the door. Liz shields herself with her hands instead of reaching for the weapon on her waist.

"Wait, I can help!" she yells, cowering against the wall. "I can draw Jewel's blood so that he won't have to bite her. Please, I'm worried about her. Some of those bites look infected."

Kingston picks Liz off the floor and holds her up. "And why should we trust you? You're a Blood Rebel."

She purses her lips. "I'm not. I swear. I give you permission to open my mind and ask me. I have nothing to hide. I just want to help."

"Why?"

"Because I'm afraid he'll kill her if I don't."

I realize that Kingston already captures Liz in his gaze, opening her mind up to him. Her body slackens in his hold, and I turn from Austin and Diego to cross the room to them.

"He won't kill her. He's in love with her," Kingston responds out loud. "And those bites look infected because they were intended to transform Jewel. They'll heal on their own."

Liz doesn't respond because he doesn't ask her anything specific. I'm kind of surprised he reveals any information at all.

"Now, about the Blood Rebels. How many are there?"

"I don't know," Liz responds.

Kingston leans into her. "Tell me."

"I don't know." Liz's face remains calm.

Without breaking eye contact, Kingston says, "She really doesn't know. No one has manipulated her mind."

I rest my hand on Kingston's shoulder to steady myself as I get a better look at Liz. "What's the Blood Rebels' plan?"

Kingston licks his lips. "Answer Jewel."

"I don't know," Liz says.

"Are you even a Blood Rebel?" Kingston asks, digging his fingers into her cheeks.

Liz's eyes remain drawn to Kingston's. "No."

Kingston releases her and turns to his brothers, his eyebrows furrowing. "What do you want to do? Wipe her mind and send her off?"

Austin groans. "Let her draw blood from Jewel."

"What?" Kingston and Diego say in unison.

I meet Austin's gaze, noticing the worry in his eyes that now blink between glowing silver and green. If he's willing to allow someone other than himself to handle my blood, he must really be struggling. And I won't let Kingston and Diego push him if he's even a little bit doubtful of his control with me.

"You're seriously going to—"

I swat Kingston in the arm. "He's not going to anything. I'm allowing Liz to extract my blood for Austin. If you stop glowering and complaining, you can have some too."

That shuts him the hell up, and he closes his eyes to get his face to cooperate.

Liz straightens her shoulders and stares at me with a dozen emotions crossing her face. For being an exempt, she handles this situation incredibly well and hasn't even tried to draw her weapon once. I thought she acted differently when I first met her and was impressed by the way she handled Mitchell, and now I'm even more intrigued with how she's handling my guys.

"Before I extract Jewel's blood, I need help bringing Brody back inside. The last thing we need is to have someone stumble upon him on the front lawn," Liz says, motioning to the broken door.

"He's still here?" I ask.

"Is he...?" Austin's soft voice trails off.

Liz shakes her head. "I knocked him out and restrained him."

Kingston disappears from the room only to return a moment later with a hoodie that he pulls tight to hide most of his face. He grabs a throw blanket from the couch and wraps it over him, protecting the rest of his exposed skin from the sun. A second later, the door flies open, blinding me with a burst of sunlight. Kingston flies back in, tossing Brody on the floor. The guy tumbles a few feet and lands face down in the middle of the living room. Liz hurries to fix the door the best she can, using Kingston's discarded blanket to block the sun.

"That should hold up until it can be repaired," she says, dusting off her hands.

"But maybe we should move somewhere that I don't have to worry about you three getting sunburned," I say, motioning to the stairs.

Liz gapes at me from her spot.

"What?" I ask, shifting my feet under her scrutiny.

She lifts and drops her shoulders. "Trying to wrap my

mind around everything is all. I had expected a challenge upon notification of your transfer here, but I wasn't expecting this."

I glance to each of my guys. "I'm not sure what you mean."

"They really love you," she says, nodding to Austin, Kingston, and Diego.

"Is that so hard to believe?"

She nods. "You don't fear for your life?"

"Never. They're the only ones I feel safe with. Everyone always seems to be out to get me." I wave my hand at Brody. "Like that guy. Who knows how many others are in Haven Springs."

She doesn't react.

"They're the only ones I can count on. Even my own sister turned against me. I feel so lucky that they love me. And I love them. Plus," I say, turning to my guys. I know I shouldn't pick now to tell them about Orlando, but I suddenly can't get my encounter with him off my mind. How he tried to give me his blood in an attempt to feed me. "I'd die without them."

"You underestimate your strength, beautiful," Diego says, speaking up.

I offer him a weak smile. "Maybe so, but that's not what I meant."

Austin frowns, his eyes finally under control, no longer flashing silver. "Then what do you mean?"

I clear my throat to whisper too silently for Liz to hear. "You're not the only ones who survive on blood."

Kingston's eyes widen. "What? Do you mean—" He flies at me and cups my face. "Show me your teeth."

I bare them, making him frown. "No fangs, dude. But I still survive on blood. Just not human blood. Whatever happened to me...what my dad did. Whatever Orlando did. It changed me. And I think Katherine's bite—your bites— triggered my progression, and the lack of blood makes me...super friggin' hungry for it. I'm only going to get worse."

"How can you know for sure?" Diego asks.

I lick my lips, my nerves at the memory getting the best of me. "Orlando visited me on the way back here. It's why I was late. Why I nearly ran into Hayden and overheard him planning something with this guy."

Kingston combs his fingers through his hair. "Fuck, babe. Start with this shit next time."

"But Liz—"

"Can have her mind wiped."

Liz frowns at Kingston materializing in front of her. He locks her in a stare. "Forget what we've talked about. You will never repeat anything we say."

"Give our girl a break, Kingston," Diego says. "The whole situation is overwhelming. She wasn't expecting Liz to be here and to be attacked."

Kingston turns to me. "We'll handle everything from

now on. You're too fucking fragile, no matter how badass you are. You're not leaving this house."

"Now that kind of attitude puts our girl and us at risk," Diego argues.

"Then we gotta get our girl out of here so we can properly protect her. We need to run tests to make sure she's okay," Kingston says, sounding like Austin. "We'll leave tonight."

"What about our deal with Mitchell?" I ask, grimacing. Kingston's impulsivity, while most definitely hot in the right moments, also makes things complicated. He reacts first and thinks later. Right now, we need a clear head and to agree on how to move forward.

Kingston flares his nostrils. "What about it? I don't fucking care about appeasing him. You're more important, babe."

I place my hands on my hips. "I don't think Mitchell will see it that way. If he's already questioning your loyalty..." I can't even think about what will happen if he's sure they put me first.

"Jewel's right," Diego says.

"It doesn't matter. I'm siding with Kingston," Austin says. "We should leave tonight. I need my lab. We need to know what we're dealing with. If Jewel needs our blood, we need to be able to provide it to her. I can't do so without properly being satiated myself." Austin meets my gaze. "If you're suddenly craving blood—vampire blood—that takes precedence, especially if Orlando knows."

"We can use this to our advantage. I'll drink less if you're worried, Austin," Diego offers. "I'm with Jewel. I don't want to risk Mitchell questioning our loyalty. He expects us to take care of the Blood Rebel problem, which might no longer connect to Orlando by what Jewel mentioned about Hayden."

"Then we'll tell Mitchell," Austin says.

"Are you fucking kidding me?" Kingston asks. "Tell him what exactly? That our girl is special? He's already trying to use our girl. Imagine what he'd do if he found out."

"I have a lab," Liz says, speaking up.

None of my guys hear her as they continue to argue over what to do next. My head spins at hearing all of the what-if scenarios they play out, all ending with me either hurt, dead, or caged. They speak freely and unfiltered in front of Liz, and she listens intently, absorbing all of the information.

"I change my mind. Jewel stays here," Kingston says. "You can go back to Dark Terrace Ranch, Austin. Take our girl's blood back with you."

Austin clenches his fists, his eyes turning silver again. Blinking, he pulls himself together. He tightens his jaw, still obviously on the brink of losing control again. I think the only reason he hasn't is because the threat to my life subsided, but now he might think his brothers are putting me back in the line of fire. "I'm not leaving Jewel."

"You can use my lab," Liz says again.

I crinkle my nose at her, knowing exactly what it's like to be ignored by vampires.

"Well, then you better fucking learn to keep yourself in control or—"

Before Kingston and Austin start throwing punches, I step right between them, slapping my hands to their chests. Liz audibly gasps and reaches for the blade on her belt. Diego's quick to put his arms around me, ready to rip me away, but both Kingston and Austin freeze. Liz does too.

"Chill out," I say. "Both of you. If you guys would just listen, Liz offered her lab for us to use. We can stay and not risk upsetting Mitchell. Maybe we can use that guy—" I point to Brody. "To get control of the Blood Rebels. He's working with Hayden, remember? And Hayden expects him to deliver him a key to our house. We can set a trap. Then, maybe we can finally go home."

Kingston groans and laces his fingers through his unkempt, dark tresses. "Fuck it. Fine. Your idea is better."

Diego smiles at me, puffing his chest out. "Nice strategizing, beautiful."

Kingston dramatically rolls his eyes. "Just because you're brilliant, babe, doesn't mean you're in charge."

I dip my chin toward my chest and raise an eyebrow. "You're right. We all have to agree."

He narrows his eyes. "Agree to handle things my way, you mean. I'm not risking you getting hurt. You're not allowed to leave this house without us. Understand?"

"Seriously? But the sun. Haven Springs runs on a daylight schedule," I say, placing my hands on my hips, ready to full-on argue. "We can't let anyone know what's up. You are not going to risk getting burned. I won't allow it."

That makes him chuckle. So does Diego. Austin continues to stare at me, keeping his face expressionless.

"I agree with Kingston, beautiful," Diego says. "As hot as your protectiveness—and bossiness is—we can manage."

"We'll figure out how to stick to the shadows," Austin adds. "If Orlando's lurking..."

I sigh. "He doesn't want to take me yet. He wants to see this play out."

Kingston scoffs. "Like that matters. We trust no one."

"You could get hurt. They shoot on sight." I groan. "I don't like this."

Kingston throws his hands up. "You think we do? You're lucky I don't babenap you."

"What if I protect Jewel?" Liz asks, braving to step a few feet closer. I think my guys forgot she was standing nearby, because they all turn their intense gazes toward her, making her heart pick up speed. I can't blame her. Being under vampire scrutiny always makes me squirm.

Diego gives her a serious once-over and not a good one. "Now why would you do that?"

Kingston flashes his fangs. "And you better not say you're acting from the goodness of your heart."

Liz squares her shoulders. I admire her bravery. I thought she acted this way toward Mitchell before because he was merely present on the projection screen, but she doesn't back down with my guys all wound up right in front of her. "You're right. I'm not. I have a request to make."

"And what's that?" Kingston asks.

"Figure out how to breach my grandson's contract to bring him here. I want him to gain exemption status. I want my family back together."

Kingston, Diego, and Austin all look at each other for a moment. "Done," they say in unison.

Liz nods her head without smiling. "Then let's hurry and get you fed and under control, then I'll show you around."

LUCKY

LIZ OPENS THE DOOR TO a concrete building near the far north wall of Haven Springs. It's a little too close for comfort to a row of houses, but the empty street and the lack of voices helps my bunching nerves.

"The best time to come here is at night," Liz says, motioning to us as we stand protected from the sun under a thick oak tree.

Diego rushes to the building first, carrying Brody on his shoulders. Austin races with me inside next, and Kingston follows last.

Liz closes the door. "If you must come during daylight hours, this time is best. School doesn't get out until three and most residents are out and about. Four of the houses on this street remain vacant for now, and my house is at the end. My daughter and grandchildren live there, so please, stay away from them."

"That won't be a problem," Austin says, squeezing my fingers.

He hasn't let go of me since Liz extracted my blood. I had for sure thought Austin was going to yell at her when she struggled to find my vein. If I didn't know any better, I'd have thought Liz was performing a life or death procedure with the way all three of them hovered close.

I thought they were protective before, but now that I'm no longer at the Divinity Estate with them, they're extra on edge. And when they're on edge...all I know is that they're going to need me to constantly calm them down.

"Good," she says, peering around. Strolling across the room, she opens the door to what appears to be a supply closet. "Everything you might need can be found in here. If it's not, let me know, and I'll see what I can do. Unfortunately, what I have access to is quite limited."

"Thank you," Austin says. "All I'll need right now is some tranquilizers for the rebel."

"And restraints," Kingston adds.

Liz motions for Kingston and Diego to follow her, leaving me with Austin. They must realize how much we need a moment alone with each other, because they ask Liz to show them around the rest of the facility and disappear down a long hallway.

"I'm sorry, Jewel," Austin murmurs, turning to face me. He doesn't explain why, because we both know the reason.

I pull him close to meet my lips to his. "You don't have to apologize. I should be the one to do so. You'd have never lost control if—" My cheeks burn at the memory of my body fully setting itself on practically devouring Austin. "God, what the hell is wrong with me? Do you think I could've hurt you? I'm so embarrassed. It was like I couldn't stop."

Austin slides his hands around my waist and pulls me with him to perch on the edge of a cot. I sit on his lap and snuggle against him, swiveling to rest my cheek on his chest. "That sounds a lot like how I feel when I don't have enough to eat. Except you were hella sexy latching onto me. You might not have wanted to stop, but I was certainly prepared to let you continue."

I giggle, warmth blossoming on my cheeks. It's been a while since he used a back-world term. "You sound like my perfect nutrients match."

"Well, I was your first."

I hum under my breath, my body shivering at the thought. "One percent still doesn't make a difference. You're friggin' delicious."

"And you're making me jealous as hell, beautiful," Diego says from the hallway.

"Not me," Kingston quips. "You can count on the fact

that I'll never be your nutrients match."

I stick my tongue out at him. "That's too bad."

Diego elbows him. "Yeah, bro. You'll never know the wonders of our girl's mouth."

Kingston releases a low growl, pursing his lips. "Fucking A. Now I'm jealous."

I hunker down against Austin, shaking my head. He scoops me up with him and carries me toward the door.

"Before your comments ignite Jewel's face brighter than a massive sunburn, I'm taking her home. You two got it handled here?" Austin asks.

"Yeah, sure," Diego responds first.

"Don't forget. It's house sixty-two," I remind them. "And you better be careful. Stick to the plan. I don't want a repeat of the last time we were here."

Diego and Kingston glance to each other. "Yes, Jewel."

Diego leans in. "I love her like this."

Kingston breaks his serious expression and chuckles. "Of course you fucking do." Turning his attention back to me and Austin, he says, "You sure you're good?"

Austin's jaw tightens. "I'm good."

Kingston turns to me. "Babe?"

I bob my head. "Great. Not even a little bit bitey."

Austin kisses my cheek. "That's too bad. I was looking forward to feeding you."

I laugh. "Hmmm, maybe just some solids."

"You bet." Turning to his brothers, he adds, "Come get

us when the blood runs its course in the rebel. I want to be here for that."

Liz strolls up behind Diego, and he and Kingston look at her. "And what about my deal?"

Kingston glances to me and back to the woman. "We'll talk tomorrow night. Jewel must survive her first official day as a Haven Springs resident."

I frown. "Please don't tell me that means what I think it means."

Diego twists his lips. "Sorry, beautiful. He's right. If we're going to make this work and do as Mitchell requested, you have to play the part."

"So, you're really going to trust her?" Because really, she would never stand a chance against Orlando.

"Fuck no. Not alone," Kingston says. "She'll be able to watch your back in the sun, though. One of us will be nearby at all times, just in the safety of the shade."

"Come on, beautiful, don't make that face," Diego says.

"I'm not making a face," I argue.

Austin pokes my bottom lip. "You kind of are. But don't worry. I'll fix it."

I don't even get the chance to say anything before the world blurs. Austin covers my mouth to stifle my sudden screech and then switches his hold on me to kiss away any and all noises. I don't know how he manages to navigate us back to the house without getting in the sun with his attention on me, but he does, and I find myself in the middle of our living room.

"Shit." I gasp for the breath Austin stole from me.

He chuckles and sets me down before shrugging from his hoodie. A little pink spot from the sun runs along his forehead. "That's better."

I laugh and pat his chest. "Not quite."

Humming under his breath, he says, "You're right. I can do much more."

Austin scoops me back into his arms and spins me, blurring the world again. I raise my eyebrows in surprise as I peer around a gleaming stainless steel and dark marble kitchen. I hadn't even bothered to look around the house yet, and I can't help staring at how impressive it is.

A blip of sadness sneaks up on me at the sight of a few photos stuck to the fridge, including one of my cousins with my sister taken at the table in the corner. This was supposed to be their lives, living in this house, taking part in this community outside the infrastructure put in place by vampires. Now, here I am with my three matches, crashing in and turning my cousins' normalcy upside down while completely trying to ignore the fact that Ramona isn't here.

Austin kisses me tenderly, touching my cheek to smear the stray tear without pointing it out. Instead, he heads to the fridge and opens it up to peer inside. "French toast, waffles, pancakes, or all three?" he asks, glancing at me from over his shoulder. His distraction works, stopping me from complaining.

"There's no way I could possibly eat all three," I say, smirking. "But since you offered...yes, please."

He chuckles and grabs an apron from a hook, making me crack up when he puts it on. It was obviously picked out by Fallon with its pink ruffles and sequins, reminding me of the one Aunt Dottie used to wear.

Austin blurs around the kitchen to gather what he needs and sets up everything beside me. He kisses me between mixing the batter, feeding me pieces of cut up fruit along the way. I've never seen him cook before, and it's just as entertaining as watching Diego work out or Kingston dance, because Austin obviously loves it, even if he can't enjoy his creations.

He flips a pancake in a skillet, and I laugh and clap. "I could get used to this. I had no idea that you had cooking skills. I assumed the chefs always prepped everything."

Grinning, he slides the food onto a plate. "Not always. And if I had known how excited this made you, I'd have done so in front of you sooner."

"I think you underestimated my love of food. In The Boxes, we didn't have most of this stuff. Just basic things like bread, potatoes, occasionally meat on special occasions. I got fruit when I was a kid. I think for a birthday or something. I can't remember."

Austin swipes a bottle of syrup from the cupboard and squeezes it on the mountain of pancakes. He cuts a piece with a fork and holds it up to my mouth. "I plan to assure you enjoy every bite while you still can. Your tastes will change when you completely transition."

I savor the rich flavor of the pancakes and nod my head. With how certain he says it, I almost believe that it'll happen. That my guys will figure out how to undo whatever Orlando and my dad did to guarantee our forever.

"It'll be worth it," I say.

Austin picks up the French toast with his fingers and feeds me a bite. Powdered sugar coats my mouth, and I lick my lips.

"Though, I might miss the sweetness of your kiss," he murmurs, shifting closer.

I open my legs so he can stand between them and hug him close, knowing how much he suddenly needs my affection. Today was rough, and there's nothing more I want to do in the world than to assure Austin's okay. To assure him that I'm okay. We're amazing.

"I guess *you* better enjoy it while you still can," I murmur, meeting his lips again.

Austin reacts to my love, kissing me deeper. His tongue slides into my mouth, brushing over mine. My body alights with desire, craving his closeness. Scooting forward, I sink against him, letting the length of his excitement press into me through our clothes.

"Can I take you to our room?" he whispers against my throat. "I just...I need to be with you. Even if it's just to cuddle and feed you in bed."

I slide off the counter and into his arms, making him chuckle as I grab the rest of the French toast and shove it in my mouth. He kisses me again, strolling toward the stairs, careful to avoid the sun's rays in the living room. Instead of moving at a vampire's speed, he moves at an incredibly torturous pace, just trailing his lips along my jawline, savoring every second.

Austin carries me to the door on the right, and I peer around the small bedroom with the purple comforter, a projector screen covering one wall, and a vanity table with a mirror. A few beauty products sit in a clear container, ready to be relocated. It looks like Austin decided to wait before touching the rest of Dana's stuff.

I smile and look around for a second.

"You like it?" he asks, eyeing me. "You know, we can change anything you like at home. More than just adding flowers."

I shrug. "I like it because it...I don't know. It's exactly what I had hoped for Dana after Blood Matching. It didn't really feel all that real until this moment."

He sits with me on the bed. "What do you mean?"

"It's hard to explain. I'm just—" I suck in a breath. "I can't believe we're here. Even if it's temporary. Don't get me wrong. I friggin' hate this place, but I love this."

Nodding his head, he leans closer. "I love it too, Jewel. More than you know."

I smile and meet him for another kiss that sends his heart racing. Austin's hands play with my hair, his lips molding to mine, devouring every ounce of my attention. Linking my fingers to his shirt, I tug it off his head and trail my lips down his neck to graze along the taut muscles of his shoulders.

"Jewel," he says, whispering my name. "If you suddenly have the urge to bite me—"

"I'll stop," I say, turning my gaze to him.

He slides his hands up my body to cup my face. "Only if you want to. What I was going to say was to let me know so that I can prepare myself."

Blush warms my skin, and I suck my top lip between my teeth. As much as the thought of Austin letting me bite him turns me on, I'm friggin' nervous as hell. Not by the act but by the feeling of being so out of control.

"Austin, don't let me," I finally say. "If I—I—" I can't even get the words out.

Austin combs his fingers through the hair that I purposely let fall in my face to veil me from him. "You don't have to explain. I get it."

He, out of anyone, would.

"And if you're too nervous, we can just hang out. I love being with you no matter what. Whatever you want."

His words make me smile like crazy, and I push him back and kiss him again. What I want is to be with Austin in the way that leaves my body zinging and my heart on the verge of exploding. I want him to feel the strength of our connection, how much I love that he gets me. That despite everything, nothing between us has changed. He's still my perfect match.

Austin's hands travel to the hem of my shirt, and he tugs it over my head and breaks his mouth from mine to kiss along my neck and to my clavicle. His fingers unhook my jeans, and he flips me over to tug them off me. He smiles, taking a moment to drink me in, and then leans in to kiss me again, sliding his fingers between my legs to touch me in a way that has me gasping into his mouth.

His hands push under me, and he unclasps my bra, bringing his mouth down to kiss the goosebumps prickling over my skin. I grab at the waist of his jeans and unfasten the button to feel exactly what I do to him. He moans at my touch, easing back only enough to let me tug his jeans down until he's able to kick them off.

I lift my hips, and he grins as I silently give him permission to finish undressing me. He licks his lips, taking in the sight of me for a moment, his heart thumping so loudly that I reach up to press my palm to it so that I can feel the sensation over my skin. Austin grabs the comforter and pulls it over us, blocking out the rest of the world.

I ease my legs open for him to lie between, and he smiles again, taking an extra moment to kiss me. Warmth builds between us, my body warming his, and he slowly enters me, releasing the sexiest noise that vibrates across my lips and makes me shiver.

My whole body tingles under his weight, his hand expertly drawing up to cup my breast while his other one keeps my body in perfect rhythm to his. A dozen emotions cross his face as he stares at me, and I smile before leaning up to kiss him.

"I can't believe how lucky I am," he whispers into my ear so softly that I wouldn't have been able to hear the words if I didn't have super hearing.

"I love you, Austin." I trail my fingers down his back, feeling his muscles shift and move.

"So lucky," he murmurs, grazing his teeth over my shoulder before brushing his lips to my skin.

He kisses me a dozen times, our breaths mingling, our hearts banging against each other. My whole body awakens to his touch, to his love, his affection. Everything about this moment with Austin is beyond perfect. I had no idea how much I needed his closeness to reassure me that even if things are out of control that no matter what, we have each other to get through things.

I arch back at a burst of amazing sensations Austin creates with his hand, adding to the pleasure that builds between my legs to swallow the rest of me. I squirm and hug Austin, clenching my jaw, trying to keep my mouth shut until there's no way I can any longer. He murmurs into my ear, his breathing turning into a hum deep in his throat until he brings his mouth back to mine, drawing his hand back up to sink under me to pull me harder against him. Austin shuts up my loud ass mouth with another kiss that turns into his own moan that he releases into the pillow.

He slows, still hugging me close, and eases his weight onto me as we both catch our breaths. Looking at me again, he gives me a smile I never want to see him without. It lights up his whole face, reflecting my own happiness and contentment back to me. I never imagined a life such as this. A life so important to me that I'd risk everything and do anything to keep. I don't even care that we're in Haven Springs. I don't care that the world might be against us. All I care about is that my guys know how much they mean to me. How much better my world is because of them.

"How about I go grab you the rest of breakfast? I want nothing more than to feed you in bed and cuddle until we have to go," Austin says.

"And you think you're the lucky one?" I tease, kissing him again. "Why don't you grab the kit and let me feed you too?"

He snuggles against me. "Like I said. I'm so lucky."

TROUBLE

STEAM CLOUDS THE BATHROOM FROM the shower, and I turn and draw a heart on the foggy mirror. Austin stands before me and dries off. He wraps the towel around his hips, his muscular stomach still damp from the heat of the water. If I knew that Kingston and Diego wouldn't call us at any minute, or that my cousins wouldn't be home from school soon, I'd have stayed in the shower with Austin for the rest of the day, possibly the night.

A dull ache burns from my shoulder, and I swipe my long, wet hair out of the way to get a better look at one of Diego's bite marks. Austin hears the low groan I let escape and shifts me to swivel back around so that he can get another look at it.

"Does it still hurt?" he asks to confirm that he correctly deciphered the noise I made.

"Just a little bit. I'm more worried about the way it looks. I don't remember Katherine's bite looking like this. Hers just bled a bit longer, remember?"

He presses his lips into a line and takes a minute to inspect the other two venomous bites on my arms. The ones he and Kingston gave me don't look much different than Diego's. And now that I'm staring at them, they hurt too.

Austin pulls open drawers and digs through the cupboards until he finds a first aid kit equipped with basic human supplies. Instead of the synthetic skin Austin favors, he pulls out a couple of colorful bandages and some ointment.

"This should help until I can get my hands on better supplies. I'll make a trip to Midnight Valley tonight if I have to since it's closest. Haven Springs isn't exactly medically advanced. They wouldn't need the same stuff the city facilities carry." Applying the ointment first, Austin gets carried away and ends up bandaging all eight bite marks, even the properly healing ones from my guys last night.

I swipe my hand across the mirror. "I look ridiculous."

He chuckles and kisses my bare shoulder. "Just wait until my brothers see you."

"They're going to thank you for taking care of me and then keep their mouths shut," I muse.

He laughs again and shakes his head. "We'll pretend they did. Just brace yourself. It was excruciating to cover you up." Trailing his finger up my arm, he stops at the green bandages I commented looked like his eyes. "We try our bests not to go all possessive on you, but it's a deep-seated urge that drives me crazy."

"Is that why people always comment about you killing each other?" I ask, running my fingers over his bare shoulder.

"Something like that. But you never have to worry about us, Jewel, okay? It's the rest of the world that should worry. Especially now."

"Because I'm yours despite the voided contracts?" I tease.

"Because we're yours," he corrects. "Always."

I watch Austin get dressed. I know he's slow to do so because I can't take my eyes off him. He grins at me, draping his shirt over his shoulder instead of putting it on and closes the space again.

"I thought I wanted to be there for the rebel interrogation, but...maybe we can let Kingston and Diego handle it? I'm not much use in mind manipulation anyway. I can perform the basics, but they're better at it."

If he didn't look so friggin' hot and all smiley, pleading to me with his vibrant green eyes to agree, I'd beg him to take me anyway. But I can't resist him, and he always gives me what I want, so I want to do the same for him. It's our day—and night—together anyway. "I wouldn't be as much help either, huh?" I say, reaching my hands out to him.

"I'm sure you could be," he says. "But I'd be lying if I didn't want to keep you far, far away from that asshole."

"Then we'll stay here. But you have to promise me that I'll get to cuddle you all I want."

His smile widens. "I think I can manage."

"No, I mean it. You have to let me smother you with all my love and affection."

He leans in and kisses me. "I accept your condition."

Austin helps me off the counter and wraps me in the fluffy robe my guys packed for me when they were forced to transfer me here. If it wasn't for the few familiar things they ensured left with me, I might be going a little crazier. I know they're only possessions, but I never had many to call my own until I Blood Matched, and I grew attached.

Tugging me the few feet from the bathroom to the bed, Austin motions for me to sit down. He flops beside me, sinking against me while sneaking his cool hands inside my robe. I love the mood he's in, and I devour every bit of his physical attention.

I giggle and shiver, pulling the blankets up, but we don't even get to kiss before the private communication line in the room I share with Diego chimes. Austin sighs while I frown, and then we both laugh. If we weren't expecting a call on the only unmonitored line in the house, we'd ignore it. Since we don't know exactly what we're dealing with, my guys have decided only to use their com devices in emergencies. It keeps Mitchell more out of the loop. He's most definitely ruined a part of his relationship with my guys with the stunt he pulled. It's not a wonder he worries about their loyalty.

"Should I get it?" I ask, sitting back up. "What if it's the council?"

"I'll go see. Wait here for me and keep my spot warm."

Austin nuzzles his nose to mine and doesn't give me the chance to respond before he disappears to head down the hallway. I listen to him cross the room and answer the phone. Unlike at the Divinity Estate, the rooms are close enough that there is definitely no privacy at all here.

"It's worse than we thought." Kingston's voice sounds through the air, and I scoot to stand up. "I think Orlando personally worked with this Blood Rebel. The guy passed out after only a minute of interrogation."

"You were supposed to let me know first," Austin says.

"Yeah, whatever. You look like you've been just dying for news. Where's Jewel, anyway? I want to see her."

"You don't trust me?" Austin asks, his voice growing in annoyance. Having them question each other about me is the last thing I want. Looks like I need to remind them that I can handle each of them.

I sigh and stride toward the door. "Please, don't start. Austin's taking excellent care of me, Kingston. And Austin, you know your brother enough to know that he would ask to see me regardless of the situation."

I make it a foot into the hallway when sunlight explodes through the room behind me. I release a small gasp, watching the curtain shift and a leg step into the room. The person has to have climbed up something to get in. I mean, eff. We're on the second floor of the house.

"Au—"

Strong hands pull me back and out of the glowing sunlight. Austin covers my mouth to stifle my surprise, and we listen to the thump of a body falling to the plush carpet. The person is loud as all get-out, but why would they try to be quiet? It's a human community. Most people wouldn't hear the intruder.

"Stay behind me," Austin whispers, holding up a scary ass dagger he must've taken from the other room.

I nod my head, and we listen to the intruder move about. The lack of stealth might be because no one's supposed to be home. The council had planned a full day for me...shit. I wonder if everyone's schedules are common knowledge or if a traitor works on the council. The idea of people knowing where I'm supposed to be freaks me out. It exposes me to unnecessary danger. I'm not an average exempt. The people here aren't rushing to hug me and accept me into their lives.

I don't get the chance to tell Austin my thoughts. The sunlight vanishes, but the noise persists. It sounds like whoever it is messes with my cousin's things. If Austin wasn't holding me, I'd charge in there. Or not. My mind conflicts with my body. I realize it's me holding onto Austin, stopping him from rushing in. I grip onto the back of his shirt, practically gluing myself to him.

"I want you to stay here, Jewel," he whispers, readying himself.

I squeeze his arm, not wanting him to leave me, even if it's only a few feet. I relent, though. I'd rather him surprise the intruder. He'll be fast enough that the person won't have a chance to fight back, which is good, considering all of the exempt seem to be heavily armed all the time. Austin will take an injury over just killing someone as much as it goes against his nature.

"Be careful," I whisper, touching his shoulder. "I don't want to have to save your ass."

He smirks and vanishes into the room. A masculine voice yells out, and something crashes. Panic squeezes my chest. I accidentally groan way too audibly. Even a normal human could hear the strangled noise that escapes me.

"Fuck!" the voice screams. "Don't hurt me. Please!"

The terror in the guy's voice doesn't sound like Hayden or a cocky-ass Blood Rebel. Those people would stand in silence as a vampire rips their throat out. It's also obviously not Orlando. And I'm nearly certain a Blood Rebel wouldn't sob uncontrollably. It's enough to get me to unlatch my fingers from the wall.

Steeling myself, I inch closer to the doorway and poke my head in. I'm glad I do. "Shit, Austin. Stop," I say, stepping into the room. I don't rush forward, trying to stay calm though my heart thrashes.

"Jewel! Run!" Berto screeches from the floor. Austin aims his dagger right at the back of Berto's neck and flashes his fangs.

"Austin," I call again, drawing his attention to me. He's in full-on fight mode, his eyes glowing silver. At least he doesn't have the unnerving hunger in them. "He's not an intruder. That's Dana's boyfriend."

Austin blinks and pulls the blade away. Standing up, he darts to my side and hooks his fingers to me, squeezing my arm like he needs to touch me. He inhales a few breaths, his eyes flickering between green and silver as he regains composure. I lace my fingers through his and bring his hand up to my mouth and kiss the back, just hugging his arm to me while Berto sniffles and pushes to his knees to get up.

I only let go of Austin when his shoulders relax and I'm certain he's back in control. Crossing the room, I head to Berto. I raise my hand to keep Austin back despite the grimace marring his handsome features. If it were Kingston or Diego, I'm sure they'd ignore me and stick to my side, but Austin lets me handle things for a reason I can't discern. Possibly because he recognizes the kid's fear cues. If he steps closer, it might make things worse.

And I'm glad for his thoughtfulness. Berto wasn't born in Haven Springs. He grew up with the same fear of vampires that I did. Any sudden movement on Austin's part might make him react.

"Berto," I say, kneeling next to him. I don't touch him or anything, just sit close enough that he won't be able to ignore my presence. "You're safe. I promise. Just take a breath."

"Fuck," he murmurs, reaching for his belt.

Austin charges him, ripping the gun from its holster before Berto has a chance to draw it. I hold up my palm to Austin, stopping him from trying to lift me to my feet. He stiffens, his hand fisted so tightly around the gun that the metal crunches under his strength, sending drops of his blood to the floor.

Berto swears again.

"Berto, chill out. Austin's my match. He won't hurt you...as long as you don't try to hurt us," I say.

"You don't have a Blood Match. You were released from the program," he says, finally managing to find his words to say something other than profanity.

I rub my lips together. "Then he's my...boyfriend?" Boyfriend? That term sounds so wrong applied to my relationship with Austin.

"Boyfriends don't bite."

I laugh. I can't help it. "Well, if you like it."

Berto's face distorts like I said the most revolting thing in the whole universe, and it elicits a just as strong reaction from Austin. He scoops me up and sets me on my feet behind him, releasing a deep growl.

"Get up," Austin commands.

Berto remains utterly still, acting how Dad always taught us if we were to ever come face-to-face with a vampire on Starlight Row. According to my dad, fighting would make it worse. The more I've become immersed in the vampire world, the more I realized the falsity of his teachings. Playing dead or running won't work on a starving vampire. Like Diego taught me—it's about strategizing. It's about—

The slamming of a door draws my attention away from Berto. I expect Kingston and Diego to materialize in front of us, but Dana and Fallon both call my name.

"Dana, run!" Berto yells out, surprising me. "Vampire!"

Footsteps clomp up the stairs as my cousins ignore Berto's warning. Dana appears first in the doorway, her eyes wide as they dart from me to Berto and then to Austin. Fallon stops short behind her, carrying Dougie in her arms. I'm as surprised as Berto to see Brayla's little brother. The last thing I knew was that the Diggs were getting re-evaluated by Donor Life Corp because of Orlando and his getting into Mr. Diggs' head, attempting to use him to threaten my cousins to get me to comply.

"Tin-tin!" Dougie says, wriggling in Fallon's arms.

Dougie wiggles so much that Fallon automatically sets him down, and he toddles right toward Austin with his arms stretched for Austin to pick him up.

"No!" Berto yells, scrambling to his feet.

Austin ignores him and lifts up Dougie, rubbing his

nose to the little guy, making him giggle the sweetest laugh.

Berto loses his good sense and charges toward Austin and Dougie. Dana yells his name, and Fallon tries to get between them. Berto has the nerve to shove her out of the way. My mouth drops open at the sight, and I don't even think before I tug Austin back by the shirt, making him shift. I swing my hand out and slap Berto across the face.

Berto freezes, clutching his cheek. Dana rushes toward him and flings her arms around him, pulling him with her. I stare in silence, my chest heaving. Austin hands Dougie back to Fallon, ready to intervene.

"Berto, calm down. Austin's not a threat. He's here to protect Jewel," she says, forcing him to keep looking into her eyes by spinning him slightly so that he can't look past her at us. "Blood Rebels are after her."

"You knew he was here?" Berto asks, his teeth clenching. "Why didn't you tell me?"

"Well, I—"

"What I want to know is why you were sneaking into our house through the window," I say, cutting my cousin off. I ease my hand from Austin's, stopping him from following right behind me as I close the space. "I mean, everyone else just barges in through the front door."

Berto swallows and turns his attention to me. "Dana told me she wasn't allowed to have guests yet. We always hang out, so I tried to surprise her. You weren't even supposed to be here, Jewel. Especially with a—with a—"

I don't know what annoys me more. The fact that he ignored Dana telling him that he wasn't allowed here or that he can't even spit out the word vampire.

"You can call him Austin," Dana says. She glances toward Austin. "I mean—if that's okay."

Austin tightens his jaw. "No, sorry. He won't be calling me anything. I can't allow him to leave here wi—"

"You're going to kill me?" Berto asks, his dark eyes widening. "Fuck! Dana. Do something."

I step in front of Austin. "He's not going to kill you. You didn't let him finish."

"Careful, Jewel. Distressed humans tend to be—"

Berto grabs onto Dana and pulls her back with him, making her screech in surprise. He yanks on the curtain, allowing in a burst of sunlight. Austin flies back, covering his face, hitting the wall instead of falling through the doorway to the hallway.

"Berto!" Dana yells. "Let me go!"

"No. I'm protecting you. I love you. You can't stay here. People need to know the community is in danger. He's manipulating you all."

Fuck me. I grab onto Austin and yank him toward the hallway and out of the sun. His face blisters, and he flashes his fangs, growling scary-loud that my heart races harder. Austin locks his fingers around my wrist, holding onto me, but there's no friggin' way I'm letting Berto jump out the window with my little cousin. All he would have to do is start running and yelling to get someone's attention. My guys can't do much with the sun, and the whole community will have time to prepare for the night.

"Austin, you have to trust me, okay?" I tell him, wrapping my fingers around his wrist.

He turns to hide his burned face from me. "He'll hurt you."

"The whole place will try to hurt you," I argue. "Please, he can't leave."

"Just get the curtain closed."

"Got it."

Austin prepares himself to run back into the room behind me but waits just outside for me to take care of the sun for him. Fallon grabs onto Dana's hands, yanking on her arms, trying to stop Berto from tossing her out the second-story window.

With one look at me, Berto yells and rips Dana back. Fallon doesn't let go of her sister. I scream as I watch the three of them crash through the window. My heart sinks into my stomach at the thuds of their bodies hitting the grass. Rushing to the window, I stick my head out and peer down. Dana groans from on top of Berto, and Fallon clutches her oddly bent arm.

"Run!" I yell to my cousins.

Berto comes to his senses and hooks his arm around Dana's waist. He drags her a couple of feet, ignoring her thrashing. Fallon remains on the grass, screaming for him to let Dana go.

Panic collides over me in a cool wave, and I do the only thing I can think of. I hike up my robe and swing one leg over the window sill.

"Jewel, stop," Austin says.

"He's taking her!" I yell.

"Jewel," Austin repeats. "Don't jump. Listen to me. Look at me."

I swivel my waist, half in and half out of the window to look at him.

Austin uses his shirt to shield his face. "He's not going to hurt her. He thinks she's in danger."

"But he's making too much noise. I have to stop him. I have to protect you."

Austin groans and flies into the room, snatching the comforter from the bed. Before I have a chance to demand he let me handle this, he jumps out the window with me in his arms, the blanket being the only thing protecting him from the sun.

"Berto!" I yell from Austin's arms. "Stop."

He doesn't, and Dana cries louder.

Austin releases me and zooms toward Berto, yanking Dana away. He swings the guy by his arms, tossing him into the shade of the nearby grove. Snarling, Austin closes the space and lifts the kid to his feet, smashing him into a tree to get into his face.

"Don't fight. Don't scream," Austin commands, flashing his fangs.

Berto freezes and slumps in Austin's arms.

I hook my arms around Dana and pull her against me. Slapping my hand over her mouth, I stifle her cries. "Austin won't hurt him," I whisper into her hair.

"You will forget me. You will forget you were ever here. Do not come back uninvited," Austin says, his voice deepening. "Go home. Call Dana when you arrive. Understand?"

"Yes."

Austin releases Berto and the guy falls to his knees. I loosen my hold on Dana and nudge her toward Fallon. Her sister bites on the collar of her shirt, tears flooding down her face. Austin blurs by me and scoops Fallon up, relocating her back inside.

"Please, Jewel. Hurry. Don't let him see you," Austin calls.

I rush to get Dana back in the house with me. She hurries to Fallon's side and releases a strangled cry, doing her best not to let her emotions give away her being here. Dougie's soft crying sounds out from upstairs, and I motion for her to go get him.

Austin leans his back on the wall, his whole body trembling. "Jewel, call Liz. I can't help Fallon right now."

"I got it," Dana calls, coming down the stairs.

I close the space to Austin and ease the blanket off his head. I try not to react toward his burned flesh from the sun.

"I'm okay," he whispers.

I fail to keep my face expressionless and blink, sending tears cascading down my face. "I'm sorry. I'm so sorry. Let me help you."

Austin turns away from my outstretched arm. "No more bites. I'll wait for Liz."

"But Austin."

"Jewel, please. You need to heal."

"And you need to let me take care of you," I murmur.

He shakes his head. "Please."

I frown and slide into his open arms, silently begging me just to hug him. So I do.

"It's going to be okay," he whispers.

If only I could truly believe his words.

SURVIVE ON BLOOD

"I TRUSTED YOU." MY VOICE sounds through the air, bouncing off the stone walls of the buildings creating shade in the alley. "How could you do this?"

"You have always been my top priority, Jewel," Orlando says, closing the space enough to make me step back and hit the wall.

"But a blood debt?" I ask. "He's my dad. What you did—"

"Was for the best. It's part of the plan. Trust me."

I lift my hands and press them into Orlando's chest. "Trust you? How can I now? My da—"

Reaching up, Orlando brushes the stray strands of hair from my face. "Cared so little about you. He was willing to risk your life. Your very existence. He made you donate instead of looking out for your best interest. He abandoned you.”

“He didn’t.”

“There are a lot of things you don’t understand. If you’d agree to come with me, I’ll see what I can do.”

“But my sister. My cousins. We’ve run out of time.”

“They’re not your responsibility.”

“Orlando!” I snap.

“He always put them ahead of you. It’s time for you to do something for yourself. For our future. You need me, Jewel. You know what happens if you don’t drink my blood. It’ll only get worse.”

I tighten my jaw, thinking about his words. The excruciating hunger flits through my memory, but I suppress it the best I can. “My mind is set. I’m applying to Blood Match. My family comes first.”

Orlando snarls, punching the wall beside me. “You won’t be able to go another month.”

“I don’t care.”

Cupping my face in his hands, Orlando leans in, capturing my gaze before I can look away.

“Don’t do this. No more,” I whisper.

“You will forget me, precious Jewel. Take the long way. I’ll see you around.”

“Jewel, Jewel. Wake up,” Austin’s voice wraps around me and yanks me from the weirdest dream of Orlando.

I groan and rub the heels of my hands into my eyes. "Fuck."

Austin tugs me up, embracing me in his arms. "You need more blood. Drink this."

A warm glass touches my lips, and I automatically open my mouth and let the sweet liquid coat my tongue. My foggy head clears, and I frown, glancing around the small room. For a second, I thought we were back at the Divinity Estate.

I moan, the pain in my stomach subsiding. I clutch my fingers around the glass, taking over holding it from Austin. A low noise escapes his throat, and I lift my gaze to glance at him. Thank friggin' God. His burns have all mostly vanished, and he looks incredibly sexy watching me drink, his mussed hair sticking up.

"Do you want more?" he asks.

My head bobs without consulting with my mind.

Austin pours more of my guys' blood from a canister, filling it completely to the top. I gulp the whole thing down faster than even Kingston drinks blood. A dozen emotions cross Austin's face as he stares at me, studying me intently enough that I squirm and look at the wooden board screwed over the broken window.

A knock sounds on the door. "Mind if we come in?" Diego asks.

"It's fine. I might need more of your blood for Jewel anyway," Austin responds.

The door to the room flings open, and Diego enters with Kingston behind him. The two of them narrow their focus on me.

"Please tell me those sexy ass noises you were making were because of dream-me," Kingston says, stopping next to the bed. "Only half a day and I can get you alone."

I smirk. "I wish it were about you."

He groans. "Fucking nightmare."

I lift and drop my shoulders. "More weird than any-thing."

"Maybe we need to increase her blood intake?" Diego says to Austin. He bites his arm and holds it out so that his blood can trickle into my glass before he hands it for King-ston to top off. "She should've had enough to help suppress her dreams."

"It's probably because Austin needed more of Jewel's blood than usual." Kingston doesn't complain or throw it into Austin's face about the incident with Dana's boyfriend that left him injured. Both he and Diego were concerned when they found us, and it still pulls at my heartstrings to see their loyalty. Turning to me, Kingston adds, "You should give him more in case until we can bring in some gen. pop."

Austin shakes his head. "I'm fine, honestly. And I want to monitor Jewel for a few days before changing anything. If she needs vampire blood like we need human blood, it's better if we don't overdo it. She'll get used to the increased amount and might lose control or something."

Diego plops down beside me and bumps his shoulder to mine. "And you know we're all goners if she does. I mean, look at our girl. I'd die happy."

I blush and crinkle my nose. "Diego."

"It's okay, babe. Austin and I accept Diego's sacrifice."

Diego tips his head back and laughs. The gesture shakes the bed, and Austin finally smiles again. Kingston too. I whip my head, hitting Diego with my hair, a wave of happiness crashing over me in the best way possible. I for sure thought my guys would be brooding messes after the incident, but they manage to still joke around. The universe feels less scary now.

I throw my arms around Diego and shower him with a dozen kisses. "Be careful. I might take you up on your offer."

"Fuck," Kingston says. "I volunteer. Bring that mouth over here."

I shift and grin at him. "I bite."

He narrows his eyes at me. "So do I."

We both snap our teeth at each other, and Kingston chuckles, braving to climb onto the bed and in between me and Austin. I roll onto him, snuggling close, and stretch my arms out to hug all three of them the best I can.

"This is exactly what I wanted to wake up to," I murmur, just lying with the three of them, listening to all of our hearts beating. "Because that dream—ugh."

"Want to talk about it?" Diego asks, propping himself up on his elbows.

I consider telling them no, because there's nothing more I hate than bringing up Orlando, but the dream still lingers with me. It felt so real.

"You can tell us anything, Jewel," Austin adds. "We're in this together."

I bob my head, and Kingston helps me sit up so that I can better look at the three of them. Scooting back, he makes room for me to sit in front of him. Austin and Diego each take my hand while Kingston clasps my bent knees.

"I don't want you to flip your shit, but—"

Kingston leans in and rests his chin on my knees, getting super close. "No promises, babe."

Austin swats him. "I'll keep him under control."

"And I'll keep both of them cool," Diego adds.

I smirk and inhale a breath. "You better. It was about Orlando."

"Fucking asshole is still in our girl's dreams," Kingston mutters.

Austin elbows him but doesn't say anything. All three of them continue to watch me in silence, giving me all the time I need to get the words out.

I meet Kingston's dark gaze. "Do you remember the first day we met? How Ms. Sybil told me that my appointment was canceled?"

"And nearly ruined this? How could I forget?" Kingston asks.

"My dream was about the trip to the center from my apartment. Orlando wasn't just trying to stir doubt over our Blood Matching. He really did stop me, trying to intervene. I think we had an argument over my dad. I was so angry. And then he manipulated my mind, telling me to go the long way."

"Because he was trying to make you late," Kingston says. We all know it's true, but just putting the words out there makes things feel even worse.

"Tell us everything you remember from your dream," Diego says, pulling my hand up to his mouth to kiss. "It might not be completely accurate, but maybe it can lead us to some answers."

I do my best to summarize the conversation I had with Orlando in my dream. My head pounds just talking about it, and my voice breaks as I mention what we've already confirmed about me needing vampire blood.

"I bet he wasn't expecting Austin to give you his blood that day," Kingston says.

I shrug. "I honestly don't know what he expected. I still don't know what he expects or what he gets out of being around here. My dad is dead. He has Ramona for whatever the hell my dad got himself into. And me? I have the three of you to sustain me."

Diego smiles at me, stopping me from frowning for long. "Hell yeah you do, beautiful. You're my dream come true. We can survive on each other."

I lean over and kiss him.

"Partly survive," Kingston says. "Our girl still eats food. And let's not forget that I'd much rather have forever."

Diego backhands him. "Says the guy who doesn't touch gen. pop. blood anymore."

"Knock it off. You know Kingston would if he had to." Austin laces his fingers through mine and draws my hand to his face to feel the weight of our fingers together against his cheek. "Do you happen to remember anything else? Maybe something about why you have to drink blood? Why you need it, I mean? Why you haven't transformed with our venom?" It sounds like he might be asking himself the questions as he says them.

I know my half-transformation has always been on his mind since Mrs. Diggs said my dad had managed to get his hands on a vaccine, but I now know it's more complicated than that. She said both me and Ramona, but I'm certain whatever my dad did was just to me. They never told my sister. She never had to visit with Orlando. My dad wanted to save her and my cousins. But what about me?

I pucker out my bottom lip. "I wish I did, Austin. But there's only one person who really knows now that my dad is dead."

"Then we need to figure out how to get him to talk," Austin says.

"It'll be risky," Diego says. "Orlando is as powerful as

Mitchell. It would take all three of us to overpower him alone—"

Kingston flings himself back to stare at the ceiling. "And fucking Brayla now—"

Austin scoots closer to slide his arm around my back. "Not to mention one of us has to be with Jewel."

I straighten my shoulders, listening to my guys spiral down a path where they imagine defeat. It's a place I want no part of. I've never once doubted their abilities. I still don't. I know that we're strong enough together to keep each other safe, but I also know that I don't want to risk anyone getting hurt in a fight against Orlando.

"What if we didn't fight him?" I ask, staring at the bandages on my arm instead of my guys' burning gazes penetrating me at my question.

"*We?* It was never *we*," Kingston says.

Diego shoves him. "Jewel's a better fighter than you now." It's not true, but I appreciate him standing up for me.

I nudge Kingston with my knee before he retaliates. "Hear me out."

"No."

Austin punches him in the arm. "Go on, Jewel. Don't listen to Kingston. Your ideas matter too."

Kingston growls. "That's not what I said."

"You just implied it."

"And you're being an asshat," Diego adds.

Fuck it. Grabbing the hem of my tank top, I yank it over my head and toss it at Kingston. My guys immediately stop arguing and turn their attentions to me. If it's not my blood or me jumping in between them, it's my boobs that can stop their fighting long enough for me to regain their focus.

"Really, babe?" Kingston asks. "Pulling the tits out? Not fair. You know how fucking horny I am, and we still have at least six hours until you can pull the 'I don't feel good, Liz. I'm calling it a day' card. She'll be here shortly, and I'm pretty fucking sure Austin's not going to let me start my time even a minute early."

Austin smiles at me, drinking in the sight of my silk and lace bra. "He's right about that."

"I'll just enjoy our girl for as long as she realizes that she not only distracted us but herself toward whatever plan she had imagined." Diego licks his lips, making me blush like crazy. I should learn my lesson by now. Shit always backfires. "Though, I'd really enjoy it a lot more if you'd lose—"

It's Kingston who knocks him upside the head. "Don't give her any ideas. My nuts won't recover."

Diego hits him back. "I was going to say bandages."

"Same fucking difference."

"Ah hell," I mutter. "Stop talking right now."

Kingston and Diego both smirk at me. "Maybe you'll think twice next time," Kingston says.

Austin releases a small growl and pulls me to him, wrapping us both in the blankets. Kingston narrows his eyes but doesn't say anything. At least the three of them stop arguing and trying to plan something that could get them hurt or worse.

"Go ahead, Jewel," Austin says. "What did you mean about not fighting Orlando for answers?"

I tilt my head to look at him directly. He's less likely to react adversely like I know Kingston will. And at least now, with Austin's arms around me, Kingston won't try to do something crazy like take me away from here.

I clear my throat. "Orlando knows you're here, but what if we make it as if Mitchell calls you away."

"You better not be suggesting we let him get a foot near you," Kingston says.

"That's exactly what I'm saying," I say. "He's been visiting me to...give me blood. Since you guys have been away."

Kingston growls.

"And if he thinks you guys aren't here to give me any, he'll think he can manipulate my mind again. I can find out what happened to me."

"No," all three of them say in unison.

Diego frowns. "It's not worth the risk, beautiful."

"Having you fight him or bring Mitchell in or whatever isn't worth the risk either," I say. "Might as well use this messed up situation to our advantage. I know you won't let me get hurt. We'll prepare."

"No," Kingston and Diego say this time.

I touch Austin's cheek. "Will you at least think about it? I'm scared for you."

"We're fine, Jewel," Kingston says, saying my name. It sounds soft on his lips while his hand gently touches my knee. "You shouldn't be scared. I doubt Orlando would kill us. He had the chance before and didn't."

I crinkle my nose. "What?"

Austin buries his face into the crook of my neck. "It's nothing to worry about. We're all fine and that's what matters."

"We're Divines, Jewel. Powerful." Diego hugs his arms around me and Austin and then Kingston joins us. "So like Kingston said. Don't worry. We're fine. Don't be scared that Orlando will kill us."

I sniffle, tears burning my eyes. "But it's not Orlando I'm worried about. It's me. What if I get worse? What if I hurt you? You wouldn't fight back."

None of them laugh or disregard my feelings, and for that, I'm thankful.

"Jewel," Austin says softly, breathing into my hair. "We can handle you. Promise."

"Even if I try to devour you?"

Kingston offers me a small smile but worry still lines his midnight eyes. "We'll assure it's only in the best way possible."

I release a breathless laugh. "Kingston."

My stomach rumbles, practically screaming at his suggestion. All three of them stare at me with wide eyes, and blush warms my face.

Kingston purses his lips. "Fuck. Get it together, babe."

Diego punches him and holds out his hand to me. "I know what that sound means. Time to eat."

Austin gets to his feet. "Eggs, toast, and bacon...or me?"

I groan. "We're not done discussing this. You can't distract me with food."

"You fucking bet we can," Kingston says.

Austin helps me into my shirt and meets my gaze. "Let us think about it?"

I nod. "Okay. That's all I ask for."

My stomach rumbles again.

"And maybe something to eat," Diego says, smiling at me.

"Fuck, me too. I'm starved," Kingston says. "Come here, babe. I'll be fast and gentle. Promise."

Austin blocks him. "Later. From a cup. Just in case."

Kingston gives me a once-over but doesn't argue. "Whatever is best."

I run my hand over Kingston's shoulder and stand on my tiptoes to kiss his throat. "Thanks, dude. As soon as some of these are healed, I'll let you bite me exactly how you like."

He practically purrs. "You're worth the wait."

"So are you," I tease, snapping my teeth.

"Fuck," he breathes.

Diego howls a laugh and smacks Kingston on the back. "She's wearing you down, bro."

Austin hugs me to him, strolling next to me. "It won't be long."

"Fuck," Kingston repeats. "How could I resist?"

OFFICIAL RESIDENT

"I VOLUNTEER," KINGSTON SAYS, LACING his fingers through mine.

"You complain if you're in the shade too long," Diego argues.

Austin links his fingers to my other hand. "Plus, someone has to stay here and make sure no one intrudes again."

"You should've just killed him."

I yank up my twined hand with Kingston's and slap the back of his own hand over his mouth. "Shut it. Dana will hear you. Berto's her boyfriend."

"Still? He's gotta go, babe. That's another Ramona fiasco waiting to happen. I mean, shit. He dragged her out a window and tried to run off," Kingston mumbles against our hands.

"She loves him," I say.

"Loves? They've been holding hands for like, what? A few days. It's not like they're bon—"

"Kingston!" Diego slaps both his hands across Kingston's mouth from behind, silencing his words.

Kingston jerks and spins around, breaking free and taking both me and Austin with him.

I let go of Austin and slide between Kingston and Diego but face Kingston. "Almost as long as I've been with you."

"You're our perfect match, though," Kingston says. "You agreed to spend your life with us the second you submitted your application. It's different."

I raise an eyebrow. "I don't know. Berto was pretty set on destroying the world for Dana. You two have a lot in common."

"You did not just take a jab at my need to protect you," he says.

"What are you going to do about it?" I tease. "Destroy the universe next?"

Kingston releases a soft growl and tugs me away from Austin and Diego before they have a chance to initiate a game of keep away with me. Kingston spins me, blurring our world, and presses my back to the wall of the downstairs bathroom and out of the view of his brothers. He meets his lips to mine for a kiss, and I giggle into his mouth, still clinging to him, trying to let the world catch up with me.

"I hope you don't mind," he whispers. "I just—I need a moment with you." Kingston's hands run down my back until he squeezes my ass. Grabbing me by my hips, he lifts me up, squishing me harder into the wall until I feel every hot inch of him awaken against me.

I gasp and shiver. "I don't mind. I love our moments."

"Yeah?" he asks, smiling, shifting me to align our bodies perfectly.

I hum my agreement through another kiss.

"I'm going to make you reconsider even leaving this house," he murmurs against my mouth.

"Is that so?" I smile as his lips leave mine to send tingles over the sensitive skin of my neck.

"Or make you yearn to hurry back. Leave you flustered. Horny as hell. Dying to just be with me." He brings his mouth back to kiss me and slips his tongue into my mouth at the same time his fingers sneak up to rub between my legs through my pants.

I release a breath and tilt my head back. "Try harder."

He grins through kisses, shifting to set me on the sink. I grab the waist of his jeans, loving seeing him in a pair and casual compared to the suits he loves, and pop the button open. He moans into my shoulder, letting me reach into his pants to feel his raging boner.

Footsteps clomp overhead, and Kingston rushes to try to unbutton my pants. "Tell your cousins you're sick."

"Kingston," I whisper, letting him continue despite knowing my cousins head down the stairs.

"Tell my brothers you changed your mind about going out. Please. I want you to stay with me."

I nearly agree, feeling the desperate pressure of his fingers tease me. "I can't. Not again. But I'll be back."

"The wait's going to kill me," he mumbles.

"Try to survive. I've missed you," I whisper.

Kingston slows down, kissing me softly for a moment. "I still miss you. So. Damn. Much."

My cousins call out my name, and a soft tap sounds on the door, making Kingston slump his shoulders and lean into me, breathing deep breaths against my chest.

"Do you need another moment, Jewel?" Austin asks. If he's jealous or anything, he hides it well. Always has.

It's Kingston who straightens his back and fixes his pants first. "No, we're coming out now."

I smirk at him. "You sure?"

He shakes his head at me. "No, but if we don't, I'm not so sure I'll let you. My restraint is weak these days. Just think about me the whole time you're gone. Come back ready."

I smile and slide off the sink. "It's going to be a long day."

"An eternity."

Kingston opens the door to an empty hallway, and he links his fingers through mine and kisses me once more before tugging me to the living room. My face burns the second I meet my cousins' gazes. Liz sits erect on the couch, her hands firmly placed on her lap.

"Sorry," I murmur, shifting to hide my face behind my hair. "I didn't mean to keep you all waiting. Kingston…"

"Doesn't want Jewel to go with you," Kingston says, sliding up behind me. "I'd prefer to keep her here where she's safe. And happy. And content in my arms. This fucking day schedule blows."

Austin and Diego both look at each other. If everyone wasn't standing around, intently listening, they might whisper something. But they know I'll react—either blushing or groaning—and the whole vampire whisper thing and my super hearing are secrets, especially to the exempt.

Fallon cracks up from next to her sister. Her broken arm hides in the thick cast kept close to her body with a dark blue sling. "You were totally right, Diego. He is as dramatic as a—"

Kingston hisses, and Fallon screeches and laughs again. Diego throws a pillow in our direction. I catch it and swing it over my head, clobbering Kingston with it. He only snickers and chucks it back at his brother.

Liz pales, remaining utterly still. I guess pillow fights with vampires aren't exactly on her to-do list. I'm not going to intervene and make everyone stop for her sake though. I want my cousins to feel comfortable around my guys. We're family.

Dana grabs the pillow from the floor and tosses it at Kingston, who lets her hit him right in the face. She laughs and high fives Austin. Liz stares in silence, her face turning an odd, sickly color.

She turns toward the door, finally gathering her nerve. "We need to get going. Jewel's day is packed. We have the tour and the newcomers meet and greet session. They sometimes run a while. People are so happy to be here."

"I'm sure to fit right in," I mutter.

Kingston's the only one to laugh at my sarcasm. "I'll be right here waiting." He turns to Diego. "And you know what to do if, you know." He doesn't say Orlando's name. He wouldn't. By some miracle, Kingston and Diego decided to get on board with my idea of using Orlando's intrusion to our advantage. They're supposed to keep hidden completely so that he comes out again. I just hope it's not today. Everything else is enough.

I kiss Kingston before heading to Austin and Diego. Liz makes me feel awkward as all get-out as she watches me kiss both Austin and Diego too. My cousins just stand there unfazed. Out of everyone in the world, they're the ones who are most accepting of my matches. For that, I'm grateful. While I wish the six of us were somewhere else, my cousins were right. Being together is more than I could have hoped for. The world could be collapsing, but having my cousins close and my guys here to watch our backs, makes this shit show somehow okay.

Diego hands me a sheathed dagger, drawing my attention from my thoughts. "Just in case. You know what to do."

"The community has a mandatory weapons training program that you'll start as soon as you're situated, Jewel," Liz says, eyeing Diego as he helps me conceal my weapon. "Knives, guns, explosives, you name it."

Diego tilts his mouth downward. "I thought the explosives belonged to the Blood Rebels."

She shrugs. "It's all just in case. Don't think our community is disconnected from the rest of the world. While Donor Life Corp has provided adequate assurance to the safety of Haven Springs, we're not going to pretend that the possibility of something happening isn't out there. We're not going to sit around placated if another round of divisions suddenly take place."

I frown at her mention of The Divide. I never even considered it could happen again, but she does make a point. If something happened to Donor Life Corp... I shake the thoughts away.

"I can respect that," Diego responds to Liz, surprising me.

"Good."

Liz motions to my cousins to head out before us, and she offers her arm to me like if I slide my arm through hers, I'll somehow be better protected. I ignore her gesture and stroll outside after my cousins, peering once at my pouty as hell vampires. Diego won't be far behind us, but it's better if he leaves separately and out the back with the better shade. Austin plans to head to the lab to see what he needs. And of course Kingston will probably leave the house anyway to follow me. Everything else will wait until tonight.

Dana and Fallen slow so that I can catch up to them. They each walk at my sides and watch me in their peripheral vision. I can see the hundreds of questions on their minds already.

I don't wait for them to bombard me. Instead, I glance to Dana first. "Tell me what's up."

She puffs air through her lips. "I wanted to apologize for Berto's actions."

I frown. "Apologize? You don't have to apologize, Dana."

"I had no idea he'd act like that."

I tilt my head. "He was from Dark Terrace Ranch. Of course he'd be freaked the heck out over Austin materializing out of nowhere to restrain him. I'd be scared too."

"They're not going to hurt him, are they?" Fallon asks, speaking the question clearly on Dana's mind.

I stop, turning to the both of them. Liz doesn't crowd our small circle, but from her curious stare, she's obviously invested in my response as much as my cousins are. Taking each of my cousins' hands, I hold them for a second, trying to gather my thoughts.

"No, of course they're not going to hurt Berto. There is

something I need you both to understand, though. Diego, Austin, and Kingston are different than other vampires, but they still carry the same instincts and needs. If someone tries to hurt me—us—they're going to react. So, I need you two to do your best to keep your lives here separate from us, okay? No one is as understanding or as brave as you two."

"Us, brave?" Dana says. "No way. You're the brave one, Jewel. I mean, I can't get over how long and sharp Austin's fangs are."

Fallon flings out her good arm toward the sky. "And Diego is massive."

Dana bares her teeth. "Don't even get us started on the scary ass growls Kingston's always making."

My cousins glance to each other and back to me. "And you let them all bite you."

Warmth rushes into my face, and I tip my head back to soak in the sunlight beaming down. This wasn't exactly the direction I wanted the conversation to head in, but I can't blame my cousins for being curious.

I sling an arm around each of them and push them to start walking again. "Let's not go there," I say. "And I'm glad to hear that you still have a little good fear toward vampires. Like I said, my guys are different. You should most definitely avoid all the rest."

"So should you," Fallon says, crinkling her nose.

I eye her and shake my head to get her to stop talking in front of Liz. "Oh, I try."

Both my cousins hug me. "Good."

"Dana! Fallon!" I tense at the familiar masculine voice as it sounds through the air, drawing all our attentions toward City Hall. Berto and Raul stand up from sitting on the bottom step. A small group of three people hover nearby and all peer in our direction. Dana and Fallon both hug me once more and break off to meet up with their boyfriends.

I look away so that I can pretend Dana didn't just kiss the boy who was responsible for Fallon's broken arm. But he won't know. Austin assured he wouldn't remember anything. I just hope the thought doesn't get to my cousins too much. They have to carry the incident forever.

"They'll be okay," Liz says like she could read my thoughts. "The younger exempt here are rather resilient."

I bob my head. "I know."

She squeezes my shoulder. "I also wanted to say that I was rather relieved to hear that you still have some good sense toward your...relationships with the Divines."

"It was more for your benefit," I say. "You looked ready to pass out at my house."

She tightens her jaw. "It was a little unsettling."

"What? A vampire pillow fight?" I laugh. I can't help it.

A soft chuckle sounds from nearby, and my shoulders relax at the familiarity of Diego's laugh. I peer around for a moment, but I can't see him anywhere. But that's how it's supposed to be. If I can spot him, others might. He needs to stay completely hidden to make sure if Orlando's nearby, he doesn't get tipped off.

Liz wags her head. "Among other things."

Turning away, she takes a few steps toward City Hall, completely ignoring the grimace crossing my face. I knew she was judging the hell out of the fact that I kissed my guys in front of her, but there was no way I was going to not do it just because she was uncomfortable. We'll be sort of apart all day. I need their affection as much as they need mine to get through this bullshit situation Mitchell and Viorica put me in.

"Ms. Matthias," Mr. Barton calls from the doorway to City Hall.

I don't even try to suppress my annoyance and just glower at him.

"I'm happy to see you managed to get Jewel out today," he says, eyeing me like I'm not standing a few feet away.

"Had nothing to do with me," Liz says.

I place my hands on my hips. "I told you I was sick and adjusting. I feel better now."

Mr. Barton gives me a once-over, making me shift on my feet. His eyes narrow on my shoulder to the spot he knows I was bitten. With how intently he stares, I almost think he can see through my hoodie.

I peer down to make sure I'm not bleeding or anything, which I'm not. Because the bite completely healed already. The only ones still left were from the venom bites in my guys' last effort to keep me from Haven Springs. Even those look slightly better.

Mr. Barton rubs his lips together. "That's nice to hear. I was rather concerned you'd be more difficult."

Ugh. This guy.

"The only difficult thing is people assuming I'll be difficult," I say. "Haven Springs isn't exactly the Divinity Estate, but it's livable. Better than The Boxes or anywhere in Dark Terrace Ranch, to be honest."

The rise in my voice draws the attention of the small group of people hanging around.

Two older male adults and a guy probably a bit older than me hover by anxiously. I can't tell if it's because of my presence or because of something else—either way, I try my best to calm the hell down.

"Hey, Jewel," Fallon calls, and I force myself to look at my cousins. "We're going to hang out with some friends after school. That okay?"

I blink a few times and shrug. "Uh, yeah. That's fine."

A small blip of sadness washes over me that I suppress with a smile and a wave as I watch my cousins head around the building to the mysterious school they go to.

It's felt like so long since I've been treated like their guardian that the small moment stirs up so many memories from our time over the last year. How they came to me first before my dad. How much they relied on me until they couldn't. Until my matching and Ramona's transfer out made them rely on only each other.

"They're doing great, aren't they?"

I startle at the chipper sound of Mrs. Diggs' voice. I was so focused on my cousins, I hadn't heard her approach. Shifting on my feet, I turn to face Brayla's mom, trying my best not to react. I knew she was here after seeing Dougie, but with everything that happened with Berto, it slipped my mind. None of my guys even mentioned any concern over her, so—

"Smile and tell her hello," Diego whispers from somewhere to my right. I automatically look in his direction, but still can't see where he is. "Mitchell and Viorica thought it was in their best interest to keep Mrs. Diggs here and under surveillance since Mr. Diggs vanished."

It takes everything in me not to ask what the hell and why no one told me. I guess my guys have their priorities but still.

"They think he'll return for his wife and will capture him for information when he does," Diego adds. "Now, say something to her. Act normal."

"Oh, uh, hey, Mrs. Diggs," I respond a little too late. Diego's words swirl through my head. I should be happy that Brayla's mom is here and that Dougie is safe, but I can't shake the negative feelings brought on by the memory of Mr. Diggs threatening my cousins. It wasn't his fault that Orlando manipulated his mind to do it, and I keep reminding myself that, but being around Mrs. Diggs officially freaks me the hell out.

"I'm glad to see you out and about." Mrs. Diggs offers me a smile. "I was a little worried when you didn't show up for yesterday's tour of Haven Springs. There was a nice boy there. I bet you'd have liked him."

Seriously? "I'm not really interested in meeting any guys."

"You tell her, babe," Kingston whispers. Looks like he lasted all of twenty minutes alone at the house. I flick my gaze around and spot him waving at me from the side of a house before Diego yanks him by the collar, and the two of them disappear.

"I don't know if you know this, but I had a boyfriend before I met Mr. Diggs," she says, not noticing that my attention wanders elsewhere. "He was everything I could hope for. Brave. Strong. Worked at the lab in Dark Terrace Ranch."

I bob my head. "What happened to him?"

She purses her lips. "His family got a transfer out, and I couldn't leave my mom. A donor union would have only allowed me to leave."

I give Mrs. Diggs my undivided attention at her words. I can't help it. Neither can everyone else. Liz and Mr. Barton stop talking, and the small group of newcomers inch closer. "Why didn't he stay?" I ask.

"I wouldn't let him. It was in his best interest to go. Safer. Last I heard, he had gotten accepted into a non-bite household in another region. It was better than I hoped."

I frown. "You didn't miss him?"

"Of course I did. I still do. Even though my heart now belongs to Mr. Diggs, I sometimes still think about Tucker."

I turn my gaze in the direction I last saw my guys.

"Donor Life Corp manipulated her to think Mr. Diggs is away doing something important," Kingston whispers, answering my question about how Mrs. Diggs could be so cool right now, talking like everything is normal.

She touches my hand. "But, the point is that sometimes something might feel bad, but it's for the best. I'm sure the Divines wouldn't want you to live in misery. They did what I did with Tucker. Allowed you a better life than any of them could have offered."

A small growl sounds out from where Kingston and Diego lurk. It's too soft for me to decipher which of them made the noise, but I turn my gaze and glower at Mrs. Diggs, feeling exactly like them. Because, what nerve.

"And you know what else?" she continues, smirking at me.

I don't respond. I can't even find the nerve to keep a straight face.

"The thing that helped me the most was meeting Mr. Diggs. So, you might say you're not interested in meeting anyone new here, but you never know."

I open my mouth to tell her that I do friggin' know, but Mr. Barton claps his hands.

"As much as I'd love to stand around and listen to stories from the outside, I have things to do," Mr. Barton says. His sudden interruption shuts me the hell up before I lose my shit. "Everyone enjoy their tour today. I'm sure I'll see you all around. Come by my office any time. The door is always open." Yeah, because this place doesn't believe in locks.

Mr. Barton shakes the hands of the guys waiting for the tour and purposely skips over me. No one seems to notice, and I couldn't care less. I'm just relieved he's not joining us. We all watch him ascend the stairs two at a time and disappear inside the building.

Mrs. Diggs shifts and smiles at the group, her eyes turning to Liz for the first time. "Oh, Ms. Matthias. Where are my manners? Was there something you needed?"

Liz smiles and shakes her head. "No. I'm actually escorting Jewel today. Just pretend I'm not here."

She makes it rather easy from her silence. I consider asking her more about herself, but Mrs. Diggs distracts me by slapping a nametag across the front of my hoodie. I jump back in surprise, nearly ripping the thing off, but the curious gazes from the others freeze me in place.

"You always did startle easily, Jewel," Mrs. Diggs says smiling. "But worry not. You'll adjust." She turns to the others. "As will the rest of you. And today, I'll prove it."

"How so?" the oldest man of the group asks. "It has been days since I arrived, and I'm still scared."

Mrs. Diggs beams. "We're going to spend most of the tour walking through the shadows."

"What?" all three newcomers say.

"Don't worry, you three. This is Haven Springs, remember? You can relax, and this tour will help you."

"I don't know," the man says.

Mrs. Diggs steps forward and drapes her arm around his shoulder. "You'll be safe. Promise. And tell you what. I'll send Jewel into the shadows first."

I grimace. "Me?"

She nods. "You cannot tell me you're scared."

I blanch. "No, but—"

"No buts. It's our last tour for a while, so I want to make it count. This will be good for everyone."

I frown at Liz, who shrugs.

"This is normal," she whispers to me.

"But—"

"It's not like you have anything to worry about," she adds.

Except I do.

"We're right here, beautiful," Diego whispers. "Just play her game. It'll make the board happy to hear."

I groan. "You owe me," I whisper back to him.

"Whatever you want," he replies.

"From me," Kingston adds.

I suck in a long breath. "Fine, whatever," I say out loud, answering Liz. "Let's do this."

Mrs. Diggs smiles. "That's what I like to hear. You were always tough, Jewel. A fighter."

Her words stir familiar fear in me, but something deep down hopes she's right.

NEW ALLIES

"SO, YOU WERE BLOOD MATCHED?" the young guy of the group asks, walking next to me.

"Yup." I don't elaborate, training my eyes on the buildings around us. One of the things my guys practiced with me was providing the least amount of information as possible. It's come in handy when acting like vampires could manipulate my mind, but it also comes in handy now.

"My sister Blood Matched," he says.

My eyes widen. "Oh." That's new. Most male donors would enter the program before their female family members. I thought he might've been with the other guys. They went on and on about their brother, who lost his life in an accident as a feeder at a party. My guys told me it was rare, but it does happen.

"It was supposed to be me, but she somehow managed to snag an immediate appointment when mine was scheduled a few months out. She went behind my back because she heard that the lifespan of a male donor was nearly half as long as a female in the program," he continues. Interesting. I guess the board makes exceptions...probably because she's female.

Tilting my head, I meet his gaze for the first time. I never heard that statistic before, never really asked about it either. I'll have to ask Kingston if it's true. All my guys have ever talked about is how there tends to be tension between Blood Matched donors and their heirs. The exempt sometimes carry guilt over what their family member gave up. It's obvious from the few sentences that this guy does as well.

"Possibly because females are more desired since there are fewer of us to go around." I regret the admission immediately.

He smooths his stern reaction with the heels of his hands, dragging them down his face. Looking back to me, he says, "My sister matched with a female vampire. Do you think I should worry more or less?"

I stare at him, trying not to react. I'm not even sure how to answer him. It depends on what would worry him.

"If it's a guy, he might not use her strictly as a blood source...right?" he continues.

All I can think about is Master Caruthers, and his disgusting ideas for my future had my guys not have torn him apart. Kingston did assure me that he was an exception. Elite vampires still carry some sort of morals, and there is nothing worse than being hated by your exclusive blood source.

I shudder and straighten my shoulders, pushing thoughts of Master Caruthers away. "Instead of asking about something that doesn't really apply to her, how about you tell me the household she matched into. Maybe I know of them."

His lip quivers until he tightens his jaw again, and I realize he misread my reaction. Now, he probably assumes I experienced the worst. "Sorry, yeah. Of course. She matched with Samantha Vaduva of Midnight Valley."

"Samantha?" I repeat, surprise washing over me. Now it makes sense. Viorica would never allow the board to postpone an opportunity for her daughters.

"You know of the vampire?" Yellow flecks sparkle in his brown eyes that complement the hue of his dark skin. His mouth tightens, his thin lips disappearing. "Is she doomed?"

I open and close my mouth, wondering exactly how to respond. "Um, no. Samantha is like the kitten to her coven of a bunch of lionesses. Sort of."

He grimaces. "I'm not sure I understand."

"She's—"

A few gunshots ring through the air, and I jump in

surprise. A body crashes into mine, sending me stumbling forward into the dirt. I heave a breath and cough. Digging my fingers into the ground, I attempt to push up, but the weight on top of me keeps me pinned.

"Stay down," Liz commands in my ear.

More gunshots pop, and something cracks. Glass shatters.

"Shit balls," I whisper. "What's happening?"

Footsteps thud, crunching through the nearby grove. A dozen thoughts swirl through my head, and I nearly scream out to Diego and Kingston. Liz's heart pounds against my back. Heavy breathing draws my attention to my right, and I wiggle and peer at the young guy next to me. He lies flat on his stomach, his hands protecting his head. The two men and Mrs. Diggs duck under a nearby bench, both guys more freaked out than the older woman.

"Is everyone okay?" a deep voice asks, the footsteps slowing.

Liz's weight falls off me, and she gets to her feet. I scramble to stand next, wanting nothing more than to run away. The young guy pushes up to stand next and jogs to help Mrs. Diggs up. The two older men look scared out of their minds, remaining in their spots.

"What's going on here?" Liz asks, placing her hands on her hips.

"There was a vampire sighting."

I jerk my attention to look at the man, recognizing him

from my short meeting with the council. He pretends not to notice me, focusing on the rest of our group. I take in his rugged face, his long hair spilling out from beneath a hat. Adorned in what appears to be protective body wear, he looks ready to lose his life in a battle against a shit ton of shadow dwellers.

"What do you mean a vampire sighting? It's daytime," one of the older guys asks. "This is Haven Springs. Vampires aren't allowed."

Tipping his head back, Mr. Vampire Hunter releases a loud laugh. I thought he might've been a Blood Rebel before, but now I'm nearly certain. "You think the 'No Vampires Allowed' sign posted on the wall actually works? We don't arm ourselves for nothing. The blood suckers don't give a shit what Donor Life Corp says. If they're hungry, they'll try, even in the sun. Walls don't stop them."

Liz and I glance to each other. There's no way it was one of my guys. They're great at hiding. The only time they'd out themselves is to protect me. Ah, hell. What if...

"But none of you need to worry. It's all covered," the man says. "Unfortunately, I'm gonna have to cut your tour short today. Better safe than sorry."

Another man strolls from the grove. "All clear, Jeremy."

Mr. Vampire Hunter, Jeremy, nods. "Great. Now, if you four can follow Topher back to town, that would be great." He looks to me and Liz. "Ms. Matthias, Ms. Jordan. I'm gonna need you to follow me."

"Where?" I ask, stiffening. He calls me by my birth last name despite the whole community knowing I'm now a Divine. He had mentioned his annoyance about that when I first met him, and I know he purposely calls me Jordan to remind me of where he thinks my place should be.

"The safety bunker. It's protocol," he replies, looking at Liz.

I glance to her as well, and she slowly nods her head without saying a word. Her eyes flick toward the trees, and I know something is wrong without her having to say anything. Jeremy adjusts his gun on his shoulder, motioning for us to walk ahead of him by tipping his head forward.

I touch my hand to my knife, wrapping my fingers around the cool metal. "Protocol," I repeat.

He hums his confirmation. "All of us council members must comply. Don't worry. You'll be safe. Right, Ms. Matthias?"

Liz swallows. "Right."

Taking a breath, she straightens her head, keeping her chin high. She motions for me to walk with her. Everything in me doesn't want to turn my back on the guy. The same fear I used to get walking near the shadows on Starlight Row engulfs me now. Except I'm in the direct sunlight. I'm not afraid of vampires. I'm afraid of someone that I shouldn't be scared of.

Taking slow breaths, I try to steady my racing heart. "Diego," I whisper.

"Right here, beautiful. Don't panic."

I swallow the burning in my throat and try to whisper out. "He's lying."

"What was that?" Jeremy says from behind me.

"No more talking, babe. You can't control your voice when you're scared," Kingston says.

I'm beyond scared. I'm terrified.

"It's dangerous for us to talk, too. In case, you know."

"So. Not. Helping, dude."

Something hard pokes my back, tensing my muscles. Three distinct growls hum through the air. I don't have to see Austin to know he's joined his brothers. I'm sure he's been focused on us this whole time, seeing as the lab isn't that far from here. Haven Springs is big, but it's not Dark Terrace Ranch big.

Jeremy swears from behind me. "Fucking shit." He shoves me with his hands farther into the sunlight. "They were right."

"What are you talking about?" Liz asks.

Tightening his hold on my shoulder, he gives me a shake. "The donor. She's come here to destroy this place."

I break free of his grip and spin around. Grabbing my knife, I pull it free. "Are you friggin' kidding me?"

Jeremy aims his gun at my chest, and I freeze, panic colliding into me. It would be so easy for him to pull the trigger. He could end my life right now, and I'm not so certain my guys could reach me in time. I might be stuck in a transitional state, but I'm not bulletproof. I can't handle the same amount of injuries and fight through it like a vampire can...I think. I don't want to find out now.

"Don't move, traitor," he says. "Tell your masters they better back the hell down, too. You hear m—"

A loud pop startles me, and I cover my ears. My head spins from the piercing sound, and I don't have time to react before Jeremy stumbles forward and crashes into me. I hit the dirt hard, my breath heaving. Warm liquid seeps through the front of my shirt, and I squirm, ramming my hands into the guy's chest, trying to push him off me.

A shadow blocks out the sunlight, and I blink the starbursts away until Liz's face comes into view. She hooks her fingers to the back of Jeremy's gear and rolls him off me, dropping his dead body to the ground.

"Jewel? Jewel? Look at me," she commands, kneeling beside me. "I need you to get up."

She yanks my hand, pulling me to my feet. I can barely focus on anything apart from the hot blood on my skin, the deafening ringing in my ears, the sunlight burning my eyes. I can't hear Diego, Austin, or Kingston at all.

Liz squeezes my shoulder to draw my attention to her. "Grab his feet."

"Huh?"

She stops and puts her hands on her hips, turning toward the trees. "She's disoriented. She might have hit her head."

I glance in the direction she looks and spot Diego pointing at Jeremy. His lips move, but I can't hear what he's saying.

Liz nudges me with the back of her hand. "Jewel, you have five seconds to help me before you force one of the Divines to brave the sunlight."

I shake my head and rub my ears, trying to hear past the dumb ringing. Liz strolls around Jeremy's body and wraps her hands around his wrist and tugs, barely getting him to move an inch. He's bigger than us by a few inches and solid. The gear probably doesn't help.

I blink a few more times, finally finding my focus. "Here. I'll take his hands. You grab his feet."

Liz releases a breath when I pull my ass together and move from my spot to help her. I lock my fingers around Jeremy's still warm hands and lug him up an inch, dragging him in the direction Diego motions for me to hurry.

"You're stronger than you look," Liz says, grunting as we stop-start, carrying the body a couple of feet at a time.

Groaning, I lift the body higher, using all my strength to lug him without dragging him. "I get that a lot."

Liz grits her teeth, her muscles flexing. "I guess you'd have to be since you were in Divine care."

I twist my lips to the side. "Not because of my guys. They treat me like I'll die at any second."

"Not Diego," Kingston mutters.

Glancing up, I smile at him. I can't help it. And I'm so

happy to hear his voice. It makes the whole carrying a dead guy thing a lot less awful. It's even worse than helping Brayla carry a bunch of mind manipulated accused criminals around the Divinity Estate. My guys didn't help me then, either. Though I know they wanted to. They want to help me now. Stupid sun. It's not worth the risk. Sun exposure weakens them, and everyone needs to be in fighting mode.

"That's it, beautiful. Five more feet," Diego says, holding his arms out.

The second I step into the shade of the building, Diego takes over and drags Jeremy out of my reach. Kingston beats Austin and lifts me into his arms, kissing every inch of my face and neck in a dozen kisses.

"Fuck this shit. No more adventures for you." He rests his chin on my shoulder, refusing to let me go. "You hear that, Liz?" he asks, probably glaring at her. He doesn't let me move to look to see her. I'm pretty sure it'll take his brothers to get him to release me.

"Let's not overreact," Liz says.

Uh-oh.

"Overreact!"

I grip Kingston's face and crash my mouth to his to distract him before he blows the hell up at Liz. His fangs accidentally pierce my bottom lip, and he freezes, inhales a breath, and holds it. One second I'm in his arms, and in the next, Austin cradles me against him, spinning me away. Diego slams Kingston into the wall of the building, holding him in place as his eyes flash crazy silver. Liz aims her weapon at the two of them, her hands steady, her eyes narrowed.

"Kingston, calm down. You're scaring Jewel," Diego whispers. "I'm sure Liz didn't mean to downplay the seriousness of the situation. She was only trying to get you to keep your cool."

"I don't fucking want to keep my cool," Kingston mutters, keeping his voice too low for Liz to hear. "I want to devour every last one of these entitled donors."

The second the words leave his mouth, he jerks his head up to look at me. I bite my lip, still tasting my blood, trying my best to keep my face expressionless to his admission. It's been weeks since he referred to humans as donors. He's made a point not to because of me.

"Jewel," he whispers. "I'm sorry."

I force myself to smile. "Dude, you better be. The idea of that mouth of yours on anyone's body but mine makes me extremely jealous."

He forces his own smile, though his dark eyes remain pouty as hell. "I can fix that."

Austin clears his throat. "As much as I hate saying this, maybe you should take Jewel home, Kingston. We need to figure out if this was a planned incident or if this guy was taking advantage of the situation."

"That's easy to figure out," Liz says. "He said vampires were spotted. Was it you?"

Shaking his head, Diego says, "No. We're the only ones

around. I highly doubt Orlando would have allowed himself to be seen. Other vampires wouldn't risk sun exposure without a sure bite either."

Liz relaxes enough to lower her gun. "Then let me report the situation. We'll handle it properly."

"What about the other guy?" I ask.

"We'll take care of him," Diego says.

Liz remains expressionless. "And then hand him over to the council."

"Fuck that," Kingston says. "He's dead—"

My body reacts to his words with a whimper before my brain can shut my mouth up. Kingston's glower softens, and he dodges Diego to close the space to me. For once, Austin doesn't play keep away and lets Kingston pull me from him.

Kingston runs his thumb across my lip, smearing whatever blood that is still on my mouth. "I'm sorry, babe. We'll do it Liz's way. I'm just so—"

"Angry?" I ask.

"Pissed the fuck off. Furious. Mitchell is endangering your life. He doesn't even care," he whispers, squeezing his eyes shut. "I hate him."

"So do I." I rest my forehead to his cheek.

"I want to run away with you. Please, let me."

I release a breathless laugh. "Not this again. You know we can't. Not to mention the fact that your brothers will never give you another minute alone with me if you start threatening to again."

He groans. "Shit, you're right. Can't have that now."

I nuzzle my nose to his. "Nope. Because I could use some cuddles."

"And kisses?"

"Lots of kisses."

"Maybe let me bite you a little. All that blood on you is making me starved."

I tip my head back and laugh. "We'll see."

He slides his hands lower to squeeze my butt. "I'll let you bite me."

"Don't tease me," I say, licking my lips.

"I'm not." Spinning around, Kingston faces his brothers. "You good?"

"We're good," both Diego and Austin say in unison. "We'll get you if we need anything."

"I'll call Mitchell," Kingston adds. "After I assure our girl is okay."

I swivel and motion for Austin and Diego to come closer so that I can kiss each of them. They sandwich me between their muscular bodies for a minute, letting me feel the strength of all three of them.

"Don't forget to feed Jewel. Do it first," Austin says.

Kingston groans. "I know how to take care of our girl."

Smirking, Austin swats Kingston with the back of his hand. "I meant blood. Her thermos is on my bedside table."

"I thought I'd just let her have at me." Kingston flashes

his fangs.

Diego punches his other arm. "Good luck, bro. We'll take good care of Jewel when you're dead."

I glower. "Diego."

He laughs. "I'm only kidding. Be nice to Kingston, beautiful. We like having his annoying ass around. Sometimes."

"I will."

Kingston wags his eyebrows. "Damn straight."

"But not too nice," Austin says.

I laugh. "Deal." Turning to Liz, I say, "Thanks for saving my life. You'll be rewarded."

"I just want you to hold up your end of our deal," she says, pressing her lips together.

Diego nods. "We're already on it."

SATIATED

"WHAT THE FUCK IS HE doing here?" Kingston sets me down in the shade of a lush oak tree, keeping us out of view from the front porch.

"No idea," I say, peeking around Kingston.

He holds my hand. "It's because you were nice."

"Don't even start, dude." I smirk at him, though he doesn't take his eyes off the guy from the tour whose sister matched with Samantha.

"You bet I will."

I shake my head and pat his chest. "Behave."

"Never."

"Dude."

Kingston sighs and links his fingers onto the back of his

head, sliding them into his hair. "Fine. Go find out what he wants and send him away."

"What? No mind manipulation?" I ask, raising my eyebrows. I for sure thought he was going to ask him to send the guy over here so that Kingston could assure he wouldn't come back. I nearly ask him to. The guy seems nice enough, and I'll agree to anything so that my guys don't do something crazy by accident.

He sighs. "And risk a Widow's wrath? I heard that his sister matched with Samantha. She'd flip her shit if we did something to upset her Blood Match. Messing with her heir would be on that list, don't you think?"

"He did mention that his sister went behind his back to do so because he was planning to enter the program," I muse.

"Yeah, so no mind manipulation." Kingston nudges me forward. "Now hurry and get rid of him. I'm getting fucking hot. And I'm hungry. Do I need to mention horny too? I might risk a sunburned ass just to bone you right here. Right now."

"Kingston!" I laugh so loudly that Kingston holds his fingers to my lips while covering his own mouth as he chuckles at my reaction.

He pushes my back into the tree and kisses me. "I'm only slightly kidding, babe."

Without giving me another moment to continue kissing him, Kingston helps me out of my bloody hoody and nudges me away from him. He motions for me to head toward the house, purposely giving me a long once-over until I have to turn away from him before I run right back.

I meet the brown gaze of the young guy. "What are you doing here—sorry, I don't remember your name." I barely looked at anyone on the tour's nametags.

"Cyprus Bradshaw," he says, rocking on his heels. "You're Jewel, right?"

"Yup." I close the space to him and peer behind me, trying to glimpse Kingston. "Nice to officially meet you."

He grins and extends his hand to me. It's then that I realize my fingers are covered in blood, and it's too late to pull back. I take an automatic step away, bracing myself for his oncoming reaction.

"Whoa, shit. Are you hurt?" he asks, sucking a breath between his teeth. "I know first aid. Do you have a kit?"

I rub my hands on my pants. "It's fine. The blood isn't—" Shit balls. One glance at Cyprus has me taking another step back.

His wide eyes look me up and down. He takes his own step away.

"I'm sorry. I..." What the hell do I even say to this guy? He looks ready to run away screaming. Probably my name while accusing me of murder.

"Tell him the truth, babe," Kingston whispers. "He's new. His Blood Match is a Divine ally. Use those big blue eyes of yours to your advantage."

"I need you to leave," I say, turning toward the door. "And please, don't tell anyone. It's not safe."

Cyprus furrows his brows. "What do you mean?"

I glance around again.

"Is it the vampires?"

Shaking my head, I say, "No. That man lied. There weren't any vampires. He only wanted to get me alone so that he could—" Real tears burst from my eyes at the memory. The fear. The feeling of his gun at my back. "He was going to kill me."

Two arms wrap around me, startling me. Cyprus pulls back and crosses his arms, frowning deeper. "I'm sorry. I didn't mean to make you uncomfortable. I just—you looked like you needed a hug."

"What I need is to get inside and wait for Liz. She was there. She—she was the one who—shit. You should go. It isn't safe. Don't tell her I told you. She told me to trust no one. I just figured since the Vaduvas are allies to the Divines." The words tumble from my mouth, my habit of talking too much when I'm nervous benefiting me for once. Because Cyprus listens intently to my every word, his concern obvious on his face. "What am I even saying? This is Haven Springs. I don't have allies. I didn't even want to be here. My sister—"

"You don't have to explain. I heard the rumors, but I couldn't believe them. No one who enters the Blood Match Program would trade places willingly. I should know." Cyprus reaches out and touches my shoulder. "And I won't say anything about this. Promise."

I bob my head and force myself to smile and touch my doorknob. "Thanks. Now you might want to get out of here. You don't want people to associate you with humanity's traitor. Not on your first day."

He shifts on his feet. "Can I at least take a look around to make sure it's safe?"

"Um..."

"Just let him, babe," Kingston whispers. "He won't leave unless he can be your hero. Guys like that shit. You were way too good. I mean, tears? Are you trying to kill my boner?"

It takes everything in me not to react to Kingston. "Yeah, okay," I say to Cyprus, bobbing my head. "Just be careful. Don't mind the mess...I've been upset since I woke up here and destroying things helps."

He smirks. "They drug you too? These houses aren't as sturdy as the apartments in the West Tower."

"You really didn't want to come here?" I ask.

He opens the door and peers inside the house. "Like I said. I wanted this life for my sister, not me."

"Looks like you might be the perfect ally," I murmur.

"Us traitors to humanity must stick together, right?" he asks.

"Right," I say, my voice cracking with my sudden nerves. "But why are you a traitor?"

He steps inside of the house and hesitates. "Because I don't want to spend the rest of my life as a donor."

I study him a moment. "You want to be a vampire?"

Grinning, he says, "Hell yeah. I want nothing more than to say screw it to this stupid, shitty, human life."

"Dude, relax," I say, concentrating on Kingston's form. He blurs around me as he paces the room at vampire speed.

"I can't. Mitchell never misses my calls. He's up to something," Kingston pauses to glance at me for a second before zooming around the room again.

The second Cyprus left, Kingston hurried to call Mitchell. But Mitchell didn't answer. And then the line wouldn't even connect when he tried again a few more times. Kingston said that only happens if our call had been blocked.

I jerk out my arm to try to snatch the back of his shirt and miss. "He's always up to something. Everyone's always up to something."

"You're right, babe." Kingston slows down.

"I know," I say with a smile. "Even *I'm* up to something."

He raises an eyebrow to give me his full attention. "And what's that?"

I twist my shirt between my fingers. "Come closer and find out."

Kingston chuckles and closes the space to me. I tug him with me by his jacket and spin him around to get him to sit on the bed. Combing my hair away from my shoulder, I expose my neck to him. The familiar click of his fangs extending sounds in my ear, and I shiver as he breathes against my skin.

"Let me feed you," I whisper, shifting on his lap. "I know it'll help. And then we can do whatever you want. I don't want you to stress. This is our time together, and I refuse to let anyone ruin it."

"Whatever I want?" he asks, kissing the crook of my neck, gliding his tongue up before brushing his lips to my jaw. He doesn't bring up my other thoughts. He's a master of changing his focus the second I distract him. I love that he can't help it.

"Within reason," I murmur. "No running away."

He groans and tightens his hold on my waist, pulling my body closer so that I feel the hard length of his desire press between my legs. I slide my hand down and rub over his zipper to tease him just a little.

"No running away," he repeats. "Never leaving this room."

Kingston steals my laugh away with a kiss that leaves me gasping. He surprises me by biting his arm and holding it to my lips. My heart thrashes at the sight of his deep red blood starting to drip from the two circular wounds.

I suck in a breath. "Kingston, I—"

"I want to feed you first," he whispers. "Let me. Please."

Hearing him say the words should weird me out more than they do. I struggle to accept the knowledge that I need vampire blood despite my desire to spend eternity with him. I had the idea I'd drink human blood from the general population. Not my guys' blood.

And now that he offers me his arm? My stomach burns with the need I know he feels glimpsing mine.

Panting, I resist closing the space to his arm. Because, what if I lose control? What if he can't get me to stop? But shit, my body wants to risk it. To experience such a moment with Kingston. I've never drunk his blood like this, in a time where it wasn't out of necessity or without his brothers. And now that he wants me to? God, he looks so hot, biting his own lip in anticipation, dead-set on giving me what I need.

I open my mouth, gliding my tongue over my bottom lip. "Kingston," I whisper, my voice barely audible. "I—I want to. So. Damn. Much. But it scares me. I'm scared. What if I hurt you?"

He smirks like it's the silliest thing in the world. And maybe it is. It helps my nerves that he thinks so. Instead of pointing it out, he says, "I know you'll be careful, Jewel. And if you use your zombie teeth, I'll heal. You don't need to be afraid of your needs or letting me take care of them. I'm better at this than cooking you something, anyway."

"You sure you want to risk it?" I ask, his words making me all sorts of excited.

He offers his arm out again. "Fuck yeah. I want that pouty mouth all over me. Now drink."

I glide my tongue over his arm, gingerly tasting his blood. He releases a low moan, shifting under me. His body tenses and relaxes, his breathing quickening, his desire clear of where he hopes this heads. Where I can't wait to take it.

The sugary, slightly spicier flavor of his blood awakens my body, and I mold my lips over his bite mark and suck harder. His dark eyes flash silver, his fangs peeking from beneath his lips. He runs his fingers through my hair, watching me with an intensity that burns through me in the best way possible, heating my skin so that he can absorb my warmth.

I ease my mouth away, so friggin' turned on by the hunger he has for me in my entirety blazing in his eyes that far exceeds his deep-seated nature to survive on my blood.

"Your eyes," he whispers, running his knuckles over my cheek to push my hair behind my ear. "They're so beautiful. Like the moon reflecting on the ocean."

"They're silver?" I ask, blinking, wishing I could see myself.

He nods. "Because you need more to eat. It's one of the reasons why a vampire's eyes turn silver."

It makes sense. Kingston first noticed a change in my eyes after not consuming their blood for a while. "Oh, okay," is all I say to that. I'm not sure I want to think more about my newish diet. So I decide to change the subject to distract him—or me—some more. "You know, you're romantic when you want to be. Moon reflecting on water?"

He chuckles. "What? It's true. But mostly, I just want in your pants."

I giggle and pat his chest. "And I want you out of yours."

"I fucking love you, babe."

Kingston wastes no time stripping my shirt off before doing the same with his. I lie back and rest on my elbows, arching my hips up to let him undress me. He drinks in the sight of me for only a second and rushes to get his pants off.

He flops on the bed next to me, making me laugh until he kisses me again long enough that I reach down to feel the extent of him with my hand. He moans and gently shifts me onto my side to lie against me. Pulling the blankets around us, he snuggles close to my back, sliding his arm under me to hold it in front of my mouth.

"Is this okay?" he asks, kissing my shoulder. "I want you to drink as much as you feel you need. I'll stop you before it's too much. I want this to be the best experience for you."

A mixture of emotions flutters through me at his words. "What about you? I want the same for you."

"Oh, I have no doubt it will be, babe. It's just—I know we've been worried about you drinking too much of our blood, but now I'm—*we're*—concerned we've been starving you. Maybe you won't feel so out of control this way," he adds. "It used to help me and Diego. It still helps Austin."

"Are you sure I should from you?" I ask him. "Wouldn't it be better if I just drank from a cup?"

He chuckles. "You could, but what's the fun in that?"

I shift to kiss him once more before he bites his arm again, igniting something crazy intense inside me. Kingston whispers how hot he thinks I am in my ear, grazing his fangs along my shoulder, turning our moment from need to desire.

"Can I bite you now?" he murmurs, kissing the crook of my neck.

His soft voice pulls me from the pleasure of my humming body, of how Kingston fills me up on every level I had no idea I needed. And I know why he chose to cuddle me and tease me, turning the act of my necessity for blood into more than just satisfying the uncontrollable hunger threatening to consume me. He wants this to be more than an act of survival for the both of us. He wants it to be an act of love. Of living and breathing and being together.

"I'd like that," I mumble, my body now warm and tingling—anticipating.

He slides his arms away from my face, aligning his body to mine, letting me feel him between my legs. It's me who guides him with silent permission. He moans the same time I do, his love for me a breathless whisper on his lips.

And then he bites me, his fangs so quick and gentle, I only feel a tiny bit of pressure before his mouth takes over, and we lose ourselves to our desire more so than ever before.

"How do you feel?" he asks when he's certain I'm content and satiated on every level.

I twist in his arms and meet him for a kiss. "Incredible. Perfect."

He grins at me. "Just how I love you to be. I could get used to this."

A strange noise from outside stops me from telling him what's on my mind. From telling him that he might have to get used to it, but I keep the thought to myself. I suppress it completely. Kingston freezes, holding his breath. The noise wasn't my imagination.

The private line rings, cutting through the house and over the movement of feet.

Kingston scoops the tablet off the night table, knowing it can only be Mitchell or his brothers. I offer him a small smile and rest my head to his chest, listening to his heart beating for me while he answers the phone.

"Get out," Diego says through the line. "Hurry."

I don't have a chance to react. Kingston rushes to get us both dressed, grabs the comforter to wrap around us, and flies toward the window.

The last thing I hear is the sound of the front door crashing open and the thudding of footsteps. Something explodes, shaking the ground. And then the house catches fire, sending a cloud of smoke into the air.

I watch from Kingston's arms as our world goes up in flames.

UNWELCOME

"IF MY COUSINS WERE HOME, they could've been killed," I say, wringing my hands together. I've never been so thankful for something in my life. The explosives some of the exempt assholes set off were right below their rooms. "What the hell is going on? What do we even do? Why hasn't Mitchell called? I want to take my cousins and leave."

Kingston hugs me against him without a word. He's in as much shock as I am and hasn't let me go since we got out of the house before it blew up. Now, we all hide in Liz's lab, and I'm freaking the eff out worse than ever. It was one thing to take advantage of a weird opportunity, but to come after me directly? What did I do to deserve this?

"There is still an hour of sunlight left. Mitchell could

be busy. We left him in an uncertain state against the Monroe Region," Diego says, rubbing circles on my back.

I groan, resting my chin on Kingston's shoulder. "I still think we need to do something."

"The only thing I want you to do now is to take a breath," Austin says, touching his fingers to my cheeks from over Kingston's shoulders. "Come on. Inhale and exhale. Your heart is out of control, and Kingston's not going to let go until he's certain you're not going to flip out and do something crazy like run out into the sun."

I do as he says, closing my eyes to try my best to settle my shot nerves.

"That's it, Jewel," Austin says, resting his forehead to mine. "Do it again."

Kingston's grip loosens, but he still doesn't let go of me. I think Austin might be slightly wrong about Kingston holding me to assure I don't do anything rash. I don't point it out, though, and I'll give Kingston another minute more.

I shift in his arms and lean back to meet his glum face. "I think I'm okay, Kingston."

"I'm not," he says. "I should've reacted faster. I heard them outside. I just didn't expect—"

"You couldn't have known the exempt would attack the house, bro," Diego says, squeezing Kingston's shoulder. "Don't hold onto that shit. I'd have thought the same as you."

Austin joins our hug. "You got Jewel out, and you're

both safe and unharmed. That's what matters."

A soft, weird ass cooing noise escapes my mouth. I can't help it. I love this so much that it makes all the other stuff seem not so bad. I've always admired my guys' brotherly loyalty and their ability to be there for one another. It makes me so incredibly happy that despite the disaster, they don't try to blame anyone but the exempt and that they also won't allow Kingston to carry unnecessary guilt.

"See?" Austin says, smiling at me. "Jewel thinks so."

"Is that what that cute ass noise meant?" Kingston asks, raising an eyebrow at me.

I bob my head, smiling. "I just love that you love each other so much."

"I wouldn't go that far," Kingston teases.

"Yeah, Kingston's always one second away from brotherly annihilation, especially if I find out he forgot to feed you." Diego smacks Kingston on the back, laughing.

Kingston hums deep in his throat and kisses my forehead. "Oh, our girl is nice and content. I did exactly what I was supposed to."

"And you feel okay, Jewel?" Austin asks.

I wiggle in Kingston's arms until he finally sets me on my feet. The three of them continue to surround me, caging me in with their delicious, muscular bodies like there is no friggin' way any of them will ever let me out of arm's reach.

I bite my lip and flick my gaze away from Austin to Kingston. "Yeah."

Diego grins at me. "You owe me half a night, Austin. Told you our girl could resist devouring Kingston. Apparently that one percent does matter when it comes to nutrients."

My face burns at his statement, and Austin punches Diego in the arm. Kingston just grins with the cockiest expression I've ever seen on him. Dude is proud as hell, and I'll give it to him. I mean—I was nervous, and he helped me through. Obviously the three of them somehow managed to plot how this would work between us.

"Just look at our girl. She managed to pull herself away right now and doesn't have the same side effects toward him as she does us," Diego adds.

That makes Kingston growl. "Because you look at them as side effects. I just took care of Jewel exactly how she need—"

Austin punches Kingston next. "That's enough. You know our girl doesn't like it when we discuss her like she's not standing right here, right Jewel?"

I bob my head. "Thanks, Austin. My face is never going to cool off."

Kingston chuckles. "I don't mind. Can't you see it helps all of us? I no longer have the urge to murder everyone as long as I can make you blush like crazy."

"But we have more important things to do," Austin says.

Kingston pulls me back to him. "Your priorities are

off."

So much for all the brotherly love.

Straightening my shoulders, I tug back from Kingston before he does succeed to distract me again. I'm thankful that my guys calmed me the hell down, but Austin's right. We have to figure out what to do.

"They are not—"

I press each of my hands to Austin and Kingston's chests, feeling the thumps of their hearts on my palms. "Please, stop. Arguing won't help."

"You're right, babe. The only thing that will help is if I hunt down that asshole Cyprus and rip his heart out to mail to his sister." Kingston's eyes flash silver.

I frown. "Huh? Why?"

Kingston crosses his arms. "He was the last one at the house, and you told him about what happened. He obviously spread the word about the incident and told people you were home alone."

"We can't hurt the guy, dude." I glance to Diego and Austin, who remain expressionless.

Neither of them takes my side. I'm pretty friggin' sure they agree with Kingston without them having to say so.

"He's the heir to a Vaduva Blood Match," I remind the three of them. I turn to Austin. "As much as Samantha annoys the hell out of me, I think you should take her feelings into consideration."

"She's why you ended up here!" Kingston shouts.

Diego flies at him and covers his mouth with his hand. Kingston reacts by twisting and elbowing Diego hard enough to send him crashing into a table, spilling Liz's medical supplies across the floor. The clattering of metal echoes through the lab, and Diego and Kingston freeze, managing to keep their shit together before they do more damage.

"You guys need to chill out," I say, hugging myself.

Austin reaches me first and pulls me in for a hug. I jump up and let him hold me, knowing how much he wants to. Without him having to say it, I know he's been wanting to since Kingston and I met him and Diego here, but Kingston wouldn't let me go.

Now I'm not so sure Austin will.

He brushes his fingers through my hair and swivels to meet his brothers' gazes and steals my view of them in the process. "Jewel's right. Our alliances are fragile with other regions. We can't risk the tension with the Vaduvas. I say we wait for Liz to return with an update and try to call Mitchell again. If he doesn't answer, we'll call Viorica."

"And if we can't reach anyone?" I ask.

"Then we'll leave," Kingston says. "Staying here is not fucking worth it."

Austin and Diego nod their agreement, and I release a small breath in relief. I just can't seem to see another way out of this. I know it might risk my future—our futures—with the Divine name, but I might not have a future otherwise.

Soft footsteps draw our attention toward the front door, and Austin zooms me to the back hallway to take cover. Kingston and Diego guard us, the three of them ready to conquer any and all possible threats.

"It's me," Liz says before opening the door. "Don't attack."

A streak of sunlight beams across the floor but nowhere near us to cause my guys to flinch. It disappears just as quickly, and heavy boots clomp across the tiled floor. Kingston and Diego step from the hallway to the main room of the lab, but Austin keeps me nestled in his arms and out of sight.

"Did you find the assholes responsible?" Kingston says, his voice deep and throaty...super hot. I like hearing him all protective.

Liz clears her throat. "One of them, but please. You have to let the council handle the situation."

"Handle the situation? How? Your laws are far too tame to deter anyone from going after Jewel again."

Austin strolls closer to peer into the main room. I twist in his arms to see Kingston balling his fists, his eyes flashing silver. He looks on the verge of attacking Liz. She holds onto her gun but doesn't aim it. Diego stands between them, his tall form enough to block them from each other if he feels the need to intervene.

"No one will come after Jewel," Liz says, her jaw tightening.

Kingston throws his arms up. "You don't know that."

"I do. They think she's dead," Liz says, turning her attention to me. "The whole community does."

"What?" I ask.

"It helps that your heirs—"

"Dana and Fallon think I'm dead?" My voice screeches through the room, and I push my hands into Austin's chest, not giving him a choice as to whether or not to let me go. The sudden force of my unexpected strength throws him off balance. Strong arms hook under mine, stopping me from hitting my ass on the floor, and Diego rights me on my feet. Austin stares at me with a startled expression that he turns to his brothers, but none of them say anything.

"Take a breath, babe. I'll go get them—"

A soft chime rings through the air, cutting off Kingston's words. We all look to Liz, who stares at the blinking light on the wall next to a communications box.

"Go on. Answer it," Diego says, motioning across the room.

The four of us return to the hallway and out of sight. Liz strides across the room, her shoulders straight. She looks far better composed that I am, which is crazy because she killed someone to protect me. I don't know how anyone can remain so unfazed like that.

The thought reminds me of Ramona, leaving a funny feeling in my stomach, but I know Liz isn't a Blood Rebel. Her mind manipulation proved it.

"Mr. Divine, Ms. Vaduva. What may I owe this unexpected call to?" Liz asks.

The world blurs around me, and I find myself facing the projection screen on the wall. Mitchell and Viorica sit beside each other, their steely expressions giving nothing away. Mitchell's gaze trains to Kingston first while Viorica looks at me in Diego's arms. Neither of them gives Liz any attention, ignoring her completely.

Kingston shifts his jaw. "We're removing Jewel from Haven Springs tonight."

Mitchell's eyes flash silver, and Viorica reaches out and surprises me by placing her hand on his chest.

"You will not do anything rash before you catch us up on the situation, Kingston," Viorica says.

"They blew up the house!" Kingston's voice yells through the room, startling me. His anger, even not directed at me, prods at my human rationale and sends panic sneaking up on me.

Mitchell and Viorica turn to each other, sharing a silent look that speaks volumes. They don't see the situation the same way my guys do. If they did, they would've reacted with concern, maybe find out if we were okay. But no. The jerks just continue to converse like they knew that this could happen.

"Blood Rebels?" Mitchell finally asks, turning his attention back to us.

"No, regular exempts," Diego says. "It was the second

attempt on Jewel's life. Had we not been here—"

"Settle down, boys. It doesn't matter what would have happened had you not been there, because you are there, and Jewel looks fine. I don't see why you're reacting so intensely."

It's Austin who reacts. Flashing his fangs, he yells, "Did you not hear us? They attempted to kill Jewel!"

"So handle it appropriately. That is no reason to leave. Haven Springs will assume they can get away with anything they want." Mitchell's voice remains even, though he looks like he could explode right back at Austin for raising his voice.

"We're not going to expose our cover," Kingston says.

"It's all we have against Orlando," Diego adds.

Viorica sighs. "He's the least of our concerns right now. And your father was not suggesting to reveal that you've been staying in Haven Springs. That kind of knowledge will lead to more tension. If the board notices a decline in donor applicants to the Blood Match Program because word got out that we allowed the three of you to remain with Jewel, our alliance will be over."

"Wait," Kingston says. "You better not be fucking suggesting that we let the humans take care of it."

Mitchell flares his nostrils. "Of course not. It is Jewel's responsibility to put them in their places as my Divine Heir." For the first time since calling, he flicks his gaze and focuses solely on me. And I wish he hadn't. Because holy shit balls. He looks like he'd murder me if I were in the same room as him. "Do you understand, Jewel?"

I swallow, the words hard to summon against my fear. My whole body betrays me, and I tremble in Diego's arms, making him hold me tighter.

"Jewel can't. They believe she's dead, and we'd like to keep it that way for her safety," Austin says, managing to keep his voice even.

"I'll take care of the punishment," Liz says. She steps right next to me and gazes at Mitchell and Viorica. "It is already in council hands."

"No," Mitchell says. "The fact that my sons have allowed you to keep this knowledge is bad enough."

"But—"

"I said no!" he yells, his eyes flashing silver. "Jewel will take care of the problem the Divine way. If she does not, I can assure you that a few donors will be the least of all of your worries. Do you understand?"

"You fucking—"

I slap my hand over Kingston's mouth, shutting him up. "Yes, I understand," I say. "I'll take care of it. Promise."

Viorica smirks, looking smug as all get-out. "We expect an update later tonight."

"And a body," Mitchell says.

My stomach rolls at the thought, and I clench my jaw. The projection screen flicks off, leaving the room in silence.

"She's going to be sick, Diego," Austin says, hurrying

to hold out a trashcan.

I cover my mouth with my hand, my stomach heaving, and despite all my efforts, Austin was right. Sweat dampens my hair, my hands trembling so hard, my heart attempting to escape through my ribs. I can't believe this is happening. I can't believe I've just been put in a position to uphold the vampire law against a human.

"Is that blood?" Liz asks, her eyes focusing on the trash can. "Oh, God. Let me get a look at her."

Austin blocks Liz. "Stay back."

Diego shocks me by capturing Liz in his stare, and he says, "You will not say anything more about Jewel's blood consumption. You won't even think about it."

"Diego," I whisper, fear shaking my voice.

"It had to be done, beautiful."

"It's just—shit balls."

I know I shouldn't be so freaked out about everything. Liz can't know about me, and it's not like the ones who came after me were innocent—they *did* try to kill me—but now I'll prove their thoughts right. I'll really be a traitor to humanity, upholding vampire law in a community that was supposed to be held outside it.

Kingston rubs circles on my back while Diego keeps my hair out of my face. Liz brings me a glass of water, and Austin takes it from her to hold up to my lips.

"You don't have to do this, beautiful," Diego says.

"You're not going to do it," Kingston adds.

"But Mitchell said—"

Austin touches my cheek. "We don't care what Mitchell said, Jewel."

I sniffle, curling in on myself. "I do. I know you guys want to do everything to protect me, but we can't risk what happens if Mitchell thinks that your loyalty has shifted to me."

"We can risk it," Austin says quietly.

I shake my head. "No."

"Babe."

I look at Kingston. "I mean it. I'll do anything for you, and if it means..." I can't say the words out loud. I can barely even think them. Instead, I turn to Liz. "Call a town meeting."

"Jewel—"

"I said call a meeting!" I yell at her, anger tinting the edges of my vision in shadows. "Right now. I'm getting this over with."

"It can wait until dark." Diego tries to hold me in his arms, but one look at him has him placing me on my feet.

I cross my arms and straighten my shoulders. "No, it can't. This has to be done."

LOYALTY

"USUALLY, I THINK YOUR BOSSINESS is hot, but fuck, babe," Kingston mutters, crossing his arms. "I want to lock you in the closet until you stop acting like a—" Snapping his mouth shut, he doesn't finish his words.

"Go on. You can tell me what you think I'm acting like," I say, sighing.

Kingston puffs out his bottom lip and shakes his head. "It won't help."

I raise an eyebrow. "You're picking now to think before you speak?"

He smirks at me. "Weird, huh?"

I meet his smirk with a frown. "I don't like it. I like your unfiltered honesty."

"Kingston's just trying to tell you that you can change your mind and not go through with upholding vampire law within Haven Springs," Diego says, sliding his arm around my waist to turn me away from an incredibly pouty Kingston. "We'll figure it out."

"I already have figured it out. The guy deserves it," I murmur.

"Hell yeah, he does," Kingston says.

"But you don't deserve this." Austin stops in front of me, standing next to Diego. "It should be the council or us."

My lip quivers. I can't help it. No matter how much I keep telling myself that people do what they have to do—me included—it doesn't feel right. I'm not a killer. I never imagined I would be, though after Katherine, I know I'm capable of it. But she was different. Right? Now I'm not so sure.

"That's it. He's dead. I'm killing him." Kingston disappears from in front of me, but he doesn't make it far. Diego grabs him by the shirt and yanks him back.

Diego shoves Kingston into the wall. "You can't go out there. People are gathering."

"I'm not letting our girl do something she doesn't want to," he snaps. Snarling, he shoves against Diego until he steps back.

"Sometimes we have to do things we don't want to," I whisper, the words my dad used to tell me now truer than ever.

"Bullshit." Kingston returns to me, his nostrils flaring, but he manages to keep his fangs in check. "I won't accept that damn excuse for you."

I drop my gaze to the floor under the intensity of his stare. "It's not up to you, Kingston."

"He's right, Jewel." Austin laces his fingers through mine and pulls me closer to him. Peering at me with his green eyes, he attempts to get me to focus on solely him. I relent and gaze at him, taking in the worry lining his eyes. "I promised to always take care of you, and that includes your heart and mind."

"Yeah, we get that you want to protect us, but killing someone, beautiful?" Diego asks. "That's not you. I promised that I'd make sure our lives wouldn't change you into someone you hate. Eternity is a long time. I know you might not feel like it's attainable right now, but it is."

"And I promised never to let you kill my boner again. So come here and let me take care of you." Kingston inches closer, holding his arms out to me expectantly.

"Kingston, really?" Austin asks, not letting me go. "Now's not the time."

"It's always the time to kiss that pouty mouth of our girl and lock her in a closet, with me of course, so she doesn't turn into a—"

Diego punches him in the stomach, making him growl. "Kingston."

"What? I don't want Jewel to fucking kill someone, all right? If it means I stop her myself or kill the fucking bastard, I'm going to do it. I don't want Jewel to turn into Brayla or a Widow or like Mitchell. Fuck, I don't even want her to be like me. I don't want her to change."

Tears cloud my eyes. "Kingston," I whisper. "Is that your deal breaker? Me changing?"

The second the words spill from my mouth, Kingston meets me with his wide eyes. He links his fingers on the back of his head without saying anything. A dozen emotions flicker across his face, dark eyes flashing silver, his fangs protruding from underneath his lips.

Clearly, I struck a nerve.

We've only talked about what my guys could do to put a strain on our relationship, but they never mentioned me. And we only talked about it because Kingston brought it up. I never thought of my life without them. But they're scared. They don't have to admit it for me to know. And it's one of the reasons I know I must follow through with Mitchell's demands. Our relationship has always leaned heavily toward my needs. It isn't fair. They have needs too, and one of them is to feel powerful. Feel good enough. To be brave. I'll do whatever to assure that they don't have to fear. Because fear friggin' sucks. I should know.

Kingston slumps his shoulders, the shock of my question wearing off. "Jewel, no. That's not a deal breaker. If you turn into a psycho bitch, you'll still be my psycho bitch, but you better fucking believe that I will do everything I can to stop that from happening. Even if you end up devouring me in the process."

"It's a good thing there are three of us," Diego jokes, trying his best to lighten the mood, knowing that I need it.

Austin motions for his brothers to close the space, and the three of them engulf me in a hug I want nothing more than to lose myself in. Because Kingston isn't the only one afraid of what Mitchell's demands will do to me. The last thing I want to have is another life on my hands, but what the hell else am I supposed to do? I don't want this on my guys' hands either. I don't care if they've done it before or that they're capable. Kingston might be afraid of me changing, but what if this changes them too? I don't want to find out.

Austin snuggles his face into the crook of my neck. "What they mean is that we're yours, and we'll assure that you won't turn into someone you don't want to be, okay? So just let us take care of this."

"And let me take care of you," Kingston adds.

I want with everything in me to just say screw it and let them do whatever the hell they want, even lock me in a closet, but I can't. I just can't. If I don't prove to Mitchell that I can follow his orders and do what he thinks is best, something terrible will happen. I know it. I feel it deep inside me.

No matter what, things will suck, but Mitchell scares

me more than Haven Springs. The damage he can cause on our lives is far greater than the damage I'll inflict on my soul. I've been doing things I haven't wanted to do all my life. Like my dad used to say, I do them because I have to.

Gathering my nerve, I glance up and meet each of their gazes. "No."

"What do you mean *no?*" Kingston asks, his voice rising in pitch.

"You heard me. No. I've already made my decision."

"That's it!"

The world blurs around me as Kingston relocates me before I can argue. He sets me on my feet, kisses me so passionately that I can't orient myself to what's going on, and then he vanishes. A door slams, and I stare in shock.

"Kingston!" I yell. "Are you friggin' kidding me?"

I rush to the door and jiggle the handle. I know he threatened to lock me in a closet, but I didn't actually think he'd do it, especially without him. Glancing around, I gaze over the organized bins with everything from blood draw equipment to medications to fresh linens. Nothing looks useful enough to unscrew the hinges, and I doubt I could use anything to try to break the door down.

"Austin?" I call next, listening to the three of them mumble too softly for me to hear.

"Jewel, please give us a minute," he responds.

I slap my hands to the door and rest my forehead against it. "Diego," I try next. "Please, let me out."

"Just a sec, beautiful."

I groan and jiggle the door handle again, but it doesn't budge. It's then that I realize that I'm not exactly locked in. Kingston probably holds the door on me, stopping me from getting out. And I'm annoyed as hell. But instead of throwing the fit I so desperately want to unleash, I take a breath to calm down.

"Fuck," Kingston whispers. "She's plotting. I can practically hear her thoughts."

"I can hear you, Kingston," I mutter, tapping my fingers to the door. "And what you're doing. Not cool. How would you like it if I locked you in a room?"

"I'd love it, babe."

I glare, hoping if I do it long enough, he'll feel my burning gaze. "Alone?"

He grumbles something I can't understand, going all back-world on me.

"Please, dude. Just open the door. I hate this. I could seriously use a hug." I keep my voice soft, trying not to whine. But damn him. I don't have time for this. "Please. Pretty please. You can't seriously want to leave me in here. I need you. All of you." I fake sniffle for good measure.

Something thuds. "Stay back, Austin. She's playing with your affection. I should know. She learned it from me," Kingston whispers.

"I don't care. Listen to her." A low groan sounds through the door. "We have to figure something out."

"Austin," I say, trying again.

"Shit," Diego whispers. "Beautiful—"

"I swear for fuck's sake, neither of you come an inch closer. We're supposed to be together on this," Kingston says, talking louder. I can almost imagine him waving his fists. I check the door to be sure, but it doesn't budge. "Think about the consequences. Think about our girl."

"I *am* thinking about Jewel." Austin's soft voice trickles through the door. "And I agree with you."

"So do I," Diego says. "But one of us needs to go in there with her."

I glower at the door. "Seriously?"

"Yeah," they all say in unison.

"Just let me the eff out!"

"No, babe," Kingston says.

I bang my fists on the door, frustration grabbing hold of me. I can't keep my cool any longer. What they're doing is ridiculous. "You can't keep me locked in here. You're all going to be in so much trouble."

Kingston scoffs, his laugh more strained than anything. "*We're* going to be in trouble?"

"You're the one being unreasonable. You just need to take a breath and to really think about things. We know you feel like you're out of options, but it's only because you can't see all of them," Austin says.

I thump my forehead to the door. "The options are plenty clear, Austin. This is the best way."

"It's not. You're not a killer, and we know you don't want us killing anyone," Diego says. "So..."

His voice trails off and he mumbles something I can't hear. My guys continue their conversation without me, making me all sorts of frustrated. I kick at the door a couple of times and then ram my shoulder into it until my arm throbs.

"Stop, Jewel. You're going to hurt yourself," Austin says.

"Yeah, babe. You're not getting out of there until we're good and ready to let you out. Call this pretend privacy."

I punch the door and immediately regret it. "Shit balls! Ouch! Just tell me. We're supposed to be together on this. This is unfair. It's my life."

"It's technically our lives, beautiful."

OhmyeffingGod. "Let me the hell out!"

"No," Kingston says. "And chill out. Don't make me come in there."

"I dare you," I say banging my forehead against the door. "If you let me out, I promise—"

"Not gonna work, babe."

"Whoever lets me out first will—"

"Still not working. Now, be quiet. Someone's coming."

The sound of a door opening and closing silences my guys, and I press my ear to the door to listen to Liz's familiar footsteps clomp across the room. I don't even have to see her to imagine the way she stands guarded, hand touching her gun, fully ready to fight if she has to.

"Haven Springs is nearly gathered. Topher is in council custody," Liz says. "Where's Jewel?"

"In the closet." Kingston taps on the door. "There has been a change of plans. She's not participating. We're handing authority over to the council to reprimand your citizen."

"What's the catch?" Liz asks. "You know there is a vote, and no one will vote to execute one of our best fighters."

"That's the catch. You have to murder him."

"Me?" Liz asks.

"Well, who else is going to? You killed the other asshole, so it's not like it's much different."

"It kind of is," I say through the door. "She was protecting me."

"If I do it, there will be worse consequences. I cannot have my authority tested like that. If it means you won't get my grandson back, then so be it. I'm sorry. This is my home. I can't just change the foundation of our community like that—"

"What if we sent Jewel out to order it?" Kingston asks.

"How is that any different," I ask.

"The blood won't be on your hands, beautiful," Diego says.

A phone rings, cutting off all arguments, and I hear Liz stroll across the room. Closing my eyes, I listen to the soft shuffling of my guys' feet. They move to wherever she is, leaving the door unattended. I wiggle the handle again, but it doesn't budge. Son of a b—

"Is everything in order?" Mitchell's voice booms through the air, making my muscles automatically stiffen.

"Almost," Kingston says.

Mitchell hums under his breath. "I'd like to speak with Jewel."

"She's already away."

Silence greets Diego's words.

"Then you wouldn't mind if I connected to the main surveillance to watch," Mitchell finally says.

I cringe.

Kingston growls. "You only asked for a body."

"Is there a problem?" Mitchell asks.

"Fuck yeah there is a problem. What you've asked Jewel to do is complete bullshit, and we're not going to—"

"Kingston!" Mitchell roars, his voice echoing so loudly that I'm pretty certain I can feel the vibration against the door.

"If you have a problem, then come here yourself," Diego adds.

Austin releases a scary ass noise that sinks into my bones. "We've already decided."

I bang my hands on the door. "Stop! No one has decided anything."

Sucking in a deep breath, I jog to the end of the closet and brace myself. I dash forward as fast as I can and ram my shoulder into the door. It flies off its hinges and crashes into something heavy that clatters to the floor before skidding across the room. Metal instruments scatter everywhere. I gape at the heavy metal cupboard that Kingston must've used to lock me in the room. There is no way I should've been capable of moving it.

Diego, Austin, and Kingston all stare at me with startled expressions. So does Liz. And thank the universe that Mitchell's projection lights up the wall perpendicular to me or else he'd have just seen me bust through a heavy ass barricade.

But just because he can't see me, doesn't mean he can't hear me.

"My sons." Mitchell's accusatory words speak volumes.

"Mitchell, please. You can't blame them. It's all a misunderstanding. They're just trying to show me how powerful they are—that they can uphold their Blood Vows to take care of me." The words tumble from my mouth too quickly for me to fully process.

"They forgot that this isn't about you, Jewel," he snaps.

I rush from my place to stand in front of my guys like my small frame could possibly shield them from Mitchell's flashing eyes. "You're right. And they're sorry."

"Do you speak for them now?"

I swivel and beg my guys with my eyes to play along. "No, but—"

Kingston slides his arm around me and presses his hand to my lips. "We're not sorry, Mitchell, and this shitty ass position you've put us in has made it quite clear where our places are with you."

I step on Kingston's foot, trying to get him to stop.

But it's Diego who says, "And because of this revelation, we're overruling your decision. Jewel is our future."

"Not yours. You can't use her like this," Austin adds.

"She is a Divine Heir! She will do as I say or else you will discover your true place."

I elbow Kingston and pull away from him. "I will!" My voice screeches. "I swear my loyalty to you. Please, just give us a couple of minutes. You can watch for yourself. I don't care."

"Jewel," all three of them say.

"You can't keep protecting me," I say. "You can't keep me from the vampire world. I'll never survive if you continue this. This is my decision, and it's final."

Mitchell flashes his fangs. "If you do not, you will not have a future as a Divine, understand?"

I nod. "Understand."

"Good. I'll be watching."

The line clicks off, and I turn to my guys. "Are you crazy?"

"No, he is if he thinks he can threaten you like that, babe," Kingston says.

I reach out and grab his hand. "Kingston. We've always had a way of doing things."

Austin takes my other hand. "It obviously wasn't working."

"But Mitchell will ruin our lives," I argue. "You guys know that. We need the Divine name."

Diego slides his arms around me from behind. "We can survive without it."

I twist my lips to the side. "How are you so sure?"

No one answers. They can't.

"That's what I thought," I say, my voice trembling. "So, I'm not letting you risk things. Mitchell can't doubt your loyalty. You can't stand against him. Not now."

"But—"

I kiss Kingston before he can argue, keeping my lips to his until I'm certain he won't say a word. Turning to Austin, I brush my lips to his next and kiss him until his shoulders relax. Diego spins me around and kisses me first, pulling me into him, allowing his brothers to crowd our space until it feels like us against the world.

"You're our badass girl, you know," Diego whispers.

"And infuriatingly stubborn," Kingston adds.

Austin sighs into my hair. "Too good to be a Divine."

"But not too good for you," I say, inhaling a deep breath.

The three of them stare at me with the poutiest faces in existence, and it nearly stops me from turning to Liz. But Mitchell's silver flashing eyes and fury flit through my mind, stealing my warmth.

"I'm ready," I tell Liz.

She looks at me with sad eyes. "I hope they're worth it to you, Jewel."

I nod. "That's the only thing I have ever been certain of."

THE EXECUTION

"IF JEWEL GETS HURT AT all—"

Liz raises her hand, cutting Kingston off. "You have my word that she won't."

Diego sets me on my feet, and I hug him again. "We'll be right here, beautiful. Once it's done, run this way, and we'll get you. Promise. Don't stick around. Don't give them any time to process or react. Do it and run."

I swallow the knot in my throat. "G-got it."

"You can still change your mind," Austin says, hugging me next.

All I do is squeeze him tighter.

Kingston opens his arms for me to fall into. "Just remember, he worked with the asshole who tried to hurt you.

He knew about the people who tried to blow us up."

I bob my head. "He deserves to face the consequences for his actions." At least, that's what I keep telling myself.

"Damn straight."

Liz motions for me to hurry up, and I give my three pouty vampires one more hug together, just savoring the strength of their arms around me. Following Liz, I force my legs to keep up with her fast stride despite the hum of voices growing louder the closer we get to City Hall.

And the front area is packed. More so than my first official visit here as a Divine.

"Shit," I whisper. "There are a lot of kids here."

Liz clears her throat. "Some people think that the worst thing they can do is hide the reality of the situation from their children. Because many aren't exposed to the workings of the world outside of Haven Springs, they need to be taught the truth in case."

She makes a point. I bet most of the children and the people born in Haven Springs have never even been in contact with vampires. My dad protected me all my life, but vampires were always there. I knew the consequences of stepping into the shadows at a young age.

Whispers turn into murmurs the second people realize who I am. Strangers meet me with wide eyes. The fear radiating from some of the townspeople is so strong, it's palpable. I can feel it jabbing at me.

"We're screwed," a man whispers into a woman's ear.

"Go home and grab the bags. I'll follow shortly."

I blink, trying not to react, considering I shouldn't have been able to hear him.

"Oh, thank God she's alive," a woman whispers.

"Maybe we'll survive this after all," her blonde friend responds. "I hope they throw Topher to the shadows for this. He put us all at risk."

"She deserved it," a man says. "This has been a long time coming."

The blonde glares at him. "Excuse me if I enjoy living."

Liz reaches out and grabs my hand, tugging me along because I can't help slowing down to listen to everyone process my arrival. Even though I'm here, I can't imagine what life must be like for them. I feel bad that everyone lives like the end is coming—and maybe it is. I always felt the same about my life—at least, since my dad had left us.

"Jewel! Jewel!"

I search the crowd for my cousins, hearing Fallon call out my name. I spot the two of them with Mrs. Diggs. Berto and his brother stand nearby, and I catch sight of Cyprus hovering a few feet behind them. Our eyes meet, and I can't help darting my gaze away. What if he was the one responsible for the attack on my house? Kingston was right about him being the only one to know I was there. He could've set me up.

But part of me doesn't believe it. If he wanted to hurt me, he could have tried and he didn't.

Dana breaks away from Berto and rushes to me, stealing my attention away from Cyprus's curious eyes. Throwing her arms around me, Dana engulfs me in a hug that nearly knocks me over. Fallon hooks her good arm around the both of us, and I try my best to stay calm.

"Thank God Berto was right about you being alive. We were so scared after we heard."

"I'm okay. It's okay," I whisper. I glance up and stiffen. Everyone's watching. "I wasn't home."

I must say the words too loud, because Cyprus raises his brows at me.

Tugging my cousins with me, I guide them toward Liz. "Come on. I want you to stand by Liz."

"What's going on?" Dana asks.

I close my eyes for a second. "I have to do something that will cause a lot of panic. I want you two close by in case. We're going to have to make a run for it."

Fallon's mouth falls agape. "Raul was right."

"Right about what?"

"The execution."

I jerk my gaze up to stare at the two brothers blatantly watching us. There is no way they should know about the execution. Liz said that they don't kill people here. Even the rest of the council doesn't know. They think this is a public hearing. "What else did he say?"

"He said the explosion was going to be everyone's wakeup call to fight."

No. No. No. No. Shit. I was wrong about Cyprus being behind the explosion. As for Topher and Jeremy? I'm not so sure they would have risked such a thing either. Topher is only here because he was an accomplice in Jeremy's failed attempt to hurt me. But the town doesn't know that. They think he's behind the explosion. My guys said he only knew about it.

I stop short of the steps to City Hall and spin toward the crowd. Thousands of voices blend and blur, growing in volume, making it hard to concentrate. I take in the strangers standing in wait before me. Everyone glowers like I'm the devil, and it takes everything in me not to lose my shit. Because I know this is what the Blood Rebel's wanted. They wanted to get those who comply with Donor Life Corp's laws to be outraged enough that they no longer turn a blind eye as long as they're safe. It'll be impossible if I execute Topher.

"Come on, Jewel," Liz says, drawing my attention to her.

I ignore her and turn in the direction of where I know my guys are hiding. "Guys?"

"Need us to get you, babe?" Kingston asks.

I rub my lips together. "I—I don't know. Fallon just told me something. Her boyfriend said that this was supposed to be a wakeup call for Haven Springs."

Austin swears. "Berto is a Blood Rebel."

I frown, turning away so that my cousins don't see my

mouth move in a whisper. "You manipulated his mind. If he was a Blood Rebel, he..."

"He would've known how to act his way through. I never manipulate minds, Jewel. I missed the signs. I didn't double check. The explosion wasn't intended for you. You were supposed to be out of the house, remember? It was for us. Berto knew I was there."

"Fuck, I knew I should've hunted him down to make sure," Kingston says.

"We'll call Mitchell and let him know," Diego says. "Just stall."

"Ms. Matthias, Ms. Divine," Mr. Barton says from the top steps, drawing my attention away from my guys. "Nice of you to finally join us. We're ready to proceed with the hearing."

I suck in a breath and focus on pushing away the noise the audience makes.

"Nice to see you, too," I mutter under my breath because he doesn't even mention the fact that I'm not dead like people thought. "Glad you weren't actually blown up, Jewel. So sorry the people here suck."

Mr. Barton turns to me. "What was that, Ms. Divine?"

I force myself to smile. "Oh, nothing. Just want to punish this asshole and get home...oh, wait. I don't have one."

Kingston snickers from somewhere close by. He must've moved.

"You will be relocated after the hearing," Mr. Barton responds, unfazed by my sarcasm. "House number sixty-two."

My steps falter. "Sixty-two?"

He glances at me. "Yes, it's a lovely two-story not as isolated from the rest of the community. The council agreed that threats might not persist if other lives are at risk."

Except sixty-two is the house number that Hayden had asked the asshole Brody to deliver a key to my place to. Eff. It was also the abandoned house Orlando took me to. No one was there.

Liz's com device chimes from her belt, and she yanks it free and glances at the screen. A deep frown wrinkles her face. "It's the board of Donor Life Corp," she says, looking at me instead of Mr. Barton.

"Jewel," Austin whispers from nearby. He's moved as well. "You need to run to the end of the building to me."

I blink. "Why?"

"How are we supposed to know?" Mr. Barton says, responding to my question intended for Austin.

"Mitchell wants you to go through with the execution anyway. He doesn't care if it puts your life in even more danger. He sees this as an opportunity," Diego says. "He wants the community to be outraged. He wants to make a point. This steals your element of surprise."

I close my eyes, trying to calm my racing heart. "Fuck."

"They will kill you, babe," Kingston says. "Mitchell

will make sure they know what to expect. This will cement you as a traitor to them."

"Did you not tell Mitchell that?" I ask.

"Jewel, I don't think you understand," Austin says softly. "This far exceeds us. Mitchell doesn't care whether any of us lives or dies. He only cares about maintaining power. You're only in Haven Springs because he wanted someone close by to bring him in contact with the Blood Rebels."

"So run, beautiful. We're at the edge of the building in the shade."

"Jewel," Liz says, drawing my attention away from the whispers. "Mitchell would like a word."

"Jewel, hurry," my guys say in unison.

When I spin to run, I crash right into Berto. He steadies me on my feet, giving me a smug ass look that speaks volumes. And shit. Taking a step back, he laces his fingers with Dana's. She remains as expressionless as I do. And then Berto has the friggin' nerve to wink. He and Raul both hold onto my cousins and block my way.

Liz grabs my hand without giving me a choice. She places her com device in my palm, and I gape at Mitchell and Viorica in the small screen. Mitchell smiles at me while Viorica frowns. I nearly drop the damn phone like it'll explode at any second.

"My sons seem to think that I don't care about your life, but they're quite wrong, Jewel," Mitchell says. "I care immensely."

"Then please don't make me do this now. I'll never make it out of here," I beg.

"You must trust me, my heir. This is exactly what the Divine name needs to persuade the board and assure our alliance."

Fuck the alliance between board members.

I open my mouth to tell him as much and that the only people I trust are Diego, Austin, and Kingston, but the phone beeps in my hand, and Mitchell's projection flashes on the building. The whole crowd draws silent at the image of him and Viorica. Mitchell told me that he wanted to watch, but he never said like this. And it makes things worse. I'm nearly certain that only the council had ever dealt with Mitchell and Donor Life Corp this way.

Dozens of clicks from people flicking the safeties off on their weapons sound through the air like they could actually annihilate Mitchell. Dead silence falls over the community. I'm not even sure people breathe. Or maybe the sudden pounding in my head prevents me from hearing it. People can't help but stare at the screen. I'd think Mitchell could mind manipulate the whole place with the way everyone just gawks.

I shift on my feet, wondering if I could make it a couple of feet away from the crowd closing in to get a better look. Glancing to my cousins next, I give them each a look, hoping that they understand that they're going to have to help me. Berto and Raul still hold them.

"Dana, Fallon," I whisper. "Do you remember the time I took down a vampire?"

My cousins frown at my question, their eyes searching my face to figure out what the hell I'm talking about.

"A really strong one?" I add.

Fallon's mouth forms an O. "Yeah."

"I need you to trust me and try it yourself if this turns to hell. We can't trust anyone. *Anyone.*"

My cousins look to each other. I just hope they understand what I mean about their boyfriends. I hope they realize what's really going on and will pick me. I'm not sure I could survive if they fall onto the same path as Ramona. I don't know what I'll do if that happens.

"Attention, the exempt of Haven Springs." Mitchell's sudden booming voice startles me. He looks scary as hell with his silver flashing eyes and protruding fangs. Viorica only smiles in amusement by his side, not feeling the same need as him to intimidate the community. "My name is Mitchell Divine, and I'm the founder of Donor Life Corp. It has come to my awareness that you've become unsatisfied with the arrangements your Blood Matched heirs have established by entering into our program."

"Mr. Divine," Mr. Barton says, speaking up. "I'm not sure I understand. No one here is unsatisfied."

"And yet they continue to threaten the life of Jewel, who was granted access as an exempt under the Divine name."

Mr. Barton frowns. "I assure you, the perpetrator is being handled accordingly."

"I do not need your assurance. What I need is to make my point clear. Anyone who dares attempt to harm my heir will face automatic execution. Their families will be required to donate to the board as restitution."

"What?" a man yells. "You can't do that! We have contracts!"

Uh-oh.

"Mr. Barton, detain that donor. His Blood Matched heir will be notified of the cancellation of his heir's contract. He will be given to the household as a donor to compensate his sponsor."

"What? My Nathanial is dead because of your program," he says. "There is no way in hell you're dooming me to the same fate."

Mitchell doesn't even look in the direction of the man. "Escort him from the premises, Mr. Barton."

Mr. Barton stares in shock, a dozen emotions crossing his face. The crowd bursts into a cacophonous explosion of outrage.

"I—I," Mr. Barton manages to say. "No. I will not."

"If you do not, consider this your resignation from the Haven Spring's council," Mitchell says.

"You son of a bitch!" the man yells. "The only way you're going to get away with this is if you come here yourself."

Mitchell still ignores the guy. "Mr. Barton."

Mr. Barton swivels and turns his attention to me. "Jewel, do something. You can't possibly agree with this."

I open and close my mouth. Of course I don't agree with this. But I also didn't agree with people attempting to blow me up.

"I—"

Someone crashes into me a second before a loud pop rings in my ears, stealing my hearing. I hit the ground hard, the air heaving from me. People scream. An old lady falls on the ground next to me, pushed in the shuffle of people scattering.

"I got you, Jewel," Cyprus says. "You're okay."

"If you don't settle down, I will close down Haven Springs," Mitchell roars.

People freeze, the panicking crowd drawing silent under his threat. And I can't blame them. Mitchell might not be here, but he's still intimidating as all get-out.

Cyprus pulls me to my feet, and I swivel, looking for Dana and Fallon. My heart nearly falters that I don't catch sight of them immediately, but I spot them a dozen feet away, staying calmer than me. I search the shadows near the edge of the building for Kingston, Austin, and Diego, but I can't see them. I can't hear them with the ringing in my ears either. Tears burn my eyes, and it takes everything in me not to lose my shit.

"Marvelous job, Cyprus," Viorica says, speaking up for

the first time since the call started. "Your sister was right about you."

All he does is nod. I had nearly forgotten that he's an heir to someone Blood Matched to the Vaduva household.

"And Ms. Matthias, you've officially been promoted to head of the Haven Springs council."

At Mitchell's words, I draw my gaze to Liz restraining the man who had lashed out. A red mark already forms on his cheek from where the silver-haired woman punched him, showing off her admirable strength.

"As for you," Mitchell adds, looking at the man. "You have been found guilty of treason."

"Fuck you!" the man screams.

"If anyone has a problem, they may join him in his punishment," Mitchell says. "Jewel, execute him immediately."

I startle at his words. "What?"

"Anyone else who stands against my heir will face the same fate, understood?" His statement is directed toward the utterly silent crowd. "Now, Jewel. Proceed."

Cyprus hands me his gun, and I stare at the thing like it'll explode in my hand at any second. I've never done more than touch one. Diego never went further in his training than showing me the safety. I've never really needed to know how to use one.

I swallow. "I—I don't know how to shoot."

"I don't care how you proceed, Jewel," Mitchell says.

Shit balls.

"Don't do it, Ms. Jordan," someone whispers. A woman. She uses my donor name, and it strikes a nerve. It reminds me of The Boxes. Of the girl I was before I became a Divine. "Please."

My hands tremble, and I inhale a few deep breaths.

"I—"

"Now, Jewel. If you do not, you know what will happen."

Except I also know what will happen if I do. This guy acted out of self-preservation. He was put in a corner and wasn't going to go down without a fight. He is no different than me. Mitchell put him in an impossible situation for no other reason than that he could. He's doing the same to me.

"Jewel." The faint voice draws attention from the gun shaking in my hand. It's Austin. I can finally hear him. "Just run. I'll get you."

"If this donor isn't executed in five seconds, Haven Springs will be divided among the households of the Blood Matched heirs," Mitchell says.

"Jewel, look at me," Kingston says.

I draw my gaze to him, now standing in the open for everyone to see. But no one looks. They all focus on the man. On me.

"Five," Mitchell says.

Ah, hell.

"Just kill him!" someone screams.

"Four."

A woman touches my shoulder. "Don't, Jewel. Don't turn against humanity. You're not his heir."

I jerk away from her, focusing on Austin and Diego as they emerge next to Kingston.

"Three."

"Run to me, Jewel," Austin whispers. "Kingston and Diego will get your cousins."

Mitchell's attention draws to my guys. "Two."

I take a deep breath and aim. If I kill the man, Mitchell might spare Haven Springs. He might spare my guys. As for me? I guess I'll find out.

"One."

I startle at the loud pop of a gun, dropping the com device, causing it to disconnect. My ears ring, stealing my hearing again. Someone in a mask—a guy from the shape of his muscular body—emerges from the crowd, his narrowed eyes zoning on me. He raises his gun again and shoots.

Bending forward, I clutch my stomach, nausea washing over me at the sight of the man dropping to his knees in front of me. Blood, and what I'm pretty friggin' sure is brain matter, splashes across the front of me. I swipe my hands over my face, doing everything I can to get the blood from my skin.

People scream.

I turn to run toward my guys. Diego and Kingston already yank my cousins away from Berto and Raul. Austin rushes into the sunlight, protected only by an extra shirt over his head. Another form in black blurs out of nowhere, knocking him away.

More guns go off.

"Austin!" I scream.

Strong hands push into my back. "Go, Jewel," Cyprus says.

The guy in the mask that shot the man right in front of me aims his gun at me. "Get away from her or I will shoot you. Everyone else calm down."

I blink the surprise from my eyes. I recognize the voice.

"Austin!" I yell again.

"Jewel, stay calm," he whispers. "Do as he says."

"But—"

"Listen to your boy toy, Jewel." Brayla's sweet voice jerks my attention to her. She stands next to Austin in the shade. Diego and Kingston remain under another tree with my cousins.

"Hand Jewel your com device, Miles," Hayden says, pulling the mask from his face. "Someone bring Topher here."

Two people escort Topher from inside and push him down the steps. He lands on his stomach in front of me.

My heart nearly crashes from my chest. "Shit balls."

Mr. Barton doesn't argue with Hayden and gives me the small black device. My hands shake as I automatically take it.

"Jewel, call Donor Life Corp back. Tell Mitchell the first execution is complete. I want you then to turn the phone to show this asshole." Hayden steps closer and tugs the man onto his knees. Touching his shoulder, he says, "Thank you for your sacrifice. Your death will not be in vain."

People murmur in the crowd, but no one moves.

"Jewel," Hayden says to me. "Do as I asked."

I suck in air between my teeth. "I won't kill him."

He ignores me and says, "I said call Donor Life Corp. Now."

My fingers fumble as I tap the screen. Mitchell and Viorica flash on the screen and stare at me in silence. "The first execution is d-done."

Hayden stays out of view and motions for me to turn the phone toward Topher. My hand shakes as I do what he says, afraid he might open fire on me next. Topher straightens his shoulders without a word, but he glares at me, or maybe it's the device. Possibly both.

"I'm sorry," I say to him, my voice hitching.

And then Hayden pulls the trigger, killing Topher for Mitchell and Viorica to see.

Hayden waves his gun at me, and I purse my lips, doing my best to keep it together. Turning the phone around, I stare at Mitchell's flashing eyes.

"And so is the second. Now, please. Let me go home. The people here get it, okay? They're not Blood Rebels.

They're scared. They're only human."

"I need you to stay and remind them," Mitchell says.

Viorica touches his arm. "Maybe let her leave until things settle. She makes a better asset alive."

An asset. Great.

He glares at her. "I suppose you're right." Turning to me, he says, "Fine. You are temporarily summoned from Haven Springs."

I release a breath.

"But Jewel, I expect you to come directly to me."

ESCAPE

"VAMPIRES!" SOMEONE SCREAMS.

I don't get the chance to process anything as Kingston pulls me into his arms before Austin and Diego block me.

"Go!" Hayden yells, waving his gun.

The world blurs, and Kingston squeezes me in an equally tight death grip as I cling onto him. My closed eyelids turn from red to dark, and I peer over Kingston's shoulder from the shaded area of the grove that ascends up a small hill that will lead to the wall.

A few weapons go off, startling me again. I bury my face into Kingston's shoulder to stifle the whimper that threatens to escape. Gentle fingers rub up and down my back, trying to smooth my trembles away, but my mind barely catches up with me now.

And what the hell?

Hayden just executed two Haven Springs citizens without much thought. More importantly, he did it on my behalf.

"Babe, I know that was traumatic as hell, but I need you to keep your shit together for just a little bit longer," Kingston whispers.

"Keep my shit together? Keep my shit togeth—"

Cool lips brush mine, stopping me from chanting the only thing I can spit out. Diego hovers behind Kingston, wrapping his arms around the both of us in the process. He inhales a soft breath against my quivering mouth, staying close enough to draw my focus to him.

"Hey, beautiful?" Diego murmurs.

I puff out air through my lips, my whole body a ball of knots. "Yeah, D-Diego."

"What's your favorite fruit?"

I purse my lips.

"What kind of question is that?" Kingston asks. "It's an orange. She always picks it first. What kind of nutrients match are you?"

Diego raises an eyebrow. "Can you shut up and let Jewel answer?"

I rub my lips together. "He's right. Oranges are my favorite."

He kisses me. "Just so you know, I knew that. Now,

tell me. What is your favorite smell?"

"It's the same thing," Kingston and I say in unison.

I cuddle my chin into his shoulder but keep my focus on Diego. "What about you?"

He grins.

Kingston shifts me. "Obviously your blood, babe. Your skin is a close second. Your hair. Fuck, your sweat is—"

"Flowers," Diego says, interrupting Kingston.

Kingston hums his curiosity.

Diego smiles at me again. "They remind me of Jewel since she's always sticking her nose in them. I can smell them after when we kiss."

"You guys are going to romance me to death. What about you, Austin?" I ask, turning my head to rest my cheek on Kingston's shoulder to better look at Austin.

He stands rigid, his hands balled into fists, ready to fight at any second. "Vanilla or chocolate. Something sweet baking in the oven. My mom owned a bakery. The scent reminds me of my humanity."

A weird ass coo escapes my mouth. "You never told me that, Austin."

Kingston adjusts me so I can look at him. "Because none of us think much about our lives before our transitions."

"Because Mitchell made it difficult," Diego says, a new heat to his voice burning away the softness he used to calm me down. Now the random questions make sense.

"As much as I want to stand here and listen to your sickly romantic attempt to relate with Jewel, we need to get moving. Hayden's headed this way."

The second I hear Brayla's voice, something in me snaps. I shove away from Kingston, making him release me. No one has a chance to catch me before my ass hits the dirt. I don't stay on the ground long. Scrambling to my feet, I charge Brayla. Her brown eyes widen, and she raises her hands up protectively.

I slam into her, knocking her off her feet. I land on top of her and twist the front of her shirt between my hands. She flashes her fangs at me and snarls, but I pin her down with my hand to her throat.

"Whoa, shit," Kingston says.

Arms hook under mine and lift me off Brayla. Anger rushes over me, and I jerk in Diego's hold, but he doesn't let me go. I thrash and kick my legs, so pissed off that I can barely see the world through my blurry vision.

"I'll kill you, Brayla!" I yell, my body refusing to give up fighting to get Diego to let me go. "You better run!"

Kingston has the nerve to chuckle. "You tell her, babe."

I glower at him.

He holds his hands up in surrender. "Sorry. You're cute as fuck all murdery."

"But Jewel, you need to take a breath and calm down," Austin says, stepping in front of me. He comes closer than Kingston but slow as hell, cautiously like I might attack him. It's enough to get me to stop fighting.

I blink a dozen times, gasping breath after breath. "You're scared of me," I murmur, my fury turning to full-on despair.

What's happening? What's going on? I'm so confused.

"No, Jewel." Austin runs his fingers across my face to pull my hair from my eyes. "Definitely not. But your cousins are. Brayla is."

"With good reason," Kingston says. "She should be lucky we haven't killed her yet."

"Why haven't you?" I ask. "Why are we still here? Someone tell me what's going on."

Silence greets me as Kingston glances to Diego and Austin. They share a look that makes me stiffen. Because damn it. They don't want to tell me. It's part of their infuriating way of protecting me.

"Nu-uh. I just had someone's brain splatter across me. The least you can do is tell me what the hell is happening."

"Later, Jewel." Hayden's deep voice freezes my insides. "We gotta get out of here."

"*We?*" My voice screeches loud enough to make everyone wince. "I'm not going anywhere with you."

"By the looks of the sun, your masters still have a bit of time before they can safely evacuate the premises. If someone finds you, they will open fire. You don't want to put your cousins in danger, do you?"

It's the first time that I manage the nerve to look up at

Dana and Fallon. They stand together, Dana's arm protectively around her sister. Both Berto and Raul hover nearby. Liz straightens her shoulders when my gaze turns to her, and I try not to react to Cyprus giving me a once-over.

"You two are rebels?" I ask, waving at them.

Liz places a hand on her hip. "No. Far from it. But the Divines owe me."

Hayden scoffs. "You think they're going to give you whatever you think you deserve?"

Austin growls at him. "Liz, you have our word."

"Whatever," Hayden snaps. "Let's move."

I look at Kingston and Diego. "We're going with them? For reals?"

Diego nods first. "Don't worry. We'll keep you safe."

I rub my hands up and down my arms. "It's not me I'm worried about."

"You need to drink," Austin whispers from next to me.

"I can't. I'll throw up." I bend forward and hang my head between my legs.

Kingston rubs his hand in circles on my knee. "Well, you already did that, babe. And your stomach is growling. Not to mention your eyes keep changing. It's freaking me out."

"And you somehow managed to outmatch Brayla," Diego whispers.

He shifts from his place next to Kingston and onto the floor to position himself between my legs. I rest my forehead on his shoulder, just taking a few breaths of his sweet skin.

Kingston squeezes my knee. "Which was fucking awesome."

Austin's hand touches my back. "But I still want you to drink, Jewel. Please, try. For me."

I groan and nod, relenting to his pleading voice. Diego sneaks his hand up and pulls the collar on his shirt down to expose his shoulder to me. I don't argue with the fact that it'd be easier for Austin or Kingston to bite their arms, but then again, it's not so sneaky. I'm already leaning forward, my hair veiling the action.

"I'm ready, beautiful. Have at it."

I hug my arms across his chest and kiss his shoulder. A dozen emotions cross through me. I should be so weirded out. Nothing about this is normal, but it still somehow manages to feel right. Austin and Kingston sink closer to me, smothering me in the best way between their bodies. I know they're sandwiching me like this for a reason. No one knows exactly how I'll react once Diego's blood touches my lips. It's a surprise every damn time.

Adjusting my mouth, I bite down until warm liquid fills my mouth, coating my tongue. My whole body buzzes the second I swallow, and I dig my fingers into Diego's chest, making him release the softest, sexiest noise.

"Lucky bastard," Kingston murmurs.

"You don't think I was jealous as hell earlier?" Diego says, linking his fingers through mine.

"Knock it off," Austin whispers. "I'm sure Jewel could do without your commentaries."

I pull back slightly. "Actually, it makes this better. I mean, you guys haven't even mentioned how weird this is."

"What's weird about you drinking our blood?" Kingston asks. "You've been doing it for months."

"I know, it's just..." I choose to shut myself up and suck on Diego's shoulder again. I still can't talk about the fact that it's weird because it's more than about protecting my mind. I don't know. I haven't accepted that this could be my life. Or how lucky I am that my guys are better than okay with it. The idea of any other way of surviving freaks me out. If I didn't have Kingston, Austin, and Diego, then what? No effing way would I turn to Orlando.

"It's just our lives now," Kingston murmurs, saying my own thought out loud. "But I wouldn't trade it."

I ease away from Diego, licking my lips. I'd bite again if it weren't for Austin intercepting me. He brings his sleeve to my lips and wipes the remaining blood. I smirk, my heart still thrashing, my body humming with desire and need.

"Perfect time to work on your restraint," he whispers.

"Don't listen to him. If you want more, I'm good," Diego says, fixing his jacket.

"He's right. She's way less savage when she's content."

Kingston flashes his fangs at me. "But me next."

I play slap his leg and motion toward my cousins sitting on the couch, watching the four of us. I know they saw me, but neither of them react with more than smiles and whispers I try not to listen to, especially when Fallon muses to Dana about wondering how vampire blood tastes.

"Probably pretty good," Dana whispers to her.

I turn to Austin. "Should we tell them that Fallon already got to taste yours?"

Kingston cracks up and nudges his brother. Austin turns redder than I've ever seen him, and I giggle and grab his face in my hands to kiss both of his cheeks.

I brush my lips to his a few times. "I was only kidding. But so you know, I'd love to shout to the world about how selfless you were. I mean, look at them."

Dana and Fallon smile at us when I wave.

"So strangely adjusted. If only..." I let my words drop. No point mentioning Ramona, especially because I hear Hayden's familiar footsteps clomping up the steps to the abandoned house.

He knocks once, making the four of us get to our feet. The door swings open to show off the purpling sky through the tree branches behind him. Berto and Raul come up the stairs next and ignore us while they both gaze at my cousins. Dana and Fallon make me proud as all get-out, because neither of them looks at the two boys. I was slightly worried that they might pull a Ramona on me, but they're pissed off that they had been lying to them all this time. Neither of them knew that Berto and Raul had agreed to help the Blood Rebels watch over them after they returned here without Ramona.

"The transport is set," Hayden says, adjusting a backpack on his shoulders. "The girls will ride with us. You guys will ride with Brayla."

"No friggin' way," I say. "My cousins are with me. You take Brayla. I'm not riding with her."

"Jewel."

Liz's voice trickles in from outside, and I stroll forward to get a better view of the woman. She stands with Cyprus at the end of the walkway with several packed bags. Dozens of different weapons stick to various parts of them, and Liz looks especially badass.

"You have my word that I'll protect Dana and Fallon with my life," she says.

I shake my head. "No. They're coming with me. It's final."

No one argues, seeing as they realize I'll start screaming at them if they even try. I don't trust Hayden. Liz is questionable. I don't even know Cyprus, and hell-to-the-no for the Suarez boys.

"You heard our girl," Kingston says. "The Divines in one car—including Dana and Fallon—and all you other fucks get the van. If any of you try anything to hurt us, you will be torn apart and donated to the nearest city for the street vampires to feast on."

"Dude," I whisper.

Kingston tightens his jaw. "What? We both know murder isn't a deal breaker."

I tilt my head. "You're right. You hear that? Try anything and you're goners."

"Goners, babe?"

I shrug. "What? Sorry if I can't be as menacing as you."

Dana releases the cutest giggle-snort at our conversation, drawing our attention from each other. Everyone gawks at me like I've lost my damn mind. I'm nearly certain that if Hayden didn't want whatever the hell he thought was worth killing people over to see to it that I get out of Haven Springs, he might turn his weapon on me. I wish someone would tell me already. It has to be a pretty big deal if even my guys are allowing him to help us.

Clearing my throat, I ask, "So, are we leaving or not?"

Hayden snaps out of his intense stare and nods his head. He motions to Berto and Raul to lead the way down the stairs to where Liz and Cyprus await. Diego beats his brothers to lift me off my feet, and I moan softly at my body reacting to the side effect of his blood. Austin pulls me away and kisses me.

"We need to work on some dietary adjustments as soon as we can," Austin whispers.

"I don't know. I kind of like it this way," I murmur.

Diego touches my cheek. "You know I do."

Kingston sighs. "Diego, you're on babysitting duty. I'll cover Austin."

"Babysitting?" Dana says, crossing her arms.

I play slap Kingston in the shoulder. "He was only kidding. He knows as well as the rest of us that the two of you know how to take down a vampire if you had to."

"But don't even try," Diego warns, flashing his fangs at my cousins, making them laugh. "It's bad for my ego."

The six of us follow the others outside, and I peer around the outskirts of the grove for signs of human activity. Instead of taking the path, Hayden leads the way deeper into the grove and toward the looming wall I spot through the fruit trees. The brilliant moon casts light over the grove to illuminate our way. Diego walks with an arm around each of my cousins' shoulders, hunching to do so, and Kingston strolls so closely behind Austin that if Austin were to stop, he'd crash into us.

"It's awfully quiet," I whisper into Austin's ear. "Should we be worried?"

"No. Haven Springs went on lockdown at dusk. They're afraid that we'll come and retaliate," he says, adjusting his hold on me.

I pout my bottom lip. It reminds me of living in Dark Terrace Ranch and curfew. I absolutely hate that it's come to that here. All because of me. Haven Springs was fine before. People were happy. Content. Now? They'll fear for their lives like every other donor.

"It won't be like this forever," Kingston whispers. "They'll realize we were only here for you."

"Unless Mitchell decides to—"

Diego turns to look over his shoulder. "We won't let him."

But I'm not so sure they could stop him. I keep the thought to myself, though. I have enough to worry about right now. I have my cousins and also Liz and Cyprus. Not to mention Brayla and the Blood Rebels. I can't help wondering where the hell Orlando is too. Why send Brayla? Maybe he thinks my guys would be less reactive toward her presence. If that's it, he's most definitely right.

"Coming up to the wall," Hayden says, waving his flashlight ahead of him. "Berto and Raul, help Dana and Fallon over. Liz, I'll give you a boost."

Diego lifts my cousins up before the boys can even turn to look in our direction. I can't stop the smile crossing my face at their surprise and laughter that they muffle with their hands. It helps with the gravity of the situation, knowing that my cousins can still manage to possess their innocence and fearlessness when neither of them knows what happens next. The fact that they trust me to take care of them gives me the strength to do so.

"Shhh!" Hayden hisses. "You'll attract every damn vampire in the vicinity. The Divines might protect you, but they sure as shit won't offer me the same courtesy. So shut up."

Diego releases a scary freaking growl. "Don't listen to him. No one will come."

Dana and Fallon nod, but the cheerful smiles on their faces vanish with Hayden's scowl. If Austin didn't launch us at the wall and scale up to the top so fast that I can't make a sound, I'd have yelled at Hayden. Friggin' asshole. I refuse to let him scare my cousins into turning into Ramona.

Kingston helps Dana and Fallon on the wall from Diego's shoulders. Diego catapults over and lands without a sound on the other side. From here, I get a view of the vast landscape. In the far distance, I spot a city, which I think might be Midnight Valley, but I can't be certain.

Austin jumps with me, kissing me to stop a squeal from leaving my mouth. Kingston totally tosses Dana into the air for Diego to catch. If Hayden thought he could get away with shooting Kingston, I'm nearly certain he would. He even aims his gun, making Kingston flash his fangs.

A bright spotlight crawls across the ground to land on us. Austin rushes toward the wall and presses my back to it. Hayden jumps right into the light and waves his arms. The light blinks off, leaving us with only the light of the moon.

"How did you all manage to survive the interrogation?" I ask him, knowing that Donor Life Corp came into Haven Springs and drugged and mind manipulated the citizens to test for remaining Blood Rebels.

"Because we're bigger than Donor Life Corp," he responds.

I wait for him to say more, but he doesn't. Instead, he strides away from us and down a small incline. At the bottom of the hill, a rickety shed hides two old cars—vehicles from long ago before the Blood Hunger Plague. I've seen the Blood Rebels with cars like this before, and I'm familiar with them from the old movies, but I've never dreamed I'd be riding in such a death trap.

"Dibs," Diego says, disappearing from in front of us before appearing next to a black, hulking looking car. The paint has seen better days, and there's a crack in the windshield, but Diego doesn't care because he bounces with excitement the second he opens the driver's side door.

"No fucking way," Kingston says. "I'm driving. I used to own..." He lets his voice trail off.

"You owned one?" I ask, grinning. "Damn, dude."

He glares at me. "It was already old when I had it."

"Whatever you say," I tease, touching my hand to the cold metal. "And Diego, let Kingston drive. I want to sit in back with you."

He waves his hand for Kingston to get behind the wheel. I knew that would work to stop an argument, but now Kingston looks like he might've changed his mind at the new idea of playing lapsies with me instead.

"Try not to crash," Hayden says. "Not all of us have access to vehicles at the tap of a button."

"I'm a thousand times less likely to crash than you," Kingston mutters.

Hayden takes his place behind the wheel of an old van and motions for the others to join him. Brayla appears next to him, and she whispers something to get him to switch places. Before getting in, she eyes me, offering me a smile that I don't return. I slide into the backseat after Diego and climb onto his lap. Dana and Fallon take their places next to us, and Austin hops into the front seat next to Kingston.

I stare at the dash. "Where's the navigation system?"

Kingston chuckles. "This beast was made before that time. Even if it did have one, it wouldn't be capable of giving us accurate directions."

I frown. "What about the seat restraints?"

Diego digs his hand into the seat. "Found one."

"That looks like a flimsy ass piece of fabric."

Sliding his arms around me, he holds me close. "Don't worry. I'll make sure none of you fly out."

"And if he fails, I'll make sure to catch you," Austin says.

I mess with the strap and hold it out to Dana. "See if you can figure this out."

Kingston starts the car, and I grip onto the front seat at the sudden vibration that rumbles through the air. This car is loud as hell, and it's a wonder that the Blood Rebel's haven't been picked off already because of it. Kingston chuckles and slaps his hand on the dash, glancing at me in the dirty rearview mirror.

"What do you think, babe?"

I grimace. "You don't want to know."

Diego laughs next and pulls me back against him, hugging me tight enough that I don't feel like I'll fly from his lap at any second. Kingston messes with a stick looking contraption between the front seats, and then the car barrels from the shed, bouncing on the dirt.

"Damn, I forgot what a gas guzzler was like to drive," Kingston says. "Fucking awesome."

Diego grumbles. "Shit, trade me."

"Diego," I say, shifting to look at him.

He grins. "Sorry, beautiful."

Austin swivels in his seat. "You can sit with me."

I shake my head. "I just need to remind Diego that I'm far more exciting than a car."

"Good luck," Kingston quips.

Diego smacks him, making him jerk the wheel.

I screech and grip onto the seat as a bright flash of light ignites in front of us. Kingston swears and stomps the brakes, sending the back of the car skidding back and forth. My cousins squeal and laugh at the sudden movement.

A horn blares next to us.

Brayla rolls to a stop and Hayden sticks his head out the window. "What's going on? You're driving like a lunatic."

Kingston points out the windshield. "Does that car belong to you?"

Hayden smacks his hand on the dash. "No."

Peering at the windshield, I search the area in front of us for the car Kingston motions to. In the distance, a set of headlights illuminate the dirt road ahead of us, heading in our direction. Kingston kills the engine, and he and Austin jump out of the car. Hayden follows their lead, already aiming his gun and ready to fire.

The car stops a hundred feet away, sending a cloud of dirt into the air. I gape at the flash of silver eyes of a vampire sitting behind the steering wheel. The passenger's side door opens, and a girl with tight, dark curls and bronzey skin that sparkles with makeup in the glow of our headlights steps out and waves her arms at us. Following her lead, the driver exits the car but leaves it running.

"Samantha?" Austin calls. "What are you doing here?"

"My mother sent me," she says. "Apparently Mitchell's gone a little nuts. I'm supposed to bring you all back to Midnight Valley."

Austin turns to look at Diego and Kingston. "Not happening, Sammy."

She frowns. "But Austin."

He shakes his head. "Sorry. Just go home."

"You're making a mistake."

Turning his back on Samantha, he strolls to the car. "Tell them we were gone when you got here."

"Austin, don't be stupid."

He shrugs. "Sorry, Sammy. This is probably the smartest thing I've ever done."

Samantha collides into Austin, and the two of them fly back and roll across the ground. Dirt wafts through the air, and I try to focus on the fight unfolding in front of me. Diego shifts me onto his back to free his arms, but he doesn't have to intervene. Austin overpowers Samantha and restrains her beneath him.

"Stop fighting," he says as she tries to jerk her arm free.

"I can't let you do this, Austin. Please, you have to come with me. Do it for Jewel's sake."

He flashes his fangs at her. "I *am* doing this for Jewel."

Samantha stops struggling. "What does that even mean?"

Austin gets to his feet but doesn't help Samantha up. "I can't tell you, Sammy."

"Then maybe this will persuade you." Samantha pulls out her phone from her pocket and clicks a couple of buttons. She offers it to Austin, who flicks his gaze over the screen, his frown deepening.

Turning, he glances at me from over his shoulder. "Can you buy us some time?"

Her gaze follows his, and Samantha looks at me too. She then turns to the pretty girl she left standing by the car. "Maybe. But I'm going to need one of those Blood Rebels."

"Are you fucking kidding me? Come any closer, and I'll blow your head—"

"I'll go," Cyprus says, stepping around Hayden. "I'm not afraid of vampires or being drained."

"Cyprus!" the girl yells. "Oh, my gosh."

Samantha intercepts the girl and stands in front of her. "Evora, no. I can't let you near him. He's a Blood Rebel. He'll try to hurt you."

Evora peeks over Samantha's shoulder. "He'd never."

"I'm sure Jewel thought the same thing about her sibling heir."

I grimace at her words. What a low friggin' blow. I don't care if she kinda makes a point. But still.

"Sammy, please. If he tries anything, you can do whatever you feel is necessary," Evora says, tightening her jaw.

Kingston hums in his throat.

I point my finger at him. "Don't you dare say it."

"As long as you know what I'm thinking." Because Kingston hates Ramona. He wishes I'd have told him something like that. But I just don't have it in me to even pretend to allow something like that to happen. Ramona might have effed up in a huge way, and we will never have the relationship we once had, but she's still my sister no matter who she's become. I don't want something bad to happen to her. Assuring her fate as the debtor to Orlando is enough.

"What we're all thinking," Diego adds.

I stick my tongue out at him, getting some seriously raised brows from Cyprus as he strolls past us and toward his sister. I jump from Diego's back and jog a few feet to catch up to him. Kingston slides right up behind me, surely flashing his fangs behind my back. I take his hand just in case.

"You don't have to do this. The Vaduvas are...bitey," I say.

"Total man-eaters." Brayla's remark makes Samantha growl from her spot.

I glare at Brayla. "Like you aren't."

Cyprus crosses his arms and looks toward his sister. "What did I tell you before?"

Everyone hangs onto our conversation, expecting me to repeat to him what he told me about wanting to transition into a vampire. But I don't say it out loud. Cyprus has found himself in a weird position of being accused by Samantha of being a Blood Rebel while wanting the same eternity his sister got by Blood Matching with Samantha. Because I know Viorica wanted to bring another female into her coven, and by the looks of Evora, she looks like she might already fit in with the way she handles her Blood Match.

"Okay, well, thanks I guess," I say. "Good luck."

Samantha devours our interaction, trying to put something between us that isn't there. Her gaze darts to Austin, and then to both Kingston and Diego, but none of them react more than usual. Not like they have a reason to. I hardly know Cyprus, and I trust him as much as I trust Liz, but I'll take all the help I can get.

In this moment, I realize that there isn't much difference between the motives of humans and vampires. Both

Liz and Cyprus do things to get what they want. They're allies for the sake of benefiting, kind of how the Vaduvas and Divines are allies.

"Back at you, Jewel. I hope to see you around sometime." Cyprus nods his head and strides the rest of the way to Samantha and Evora.

Evora rushes past Samantha and throws her arms around Cyprus, and he lifts her off the ground and chuckles, hugging his sister. Now that they stand together, I can see the similarities in their features, from their brown eyes to the roundness of their chins and softer jawlines, though Evora stands an inch taller.

Austin turns to Samantha. "Are we good? You'll buy us a few hours?"

"You swear only a few hours?" she asks, looking over at her Blood Match. "You know you put me in a tough position."

I gawk at her. "*We* put *you* in a tough posit—"

Austin holds his hand out to me, cutting me off. "Promise."

When Austin turns his back on Samantha, I can see the doubt cross his face. Because he's not sure about the situation or what we're doing. And that makes me nervous.

I squeeze Kingston's hand. "Are you sure this is a good idea? I don't mind going to Midnight Valley. I don't want to piss Mitchell off even more."

"Too late for that, babe," Kingston says. "But he'll get

over it."

"We hope," Diego says.

Austin closes the space to us, and I give him the hug he looks like he desperately needs. "Austin, please tell me what's going on. What did Samantha show you?"

He tightens his jaw. "It's nothing, really. We'll be in Dark Terrace Ranch later."

"But why not just go now?"

None of my guys answer me, and I sigh.

"You guys scared of how she'll react if you tell her the truth?" Hayden asks, drawing my attention to him.

"Shut up," Kingston snaps.

Hayden raises his gun like it could possibly keep my guys back. "Jewel deserves to know what you're getting her into."

I turn my attention to Austin. "What is that supposed to mean?"

He swallows. "Jewel, don't freak out. We were going to tell you soon."

"Tell me what?"

The three of them crowd me, and Diego says, "Hayden knows about you. He knows about your resistance."

"He wants to arrange a deal for answers," Kingston says.

I frown. "What kind of deal?"

Austin brings his hand to my cheek. "Don't know yet, but we're willing to hear him out for you."

"We suspect it has to do with Ramona," Kingston adds.

"And what does Brayla have to do with this?" I ask.

Diego squeezes my other hand. "She's the only one who can get in touch with Orlando to go through with anything."

I shake my head. "Nope. Not happening. We're not trusting any of them. I don't care what they know."

"But what if they can help us help you? We want to give you forever," Austin says.

I blink the tears from my eyes. "I don't know."

"Please, Jewel," the three of them whisper. "We might not have the chance otherwise. Things right now under the Divine name are...uncertain," Kingston adds, glancing at his brothers again.

Sucking in a breath, I finally nod. "I just hope they don't make us regret it."

THE DIVINE NAME

"LET ME GET THIS STRAIGHT. You'll explain what the hell my dad did to me if we get Ramona out of Orlando's care?" I ask, placing my hands on my hips.

"No way," Diego says.

Kingston stands from his spot next to me on the old couch. I thought we'd be traveling much farther, but Hayden led us to a small abandoned farm not far from Haven Springs. "That's it. He's wasted our time. I'm ripping his fucking head off."

Hayden aims his gun. "You can try."

I cover my face with my hands. I'm just as tired as Kingston with all the secrets and games. And there's no friggin' way I'm going to argue with Kingston's murderous need. Better he come to his breaking point with Hayden than snap somewhere else. I have no sympathy for the Blood Rebel who turned my sister against me, threatened me, and ruined my life.

"Everyone, chill out," Brayla says, materializing in the room. "Kingston, sit back down. Hayden, put that thing away. Fighting isn't helping Jewel or Ramona."

"I don't care about Ramon—"

I lean over and touch Kingston's hand, the small gesture shutting him up. Swiveling, he looks down at me with a pout, his face a series of hard lines that I'm not sure even a dozen kisses could smooth out.

"Come sit with me," I say, scooting closer to Austin.

Kingston plops down and pulls me onto his lap to rest his forehead to the middle of my shoulder blades, just breathing in a few soft breaths of my hair. Austin and Diego move in and each takes one of my hands, lacing our fingers together. I avoid glancing up at all costs, the heavy gaze of Hayden burning into me like he can blow up the four of us with a glare.

"Hayden, your turn," Brayla says.

"I don't take orders from a vampire," he mutters.

"Just put the damn gun down," Liz says, getting to her feet. "I've had enough of your Blood Rebel bullshit, Hayden. It was one thing keeping the community together and prepared. It's another thing to go shooting people, causing fear, and then threatening people who can help."

I peek up from under my lashes to watch Hayden put his gun into its holster. He scowls at Liz but doesn't argue again. Instead, he links his fingers together on the back of his neck and turns to face the window.

"This was a bad idea to come here," I whisper to my guys. "I know you guys worry about me, and you want answers, but this isn't getting us anywhere. Let's just go home and deal with whatever the hell Mitchell's problem is."

"Jewel, give us one minute before you make any decisions. I want you to hear us out," Brayla says, overhearing my whisper.

I groan. Ah, hell.

"And don't worry. Your secret is safe with me," she adds. "It's the least I can do."

I blink a few times at her words. She knows. Of course she knows. Whatever she's involved in with Orlando would give her access to that kind of information.

"Brayla," I say, pushing up from Kingston's lap. Kingston follows my lead, standing behind me, his fingers locked on my hips and fully prepared to launch me away if the need arises. "Tell us what's going on. You claim to be my best friend, but friends don't keep secrets. Friends don't ruin each other's lives. Friends—"

"Do whatever they can to save each other," she whispers. "And that's what I've been trying to do this whole time."

"No, you've been trying to rip me away from the guys I

love."

"Not them. Mitchell. They're Divines. They're loyal to their father. To their coven."

"Fuck you, Brayla!" Austin yells, surprising me. "We made Blood Vows to Jewel. She's where our loyalty lies."

Brayla puts her hands on her hips. "As long as she has the Divine name."

"Not true," Diego says.

"Yet you let them put her up for a re-matching. You stood by and fell compliant as they forced her to my household. Not to mention you did nothing to stop them from transferring her to Haven Springs where you knew her life would be in jeopardy. You took two weeks to even show your faces!"

"That's not fair," I say, glaring at Brayla. "They've done everything they could to assure our lives together."

"As Divines."

I ball my hands into fists. "Stop it."

She flashes her fangs. "As the perfect heirs afraid to do anything to piss their father off."

"I *said* shut up," I say, taking a step forward.

"They're willing to take you back there even with the risk your secret poses to you. If they were loyal to you, they wouldn't allow it. They'd do the right thing and take you where you belong."

"I belong with them."

"You don't."

Something inside me snaps, and I fly forward faster than ever. I crash into Brayla, sending the both of us skidding across the floor. Plaster rains down on us as we crack the wall, and I jab my hand into her hair, jerking her head to the side. My mind doesn't even get a chance to catch up to my body before I sink my teeth into her neck hard enough to draw blood. Brayla screams, a gun fires, and then my world spins.

Shadows edge my vision, and the last things I see are Austin's green eyes as they spill tears across my face.

Growls sound out from the extravagant dining room of the Divinity Estate. I peer around in search for Diego, Austin, and Kingston but can't see anything past the shadows blurring my vision. Taking a careful step forward, I head in the direction of the growls despite my mind screaming to turn the hell around. My body moves without my permission no matter how hard I try to command it otherwise.

"Good girl," a familiar voice whispers from my right. "One step at a time. I want the anticipation to hurt."

Tears burn my eyes, but I can't even open my mouth to say anything. My feet shuffle forward while a firm hand pushes at my lower back. Fear cascades through me in cold waves that leave my teeth chattering.

"Now stop." Mitchell materializes in front of me and leans in so close that I can't see past his silver eyes and into

the dining room. "Listen carefully, Jewel. Everyone's dying for a drink of your coveted blood, but I promise only those worthy will get a proper taste."

An uncontrollable sob escapes my mouth, and Mitchell smiles and wipes his fingers under my eyes. "You will be happy to be rewarded with such an honor. If you do as you're told, I'll provide to you what you need," he adds.

My eyes dry and a strange wave of calm spills over me. My mind continues to scream to resist, to fight his manipulation of my emotions, but my body refuses to cooperate. It wants nothing more than to stay in this sudden state of bliss.

"Now, show me that stunning smile of yours, my heir."

Nudging me forward, Mitchell leads me into the dining room with creepy flags that drip blood to pool on the pristine tile floor. The shadows blend and move around me, tugging at my dress and hair, whispering my name. But I can't make out any of the vampires apart from their flashing fangs and silver eyes.

Climbing onto the table, I stand in the middle until my dress drops to the floor, exposing my undergarments to the shadows. I remain utterly still with my eyes closed, my skin buzzing as cool fingers graze my wrists and legs. A hand touches my neck and moves my hair. My heart pounds in my ears, stealing away every noise apart from the slowing beats.

I fall to my knees.

Numbness engulfs me.

"Good girl," Mitchell whispers. "Now it's time for your reward."

I snap my eyes open, the room clear of vampires, the only evidence of their existence being the blood splashed across the table. I don't look down at myself. I can't. All I can do is push to my feet. With wobbling steps, I follow behind Mitchell down a grand hallway until it dead-ends into a massive, arched wooden door.

He pulls a key from his pocket and unlocks the door to reveal a dark room. Mitchell spins me and captures me in his gaze. "Don't forget, my dear. Stop before death for this is their eternal punishment."

Shoving me inside the room, Mitchell slams the door and locks it. Freezing air engulfs me, and I shiver and hold myself until my eyes adjust to the darkness. Low growls reverberate through the air, sinking deep into my bones. A tear slips from my eye, and I rub it away with the back of my hand.

"Jewel." The soft whisper of my name tears me from the haze clouding my mind. "You must resist."

I take a cautious step closer. "Diego?"

"Yeah, beautiful. It's me. But please, stay back."

Fear clenches my chest at his pleas. "Why? What's wrong?"

Taking another few steps closer, I finally spot three forms standing out from the rest of the darkness. Then I see the silver eyes. I hear the rapid heartbeats.

"Please, babe. Listen to Diego. Don't come any closer. We're too hungry. I can practically taste you," Kingston says, his voice hoarse.

"I'm not afraid," I say, stepping closer.

"Jewel," Diego repeats.

I close the space but stop a few feet away at a deep growl that comes from neither Diego nor Kingston. "Stop arguing and let me help you. Austin, are you okay? Let me feed you fir—"

Austin snarls, jerking away from the wall. Diego grabs him by the throat and yanks him back, though there is no way he could possibly touch me because of the chains restraining him to the wall.

I suck in a breath. "Just hold him so I can feed him, Diego."

"Babe, no. Stay back," Kingston pleads.

I cross my arms. "Why are you acting like this?"

"Please."

Peering around the dark room, I search for a light switch and find one near the door. I flick it on and spin around to face my guys. My heart sinks into my stomach, and I cover my mouth with my hand.

"Holy shit balls," I whisper, taking in the sight of Diego's ravaged chest. I've never seen so many bite marks. Not vampire ones. Human. And they're not healing. "What happened? Here, you need blood. No more arguing."

I rush forward despite their pleas, extending my arms out to them. Austin jerks against his chains, trying to break free. But he's not trying to get to me. He looks scared, if anything.

His silver flashing eyes lock on mine. "What did he do to you?" he manages to ask.

I freeze at the strangeness to his voice. It's then that I look down at myself, standing exposed in my undergarments, bleeding from a dozen bite marks I don't even feel or remember getting. I blink a few times, staring at the red rivulets of blood trailing down my arms.

"I—I don't know." Confusion washes over me, and I step closer to my guys. "I think I was..."

An incredible scent suddenly wafts to my nose, and I inhale a long breath. My stomach explodes with a pain so intense that I arch my back before bending forward to clutch my knees. My eyes burn with tears, and I fall to the floor and curl in on myself. I don't know what's happening to me, but I'm terrified. I feel like I'm going to die at any second.

"Jewel, fuck. Jewel!" Kingston calls my name, but all I do is turn my head in his direction.

"Don't, Kingston," Austin warns.

"But she needs us," he says.

Diego's tall form closes in on Kingston. "She made us promise her that we wouldn't let her."

"We have to do something," Kingston says to his

brothers, begging them with his midnight eyes.

I open and close my mouth, but no words break free from the burning in my throat.

"Just a little," Austin says. "But don't let her touch you. It'll set her off."

Warm liquid splashes across my face, and I jerk upright at the sweet taste of Kingston's blood coating my tongue. I manage to push to my feet to face my guys, all staring at me with wide, watery eyes. I've never seen such despair mar their handsome faces.

I lick my lips. "That was so good."

Kingston flares his nostrils. "Stay back."

"But—"

"Stay back!" he roars, surprising me.

But I can't. My body flies forward without my mind's consent. A need so intense consumes me that my mind can't regain control.

Kingston hollers.

"Restrain her!" Diego yells, his voice cutting through the fog in my mind.

I jerk upright and swing my arms, hitting them into a hard, muscular chest. Austin oomphs, and I snap my eyes open, relief flooding over me at the sight of the vibrant green depths of his intense stare instead of the constant silver I had expected.

"I got you, babe," Kingston whispers into my ear. "You're okay. It was a nightmare."

"I bit you." I gasp a few deep breaths. "I'm so sorry. I told you I never would. I don't know what happened. I couldn't control myself. Please, you have to let me go. I can't stand the thought of doing it again."

"She's confused," Austin says, pinching my chin to get me to look at him. "Jewel, hey. Hey, focus on me, okay?"

"Listen to Austin." Diego combs my hair from my face.

"Stay away. Please, just get back. I don't want to hurt you again, but he made me." More tears pour from my eyes, my heart hurting so badly the longer the three of them look at me with their wide eyes.

"Who made you?" Kingston asks.

A sob escapes my mouth, and I turn over and curl in on my side. "Mitchell."

Kingston nestles down behind me and molds his body to mine, spooning me right in the middle of the floor. Austin follows suit but lies in front of me, holding my hands between his. He leans in and ever so softly brushes his lips to mine to stop the tremble of my mouth. Diego plays with my hair, trailing his fingers over my scalp and putting pressure on my temples.

It's enough to calm me the hell down to accept that what I thought I experienced was a vivid nightmare. It never happened. It was all in my head, except...

"Shit. Did I attack Brayla?" I whisper-hiss. "Oh, fuck."

"The zombie bites you give Diego can't even compare to the rip and spit you pulled on Brayla, babe. Total savagery. And fucking awesome. She deserved it. Made me hella proud."

I squeeze my eyes shut. "Obviously if it was enough to get you to speak back-world to me."

Kingston hugs me tighter, kissing the back of my neck. "You have no idea. Not that I didn't think you were badass before, but damn."

"Hot," Diego whispers.

"Makes returning to Dark Terrace Ranch less intimidating," Austin murmurs.

"Dark Terrace Ranch? No. We can't. Mitchell will—"

Cutting me off with a kiss, Austin whispers, "He won't do anything. He can't."

But he can. I know he can. I've seen him outmatch my guys before. He knocked Kingston out cold once. He's old as hell and powerful enough to lead Donor Life Corp. And he's angry.

"No," I repeat.

"See, Jewel. What did I tell you?" Brayla's voice flicks off my fear and turns it into rage with a single glance in her direction.

She hovers in the doorway, holding a towel to her throat. My eyes immediately zoom in on the blood staining the towel, and her eyes flash silver at me. She takes a step back and shifts her body against the wall. Her obvious fear of me sends a frown crossing my face, but Kingston and Diego smile wide as hell and Austin smirks, squeezing my hands between his.

"I don't care what you told me, but I need you to leave," I say. "This is none of your business. You lost the right to be a part of my life the second you betrayed me."

Tears line her eyes, spilling on her cheeks. "Jewel, please. You have to understand. I'm trying to save you."

"You keep saying that, but I don't believe you. You are helping Orlando. You killed my dad. You made Donor Life Corp cancel my contract. That is not saving me. That's ruining my life." My voice lowers as I say the words, my anger so hot that my whole body shakes. I sit up, trying to push to my feet, but Kingston laces his arms around my waist.

Austin brings my hands to his mouth. "Jewel, big breaths. In and out. Don't lose control because of her. She's not worth it."

"I—I—"

"Breathe," he repeats.

Inhaling deeply, I let air fill my lungs until they hurt and slowly release. Austin breathes with me again, smiling while he does so, making things feel less out of control. With Kingston still hugging me against his chest, and Diego rubbing gentle circles on my knee, things don't feel so bad. The haunting dream finally diminishes, and my need to attack Brayla again sinks to the back of my mind.

"Jewel," Brayla says quietly, refusing to leave her spot. She just won't give up.

I turn my gaze to her without responding.

"I want you to know that if you choose to go back to Dark Terrace Ranch with them, you can still call on me if you need to. Even if you don't think so, you're still my best friend."

Again, I don't respond.

She sighs, pulls a phone from her pocket, and tosses it to me. Diego catches it and holds it out. I just look at the thing like it'll explode at any second. But it doesn't.

"If you change your mind, all you have to do is tap the screen once, okay? Your fingerprint will activate it."

Brayla disappears, and I listen to the door slam.

My guys hug me between them, and I soak in as much of their affection as possible. I don't want to be in this run-down house, but I also don't want to go to Dark Terrace Ranch. All I want is to go home to the Divinity Estate and pretend none of this happened.

Kingston breaks away from me first and combs his fingers through his hair. "Come on. If we leave now, we can still make it to Dark Terrace Ranch in time for the sunrise."

I shake my head. "No. I don't want to go tonight. Tell Mitchell we'll meet him tomorrow. We have my cousins and Liz. We can't just take them into the city."

Diego twines my fingers through his. "Yes, we can. It'll be fine."

"You sure about that?" The question comes from the front door. Hayden enters the house. "My sources from the city said that the city was on complete lockdown due to a threat from another region."

Kingston raises an eyebrow. "It doesn't apply to us."

"You might want to re-check," he says, a cocky smile distorting his face. "My sources don't lie."

Kingston tugs out his phone and turns it on for the first time since we've left Haven Springs. Austin and Diego watch him tap away too quick for me to see what's going on. It doesn't help that I keep glancing at Hayden, whose arrogant smile turns to a smug as hell expression with the sight of Kingston's frown.

"My access to Donor Life Corp has been denied," he whispers too lowly for Hayden to hear.

"What?" Diego asks. "Let me try."

Diego takes Kingston's phone and taps his fingers across the screen and sighs. Austin tries next, frowning the whole time, because we all know it's pointless.

"So, what does it mean?" I whisper.

"We can't take any visitors into the city," Kingston says.

I rub my hands around Diego's, releasing a small breath. "Then we won't go. Mitchell can wait."

Kingston flares his nostrils, his eyes flashing silver. "Jewel, we have to go."

"Uh, what happened to you always wanting to run away? You told me—"

"That was different. We fucked up, okay? We have to go back. We have to get this straightened out with Mitchell."

Something about the sudden deepening of his voice freaks me out. Kingston's always been a little—okay a lot—dramatic, but he's always had the confidence to assure me that everything will be okay. Now? I'm not so sure.

"But my cousins—"

"I'm sorry, beautiful," Diego says. "We're going to have to take them back to Haven Springs."

"What?" I ask. "No."

"Jewel—"

I hold my hand up, cutting off Austin. "I said, no."

Kingston, Austin, and Diego all glance at each other, silently conversing with their eyes. And it pisses me off, because I can't tell what's going on between them. They're leaving me out of whatever it is they're thinking about.

"I'm not going," I say, pulling away from Diego. I get to my feet before Austin can try to take my hand next.

Kingston releases a scary ass growl. "You don't have a choice."

I glare at him. "Seriously? You can't—"

"We can," he snaps, his chest heaving, the words seemingly causing him pain to say them. Or maybe it's the fact that I can't stop the full-on glower crossing my face.

"Jewel," Diego says, getting to his feet. "Don't get upset at Kingston."

"Don't get upset?" I say. "Are you shitting me? You can't just tell me what to do. And I'm not taking my cousins back to Haven Springs. We're not going back to Dark Terrace Ranch without them."

Kingston closes the space to me and holds my stare. "And what do you expect us to do? We don't have the clearance anymore—"

"Figure it out."

"We're doing the best we can. You don't understand the seriousness of the situation, Jewel."

"Then tell me, Kingston," I argue.

"No."

It takes everything in me not to spin around and storm off. "Kingston."

"Babe."

I turn to Diego and Austin. "One of you tell me."

"Don't even," Kingston snaps at them. "It won't change anything and will stress her out. You both know it."

OhmyeffingGod. "Damn it, Kingston. Stop it. I'm getting tired of the secrets. I'm fed up with everyone making all these decisions for me. For the mind manipulation."

"We'd never," Kingston says.

I close my eyes and take a breath. "Still. My memory is all messed up. I feel like I don't know what's going on half the time, and it doesn't help that you're getting all overprotective and bossy. You promised me it was us against the world. Right now, it feels like you three against the world on my behalf."

"Jewel, I'm sorry," Kingston whispers. "I'm just—I'm

scared."

"We don't know exactly what we'll be dealing with going back to Dark Terrace Ranch," Diego adds.

Austin comes up behind me and hugs me by the waist. "If we could safely take you somewhere else while we deal with it, we would."

"I can take Jewel," Hayden says.

Shit. I forgot he was standing there. Glancing in his direction, I see Liz and my cousins have joined him. They all heard everything, and my cousins' wide eyes look scared as hell.

"No," my guys say in unison.

"I'll guard her with my life," Liz says.

"Please, Kingston," Dana says. "If you think something bad will happen—"

Diego forces a smile at her. "It won't, Dana. We just have some business to attend to, and Jewel's presence is required."

I wring my hands together. "I can't leave my cousins. Not again. Not in Haven Springs."

"Jewel," Austin says. "They're going to be okay."

Hayden clears his throat. "What if I could arrange transport into the city?"

I raise my eyebrows. "You can do that?"

He smirks at me. "If you agree to help me get Ramona from Orlando."

I frown. "I don't even know how to do that."

"Start with arranging a meeting with him," he says.

Kingston snarls. "No."

I touch his shoulder. "But if Hayden can get my cousins into Dark Terrace Ranch—"

"There's only one way to get Ramona, Jewel," Diego says. "And we're not letting you trade places."

"Maybe there is something else he wants," I say.

The three of them look at each other in consideration, and then Kingston turns to Hayden and says, "If you can get Dana and Fallon safely into the city, we'll arrange a meeting with Orlando. But us. Not Jewel."

"It needs to be—"

"Us, not Jewel," he repeats, cutting him off.

Hayden inhales a few deep breaths and finally nods. "Fine, but it's either getting Dana and Fallon in or the information you want to know about Jewel. Not both."

I glare. "Seriously?"

"Is it a deal or what?" he asks.

My guys silently converse again before glancing from me to glare at Hayden. "Deal," Kingston says. "For Fallon and Dana."

"Really?" I ask.

It's Austin who nods. "They're family. I can still figure out everything with you."

I throw my arms around the three of them. "Thank you. I know this is hard on you."

"You're a pain in my side, babe," Kingston says. "I

want to lock you in a damn closet again."

I smirk at him. "Only with you."

He doesn't relent to smiling at me, though I can see he's struggling not to.

"Oh, and one more thing," I say.

He sighs. "What now?"

"You have to tell me everything."

"No."

"Kingston."

"Is it a deal breaker?"

I don't respond. I can't.

He swears. "Fucking fine. But on the way. We have to go."

BLOOD FEUD

I GAPE AT KINGSTON IN the rearview mirror. An intense five minutes of silence passes between us as I try to wrap my mind around everything. For the first time, my guys are scared and not just because they're afraid of losing me. They're afraid of Mitchell and what he could possibly do.

"You can't just apologize?" I ask, shifting in the backseat next to Diego.

"Sure, that's a start," Austin says, swiveling in his seat.

Kingston doesn't react and continues to stare at the road in front of us. Pulling the information from him about what we're getting into was painful for the both of us. He's always been more secretive and overly protective when it comes to what I know about the vampire world, and I'm afraid of what kind of strain it has put on us. Because I don't like feeling like just telling me tortures him. He's supposed to be able to tell me anything. I mean, I've agreed to a Blood Vow to him.

He feels the strain too.

It freaks us both out. Austin and Diego too. We're tense as all get-out.

I sigh. "What else do you think is going to happen? He can't be so upset to just trash your bond, right? You guys are his sons."

"He's our creator," Kingston says, his voice deep, hoarse almost.

I squeeze his shoulder. "You can't talk like that. It doesn't help."

Diego pats Kingston's other shoulder. "Our girl is right. If Mitchell thinks that we've sworn loyalty to Jewel as more than our future match and a Divine Heir, he'll do something crazy."

"Crazier than betray us, rip Jewel away and put her life in danger, and threaten her into complying with his demands?" Kingston grips the steering wheel, turning his knuckles nearly white from the effort. I'm pretty sure if he doesn't chill out, he might break the wheel right off.

Diego eyes me in his peripheral vision. "Actually, yeah. You saw the notice Brayla showed us."

"What notice?" I ask.

Kingston grumbles something I can't understand, his eyes flashing silver in warning to Diego.

Diego ignores him and laces his hand through mine. "It doesn't concern you because your matching contract was canceled, but Donor Life Corp put out a notice that all future applicants to the Blood Match Program's contract will officially transfer to the coven if something were to happen to the vampire they matched with...I mean, if they were to survive."

I blink a few times. "So, no Haven Springs for them?" That was the stipulation before and one way to cancel a contract. If a vampire isn't alive, they can't have a Blood Match. But from what I know, the likelihood that a donor would survive without their match is basically non-existent. But it's a rare occurrence. Diego said it's only happened once, a long time ago before I was even born.

Austin sighs. "No."

I press my lips together. It's one less incentive for a donor to enter the Blood Match Program, but I doubt it'll affect anything. It wouldn't have changed my mind. But the fact that Donor Life Corp is instating a stipulation worries me. If they do this, what will they change next? Why are they even doing it now? What's the point?

So many questions burn through my mind, but I know my guys can't exactly answer them. They can only speculate. They're Divine Heirs, but they're not board members, and right now, they've been cut off from access to Donor

Life Corp.

"But don't worry about it, beautiful," Diego says, leaning into me. "You need a clear head to face Mitchell with us. He'll know that we gave you our blood and won't be able to manipulate your mind."

My hands shake at the thought. If he knows he can't use his mind manipulation against me, then he'll use force. The idea freaks me the hell out. It reminds me of my crazy ass nightmare of finding my guys chained in the dark room.

I groan and bury my face to Diego's chest, wrapping my arms around him so that he'll hold me. "We need a plan."

"We have a plan," Kingston says. "Grovel, swear loyalty, and if that doesn't work, tear his head off."

"Kingston, what the hell kind of plan is that?" I ask, turning my head to peek at him.

Austin scrunches his nose. "A terrible one."

"Maybe he should just wait in the car," I murmur.

Diego chuckles and shifts me off the seat so that I sit in his lap. "All right, beautiful. You make the plan. That idea was the best one of the night."

I lean into him and kiss him, sensing how much he craves my closeness. Brushing his lips to mine, he kisses me softly a few times but doesn't let his desire take control. I'd love nothing more than to forget the shitty world around us, but it's impossible. My guys are too tense. Our nerves frayed. I just wish I knew how to make things better without suggesting blowing up the world. I wouldn't put it past Kingston to try.

I ease away first but remain sitting on Diego's lap despite how close my head comes to touching the roof. If Kingston were to hit a bump, I'm sure I'd get a splitting headache. "I can try to think of something," I say, responding a little too late to Diego's joke. "Let me get things straight. The only reason we're going back to Dark Terrace Ranch is because Mitchell wants to murder you because you showed more loyalty to me than him."

"Pretty much," Kingston says.

Austin looks at me. "Not true. It's more complicated than that. Not showing up guarantees our betrayal to the Divine name. We'll be traitors. Our options are limited right now. We're not fully prepared to take on a war with Mitchell. If we show up and prove our support of the Divine name, our chances are better."

"And you don't think he'll hurt me?" I ask, trying to get everything straight.

"You proved you'd do what you had to," Diego says. "You're still useful."

"An asset," Kingston practically spits out, reminding me of what Viorica said to Mitchell in Haven Springs.

I stare at the lights of the city in the distance before shifting to glance at the headlights behind us. I nearly lost my shit when Hayden insisted my cousins ride with him, but he had a valid point about the risk of having to have them swap cars in the city past dark.

The only reason I'm even semi-okay is because Liz is with them, and Fallon has Austin's phone to track. I'm also pretty sure Hayden wouldn't test me if he thinks I'm the key to getting Ramona from Orlando. I just wish I knew his deal and what he got out of helping Orlando get to me in Haven Springs in the first place. He had to have gotten something.

"He's going to learn real quick that he can't," I say.

"Please don't make him think otherwise. Save your badassness for later. And be prepared. He's going to punish us, Jewel," Kingston says. "We have to give him a good reason not to."

A good reason? I'd think wanting his sons not to hate his guts would be a good enough reason. But I suppose this isn't about family. This is about blood. And right now, Mitchell started a blood feud with us. It's obvious my guys will only tolerate so much.

"I doubt a promise to try harder will do," Kingston adds.

The headlights from Hayden's van flash behind us, drawing my attention away from Kingston. The idea hits me hard enough that I gasp in a breath and nearly slam my head into the roof.

"Shit," I say.

Kingston swerves. "He wants us to pull over."

"Just one more minute." I slide off Diego's lap. "I have

an idea."

All three of my guys turn their attention to me.

"This whole shit show started with the Blood Rebels. If it wasn't for Hayden trying to friggin' murder us, we would never be in this position," I start.

Hayden flashes his lights again.

Kingston slows, hitting the brakes. "Okay, so...are you saying what I think you're saying, babe? I need you just to spit it out to be certain."

"Why don't we give Mitchell what he wants?"

"The fuck are we giving him you, babe."

I frown. "Excuse me?"

He blinks. "Haven't you realized that everyone wants you? They don't have to say it. All part of the need to possess what they can't have."

I try to keep my face expressionless. "Um, I meant Hayden, not me."

Diego punches Kingston. "And now you freaked her out. Good going, asshat."

Austin reaches out to me, brushing his fingers along my cheek. "You want to give Mitchell Hayden? You know what that would mean, right?"

My heart races at the thought. Because I'd be a true traitor to humanity. Mitchell will use Hayden to get the information he needs to take out the Blood Rebels. People will die.

But I don't know what else to do.

I bob my head. "I know what it means."

"Are we really worth it?" he asks quietly.

I lean forward between the seats and kiss him. "You guys can't be the only ones capable of destroying the world."

"I love you, babe," Kingston says, killing the engine as Hayden waves from the van without getting out.

Diego nestles his chin to my shoulder. "Let's just hope it doesn't come to that."

"You want us to what?" Dana asks, gawking at Hayden.

"Drink this." He holds out a canister to my cousin.

I don't have to ask to know that it contains blood. It's freaky as all hell that I can smell it. And it smells weird. Not a good weird, either.

"That's vampire blood," I whisper to my guys. "Old vampire blood."

Austin tips his head forward to meet my gaze. "It could make them sick if they're not used to it, especially if it wasn't stored properly."

"Can you smell my blood?" Kingston whispers. Of course that's the one thing he would focus on in this situation. But I can't blame him. He's a master at distracting himself. It helps with his restraint.

Right now, I'm pretty certain it's taking everything in him not to tackle Hayden and toss him into the trunk. But we still need him. Apparently, he can get my cousins and Liz into a safe house to wait for us. I just hope that Raul and Berto like my cousins enough to help Liz protect them, because from their constant glowers at me, I can tell they wouldn't purposefully do me any favors.

"When I'm sticking my nose to your neck," I whisper. "But this is new. Gross too."

"Good," Kingston murmurs.

I sigh. "Not good. We can't let them drink that."

Diego links his pinky with mine. "He's right about it being safer. It'll lessen the risk of mind manipulation."

"But it's disgusting blood from who knows what source," I complain, nearly saying the words loud enough for everyone to hear.

I watch Liz take the canister from Hayden and bring it to her lips. She swallows and coughs, her face twisting at what I know is the nasty ass taste. She looks ready to puke, but Hayden hands her a canister of water to chase it with.

I gag. I can't help it.

Kingston rubs his hand between my shoulder blades. "Our girl is officially a blood snob."

"Because you guys are friggin' delicious."

Kingston flashes his fangs at me. "And to think I thought I was more than a food source to you."

"Don't test her, Kingston," Diego whispers. "You'd be the first she'd devour, especially after all your bullshit tonight."

Kingston turns pouty as hell at Diego's words. We've been ignoring focusing on stuff we can deal with later. Surviving takes precedence over my annoyance with secrets, and Kingston did realize that he was hurting me, though I know I might have hurt him too.

I push the thought away to stop my own mouth from pouting. Liz hands the canister to Dana next, and I rush forward and smack it to the ground before she can bring it to her lips. Blood spills across the dirt, and I gag again, the stench of it worse now that it's permeating the air.

"Damn it. That was all I had left," Hayden says, glowering at me. "It'll be your fault if something happens to them."

I straighten my shoulders. "*My* fault? You were going to make them drink rotten vampire blood."

"Ew, what?" Dana asks.

Liz shudders at my words.

"It was still fine," Hayden argues.

I point at the dark liquid. "Was not."

"Whatever." Swiping the canister off the ground, he waves it at my guys. "Why don't you make yourselves useful and fill it up."

Oh, hell no. I snatch the canister from his hand. "They're not giving you their blood."

Hayden turns to my cousins. "You can thank your selfish cousin if you get your mind manipulated."

Dana and Fallon look at me with wide eyes.

Before I can react, Kingston takes the canister from my hands and bites his arm. He dribbles a small amount into it and gives it to Diego to do the same. We all watch in silence, and my dumb body chooses now to start buzzing with anticipation even though I know they didn't just pour their blood for me. Austin hands the canister to Dana with just enough of their blood that Hayden wouldn't get any leftovers.

Kingston eyes me in his peripheral vision. "Babe, just this once won't be a huge deal. It's a small amount."

"You want us to drink *your* blood?" Fallon asks Kingston.

"No, but the asshole was right. Plus, I know you two were curious. Please turn around and never mention this again. It's weird as fuck to be a donor."

I backhand Kingston's shoulder, his words turning both my cousins into flaming red blushing machines. All he does is tip his head back and laugh.

I rub my hand across my face. "That was totally unnecessary."

"But hilarious," Kingston whispers.

"Or awkward."

"Hell yeah to that, too." He hugs me and buries his face into the crook of my neck, grazing his fangs along my throat through a teasing kiss. "So kiss me. Let me bite you. Cop a feel. Do something. I need a distraction to cancel out the weirdness."

I laugh and turn my face to kiss him.

"More," he whispers.

"I'm afraid I'll get carried away and bite you," I tease.

He laughs and pulls away to look at me. His smile falters the second our eyes meet. Without having to ask him, I know my eyes might betray that I'm only half kidding about getting carried away.

"You need blood," he whispers.

"I'm fine," I say, easing away.

I turn my back and take a few steps from him.

Austin's gentle hand touches my shoulder. "Jewel, Kingston's right. You should drink some before we head into the city. Just in case."

I inhale and exhale a breath. I want so much to argue that I really am fine, but I'd be lying. Nothing is fine. The more I think about how close to Dark Terrace Ranch we are, the more out of control I feel. But it's not necessarily because of hunger. It's everything.

"Listen to your masters, Jewel," Hayden says. "You're going to need your strength."

I glower at his remark. "Stay out of it."

"I'm only trying to help. You have no idea what you're involved in and what your family did to assure the safety of the human race," he says.

"What's that supposed to mean? You constantly call me a traitor to humanity."

He shrugs. "I'll tell you a hint when you give me what I

want."

So, I'll never friggin' know.

Diego intercepts Kingston before he flies at Hayden and puts our plan into action way too early. The two of them throw a few punches at each other but manage to pull their shit together faster than usual. Austin squeezes my hand and tugs me toward the car.

"I hope you realize that the only reason you're still breathing is because of Jewel. You should thank her," Kingston mutters.

Hayden tightens his jaw. "I can say the same about you three."

"Okay, that's enough. We have to get going. I want to get in and out of the city before the sun rises," I say, intervening. "We'll follow you in."

Hayden nods. "Probably better that Donor Life Corp doesn't know you're coming."

For the first time in my life, I think I might actually agree with the asshole.

What the hell is happening to my life?

BETRAYAL

DARK TERRACE RANCH AT NIGHT is the worst. I used to think I was lucky to have survived Starlight Row with Brayla after sunset the few times we had to race, but now that I can look around, I know it wasn't luck. Donor Life Corp manages to control the shadow dwellers well, and any of them who chased me were only doing so to freak me out. They could have killed me if they wanted to. Even Chomper Jonas could've killed me.

"So this is where the shadow dwellers get their gen. pop. rations?" I whisper, peering at the long line of vampires waiting to enter the donation lab.

"Not just shadow vampires. All vampires without exclusive donors," Austin says. "It keeps the peace rather well doing it this way."

"Because those without power don't see the divide between covens as much?"

"Something like that," Diego says.

I hum under my breath, drawing the attention of a few nearby vampires. They're nothing like the ones I've encountered outside the city, and it makes me wonder if Dark Terrace Ranch truly has the shadow dwellers my dad constantly warned me about. "I have so many questions."

"You always choose the most inappropriate times to want to talk, babe," Kingston says.

I shrug. "Because you all distract me and make me forget."

He smirks. "With good reason."

I turn to Austin. "Are there any super starved vampires in the city?"

He shakes his head. "I'll tell you everything you want to know as soon as we get you to where it's safe."

"Promise?" I ask.

He motions for me to hop on his back. "Promise. No more secrets."

Friggin' finally.

I kiss Austin on the nape of his neck and hug my arms around his taut chest. Diego situates himself in front, and Kingston takes his place to protect my back.

We abandon the old car in the street with the rundown ones from long ago and head in the direction of the Blood

Match Center. If the car wasn't so loud, Kingston would have driven it right to the front of the building, but we've already garnered too much attention.

"Almost there," Austin says, picking up his speed so much that the world blurs.

One second the city lights streak by my vision, and in the next, bright lights engulf us, and it takes me a minute to orient myself to our change in location.

For the second time since I Blood Matched, the lobby to the center lacks vampires this time of night. It's usually pretty packed with applicants and staff members and the donors they matched with ready to leave to start their new lives.

"This is creepy," I murmur. "Where is everyone?"

Kingston glances around. "After your contract was canceled, Donor Life Corp put a hold on Blood Matching with exception to certain covens like the Vaduvas. The tension Mitchell caused in murdering Pierce in front of the board didn't help."

"That's another reason why we couldn't get to you as quickly," Diego adds.

It already feels like forever ago since I woke up in Haven Springs so confused and scared. "And they still haven't fixed the program?"

Kingston peels me away from Austin and sets me on my feet. I hadn't even realized it was me holding him in a death grip. "Probably because of the change in terms. Negotiations and revising contracts take time when the whole board must agree."

Austin turns and gives me a long once-over, inspecting every inch of me. "But don't worry about any of that. You're no longer in the program. You're ours."

I lift an eyebrow, smirking at his claim on me. Austin's vampire nature sneaks out mostly in tense situations, but I friggin' love it in this moment. I don't care if I sound like a possession. It makes me feel a shit ton better about being here.

I reach out and touch his cheek. He closes the space and kisses me, his shoulders relaxing the longer I graze my lips to his, just letting our breathing mingle until both our heartbeats slow. Diego hugs me next, lifting me off my feet for a moment to kiss him, and Kingston soon follows suit. The sudden affection speeds my even heart right back up.

"While I love all of your attention, it's freaking me out," I whisper, pulling them all to me in an attempt to wrap my arms around all of them.

Diego snuggles his face to my shoulders. "It's just been a long night, and you keep our heads clear."

"Sure that's it," I murmur.

Kingston kisses me again. "It is. Because everything is going to be fine. Your plan will work."

"I know. I promised to always take care of you."

The elevator dings, drawing our attention to it, but it's empty when the door slides open.

My guys all peer up at one of the security cameras blinking in the corner. We might have snuck into Dark Terrace Ranch unnoticed through a freaky ass tunnel that was supposed to be blocked off, but now we lost the element of surprise.

I just hope it's given us the time we need. A minute isn't exactly enough time to prepare for our arrival unless Mitchell has been waiting since the executions. That was hours ago. He probably thought we wouldn't show. At least that's what we hope.

"You are not to let go of Austin, babe. Understand?" Kingston asks, grabbing my hand and placing it in Austin's. If he had a pair of restraints, he'd bind me to him.

I squeeze Austin's fingers. "Got it."

He turns to his brothers. "If shit goes down, get Jewel out."

"You should be the one," Diego says.

Kingston's eyes flash silver, and he glances at me. His Adam's apple pops in his throat. "I—I—you're the better fighter, Diego. Jewel needs you more."

Coolness drips over me, stealing all the warmth from my body at Kingston's words. I can't even believe he said them.

A tear trickles from my eye and onto my cheek, and Kingston swipes it away and pulls me into his arms. He kisses me a dozen times, running his hands over my tears to assure they don't get far.

"Babe, I love you, and I'm sorry if things aren't always easy for us, but you're everything to me. I know you think I'm this super sexy, all-powerful vampire who can actually follow through with world-destroying threats in your honor, but I have my limits. I can't promise to protect you without my brothers. Not like they can protect you."

I smother him in a hug. "Shut up and don't talk like that. I know you could protect me just fine. And we're staying together, got it?"

He chuckles. "You're the boss, babe."

"Oh, *now* I'm the boss?" I say, my tears subsiding enough that Kingston takes a step back.

"For the next hour. Don't let the power get to your head."

Austin tugs me into the elevator, taking Kingston's place once more. Diego and Kingston stand protectively in front of us like the second the door slides open, all hell will break loose. But we're greeted by the open doors to the empty board room.

Austin doesn't give me a chance to hesitate, tugging me along with him behind his brothers into the board room. A soft light illuminates the dark from an open door I know leads to Mitchell's private office. He doesn't even look at us when we enter, but there's no way we're sneaking up on him. He's just not going to greet us until he's ready. Stupid vampire customs.

"Dad," Kingston says, speaking up, making sure to use

his name of affection for his creator. I hope it's enough to stop Mitchell from blowing the hell up. "We've come to make amends."

Still, Mitchell doesn't look up or react.

"I know we abandoned you during a tense time to check on Jewel, and we're sorry," Diego adds. "It won't happen again."

Austin clears his throat. "We hope you understand our reason. We love her. We made her a vow."

"You made me a vow, or have you forgotten?" Mitchell asks, finally responding. "As my heirs, it is your duty to follow in line and trust that I know what's best for this family. You should have come to me first. Now, your presences in Haven Springs caused irreparable damage."

"You think they caused irreparable damage?" I slap my hand over my mouth the second the words escape.

Mitchell's eyes flash silver, and he jerks his attention toward me.

Holy shit balls. He looks ready to murder me.

But apparently my rebel mouth couldn't give a flying fuck, because I say, "You're the reason for the unrest in Haven Springs. You and Donor Life Corp. If you hadn't just thrown me in there, none of this would've ever happened."

Mitchell materializes in front of me, cocking his head to the side. "Do not speak on topics you have no knowledge of."

"Are you kidding me?" I ask. "You have no friggin'

idea."

Austin pulls me back before Mitchell can try to touch me.

"Enlighten me, Jewel. Because from where I'm standing, you're currently my biggest problem and not because you've somehow managed to seduce all three of my heirs."

I try not to react.

"But you can fix this," he says. "The executions were a start, but I need more. I can forgive my sons for their lack of judgment. I can forgive them for falling in love with you. But, what I can't forgive them for is forgetting their place as my heirs."

"They didn't forget their place," I say.

"Then prove it."

Seriously? I barely tolerated Mitchell before, but now I can't stand him. It takes everything in me not to swing my arm out to sucker punch him. Thankfully, my good senses win, because I'm certain I'd lose my limb. "Haven't I been tested enough?"

His attention jerks from me to my guys. "Not you. Them."

Kingston steps forward. "Okay, whatever you want. We just want things to turn back to normal without all the Blood Match contract bullshit, board interference, whatever the hell else is going on. We need to be united as a coven, especially now."

I reach out and squeeze his shoulder, just letting him

know I'm here for him. Admitting as much to Mitchell is hard as hell for him, but he hides it well.

"You're right, my son," Mitchell says. "Together, we're stronger."

"So, what can we do to make it up to you?" Austin asks.

Diego steps closer to Mitchell. "How can we prove our worth?"

Mitchell's eyes flick to mine, and I take an automatic step back under his scrutiny. Because effin' A. I don't like the silent thoughts that turn his eyes silver. Neither do my guys, because they all stiffen. Mitchell doesn't have to say anything for us to know that it involves me.

"I want you to allow me into Jewel's mind. I want whatever it is that hides locked in her head." Mitchell slowly turns his attention away from me. "I want to assure she knows her place."

Panic washes over me, my nightmare replaying in my mind. "You can't be serious."

Mitchell doesn't respond to me.

"I'll do it," Diego says, turning to me. "If you let me."

I open my mouth to agree, but Mitchell wags his head. "No. It must be me."

"Why? Any of us can do it," Kingston says. "We're less likely to hurt her in the process."

Mitchell reaches out and grabs Kingston's shoulder, keeping him in place. "It's your inability to do all it takes that keeps the information locked up tight. I believe the only reason Orlando hasn't already taken Jewel is because he knows you don't have it in you. You have no idea who you're dealing with."

"Then tell us," Diego says.

"Orlando is one of the few responsible for the shift in the world. He led the uprising that wiped out humanity. The world was lucky I could get things under control with Donor Life Corp, because we'd have all been doomed otherwise. There wouldn't have been a single donor left." Mitchell's voice comes out so softly that I can barely hear it with my super hearing.

"I don't understand," Kingston says. "I remember what you told me when I turned. You said we were saving the world from the destruction caused by humanity. You said we—"

"That was the intent but others disagreed with returning to the shadows." Mitchell straightens his shoulders. "So I embraced it, as did the rest of the board. And you three helped me create the magnificence of the world today. So, don't throw it away. Let me do what is necessary to protect our reign."

All of the information swirls through my mind. My dad's conspiracy theories weren't actually conspiracy theories. He was right in a way about how the Blood Hunger Plague was unleashed to take care of the damage to the world caused by humans. He was right about it being a way to get the population under control. But he was wrong—or he lied—about how it happened. I always thought the Blood Hunger Plague was a real thing until my guys told me otherwise. But now that I know it wasn't an actual plague and that Orlando was responsible, I need to know why. What is my involvement?

But I don't want anything to do with Mitchell manipulating the answers from me. I don't trust him.

"No," all three of my guys say in response to Mitchell.

I don't even have a chance to react before I fly through the air, my head spinning. Something crashes and glass breaks. Diego catches me a second before I hit the floor and swings me out in one of Kingston's most hated fighting techniques. Like my body knows exactly what to do, I don't resist the force and kick Mitchell into the wall.

Diego flips me onto his back, and I clutch my arms around his chest for dear life, knowing he depends on me to keep a good hold to allow his arms to be free to fight.

Austin and Kingston materialize in front of me and Diego, standing tall and fierce, and scary as hell, triggering my fear cues.

Mitchell doesn't fly to stand. He doesn't come charging at us.

All he does is push to his feet and dust the plaster from his clothes. "Think long and hard what you do next, my sons. If you run, consider it an act of treason. You will no longer be welcome into Dark Terrace Ranch or the allied regions. You will lose your Divine name and all that comes with it. You will be cast to the shadows."

"Get ready," Kingston whispers.

A growl sounds from behind us.

"And don't think for one second I'll allow you out of the building with Jewel. You might have made a Blood Vow to her, but she is *my* heir. She is *my* property. If you attempt to take what belongs to me, you will meet a fate far worse than the mercy I'll show you," Mitchell says, strolling closer at a painfully slow pace.

"Listen to your creator, boys," Viorica says from behind us. "Don't force me to help him. You know what it'll do to Samantha, Austin."

I peer over my shoulder at Viorica standing in the boardroom with her hands on her hips. "Viorica, please. You can't."

Her eyes flash silver. "It was a simple stipulation, but you're making it more difficult. If you loved them, you'd agree. You'd allow Mitchell to get what he wants from you. You'd save the Divines from a fate you know they don't deserve."

I can't agree. I can't. Not because of me, but because of my guys. They would never want me to. Ever.

"Jewel, no," Kingston says.

"But I'm scared," I whisper.

"Stick to the plan," Austin murmurs. "It'll give us the chance to strategize things."

I had nearly forgotten about offering Hayden to Mitchell. "Okay," I whisper. "But don't put me in charge anymore."

"Damn straight," Kingston replies.

"What will it be?" Mitchell asks, sliding his hand into his suit jacket.

"What if I took you to one of the Blood Rebel leaders?" I say, grimacing at how squeaky my voice comes out.

Mitchell glances behind us at Viorica and then turns his gaze to each of his sons. "So my suspicions about your ties to them were correct. I should execute you all right now."

I swallow the burning in my throat. "No, it's not what you think. The Blood Rebel wanted to make a deal with me. He was the one to bring us into the city."

Mitchell doesn't react, though I can see a dozen thoughts cross his mind.

"We'll take you to him if you agree to let us all go, including Jewel. If you want to renounce our statuses as Divine Heirs, then do it. But we're taking Jewel. She's ours," Kingston says.

Mitchell slides his hand from his suit jacket and drops it to his side without the weapon I had expected. "I think we might be able to work things out."

"Really?" I ask, regretting my response immediately.

"But first, the Blood Rebel," Mitchell says, ignoring me.

I release a small breath at his words. Thank friggin' God. For a minute, I wasn't sure he'd agree.

If only it didn't still feel like our world is about to crash and burn.

TREASON

I SIT ON AUSTIN'S LAP in the back of Mitchell's sleek silver car. Diego and Kingston each hold one of my hands from their spots on each side of us, leaving the front seat empty. Mitchell hasn't taken his eyes off me from the rear-view mirror since we left the Blood Match Center, unfortunately without Viorica. I used to think I hated her, but something different about her got to me tonight. Under her cold demeanor, she might actually care. Why? I have no idea. I haven't exactly been Team Widow or whatever.

"Turn left at the next alley," Kingston says, comparing his phone to the map glowing on the dashboard.

Mitchell follows Kingston's instructions and maneuvers the car into a narrow alleyway barely big enough to fit the car. It dead-ends at a chain-link fence that leads to a re-stricted zone—at least restricted to donors. I'm not exactly sure what's on the other side, considering I wouldn't have dared enter this alley while living in The Boxes. With how tall the buildings are and how close the one across the street is, it would be guaranteed shade probably all day and where shadow dwellers hang out. And seeing that Hayden brought my cousins here? He's lucky he's already a dead man.

"Your Blood Rebel is hiding in a vampire exclusive lo-cation?" Mitchell asks, raising his eyebrows at me.

I shrug. "Is that what this place is? I'm not exactly friends with the jerk, so I wouldn't know."

Mitchell turns off the engine and swivels in the seat. "Yet he trusted you?"

"Not exactly," I say.

"I'm going to need more to go off of, Jewel. You can't expect me to believe some nonsense story about a Blood Rebel helping you from the goodness of his heart. What is in it for him? How did you come across him in Haven Springs? Why didn't you inform me immediately?" Mitch-ell's eyes flash silver, and he attempts to capture me in his gaze.

I avert my eyes. "Because he showed up after—after the executions." The words struggle to escape me. The second they do, I imagine the men dying right in front of me all over again. "And he—he..."

"Hayden is the rebel who converted Jewel's sister,"

Kingston says, finishing the words I can't manage to spit out. "He wants Jewel's help to get Ramona."

"And what do you get in return?" Mitchell asks, penetrating me with his stare, though I don't look up. I refuse to.

"He brought my cousins and a friend here for us since you denied us access," I murmur. "And so you know, I didn't agree to help him get my sister."

"Then what was the deal?"

I try to think of a million things we could possibly agree on, but nothing seems good enough. A part of me knows that if I tell Mitchell about Hayden's connection to Orlando, he'll automatically use it to his advantage. If he does, we lose any and all leverage we have. We need Mitchell to be content with Hayden. He can't know there's more. If he does, he might learn the truth about me...the truth Hayden could also give to him if he asked the right questions, but it's a risk we're willing to take.

As long as Mitchell is good on his word, we'll be free of him without a target on us. We won't get the wealth and power attached to his name, but we won't get all his bullshit either. We'll finally be free to live how we want without all the vampire politics my guys keep from me.

"I agreed to betray you," I say, the words surprising everyone. "You know, for being an asshole."

Mitchell smirks. "How strategic."

"Something I learned from your sons."

Mitchell offers me a smile, a real smile, and one I haven't seen since before the first incident in Haven Springs. "I've underestimated you, Jewel. I thought my sons were enthralled with you because of your fragility making them feel powerful, but you've grown into someone rather fitted to a life outside of the one you were born into."

"Thanks?" My response comes out as more of a question, and I shift awkwardly on Austin's lap, wishing my guys would speak up. But they won't. Mitchell doesn't include them. I can't tell whether it's good or bad, but until he shows them attention, they won't intervene unless they have to. I'm in charge tonight...sort of.

"I would like to continue this conversation later if you're good on your word to deliver the Blood Rebel to me." Mitchell turns to his sons. "If that's okay with you."

Fear sneaks up on me, his words making me uneasy. Austin tenses at my body's reaction, even though I hide it well in my expression. Because eff. No, that's not okay with me. I don't like his interest, especially after what I know about Donor Life Corp changing how the Blood Match Program works.

"Yes," Kingston says, speaking up.

I grip his hand tighter, but he doesn't react. We don't look at each other either. I just hope he knows what he's doing.

"Good. Now, boys. Why don't you go first? Disarm anyone with weapons. Kill those who fight, but keep your

Blood Rebel alive," Mitchell says. "I'll look after Jewel."

"Wait, what?" I ask.

No one moves. None of my guys even breathe. They look ready to rip Mitchell's head off for even making the suggestion.

"It's fine," I whisper. "Just be quick."

"Babe—"

I rub my lips together. "Mitchell's not going to hurt me."

Mitchell twists his lips. "That you'd even think such a thing proves just how far you've fallen from me, my sons."

Great.

"It's not that," Diego murmurs.

Austin shifts me off his lap and onto Kingston's. "We don't trust everyone else around here."

"I suppose I can't fault you," Mitchell says. "You have my word that Jewel will be safe until you return."

Diego kisses my cheek and opens the car door. I hug Austin, letting him inhale a few breaths of my hair, and then nudge him to follow his brother. Kingston doesn't move, tightening his hold on me. I turn in his lap to face him, resting my forehead to his until he closes the space completely and meets me for a kiss.

"The faster you get Hayden, the faster we can sneak away for some much needed cuddles," I murmur softly.

He groans. "I don't want to leave you."

I brush my fingers through his hair. "Trust that I can

take care of myself, dude."

"And us," he whispers. "My fucking badass babe."

I kiss him again. "Now hurry."

He slides me off his lap. "I expect more than cuddles."

"Me too."

With one more look at Mitchell, Kingston exits the car and joins his brothers. They disappear into the night too fast for my eyes to follow, leaving me with Mitchell.

Everything in me screams to fling the door open and run like hell, but a pair of silver flashing eyes on the other side of the chain-link fence freezes me in place. Mitchell turns to follow my gaze to the lurking vampire, but it disappears.

The sounds of gunshots ring through the air, and Mitchell shifts his attention toward the dark alcove my guys disappeared into. Bright light cuts through the dark alley, and the door swings open. Mitchell exits the car without a word, abandoning me to go after the few figures running from the place.

"Jewel!"

I throw the door open and rush toward the group of people. Mitchell holds Liz up against the wall, flashing his fangs. Something comes over me, and I rush forward and yank the back of his suit jacket.

Dropping Liz, Mitchell spins toward me and lifts me off my feet, ramming my back into the wall of the building on the opposite side. His silver eyes lock onto mine, his fangs extending longer than I've ever seen them.

"Mitchell, don't," I beg, attempting to press my back in the wall. "I was only trying to stop you from hurting my friend. You know Liz, remember?"

"And Ms. Matthias is a rebel," he snarls.

"But she's not."

Diego flies up behind Mitchell and grips his shoulders. "Release Jewel immediately. Liz is an ally, not a rebel. We owe her a favor for the help she provided to us in Haven Springs."

Mitchell composes himself, retracting his fangs. I half expect him to throw me over his shoulder and flee, but he sets me on my feet and straightens his suit jacket. I fix my own hoodie and run my fingers through my hair, pulling it from my face.

Diego scoops me up and holds me like he's afraid to even let me walk the few feet it takes to reach the door. Dana and Fallon rush us, each taking a spot at Diego's side, hovering so close that they practically stand on his feet. And then he lets them, wrapping an arm around each of them while I hang on myself.

My dad would probably faint or curse the universe or some shit if he was alive to see the three of us now. I'm pretty sure we're the first humans ever to hang onto a vampire like this, but Diego smiles, amused as hell by the situation. I didn't think it was possible for me to love him more, but I do.

I imagine this to be how our lives should be...but without all the Donor Life Corp and Blood Rebel drama. It should be us joking around and testing Diego's strength for fun and not because we're scared. I want the thought so badly to come true, I consider taking the dagger from Diego's pocket to go after Mitchell while his back is turned to me.

"You fucking bitch!" Hayden yells at me from his spot on the floor, his arms bound behind his back. "You're going to regret this."

Kingston slaps his hand over Hayden's mouth. "Don't talk to her. Don't even look at her. If you do, I'll rip your head off."

Hayden thrashes and falls onto his stomach, attempting to free himself from the shredded pieces of fabric—the hem of Kingston's shirt—tied around his wrists. "I'm a dead man, anyway."

"Maybe not." Mitchell's smooth voice cuts through the air as he peers around what used to be some sort of factory. Old machines lie dormant and rusted. A few gross mattresses clutter the floor, and a stockpile of rations sit on an old shelf. "It'll all depend on what you can offer me."

Hayden jerks his head up. "I don't have shit to give you."

"What about the people who reside here?" he asks. "Where are they?"

It's then that I realize Hayden's alone apart from Liz

and my cousins. Not even Raul and Berto are in sight. If there were people here, they're now gone.

"I don't know what you're talking about," Hayden says.

Mitchell charges forward too fast for my eyes to follow. Kingston disappears from Hayden's side, and I scream at the sight of Mitchell ramming him into the wall instead of Hayden. Kingston flashes his fangs but doesn't fight back.

I scream and try to break away from Diego, but he stops me, holding me tighter against him.

"Where are they?" Mitchell repeats.

Ah hell. He wasn't even asking Hayden about the people in the first place.

Mitchell shoves his hand into Kingston's throat. "There were obviously people here, Kingston, and I know you well enough to know that you would have rather let them go than hurt them because you worry what Jewel thinks."

"There was no one," Austin says, inching his way closer to Mitchell. "Dad, please. Let Kingston go. You have Hayden now as we promised."

"He's not enough! None of this makes up for your betrayal."

Mitchell swipes a blade from beneath his jacket and holds it to Kingston's chest. Kingston remains utterly still, his eyes turning away from Mitchell to search for me.

"I love you, Jewel," he says. "I'm sorry."

Mitchell roars. "You should apologize to me. Beg me to

forgive you. Plea for your life."

Kingston doesn't react, never taking his eyes off mine.

"Mitchell, please," I say. Kingston might not beg, but I sure the fuck will. "Don't do this. You want me? Fine. I'll swear my loyalty. I'll be your blood source. I'll do anything. Just let him go."

"You think my sons will allow it?" he asks without looking at me.

"Please."

"No."

I don't even have the chance to scream as Mitchell jerks his weapon toward Kingston's chest. The world blurs and my cousins scream. A gun fires, the loud pop ringing in my ears. Metal scrapes against metal. Something crashes, the boom reverberating through my bones.

"Get them out of here," Kingston says, his deep voice flooding me with relief.

Something thumps again, and Kingston yells out. I twist in Diego's arms to look behind me. Blood splatters across the floor, a streak trailing from one end to the other. My heart falters at the sight of Kingston pushing to his feet. Blood soaks the front of his shirt, but I can't tell whether it's his or not.

He waves his arm. "Get them out!"

Diego turns to take us to the door, but a low growl sounds from outside. "It's not safe. I can't protect them all."

"Fuck," Kingston says.

Two figures blur by, and Kingston disappears, crashing into Mitchell and Austin to knock them off their feet. Mitchell twists and rams Austin's head into the concrete ground, the thunk loud enough to twist my stomach. Kingston spins and kicks Mitchell with enough force to knock him away, but Mitchell's too fast and rushes Kingston. The two of them disappear in another fight. Austin pushes up to his feet and snatches a discarded dagger off the ground.

A pop rings out, and I cover my ears. Liz fires her gun from beside Hayden as the fighting forms get close. Austin joins the fight again, moving it away from her. She helps Hayden to his feet and shoves him in our direction.

"Hurry, Liz!" I call.

She freezes in her tracks and raises her gun. Diego spins me and my cousins out of the way, and glass shatters behind us. Growls sound through the air, and Diego sets me on my feet. He pushes me toward Liz and Hayden.

A vampire climbs through the broken window. Blood seeps from a bullet hole in the front of his ragged T-shirt. He cracks his neck, swinging his gaze from Diego to the rest of us. Austin snarls from behind us, and I realize the fight between my guys and Mitchell stopped.

"How many donors?" a vampire asks from outside the window.

"Five. They're with the Divines."

Mitchell steps closer, making Diego tense. "The young woman is mine. If you manage to overpower my former heirs, you may have the rest."

The vampire's eyes flash silver. "What else will we get?"

"Residency at the Divinity Estate and authorization to leave the city."

I blow a breath of air through my teeth. "Shit."

"Relax, beautiful," Diego whispers in my ear. "And brace yourself."

I try not to react to his words, but fear tightens my chest, making it hard for me to breathe. My cousins' soft whimpers don't help. Mitchell's willing to buy the shadow dweller's loyalty in exchange for me. He's willing to give them my cousins. I can't let that happen.

I grip his hands. "Diego, my cousins."

"We're fine. Now, get ready."

Diego hooks his arm around my waist and throws me into the air. I clench my jaw, stopping myself from screaming. Austin uses the distraction to punch Mitchell in the face. Kingston catches me in his arms and cradles me against him. Liz fires her gun—no, Hayden fires Liz's gun, but not at the vampires. He manages to shoot Mitchell in the back, getting him to release Austin.

"Go!" Hayden yells, pushing Liz forward.

Kingston rushes us to the window where another vampire climbs through. The shadow dwellers disappear. Mitchell snarls. Another gun goes off, this time from a human outside the window. I've never seen anything like it— the humans are with the vampires.

"Blood Rebels," Kingston whispers, reading the silent questions on my mind.

"Why are they helping us?" I ask.

"Later. No time."

Diego helps my cousins through the window where Liz guides them to a running car. Hayden follows next and extends his arm out to me. I automatically take it and drop the foot to the ground. A car peels out, driving away. Another follows suit.

"Hurry, we're losing our window," Hayden says.

Kingston slides his fingers through mine. "I never thought I'd say this, but nice work, asshole."

I blink. "You guys were working together?"

A high-pitched scream rips through the air, stopping either of them from answering. Mitchell materializes in front of us, fangs extended, silver flashing in his eyes. Diego rushes him, but he bolts out of the way.

He dodges Austin next. Kingston spins me and the world blurs. I squeeze my eyes shut, my hair blowing around me.

Sharp nails pinch my sides, and I screech as Mitchell rips me away from Kingston. Instead of fighting, Mitchell grips me tighter and runs. Kingston yells my name, and I spot my guys flying behind us from over Mitchell's shoulder.

He stops in the middle of a brightly lit street, right outside the Blood Match Center. Flipping me off him, Mitchell throws me onto the ground. Pain erupts in my back as I hit it on the curb. Shadows edge my vision, my breath hard to come by.

Mitchell drags me to my feet by my hair, and I grip onto his wrists, flailing in an attempt to break free.

"Come any closer, and I'll kill her," Mitchell says.

I don't get the chance to scream before he snarls and bites my neck.

"Don't," Kingston says. "Please."

Mitchell digs his fingers into my hair, turning my head the other way. "You deserve to watch her die."

"Just run," I whisper. "He'll kill you too."

Mitchell sinks his fangs into my throat again, sending pain shuddering through my body.

I black out.

BRAVE

"BE BRAVE, JEWEL," MY MOM whispers, combing her fingers through my hair. Sweat drenches her face, and she heaves a cough. "Your dad's going to need you to be strong."

I blink the tears from my eyes. "Don't talk like that. You're going to be fine. Donor Life Corp won't let you die. Dad will be back with the medicine soon."

She wheezes, clutching her chest. "I know, sweetie, but Dad's still going to need you. He sometimes needs to be reminded that there is more to life than the fight. I want you to remind him of that."

I sniffle. "Okay. I'll remind him."

"And I need you to remember that there is more to life

than what your vein can offer. Sometimes it's easy to just give in and give up, but don't you ever dare, no matter what."

"I don't understand," I say.

"Just be brave, Jewel. The world needs it."

"Mom?"

"Jewel." Austin's soft voice tugs me from my dream. "Jewel, wake up. Hurry."

I thrash and sit up in a dark room. "Shit balls."

"Listen to my voice. I need you to crawl to us. We only have a few minutes at most."

Instead of asking him what's going on or if everyone's okay, I crawl in the direction of his voice, my whole body aching with every move of my muscles. The icy floor sends goosebumps traveling across my skin. My hands slip across something slimy yet sticky, and I land flat on my stomach.

"Almost here," Austin says. "You're doing great. I know you hurt, but you have to push through it. Please, Jewel. Get back up."

I push myself onto my hands and knees and force my body to keep moving. Gentle hands reach for me, and I can smell Austin's blood even though it's too dark to see anything clearly. The dark room is a bunch of shadowy forms with only a tiny bit of light seeping in through a crack in the door.

Pulling me the rest of the way, Austin cradles me against him. My whole body buzzes, the scent of his blood growing stronger, and I tense, my stomach burning. I thought I hurt before, but the ache inside me can't compare to the sudden starvation blazing in my core.

"It's okay. You need to drink," he whispers, brushing my messy hair from my forehead.

Austin holds his arm to my face, and blood trickles over my bottom lip until I latch my mouth to his wrist and suck, the sweet and tangy flavor warming the ice freezing my veins. He moans softly, and I hear the click of his fangs extending.

The pain in my body lessens the longer I drink, and Austin hugs me tighter against him. "I need you to be brave, Jewel. Mitchell will be back. We're in some serious trouble."

I slowly pull away from his arm. "Where are we?"

"In a cell."

"Kingston? Diego?" I ask, my soft voice echoing around the cold room.

Austin shifts and grabs something—not something, someone—and places a large hand on mine. It's Diego's. I'd know his touch anywhere and how his hand always swallows mine with its size. "They're alive but still unconscious."

I release an uncontrollable whimper. "Oh, God. What about my cousins?"

"I don't know. Hayden took them. You were supposed to go with him."

Tears burn my eyes. "You guys should've left me." A

faint memory of Mitchell outside the Blood Match Center flits through my mind. My guys are here because of me. They couldn't leave me.

Austin snuggles me close. "Never."

"But look at us. Look where we are. I'm not worth this fate for you."

"That's not true, Jewel."

His soft voice quivers, and I feel like shit for even suggesting such a thing. Because if Austin told me that they weren't worth me, it'd break my heart. "I'm sorry," I whisper. "This just sucks. I'm scared. Kingston and Diego—"

He kisses me softly, stopping my mouth from trembling. "They'll be fine."

"They need blood," I whisper, rubbing my hand up Diego's arm. I try to pull him closer, but his heavy body doesn't budge. "Can you see them?"

"Sort of, but I don't know if you should try. You've lost a lot of blood already."

"I'll be okay. Here, bite me, but I'm going to feed them first, okay?" I reach up and press my arm to his lips.

He doesn't argue, knowing that I'm going to give them my blood regardless of how shitty I feel. Austin quickly bites down and pulls back from my arm, hitting his head against the wall in the process. It probably takes everything in him not to latch onto me, and I do my best to keep my fear in control.

I tug on Diego again, listening to Austin's rapid breathing as he attempts to get himself under control. "Can you pull Diego closer? I can't see anything." Hopefully talking to him and giving him something to do will help him stay focused on anything else besides my blood.

Austin shifts me to sit next to him before he yanks Diego's massive form up and onto my lap. "I'll hold him still. Be careful. He might bite."

I run my hand across Diego's face, feeling his closed eyes under my fingers. "Diego," I whisper. "Hey, Diego. I'm going to feed you, okay?"

I carefully touch his mouth, feeling the sharpness of his fangs as I pry his lips open.

"You have to wake up," I whisper, gently resting my bleeding arm over his mouth. "I need you. Please, wake up."

Diego groans and shifts, and Austin grips him tighter as he starts to struggle.

"Knock it off, bro. You're going to hurt Jewel."

"Diego, don't fight. It's Austin holding you," I whisper, leaning closer to his ear. "Just relax and drink. But not too much. I feel like shit."

I spot Diego's eyes flashing silver in the tiny bit of light. He gazes into my eyes, his stiff body practically melting into mine as he figures out what's going on. Combing my fingers through his hair, I cradle his head and continue to look down on him, never taking my gaze away. Diego slides his fingers around my wrist and adjusts my arm to his mouth, his warm tongue caressing over the puncture wounds. I hang my head, my hair veiling over us, and he sucks harder but not hard enough to hurt me.

"Stop," Austin whispers, touching my arm. He'll pull me away from Diego if he has to. "That's enough. Jewel still needs to help Kingston."

"And you, Austin," I murmur.

Diego sinks back into my legs, releasing my arms. "Fuck," he mutters. "How long have I been out?"

Austin pushes Diego upright. "A couple of minutes."

Wrapping his arms around me, Diego embraces me and kisses my shoulder until I caress my lips to his. "You're okay. We're okay." The words come so faintly that I know they weren't intended for me. Diego's reassuring himself.

I snuggle against his neck. "I'm a badass, remember? Now, can you reach Kingston for me? You guys are way heavier than I realized."

He hums his answer under his breath and reaches over but doesn't shift me off his lap. Diego hoists Kingston up, propping him against us. I lean over and slide my arms around Kingston and hug him, bringing my arm to his mouth.

"I swear you better not release your venom, dude," I murmur. "And if you bite, I'm going to bite you back."

I press my arm harder to his mouth, feeling my blood trickle over his lips. Kingston inhales a sharp breath and flings my arm away, sending me crashing into him.

"Kingston, you have to drink," I whisper, righting myself with Diego's help. "It's okay. It's me."

I kiss his neck softly, bringing my arm back up.

He releases a small cross between a growl and a moan. "I got enough, babe."

I frown. "You did not."

Diego chuckles. "You should thank Austin for being helpful, bro."

I nip Kingston's neck. "Seriously, dude? If it's that weird to drink from Austin's bite, then go ahead and bite me, but just so you know, I'm in pain."

Kingston shifts and pulls me to him. "Diego, feed our girl. And I swear if any of you bring this up ever again, I'll knock your fangs out."

Austin laughs. "It'll be worth it."

The softness of his voice helps push away the fear and anxiety clinging onto me. I don't know how they manage to keep their shit together, but hearing my guys tease each other, even in this crazy ass situation, gives me enough hope to believe that everything's going to be okay.

"Here, beautiful." Resting his chin on my shoulder, Diego adjusts his wrist to my lips. "Have at me."

I giggle. I can't help it. "You're ridi—"

Diego's sweet blood trickles into my mouth, cutting off my words. I graze my tongue over his puncture wounds for only a second before giving in and sucking. Kingston mutters under his breath at the murmurs escaping my mouth. He brings my arm to his mouth and quietly drinks, careful not to scratch my skin with his fangs.

"Austin, you good?" Kingston asks, easing away.

"Is it okay, Jewel?" Austin asks me.

"Mmmhmm," I murmur, warmth washing through me, feeling his lips touch my skin next.

"Here, Diego. Let me help her now," Kingston says.

This whole blood exchange should be a lot weirder than it is, but my body begs for me to give it what it needs. And my guys' blood helps me as much as my blood helps them. I just wish it wasn't in this dank cell with no clue as to what's going to happen.

Austin pulls away and presses his fingers to the bite mark he gave me, staunching the blood. He and Kingston shift closer, crowding me and Diego, and I hug the three of them in silence for a moment, just letting my mind and body catch up to each other.

"How much longer do you think we have?" Kingston asks Austin, breaking the silence.

"I don't know. A few more minutes, maybe. Mitchell promised to be back for Jewel's last breath and thought she only had minutes left," he whispers.

I frown. "What a friggin' bastard."

"That's why you're in here with us. Mitchell wanted to make sure that we saw you die," Austin says. "Part of our punishment."

I guess it's a good thing Mitchell doesn't know that I'm far stronger and more resilient than an ordinary human. But it pisses me off that he would try to punish my guys in such a cruel way—punish them at all. None of us deserve this shit. I thought Katherine was a psycho. Same goes for Orlando. But neither of them compare to the craziness that is Mitchell.

"That asshole," I say. "I'm going to kill him, you know."

Diego hugs me tighter. "We're going to have to. There's no way he's going to let all of us live otherwise."

The ding of an elevator draws our attention away from each other. I glare at the line of brightening light that comes in through a crack underneath the door. Diego gets to his feet, tugging me with him. Metal clanks, and I realize that my guys are chained to the wall.

"Jewel, go back and lie on the floor. I'll tell you when to stop," Austin says. "Stay as still as you can. He can't know that you're healing."

I breathe in a few deep breaths, my whole body trembling. "Are you sure?"

Austin kisses me. "Yes, now hurry. Five big steps straight ahead. You'll feel your blood on the floor."

Diego nudges me away before I can turn to him or Kingston, and I stride across the room until I feel the cool stickiness of blood. I drop down onto my stomach.

"Now crawl forward just a bit," Austin says. "Make it look like you were struggling."

I do as he says.

"Austin, let's see if we can rip Diego's chains from the wall first," Kingston says.

Whispering voices trickle in from somewhere outside the room, making me stiffen. Kingston and Austin make a helluva lot of noise yanking on the chains restraining Diego to the wall. They're beyond trying to hide their actions. We don't have a lot of time.

I hear the elevator ding again and then footsteps. Two sets.

"Almost there," Kingston says.

The door to the room flies open and bangs against the wall. I hold my breath and listen, struggling with the war raging inside me, part of me wanting to jump to my feet and to my guys and another part of me begging to calm the hell down, because my guys have a plan.

"Mitchell, is this all really necessary?" Viorica says, click-clacking into the room. "This kind of behavior will bring forth a lot of unnecessary speculation from the board."

"They betrayed me," Mitchell says. "They were working with rebels."

"Because you fucking left us no choice!" Kingston yells, his loud voice so full of fury unlike anything I've ever felt radiate from him. "We've been nothing but the best to you, and you lost your damn mind. Jewel was our Blood Match. You put her at risk. If you had just done things our way to begin with, we wouldn't have been in this position."

"Do not speak to me!" Mitchell roars.

"Mitchell," Viorica says. "Stop being unreasonable."

A loud slap sounds through the air, and I squeeze my eyes shut. "Shut up. I brought you here to help me punish them, not to take my traitor heirs' sides."

Viorica grunts and growls, and I listen to her take a few purposeful steps in my direction. "Touch me again, and our alliance is over. And as for Jewel, let me have her. Letting her suffer and die like this is not only cruel but a waste. I'll assure that she remains isolated in my household. Our alliance would be stronger, and no one will have to deal with the messiness of the emotions you allowed your heirs to run rampant with."

"No."

Viorica sighs. "Let me make my offer first."

"I said *no*. I've sentenced her to death. She poses too much of a risk after seeing how fiercely both my heirs and the rebels want her. I want my sons' loyalty to die with her," Mitchell snaps.

Viorica clicks her tongue. "You're a stubborn asshole and let things get too personal."

A cool hand touches my shoulder, and I try to relax as Viorica rolls me onto my back. She drags her finger across my forehead and pulls my messy hair from my face.

"Jewel," she says. "You'd have been a lovely heir."

"That's enough. Now, get over here, Viorica. I need your help with the tattoos," Mitchell says.

Confusion washes over me. What the hell is he talking about?

Kingston growls and chains rattle. "You've got to be fucking kidding me. I'd rather die than bear that mark."

A thud startles me, and I peek over to see Mitchell shoving Kingston into the wall, holding his chain up to his neck. "Dying would be an undeserved mercy, my son. I want you to suffer. I want you to regret all that you've given up for a donor."

Kingston presses against his chains. "I gave up nothing for her."

"Marking us won't change anything," Diego adds.

Austin snarls. "You're the one who threw everything away."

Mitchell ignores them and motions to Viorica. "Restrain Kingston."

Viorica blurs and appears behind Kingston, jabbing her fist into his back hard enough to drop him to his knees.

"If either of you intervenes, I'll kill him," Mitchell says.

"Fight," Kingston tells his brothers.

But Diego and Austin hesitate at the sight of the silver dagger Mitchell pulls from his bag. Kingston might say he'd rather die, but there is no way Austin and Diego will risk it. They don't want to lose Kingston as much as I don't.

Kingston snarls and flashes his fangs, causing Viorica to clutch him tighter. Mitchell pulls out a strange glass jar with a black liquid inside. I stare in shock as he dips the thin dagger into the liquid. It's then that I realize what's truly happening. Mitchell plans to painfully tattoo an outcast mark onto Kingston. I've seen shadow dwellers outside the city with them. It's a form of punishment for breaking vampire law. They're marked and thrown out until the tattoos fade. They're driven to the brink of starvation, guaranteeing they lose their civility.

Mitchell grips Kingston's hair in his hand, holding him still. Panic crashes over me, and an uncontrollable whimper escapes my mouth. Mitchell freezes and turns to face me. He flashes his fangs in a smile.

"Show your donor how brave you are, my son," Mitchell says, turning his attention back to Kingston.

Kingston tightens his jaw and glares at Mitchell. "Don't watch, Jewel."

"Request denied."

One second I'm on the floor, and in the next, Mitchell hangs me up by my hair, dangling me in front of Kingston. I screech at the shooting pain burning through my scalp, and Mitchell releases me. I hit the floor with a thud, wishing with everything inside me that I could stop myself from crying, but I'm in so much pain—my mind, my body, my blood—seeing the three guys I love, who make up my soul, trying to fight even in a moment without power, gives me more strength than ever.

I swipe my hand across my face and glare at Mitchell. "You're a monster."

He laughs, the strangled noise making me shiver. "I rather enjoy it."

Reaching for Kingston again, Mitchell grabs his hair and positions his head. Kingston closes his eyes, tensing, anticipating the torture that comes with the tattoo of an outcast mark. And I can't stand it.

"Be brave, brother," Diego says.

"Be brave," I whisper to myself. It was the words my parents always told me growing up. Be brave in a world that wants me caged. Be brave because the light will always return to push the shadows away. Be brave because it's the only thing that can't be taken from me.

I summon all my bravery and launch myself at Mitchell faster than he has a chance to react. Pain explodes in my side as he stabs the dagger into my skin. He spins and shoves me into the wall, flashing his fangs. Kingston shouts my name. Austin snarls. Diego breaks free from his restraints.

But he's too slow.

So is Mitchell.

I lock my hand into Mitchell's hair, surprising him, and jerk his head to the side. Leaning forward, I bite down as hard as I can. Mitchell yells out and thrashes, but I don't let go. I bite him again, tasting his spicy blood fill my mouth, reminding me of the time he tried to use his blood to lock my mind.

The world blurs as Mitchell tries to knock me away,

but my body reacts and grips on tighter. Something dark possesses me, and I can't stop myself. I can't yank away. Mitchell rams me toward the wall, and I lock my teeth into him, bracing myself to be squished to death by his strength, but I hit a firm chest and strong hands grab my waist.

Mitchell yells again.

Diego rips me away from Mitchell, and Austin and Kingston break free and close the space to him. Viorica stares at me with wide eyes for a moment before she disappears. Mitchell manages to shove Kingston away, but Mitchell's not fast enough to fight Austin off, and Austin shoves the same dagger he tried to tattoo Kingston and stabbed me with right into Mitchell's chest.

Mitchell thrusts himself back and disappears from the room, choosing not to fight something he knows he won't win. Diego hands me to Austin and follows Kingston out, chasing after Mitchell.

"Hang on, Jewel," Austin says, setting me on the floor.

I gasp and clutch my bloody side, fear and ice washing over me. "Shit balls. Am I going to die?"

Austin grimaces and puts pressure on my stab wound. "No. You're going to be fine. I got you."

I blink and the world shifts. I stare up at the lights moving across the ceiling. I must've passed out.

"In here," Kingston says. "We gotta be quick. The city's already going into lockdown."

"We'll hide out until dark," Diego says.

"Hey, Jewel. Look at me." Austin touches my cheek to bring my attention to him. I'm so confused. They move too fast. All I can see is the blending of light and shadow. My heart thrashes in my chest, the frantic beats the only noise I can hear apart from my guys' muffled voices.

I stare at Austin's hazy form in my blurry vision.

Austin touches the back of his hand to my forehead. "That's good. Keep looking at me."

"You're doing great, babe," Kingston says, his form materializing next to Austin's, haloed in the light stinging my eyes.

Diego squeezes my hand. "So fierce."

I open and close my mouth, trying to form words that don't come. My vision clears as Kingston swipes his fingers under my eyes. All three of my guys stare down at me with the poutiest faces I've ever seen. All I want to do is smother them with my affection and make them smile.

"Okay, done. She'll be good to go in a bit," Austin says. He trails his fingers over my jaw. "You did great, Jewel."

"Amazing," Kingston adds.

All I do is continue to blink through the pain and confusion.

Diego scoops me up and holds his arm to my mouth. "Drink some more, beautiful. We need you to be able to stay awake for a bit longer. I know you've been through a lot, but it's almost over."

"And then I'm going to treat you to the best fucking night of your life for saving me, babe," Kingston says, smiling at me. I had no idea how much I needed to see his face light up.

I release a breathless laugh, my side stinging with the movement. "Can't wait. I'm going to cuddle the hell out of all of you."

Diego smiles at me next, lifting his arm to my mouth. I drink more of Diego's blood, warmth finally blossoming in my stomach to travel down my legs and to my toes.

Kingston pets my hair. "That's it, babe."

"Do you feel well enough to stand?" Austin asks, offering me his charming smile despite the worry in his eyes.

I wiggle in Diego's arms until he sets me on my feet. I clutch onto him, my wobbly legs disagreeing with my mind for a second before I get my act together and find my balance. Austin kneels down and tugs up my shirt, checking my stomach, and I catch sight of a nasty looking gouge in my side that looks stitched up with thread.

"Try not to move around too much. I'll fix it later," Austin murmurs, tugging my shirt back down. "We need to get out of here first."

Diego keeps his hand on me, assuring I don't fall over. "And you know Dark Terrace Ranch better than us, so we need your guidance. Do you know somewhere that we can hide?"

I nod and peer around. "I think I know a place, but

you need more clothes in case. I only know the city as a donor. I've always avoided the shadows."

Kingston grimaces. "You're lucky I love you, because you're the only reason I'd ever face the sun."

PAST LIFE

"FUCK, IT'S HOT." KINGSTON CROUCHES behind me, using me as a shield.

I point. "There's an alcove twenty feet away. To the right. Security should let us in. Just don't let him get a good look at you. He won't suspect a thing."

Diego scoops me up and flies us to the entrance of Central Tower Plaza. Only a streak of shade cuts across the pavement in front of the door, and it's barely enough to shield half a body. Kingston shoves himself into the corner, pressing his face into the wall. I hold my hoodie up to help block Diego and Austin from the sun, their faces already showing a few blisters.

Pounding my finger to the security buzzer, I call for access inside. I wave at the unfamiliar security guard as he pops up from behind the desk. I frown, remembering the man Brayla and I used to call Security Steve, even though that wasn't his name. Something must've happened to him if this guy is here. Hopefully it wasn't an invasion.

The security guard picks up his radio. "Can I help you?"

"Hi, yes. I'm here to visit Mrs. Peppers on the fifth floor."

"Mrs. Peppers?" he asks.

"Yeah. Tell her Noah's daughter is here to visit."

The security guard doesn't even attempt to call Mrs. Peppers. He wouldn't this time of day. Hitting the buzzer, he unlocks the door to let me in. My guys zoom in, dragging me with them out of the blazing sun. Before the guard has a chance to even raise his gun, Diego flies at him and hoists him against the wall. The man startles, his eyes wide. The last thing he was expecting was for a vampire to rush him with the sun fully lighting the sidewalk in front of the building. If it was anyone else, the whole building wouldn't stand a chance.

"Don't fight. Don't make a sound. I'm not going to hurt you," Diego says.

The security guard slackens in his arms.

Diego's eyes flash silver. "If anyone asks, you did not see any vampires. You will forget that we're here. And when we leave, you will not react. Do you understand?"

"Yes."

Diego steals the man's gun, and I lead the way to the stairwell that'll take us up to the floor I lived on all my life before entering the Blood Match Program. Austin moves ahead of me and motions for me to hop on his back, noticing how much I'm dragging. Kingston carefully lifts me up to help me, and I rest my chin on Austin's shoulder. Now that the adrenaline has worn off, exhaustion sneaks up on me.

"Which apartment?" Diego asks, climbing the stairs two at a time ahead of us.

"5D. Right next door to my old place," I say. "Are you sure this is a good idea? You don't think Mitchell will send someone here first?"

"No, he knows if we aren't trying to leave the city, that we'll take cover and wait. He wouldn't give away his opportunity to hunt us down, but you also fucked him up pretty badly. Even he'll need time to heal," Kingston says. "We'll only stay here for a couple of hours to rest."

"I just hope we don't give Mrs. Peppers a heart attack," I murmur.

"Don't worry. I'll be fast and gentle," Diego says.

Austin sets me on my feet at the top of the landing, and I push open the heavy door and stare into the narrow, empty hallway. A dozen emotions wash over me, and I blink the tears from my eyes. I never thought I'd be back here after the day I ran from Ramona so that she couldn't stop me from making it to my appointment. But thinking back to that day, I didn't know I wouldn't have had the chance to say goodbye either. Or good riddance. Seeing the drab carpet and dirty walls makes me realize that the only reason why this place ever felt like home was because of my family. And my guys are my family now.

"This place is substandard," Kingston says from behind me.

Austin whacks him on the arm. "Shut up. Jewel grew up here."

"And I feel terrible she did."

"But it still holds sentimental value to her, so watch your mouth."

"Thanks, Austin, but it's okay. I know it's not great," I say, touching Austin's shoulder.

Kingston curls his lips and glances at me. "It's fucking awful."

Sliding past Austin and Kingston, I take Diego's proffered hand. I close my eyes and imagine the thousands of times Ramona and I raced up and down this hallway. Nothing has changed since I left. Even the same dead flowers remain in the ugly orange vase on the decorative table my mom asked my dad to build to bring hominess to the floor that everyone could enjoy.

I run my finger across the sleek, dusty wood. "My dad built this."

"Really?" Kingston asks. "Looks like he styled it after a

back-world antique."

"My great-grandfather and grandfather assured my dad would never forget the time before The Divide," I say. "You know, since vampires destroyed most references of human history."

Austin raises an eyebrow. "That's not true."

"Well, donors have limited access to it then."

Mrs. Peppers' apartment door swings open before I even have a chance to raise my hand to knock. The old woman stands in one of her familiar house dresses, and I relish in the relief flooding through me at her familiarity. She probably heard us coming from the stairwell. Mrs. Peppers' biggest thing growing up was teaching us how to be quiet as to not draw attention from shadow dwellers, even up here on the fifth floor. She probably has better hearing because of it.

"Jewel?" she asks, squinting at me. "Is that you? Come closer so I can get a better look."

"Yeah, it's me." I step toward her and let the old lady clutch my head in her hands. "Where are your glasses, Mrs. Peppers? Did you lose them again?"

She hums. "A couple weeks ago, I think. Things haven't been so easy without my little helpers around here...wait a minute. What are you doing here?"

Diego comes up behind me, drawing Mrs. Peppers' gaze to his. "Don't panic. We're not going to hurt you."

Mrs. Peppers' eyes widen, and she releases a strangled

yell, stumbling back. I rush inside her apartment with my guys right behind me. Kingston shuts and locks the door, and Diego closes the space to Mrs. Peppers again.

He holds her face in his hands. "Be quiet."

"Don't bite me!" she hollers, swinging her arm out. Mrs. Peppers surprises the hell out of all of us, slapping Diego hard enough to send his head jerking sideways.

"You said she wears glasses?" Austin asks.

I close the space to the old woman. "Yeah. She's almost completely blind without them."

"That makes things harder."

Mrs. Peppers tries to punch Diego. "Stay back!"

I touch her shoulder, getting between her and Diego. "It's okay, Mrs. Peppers. These are my matches. They won't hurt you."

She waves her finger at them. "They're vampires. It's against the law for them to be here."

Kingston crosses his arms. "Actually, it's not."

Mrs. Peppers scrambles toward her kitchen and picks up a broom. The old woman has a lot of fight in her. Austin pulls me away as Mrs. Peppers starts swinging the broom around like it could possibly stop a vampire in its tracks. Austin puffs out his bottom lip at me and shrugs. Kingston chuckles and ducks, looking amused as all get-out with his raised eyebrow. Diego just continues to massage the handprint on his cheek.

"Get out of my home," Mrs. Peppers says, rushing forward with the broom again.

Kingston lets her whack him in the arm. "We were hoping you'd allow us to stay here for a few hours."

She blanches. "What?"

"Someone find the old woman's glasses," Diego says.

Kingston tips his head back and laughs at Mrs. Peppers' attempt to stake him with the blunt broom handle. "I think she's fine without them. I can't say I've ever been attacked with a broom before."

"What if you scare her to death?" I ask, placing my hands on my hips.

He smirks. "Is that a deal breaker?"

I glare.

"She seems to be in good enough health," Austin says. "The citizens of Dark Terrace Ranch are some of the strongest."

I turn my glower on him.

"And delicious," Kingston teases.

Mrs. Peppers swings at him again.

He snatches the broom away, and she rushes toward the window.

"Kingston, the sun," Austin warns, motioning to Mrs. Peppers preparing to fling open her curtains to allow in the sunlight.

Rushing the old woman, Kingston lifts her off her feet and spins her back toward the living room. He does it so fast that Mrs. Peppers halts in confusion. It takes her a second to realize she's been relocated.

Kingston laughs again, grinning at me.

I shake my head. "Seriously?"

"Found her glasses," Austin says, closing the space to Mrs. Peppers. He slides the old woman's glasses on, and her eyes widen even more when she catches sight of him.

Kingston twirls her back around and cups her face. "Believe we're human and here for a quiet visit."

Mrs. Peppers' face softens, and she smiles at Kingston. He grins right back at her, keeping his fangs in check to play along with the mind manipulation he performed on her. I'm rather relieved he didn't ask her to sit down and be quiet, because she'd still be freaking out on the inside and unable to express it.

"Oh, Jewel. Where are my manners? I haven't even offered you something to drink. Are you hungry? I was just about to make some toast. What about your handsome friends?"

"She called me handsome," Kingston whispers to me. "Blood sucking must be her deal breaker."

"Dude." My stomach growls at the thought of food, but seeing Mrs. Peppers open a nearly empty cupboard makes me hesitate. She has already aged out of donating blood, which means that she now only gets the bare minimum to survive on, including her apartment. At least that's something. If she had children, they would be in trouble if they weren't eighteen. It's why Brayla entered the Blood

Match Program. Both her parents would have aged out, and she didn't want them to struggle with Dougie. She wanted to give them all a better life.

"I'm good, Mrs. Peppers," I say.

"I can hear your stomach growling," Kingston whispers.

"She doesn't have enough. I'm not taking anything from her."

Kingston puffs out his bottom lip. "I hate this, babe. Everything about it. I can't believe you lived like this."

I twine my fingers through his. "It's life. Can't do much about it...especially now."

He leans into me and rests his head on my shoulder. "Fuck that. As soon as we get the hell out of this city, I'm changing the world for you."

"Not for me. My world is great now."

He smirks. "We're outcasts."

I shrug. "But together."

"Such a romantic."

Nuzzling my nose to Kingston's, I take a moment just to breathe and let him hug me. Austin and Diego chat with Mrs. Peppers as she makes herself toast, and Austin brings me half a glass of water that Mrs. Peppers insists I drink.

"Jewel, you look like you've had a long night, dear. Why don't you help yourself to my bed?" Mrs. Peppers says from her tiny kitchen. "Maybe after, you can tell me all about what it's been like for you outside the city."

I bob my head. "Thanks, Mrs. Peppers. I appreciate it."

"Your dad will be so relieved that you're still safe," she adds.

Tears prickle the corners of my eyes. "Yes, he will."

If only I could be certain. It still feels like my whole world is about to explode and turn to hell.

"You should try to sleep more," Austin whispers from next to me.

"That's the last thing I want to do." I try to roll to my other side, but my tender stomach wants no part of the movement. I wince and suck in a sharp breath between my teeth.

Austin sits up, turning our blanket into a tent in the process. "Here, let me take a look."

"It's fine. Sore." I reach for him to pull him back to me, but he only gathers my hands to kiss my knuckles and eases me back.

"I swear, babe. You better not unintentionally seduce Austin. He loves playing doctor, and it feels like I'm sitting on the bed with you both," Kingston murmurs through the door. He and Diego have been taking turns resting on the couch and keeping a lookout.

I smirk at Austin. "It's going to be hard."

Austin chuckles. "Too late."

Kingston releases a throaty growl. "Damn it. Not cool."

Giggling, I reach up to play-smack Austin. "You're getting as bad as Kingston. Is that a body match thing?"

"It's a we-love-to-hear-you-laugh thing," Diego says.

Leaning down, Austin kisses my blushing cheek but pulls back before I can sneak a kiss to his mouth. He grins at me, pressing his finger to my lips, and mouths the word "later." I sigh and lean back, cringing at the stretching of my side. Austin gently tugs up the hem of my shirt and looks at his sutures.

"You're going to have a scar for a while because of the ink that the blade was coated in," he says.

I scrunch my nose.

Austin gently touches my side with his cool fingers. "Think of it as an extra spot for me to kiss, since it'll always remind me of how brave you are."

A smile lights my face at his words. That's one way to look at it. It'll be harder for me, because I'm sure the imperfection will always remind me of what an asshole Mitchell is. It'll remind me of how close we were to a fate I can't even think about.

I've been blaming my dad for screwing up my chance at forever by doing whatever the hell he did to me, but he might've saved me. If I were an ordinary human, I'd be dead. My guys would be marked outcasts, and Mitchell would continue to live his life as the Divine he thinks he is. But he has no idea. I'll use this scar to push me forward. To figure out how to change things. Change feels like the only way I'll get forever with my guys now.

Pushing the thought from my mind, I wiggle my fingers at Austin until he leans close enough for me to grab the front of his shirt. I kiss him softly, just grazing my lips to his, feeling our breaths blend and the closeness of his body until my rising anger over Mitchell subsides.

"I'm so fucking jealous right now," Kingston whispers, but his thought isn't directed at us. "I just want to get out of here."

"They should be here any minute," Diego responds, his voice as low as Kingston's.

"Who?" I ask.

Austin grazes his finger over my cheek. "Our ride."

"Who I think I hear," Kingston says. "You can go ahead and answer it, Mrs. Peppers."

Austin holds my gaze, watching me focus on what's happening in the living room. Neither of us moves to get out of bed. I'm not even sure if I can. I'm friggin' sore as hell. Footsteps shuffle around, and Mrs. Peppers' front door squeaks on its hinges.

"My girls! What a nice surprise. Jewel didn't mention you two were coming over." Mrs. Peppers' voice pulls my attention completely away from Austin. "But I don't understand. Why would your Uncle Noah allow you to come back to Dark Terrace Ranch? He worked so hard to get you out."

"Oh, Mrs. Peppers, you remember it was Jewel who

applied to Blood Match," Dana says.

"Yeah," Fallon adds. "Uncle Noah met his final dona-tion because of a stupid blood debt."

Rolling to my side, I heave a breath, attempting to push my aching body up at the sound of my cousins' voices. It's impossible to ignore the pain, but it's not as bad as it was when I first laid down. I had almost forgotten how ter-rible beds in The Boxes were. If Austin didn't know exactly how to position me to lie with him, I probably wouldn't have even gotten the little sleep I did.

"Careful, Jewel." Austin slides his arm under me and gently tugs me upright. "No need to rush. Your cousins aren't going anywhere. Promise."

I sink into him, resting my head against his chest. Purs-ing my lips, I consider asking him to carry me, but I know that if he does, it might freak my cousins out. I kind of don't want them seeing me injured like this at all.

"Fallon!" Dana's high-pitched voice echoes from un-derneath the door. "You shouldn't just go telling everyone our business."

"It's Mrs. Peppers."

"So what. We thought Mr. Diggs was our friend, too. Jewel wouldn't want us to trust anyone apart from her and her guys."

I smile at the fact that Dana calls them mine.

"Oh, dear," Mrs. Peppers says.

"It's cool, Fallon." Kingston's smooth voice cuts over

their bickering. "Mrs. Peppers will forget what you've said. Right, Mrs. Peppers."

"Right."

"And you'll forget we were ever here."

I blow out a breath and let Austin help me to my feet. He never takes his hand off me, and if I wasn't already trying to walk, I'm sure he'd just pick me up and carry me to the door. But he can see my need to pretend I don't feel like death on my feet for my cousins' sakes. There's no friggin' way I'll ever tell them what we went through either. I've already messed up enough by dragging them around with me. All I ever wanted was for them to grow up and have a life without the same fears as the general population, but obviously, as long as Donor Life Corp is in charge, I'll never get that for them.

"How did my cousins know where to find us?" I ask. I've never been so thankful to hear them arguing in my life. I was so scared something terrible happened to them.

Austin strolls next to me, keeping with my slow pace. "Kingston used the phone Brayla gave you while you were sleeping."

"What?" I ask.

"Mmmhmm."

I stop in place and glance at him, waiting for him to answer with more than a noise. His jaw tightens, and he looks to the door again like Kingston will intervene with his reason for calling the person I want nothing to do with. But if Kingston hears us, he refrains from answering. Diego too.

"Just mmmhmm?"

He bobs his head. "For now."

I crinkle my nose and rush forward, shoving the door open. It hits something solid, and Kingston peeks his head in but doesn't move out of the way to let me out.

"Babe, you look like you need to lie back down," he says, giving me a once-over. "We still have a couple of minutes."

I push my hands against the door, but it doesn't budge. "What are you trying to hide from me?"

"Nothing. It's all good. Just hanging out with your cousins until the sun disappears enough to get to where we're going."

I lean my weight against the door, making Kingston shift a bit. "And where's that?"

"Do you think she's going to be upset or pissed when she finds out?" Dana whispers.

"Mad at what?" I ask.

"Shhh!" Fallon hisses.

Dana groans. "Jeez, I thought I was being quiet."

This time, I ram my shoulder into the door, knocking Kingston enough to move. Austin stops me from falling flat on my face, and I groan and clutch my side. My cousins close the space to me but keep their hands to themselves when Austin holds up his palm.

"She's hurt," he says to them.

"I'm fine," I snap. I turn my attention to my cousins. "Wait, are you two here alone?"

They shake their heads. "Liz is in the lobby with Hayden, Berto, and Raul."

"So they're all okay?" I ask.

Fallon nods. "Yeah, it was a little scary spending the day in a shadow—"

"What!" My voice booms so loudly that all of Dark Terrace Ranch probably heard me.

Dana backhands her sister's good arm. "There was only one vampire, and he didn't even have fangs."

I swing my head to glance at my guys. "No fangs?"

Diego shrugs. "It happens."

"He was a little weird, but nothing like the shadow monsters on Starlight Row."

"Because he was a Blood Rebel. Can you believe it? All he required was a little blood for protection."

"What?" I gawk at my cousins, searching every inch of their arms and necks for signs of bites.

"Not us. Hayden," Dana says.

I blink and cover my hands with my face. "I'm so confused."

Austin must sense I'm going to pass out, because he swipes my legs out from under me and cradles me against his chest, careful not to touch my aching wound. Diego and Kingston close the space to us, and they smother me in the best possible way with their closeness.

"Just take a breath, babe. No need to stress out. We've got it under control," Kingston says, brushing his lips to my temple.

"We're going to owe Hayden too much. I don't like this," I say. "There's no way in hell that I'm trading myself for Ramona."

"Damn straight," Kingston says.

"So then what?"

The three of them look at each other and then to me.

"You promised me no more secrets."

Austin sighs, breaking first. "It's complicated, but just know that you don't have to worry about yourself. We have it handled. All debts will be paid by us."

"What's that supposed to mean?"

Diego presses his lips into a line. "Looks like we're going to prove Mitchell's fear right."

I study each of their faces. "You mean...?"

Kingston nods his head once. "We're officially Blood Rebels."

BLOOD REBELS

"NOPE. NOT HAPPENING," I SAY, stepping back into Diego's arms. "I'd rather risk running the streets and hopping the wall."

"With your cousins?" Kingston asks. "We'd never make it."

I nudge Kingston's shoulder. "Come on, dude. You guys are the most powerful vampires I know."

"Completely true, but we're tired as hell. You're injured. Your cousins don't want to even walk on their own, and I'm not in the mood to carry anyone but you around. It's just a car ride."

"Would you feel better if I let one of your boy-toys drive?" Brayla asks, swinging the door open. "Because I don't mind."

"Dibs." Diego strides forward, forcing me to go with him. "I'll have us out of the city fast."

I stretch my arms and stop him from nudging me inside. "Diego."

Kingston slides his fingers up my sides, tickling me in the process. I jerk my elbows back, and he chuckles and catches both my arms. Leaning against me, he nuzzles his nose to my neck and kisses my sensitive skin.

"Stop being a brat, babe. Get in. You can ride on my lap," he murmurs. "I need your affection. Like bad. Look at that awesome third row. I never liked them until this second."

Austin nudges my cousins into the car and helps them fasten their seatbelt restraints. Brayla slides into the front seat next to Diego, and Kingston tilts his head and smirks at me expectantly.

"While I won't leave your stubborn, sexy ass behind, Diego might because he gives me way too much credit to take care of you and will murder me if I don't, so..."

I sigh and get in. "I highly doubt that's true but okay."

Kingston chuckles and adjusts the seat in front of us before pulling me onto his lap even though there is room for me to sit next to him. Austin gets in last, and Diego takes off without giving him the chance to strap in.

Silence fills the car, and Diego braves driving right down Starlight Row. Streaks of lights zoom by the faster we speed. Kingston holds me tightly but doesn't squish me against him, even when a shadow dweller slams their hands against the window.

"Turn left at the next alley," Brayla says.

Fear sneaks up on me. "Don't."

Diego peers at me in the rearview mirror. "What's wrong?"

"I don't know. I have a bad feeling."

Brayla twists in the seat. "Then go straight."

I furrow my brows. "Really?"

She shrugs. "Human instincts tend to be accurate toward vampire threats. You look freaked the hell out, and your cousins are paralyzed with fear. So yes, really. We'll take another route." Her voice comes out too soft for human ears to hear, and I try not to react. Brayla knows about me. She knows I'm different. Now, she's being obvious to the fact.

Shifting forward, I hang my arms over the seat to hug my cousins. "You girls okay?"

Dana nods. "Yea-a-a-a-h-h-h!"

Fallon screams with her sister and points out the windshield. Kingston hooks his hands to my chest, and Austin holds his arm out across my cousins even though they're securely buckled in.

The headlights illuminate a dozen silver eyes in front of us. Diego stomps the throttle, sending the van jerking forward faster. He grips the wheel and doesn't stop. Kingston tries to pull me back in the seat, but my fingers refuse to let go of my cousins.

"Hang on," Diego says, tapping a few buttons on the dash.

The headlights brighten more, and a few vampires shield their eyes. Some scatter. Jerking the wheel, Diego fishtails and skids the vehicle to the right, plowing into the shadow dwellers that try to flee. A body hits the windshield and thunks over the roof. I turn my head to peer over my shoulder, but the vampire never falls.

A bloody hand slaps the rear window.

"Looks like we got a hitchhiker," Kingston says, glaring at the hand.

The dirty fingers scratch at the glass so hard that the vampire leaves streaks of blood. Something weird comes over me, and I peel away from my cousins. Reaching out my hand, I draw my finger over the blood like it's the most fascinating thing in the world.

"Babe," Kingston whispers. "You're acting weird."

"I—"

Two silver eyes flash in front of me, startling me. Swinging my arm back, I punch the window so hard that my hand breaks through it. My fist rams into the shadow dweller's nose, and he releases a scary ass growl, latching his fingers to my wrist in an attempt to drag me closer.

I screech, yanking my hand back, but my weird ass strength vanishes at the wave of panic crashing over me.

Kingston rips at the fissured glass and shoves his hand between my wrist and the vampire's mouth all while still holding onto me.

Kingston snarls as the vampire bites him. "Hit him again, babe. As hard as you can."

I jab my fist into the vampire's nose, and he releases my wrist. Kingston slides his arm in front of me and knocks me away from the window. Austin's strong arms envelop me and pull me to the middle seat. He brings his hand up to my face in an attempt to cover my eyes, but he's not faster than Kingston, who stabs the vampire with the same dagger Mitchell jammed into me. The same one Mitchell wanted to use to crudely tattoo an outcast mark on Kingston's forehead.

Kingston slides his arm out through the gaping hole in the fissured window, barely held together with the dark film of the window tint, and hooks his fingers to the vampire's shirt. He drags him off the car and lets him fall to the asphalt.

"Austin, swap places. I'm hurt," Kingston says, waving his bloody hand.

My cousins whimper from next to me, and I slide my arm behind them in an attempt to hug them close. Dana shoves herself closer, staying as far from the window as possible. If she wasn't restrained in, she'd probably hide on the floor.

Climbing over the seat, Austin switches places with

Kingston to guard the broken window. Kingston cradles his hand against his chest, using his jacket to staunch the bleeding. The second the sweet scent trickles to my nose, hunger burns through me.

"Someone grab Jewel," Kingston says, shifting away from me.

A cold hand grabs my shoulder, and someone snarls and growls, releasing the freakiest noise I've ever heard.

"What's w-wrong with h-her?" Dana asks, her voice squeaking.

I slap my hand over my mouth, realizing that intimidating, monstrous sound totally came from me. "Shit balls. I'm sorry." I inhale a few deep breaths, trying not to stare at Kingston's blood. "Kingston, your blood..."

"Smells delicious as hell?" he asks, daring to reach out to touch my cheek with his clean hand.

I frown, tears burning my eyes. "I'm sorry."

Kingston's amusement vanishes, replaced by his pouty face. "Whoa, hey. None of that boner killer bullshit. You're good, babe. Hot as fuck. But as much as I love how sexy you are with that look of wanting to devour me, you also look bitey as hell." He snaps his teeth at me, trying to make light of the strange situation.

"Seriously, Kingston?" Diego says. His fingers ease off my shoulder, and he tucks my hair behind my ear. "I thought Jewel was going to try to fly out the window or something."

"She did kind of look like she was going to," Brayla says, darting her gaze from the road in front of us and to me. "Even if she wasn't, can you blame your brother for freaking out and being scared of her teeth? I'm still healing."

Heat floods my face. "I wouldn't bite Kingston."

"And you deserved her savagery. Now, shut up. You're embarrassing, Jewel," Kingston says, flashing his fangs at Brayla. "Only I can do that."

Brayla flashes her fangs right back at him. "Watch it. You're not in control where I'm taking you. Your name no longer carries the power it used to."

I gape at the two of them in shock. Resting my head against the window, I hug myself, silently hoping they don't start physically fighting in the car with my cousins...who now sit in the very back with Austin. I didn't even see him move them, but they sink against him, hugging him because they know he'll protect them.

"Please, stop." My voice barely comes out a whisper.

"Our name doesn't need to carry power. We were turned with it," Kingston snaps at Brayla.

She hisses, sounding a whole lot like a Vaduva. "And so was I. You have no idea what you're even dealing with."

Kingston leans forward, getting closer to her. "Oh, we know. I've been around a long fucking time, Brayla. I didn't survive as a Divine because of sheer luck."

"You sure about that?"

"Enough!" I yell, balling my hands into fists.

Everyone stares at me, and I realize Kingston's not the only one bleeding. The glass of the broken window cut through my sleeve and scratched me. And hell, does it get even more intense. Hungry vampires are easily irritable, and the scent of my blood probably isn't helping.

"I can't stand everyone fighting right now," I say, closing my eyes. "I just need everyone to chill."

Kingston slides across the seat. "Sorry, babe. I'm just so—"

"Hungry? Pissed off? Feeling murderous?" I ask. "Because same, dude."

"Come here, Jewel." Pulling me onto his lap, he shifts me sideways to stretch my legs across the seat. "You need a hug."

I release a cross between a groan and a laugh. "What I need is to get out of this friggin' city."

"Five more minutes," Diego says.

I rest my head on Kingston's chest and peer out the windshield at the huge wall of the city looming in front of us.

"We just have to get through the guards, and we'll be good to go," Diego adds.

"What?" I ask.

Kingston squeezes me tight. "Don't worry, babe. It'll be—"

The car jerks right, the world spinning impossibly fast around us. My cousins scream, their terrified shrieks stinging my eardrums. Diego hits a few buttons, turning back on the autopilot and sensors, and the van screeches to a stop a foot away from a cement block wall of the last tower before reaching the road that leads through the vampire guarded gate.

"Kingston, take Jewel. I'll take the girls," Diego says.

"Brayla, I hope you know how to fight," Austin says.

She flashes her fangs. "I hope you can keep up so I'm not doing all the work."

The two of them disappear from the van, and Kingston carries me out with him. We wait for Diego to pry my cousins from the vehicle. Dana grips his neck, riding on his back, and he carries Fallon in front. If they didn't look ready to cry, I might laugh at the sight. Diego looks ginormous compared to their small frames. I'm glad it's him carrying them. Kingston would probably complain about them crying or accidentally snotting on him.

"Ready?" Kingston asks. "You lead. I'll watch your back."

Diego nods. "Don't fight unless you have to. Let's just run."

"That was the plan."

Kingston adjusts me in his arms so that I can wrap my legs around his waist and my arms under his and across his muscular back. If he wasn't afraid of someone trying to grab me, he'd put me on his back and keep his front free, but we can hear at least a dozen growls already.

"Go! Go! Go!" Austin yells. "There's a bounty on us."

"Fucking A. Damn we underestimated Mitchell," Kingston says.

Diego zooms ahead of us, but Kingston keeps right on his back. "Or he's still too hurt from Jewel."

"I friggin' hope so," I mutter.

Two vampires fly toward us, and Diego spins and kicks, sending one crashing into the street. The other one dodges him and rushes us. I jerk my head and hide my face in the crook of Kingston's throat. A guttural scream rips through the air, and something splatters across us. Deep ruby liquid streams down Kingston's jaw, and I inhale a breath, making him suck in his own.

Kingston digs his fingers into my back. "Try not to bite me."

"Maybe you shouldn't cover yourself in vampire blood and tempt me so much then. You're making me hungry. I just want to lick you," I tease, sniffing his neck like all the times he joked about me making him starved.

He releases a soft purr. "Not the time, babe."

"It's always the time."

"You better save this dirty talk and role playing for later."

I kiss his neck, regretting the action immediately as a few drops of blood coat my lips. The strange taste isn't anything like my guys' blood, but it's not bad either. And that freaks me the eff out. Can't my body understand that I'm not a match against vampires? I'm not a predator. I'm like a friggin' mouse who realizes it must eat a cat. This shit doesn't work. My dad must've known it, and that's why he made a deal with Orlando in the first place. But he should've told me. Someone should've told me.

"Whoa, fuck," Kingston says, his breath turning ragged in my ear. "Austin, take her. I can't concentrate."

The world spins, and I screech only to have Austin kiss away the noise. I whip my head toward Kingston, and he bolts ahead to punch his hand right into the back of a roaring vampire grabbing Brayla by the hair.

Austin cradles my head to his chest. "You're making Kingston nervous."

"Not nervous. Horny as fuck," he calls. "I want that sexy mouth of hers to give me hickies like that everywhere. Just not now when I can't return the favor."

I bring my hand up to my lips. Was I seriously sucking his neck? What the actual hell? I'm getting out of control.

"It's okay, Jewel. We're going to figure this out," Austin says, adjusting me in his arms to get me to hug him with my arms and legs.

"I'm getting worse."

"You're just hungry and tired. Kind of all over the place."

"You sure it's that?"

"Mmmhmm."

Another yell cuts through the air, and Austin skids to a

halt. Kingston and Brayla tense in front of us, and Diego releases a scary growl from right behind us. Neither of my cousins makes a sound. But it sure seems like the rest of Dark Terrace Ranch does.

"Shit. There are too many," Kingston mutters. "We should take cover and try again at dawn. It might be the only time."

Austin shifts to peer around. "Mitchell will have had too much time to strategize."

"I'm not sure we could even make it." Diego comes up next to me, and my cousins snuggle against him with their eyes closed, though I know they're listening. He probably told them not to look. Obviously, they're far better at listening and taking instructions than I am.

Kingston cracks his knuckles. "Guess we're going to die trying."

"Jewel, I'm going to need you to back me up," Austin says, setting me on my feet.

"Here, beautiful. Take my knife," Diego says, shifting to show me the nearly invisible built-in sheath. I always knew my guys carried concealed weapons, but they're usually so fast and infrequent to use them, that I never pay much attention.

"You sure you don't want me to take my cousins?" I can't exactly carry them, but I can hold their hands.

He shakes his head. "Nope. Just back Austin up. Remember what we showed you."

Austin links his fingers through mine and flies me forward with him. Spinning, he uses one of mine and Diego's favorite moves and swings me out, using me to knock a few vampires off their feet. They tumble into the street and disappear the second they manage to get themselves up.

"Jewel, stab right," Austin commands.

I jerk my arm up and the first female vampire I've seen tonight apart from Brayla runs right into my blade. She snarls, snapping her teeth at me, and I sucker punch her in the face. My hand screams in pain, but I whack her again, sending her dirty, tangled hair splaying across her face. She swipes her hand out at me, but Austin blocks her for me and twirls me out of the way. She releases a guttural sound from her throat, snapping her teeth. Another vampire grabs Austin by the shoulders, trying to rip us apart.

Austin elbows the guy so hard in the nose that his blood splatters across me and in my eyes. I blink through my blurry vision, swinging out my arm, trying to keep the vampires back. Sharp nails dig into my wrist, and the female vampire drags me closer. Austin blocks her gnashing fangs with his arm, taking a deep bite from her in the process.

I lock my fingers into her hair, surprising the hell out of her by biting her. I yank away to avoid getting a mouthful of her sour smelling blood, and Austin manages to knock two other vampires into her.

But they just keep coming.

There are too many of them.

"Keep up, Jewel," Austin says. "The wall's up ahead. Almost there."

Gunshots ring through the air, and I flinch and cover my ears at the startling noise. A few vampires scream, and the crowd of shadow dwellers starts to disperse. An explosion booms, rattling the whole world. The blast knocks me off my feet, and Austin twists to take the brunt of our fall.

My head spins as a dust cloud engulfs us. Dozens of bodies lie on the ground around us. I can't hear anything over the ringing in my ears. I search the area, catching sight of Diego shielding my cousins. Kingston already shoves himself back to his feet. He waves his hand at me, saying something I can't hear.

Austin pushes my back, struggling to get us to our feet. "Hurry. Get up. Run."

My muscles scream, my head and heart pounding. Shadows crowd my vision. I just can't get my body to work.

"Jewel," a whispered voice says to me. "Take my hand."

"Go," Austin says, nudging me. "It's okay. Go."

I blink a few dozen times, staring into Orlando's startling blue eyes. "I'm scared."

Austin picks me up from under my arms and holds me out to Orlando. "Jewel, I'm going to be right behind you, okay?"

"We're right here, babe," Kingston adds.

I close my eyes and extend my arms to Orlando.

He hugs me against him. "I was quite surprised by your

call."

"My call? I'd never call you."

Orlando shifts me in his arms. "You didn't tell her?"

I frown. "Tell me what?"

Orlando smiles at me. "No time now. But I'm thrilled to finally take you home."

THE CHOICE

I SIT ON THE EDGE of the surprisingly comfortable bed in a room I can't help but love. And I hate that I love everything about it. The soft green bedding that matches Austin's eyes. The mountain of pillows I've arranged into a sitting area. The cream colored walls with flecks of gold glitter embedded into the paint. How they sparkle under the crystal chandelier that casts fractals of rainbow light across the plush white carpet. On an ornate table, three vases bloom with rainbow bouquets of the most fragrant flowers. It's perfect.

A projector screen lights up the far wall to display hundreds of movie posters of all my favorite classics. Old books line a corner shelf next to a desk with a dozen framed pictures of my whole family—even some of my ancestors from before The Divide. On the night table next to my bed sits a framed picture of Diego, Austin, and Kingston with their arms around each other, dressed in their finest tuxedos. They look exactly the same as they do now, but the picture was taken before I entered their lives. How Orlando got it? No friggin' idea. But I love it. I love that it's here.

A light tap on the door draws my attention from the photo. "Jewel, can I come in?"

"Yeah, Diego," I manage to say, my voice still hoarse from screaming. From the smoke of the explosive that took down part of the massive wall surrounding Dark Terrace Ranch. From crying the whole way to what's supposedly going to be my new home. I've been a real mess.

The door swings open, and Diego hesitates a moment, trailing his gaze from my eyes down the length of my body. I force myself to smile and motion for him to come in. I don't know how long I've been alone in this room, but it couldn't have been more than an hour. It feels like eternity has passed by, though. I'm still not used to being alone. I don't think I'll ever be.

"You're not dressed yet." Diego peers around the hallway and enters my room, closing the door behind him.

I tug on the hem of my towel. "Nope."

"Do you want me to help you pick out something to wear?"

I shake my head. "Nope. I'm not in the mood to leave

this room right now."

Diego rubs his lips together, trying to hide the frown marring his face. Combing his fingers through his brown hair, he pushes the loose strands back, making them stick up in the process. He opens and closes his mouth like he wants to say something, but instead he just waits for me to guide him as to what I want and need. Straightening his shoulders, he tightens his jaw, and I purse my lips because he looks ready for me to send him away.

"What's with all this space?" I ask him, smiling for real when he graces me with a grin that makes everything feel normal. I motion for him to sit beside me, and he strides closer and plops down. The bed shifts under his weight, sending me sinking against him, and I slide my legs over his and hug him.

He twines his fingers through mine. "Sorry, beautiful. I didn't mean to make things weird. It's just—"

"Things *are* weird," I say, cutting him off. "I have my own room. You guys left me alone for an hour. No one has told me what the plan is or how long we're staying. Or what happens next."

Diego's smile falters. "You have a lot of questions."

I groan. "I always have a lot of questions."

"And I want to answer them, I do, but..."

I puff out air through my lips. "Orlando won't let you? Are we prisoners? Is this—"

He shakes his head to stop me from thinking of all the

worst case scenarios. "No, I just don't have all the answers yet. Orlando wants to talk to you first before anything is set."

"I don't want to," I say.

"And none of us are going to make you. Not after everything." Diego brings my hands up to his mouth and kisses the backs of each of them.

"So it's my choice?" I ask.

"Mmmhmm," he murmurs. "Whenever you're ready. Whatever you want."

I bob my head and smile. "Whatever I want, huh?"

"Within reason. I can't run away with you."

I laugh. "Do I look like Kingston?"

"No, definitely not, but you sometimes sound like him," he says, chuckling.

"Is that good or bad?"

"Depends."

Sliding my hands around his neck, I pull him closer so that I can whisper in his ear. "What if I told you I'm starved?"

He turns his face to me, meeting my gaze. "In what way?"

I bite my bottom lip, smiling. "Want to find out?"

Diego raises his eyebrows and laughs again, bobbing his head. "You always surprise me, beautiful. I was fully prepared to—"

I cut off his words with a kiss. "I'm okay. This wasn't

how I expected things to turn out, but it is what it is. I don't care as long as you guys are safe and fed and happy. As long as my family is good, I'm good."

"We're good," he murmurs into my lips. "But I want you to be better than just okay, Jewel."

I slide into his lap. "This is a great start."

Diego reacts to my affection with furious passion that sets off my own desire in waves. I don't know if it's because of all the bullshit and upheaval in our lives turning the both of us so desperate for each other's touch, but it feels like nothing in the universe matters. As long as I can feel Diego's hands roaming over my body, the heat of his mouth blazing tingles over my skin, and how nothing seems important compared to just being together in a way that leaves me feeling so incredibly hot and perfect, my life will be exactly how I want it.

Slipping my hands under the hem of his shirt, I yank it over his head and bring my mouth to his shoulder, kissing and licking my way back up his neck to suck his bottom lip between my teeth. His excitement presses between my legs, teasing me with every shift and movement of my body but neither of us rushes, taking the time to explore and taste and enjoy our kiss.

Diego trails his fingers through my hair, pushing it over my shoulder. I let my towel drop, and he leans back, panting, taking a moment to drink me in. He shifts me off of him and onto the bed, grazing his hands over the curves of my breasts, working his way down like he's memorizing every inch of me with his fingers. I stay utterly still, blush warming my chest and throat while goosebumps and tingles make me squirm under his intensity.

He leans down to kiss my flushing skin, grazing his lips over my fading bruises, his kisses truly making the aches disappear. I reach up and grab at the waist of his pants and unclasp the button. I lick my lips, trailing my gaze over his muscular body, feeling a teensy bit nervous all over again. My heart thrashes against my ribcage with my quick breathing. It feels like forever since I've been intimate with Diego, but everything about this moment is just as exciting.

Diego completely undresses and joins me on the bed, pulling the covers around us. He takes his time kissing and teasing me, working me up so much that I can't stop shifting and moving, arching my body to his and making him moan against my skin.

I mold my lips to his and slip my tongue into his mouth, caressing mine over his until he aligns our bodies perfectly. My body buzzes all over, desire and need making me crave Diego in the same way he craves me. We moan into each other's mouths as he pulls me by my ass to sink into me completely.

Sliding my hands over his sides, I clutch onto his back, savoring every kiss and touch, every tingle and sensation that explodes through me, leaving me gasping and shuddering beneath him. Diego smiles with his eyes closed. He sucks in his bottom lip, his face scrunching, and he kisses me a dozen times, slowing with his release.

"Jewel, I love you," he says, my name sounding breathless and sexy, like a whispered plea against my mouth. "More than anything."

I kiss him again and relax under his weight, relishing every bit of his closeness and ability to be strong yet gentle with me under him. "I love you too. You're everything to me. I can't imagine my life without you."

"You'll never have to."

"Promise?" I can't stop the worry from softening my voice.

"Promise. Just because we're no longer Divines doesn't mean I'm not vowing you my forever."

"It's all I want. Always."

"Always," he murmurs, brushing my hair behind my ears. "We'll do whatever it takes."

"I will too," I say, hugging him.

A strange look crosses his face like my words worry him. I don't pry him about it, though. He looks like he could use a dozen more kisses and cuddles, which I gladly give him. If it weren't for the soft footsteps sounding from somewhere outside my room, I'd remain cradled against Diego's side.

He's quick to get his pants on, and I laugh and spin, sliding into his shirt to cover up the pair of underwear I shimmy on from the drawer even though hundreds of outfits hang neatly in the walk-in closet.

"You had one job, Diego. You're so lucky I love the sound of Jewel laughing like a maniac, or I'd be pissed as hell right now," Kingston says through the door. "Now I'm just jealous."

I dance my way to the door, smiling at Diego, and he remains shirtless on the bed, leaning back on his elbows. "You can't come in unless you have food," I tease.

"I am your food," Kingston says, tapping his finger on the door.

My bottom lip puffs out at his teasing.

Diego throws a pillow at the door, closing it at the same time Kingston tries to open it. "Jewel wants something hot and solid."

Kingston pushes open the door again. "That can be me too."

Austin holds a tray in his hands, entering the room after Kingston. "Fortunately for you, I figured you might not want that, so I made you a few of your favorites."

I laugh while Kingston glares and shuts the door behind Austin. The two of them cross the room, trying to be sneaky as they look at me and Diego. There's no denying that we had sex, but neither of them say anything, though Kingston looks like he really, really wants to. Diego motions for me to return to him, and I take my spot on his lap. Austin sits next to us while Kingston pulls out the chair from the sleek vanity table filled with all sorts of glass bottles that sparkle in the light.

"How does your side feel?" Austin asks, handing the tray of breakfast foods to Kingston to prop on his knees.

I eye the food without looking up. "It doesn't hurt."

Kingston cuts a piece of the berry crepes with the fork and smiles as some of the sauce drips on my chin. Diego chuckles and swipes it with his finger, flicking it across his brother's face. I snort and nearly choke, making Kingston laugh instead of trying to punch Diego.

Austin shifts closer, vying for my attention. I know he wants to examine me to make sure I'm not lying, but the food screams my name. "Mind if I look at it?" he finally asks.

"Only if it doesn't require me to stop eating," I murmur through another mouthful.

Kingston already holds the next forkful in anticipation, not letting me take the utensil from him. "Yeah, bro. I need our girl's stomach to shut the fuck up and stop growling like I'm next."

Diego tips his head back and howls a laugh. My cheeks burn so hotly that I'm sure my face will explode into flames any second. Austin whacks Kingston, knocking the plate off in the process. Diego catches it and grins at me, ready to feed me next.

I shift and narrow my eyes at Austin. "You got lucky, because if that hit the floor, you would be next," I tease.

Kingston groans. "When you say it like that—"

Austin swats him again but keeps his smile for me. "So can I look?"

I scrunch my nose. "Fine, but no one better react."

Diego kisses my shoulder through his shirt. "Even your battle scars are beautiful, Jewel. So don't worry."

I smirk at him, his words making me feel tons better. I just can't help feeling self-conscious over the dumb scar that'll remind me for who knows how long of what Mitchell did to me. What he tried to do to my guys.

Austin touches the button on my shirt and waits for me to unfasten it enough to bare my side to him. Kneeling in front of me, he leans in to get a better look, making sure the synthetic skin he applied after removing the sutures still remains in place.

"Looks gross," I say, turning my gaze away.

"Not as gross as this." Austin rolls up his sleeve to show me the most disgusting bite mark I've seen in my life.

I press my lips together, trying not to react, and then I shudder and groan. "Whoa."

"Show her yours, Kingston," Diego says, elbowing his brother.

Kingston grimaces and whips his head back and forth, twisting away before Diego can grab onto him. "Repulsing Jewel is on my never-gonna-happen list."

I link my fingers through Austin's. "Not necessarily repulsed but...ouch."

"Vampire venom," he says. "It does more than transform humans. Hurts like hell, even to us."

"Do you need my blood? It's been a while."

Austin shakes his head. "Maybe in a bit. Your body has been through a lot of trauma, and I want to do some blood work."

"Plus, we came to an agreement with Orlando," Kingston murmurs.

I jerk my attention to him. "You what?"

Kingston sighs, combing his fingers through his hair. "It's not a big deal. We just...you can't be our exclusive blood source."

"And why not?"

Kingston takes my hand. "This is Orlando's region. His rules. We haven't gotten much into things, because we know you'd want to be included."

"And we're not in a huge hurry, beautiful," Diego says. "Whenever you're ready—"

I slide off his lap and get to my feet. "I'm ready now."

Strutting to the closet, I shimmy into some dark jeans and tie up Diego's shirt, not even bothering to change it. I comb my fingers through my hair and tie it in a knotted bun on top of my head and glance in the mirror once. I look a complete disaster, but I don't give a shit. I'm not wasting another minute and allowing Orlando to suddenly think he gets to control my life. Screw that.

Austin blocks my way out. "Jewel, you should rest for a bit more."

I poke his chest. "I'll rest once I find that asshole and set things straight."

Kingston releases a quiet chuckle and clears his throat to suppress it. "Want a weapon or something, babe? It might help."

I swivel on my feet and hold out my hand. "Actually, yes."

"Kingston, don't instigate her," Diego says, socking him hard enough to send him falling off the bed only to land in a crouch on the floor.

I tap my foot. "Weapon, now."

Kingston purrs deep in his throat and materializes in front of me to hand me a silver dagger from his jacket. "Command me to do something else. It's so hot."

I shake my head and roll my eyes. "Stay here."

He slides past me and out of the room to walk backwards. "Not happening."

"Then back me up." I turn and look at Diego and Austin. "You guys, too."

"So hot," Kingston whispers again, looking at his brothers behind me.

I stroll down the narrow hallway with no idea of where I'm going. The last time I was here at the Shadow Crest Villa in Ombre Noire, I basically ran in circles, trying not to fall through windows in the floor. But now, I'm in a completely different part of the gaudy, grand death-trap of a mansion.

"You have no idea where you're heading," Kingston says, smirking at me.

I shrug. "Nope. I figured that if I were heading somewhere I shouldn't be, you'd let me know."

"Maybe."

Obviously, none of them wants me to confront Orlando, but they know that I'm going to do so anyway. They're just not going to help.

"Or not."

I spin away from Kingston and face Diego and Austin. They stop in their tracks, and Kingston comes up right behind me. The three of them trap me between their muscular bodies, and I can't even shift my feet without touching one of them.

"One of you better just take me to Orlando or I'm going to yell until he shows up," I say.

"And bring every vampire on the premises into our wing?" Diego asks.

Austin motions behind him. "You know your cousins are three rooms that way still fast asleep."

Kingston hangs his arms around my shoulders. "Not to mention Liz is probably aiming her gun at her door too. I'd prefer none of us gets shot because she doesn't trust that she's safe here...which she shouldn't."

I sigh. "If you don't want me to confront him, just say so."

The three of them look at each other in consideration.

"It's not that we don't want to..." Austin's voice trails off.

Kingston groans low in his throat. "I fucking don't unless she charges at him with that blade."

Diego squeezes my hand. "Jewel, we just...this is new to us."

"It's new to me too."

Austin steps closer, linking his fingers to my free hand. "And we worry."

"Things are changing," Kingston says, digging his chin into my shoulder so that I can't meet his gaze. "Whether it's good or bad...well, I guess we'll find out. But first—"

I huff a breath through my nose. "Dealing with Orlando. So will you guys just take me already, before I lose my nerve?"

Austin nods and tugs me with him, taking initiative to lead the way. I trail between my guys, letting them practically smother me with their closeness, but I know none of them can help it. We don't know this place well. We don't know exactly what we've gotten ourselves into. All I know is that Orlando got us out of the city, and I'm sure he's going to expect payment in one form or another.

Vampires don't do things out of kindness. They're strategic. I should know. My guys constantly strategize when it comes to our lives. They've been doing so long before me under Mitchell and then with me after we agreed to be together.

Voices sound from behind several closed doors as we make our way to a scary old elevator I'm not sure I want to risk getting on. But Diego manually slides the cage-like door open and we all enter together.

Kingston nudges me to the back of the elevator and rests his hand on the wall above my head. "Babe, there are a few things you should know before you step out of here."

I gaze into his midnight eyes and peer past him at Diego and Austin guarding the door. The elevator comes to a halt, but none of us moves to get out. "Only a few things, huh?"

He licks his lips. "Whatever happens now, we will still be here for you no matter what."

I frown. "Yeah, I was kind of hoping that."

"And we know that you love us," Diego adds.

"Of course I do."

Austin slides closer. "But we also know that things are changing, and you do things because you feel like you have to. You always put others before yourself. And that's okay."

"Okay...why are you guys saying this?" Because even though they're assuring me for whatever reason they think they have to, it's freaking me the hell out.

"Jewel, you have history with Orlando, and none of us really know to what extent," Kingston finally says.

"Oh." I haven't even thought about that. All I know is what I know now, and I'm confused.

The three of them hug me. "We just don't want you to

stress out or feel guilty for anything."

I bob my head because I don't know what else to do. I squeeze them tighter and kiss each of them, letting them pull back on their own when they're ready. I shift on my feet, peering out the gated door of the elevator and try to listen for sounds of life, but we're still alone.

Diego slides open the gate and peers into the dimly lit hallway. Dark walls and wooden floors with red runners lead to another portion of the estate I haven't been to.

"Let one of us go ahead," Kingston says, locking his fingers through mine.

"No."

Austin tries to slow me down. "It's better to announce our arrivals in case."

"No," I repeat. "I'm sure he'll hear us coming."

Diego leads the way to a set of dark stairs that leads up in this maze of a mansion. Soft music hums through the air, growing louder as I reach the landing and peer around a half windowed hallway with a view of the sprawling lawns completely shaded by the tall cliff.

Raising his hand, Austin motions to the arched doorway that shows off a huge study with more books than I've ever seen in my life in one room. A fire glows from an old stone fireplace, casting dancing light and shadows across the gray and blue rug. Silver sconces glitter with burning candles, the place more haunting than the rest of the mansion that I've seen.

Intricately carved double doors hide another room where the music trickles in from. I straighten my shoulders and strut directly to them.

"Jewel, give me a minute." Orlando's voice hums over the music.

I don't. Instead, I twist the handle of the brass knob and crack it open. Austin touches my shoulder to pull me back, but I shrug away from him and push the door open completely.

"Out!" a masculine voice yells. But it's not Orlando. It's Hayden.

I catch sight of him standing next to Orlando in the middle of the room, his arm extended while Orlando drinks straight from his vein.

Orlando pulls back, his eyes flashing silver. I expect him to yell at me too, but all he does is drop Hayden's arm and smile at me, his lips stained red. "You're excused, Mr. Andrei. Find Brayla and she'll assure my portion of our deal."

Deal? Looks like Hayden is exchanging blood to get something he wants. He glowers at me. If my guys weren't standing nearby, Hayden would most definitely push past me and say whatever terrible thoughts about me linger on his mind.

"Close the door behind you, Mr. Andrei," Orlando calls.

Hayden slams the door without another word.

And I suddenly wish he hadn't. I wish I had better sense than to come here to confront the jerk that has been stalking and messing with my life—the same jerk that has answers.

Orlando remains in his spot, studying me so intensely that I shift and reach out to grab onto Austin because he stands the closest. "Don't be afraid, precious Jewel. We are all now allies."

"At what cost?" I ask, finally finding my nerve to look at Orlando directly.

"That's yet to be decided." Orlando reaches up and touches my cheek. "How things turn out for everyone will depend on you."

"Me?"

He nods. "Just be happy that I'm giving you a choice."

ANSWERS

I SIT BETWEEN KINGSTON'S LEGS, resting my back against his chest. Austin and Diego each sit in their own chairs beside me with Orlando across from us. The cozy sitting area gives me a view of the rest of his room with a king-sized bed, a walk-in wardrobe, and a bathroom with an old claw tub with an attached shower sprayer that hangs on the wall above it.

"Does Brayla sleep here?" I ask, peering around. Nothing reminds me of her, and I can't see any feminine clothing in the closet from my position.

"No."

I stare at Orlando, expecting him to say more, but he

doesn't.

"Why not?"

"Jewel, every coven has their own infrastructure and dynamic. Until you're a part of mine, you will not be privy to that sort of information."

Well, shit. "You say that like I will be."

"It is your choice."

I frown and twist to look at Austin first. "I don't even know what to say to that. You know I'm a..." I let my voice trail off.

Orlando leans closer, his blue eyes flashing silver. "You're a guest here. So are your matches. But with saying that, I'll offer them the same courtesy and options, but under one condition."

"That always seems to be the case," I mutter.

"They must share you with me."

I hop up from Diego's lap. "Fuck that."

"Jewel, wait." Orlando materializes in front of me.

"What for? You're a friggin' asshole monster. You came into my life and screwed everything up. You turned my best friend into a lunatic who murdered my dad. You took my sister from Haven Springs. I almost died because of you in the hands of a shadow dweller."

"We do things that we have to in this world. Donor Life Corp made sure of it," he says.

"Fuck them," I say, pushing past him to rush to the door. "And fuck you. Come on, guys. I can't do this."

"If you leave, you'll no longer be a guest in this house. I will no longer offer you my protection, Jewel. I'm offering your matches a new coven. Without one, they'll be outcasts. Shadow vampires."

"And we'll be fine."

"Are you willing to risk your life, and theirs, to find out? Have you asked them what they want to do?"

I blink a few times, angry tears burning my eyes.

"There is only so much they can do to protect you. They don't understand how delicate your situation is or how to properly take care of you. Your father failed you by trying to give you a human life when he knew you deserved more. He turned you into a donor."

"He did the best he could for my family," I say, my throat burning.

He shakes his head. "It's never been about your family, Jewel."

"You're lying."

"Your father abandoned you."

I bare my teeth at him in anger. "You stole him. You forced me to join the Blood Match Program. All of this is your fault."

"I did what I had to do to save you."

"Save me? *Save* me?" My voice rises in pitch, fury boiling through me.

The world spins and my back hits the wall. Three deep growls sound out, and Kingston, Diego, and Austin close the distance, each putting a hand on Orlando. He flashes his fangs at me, his eyes lighting silver, but just as quickly, he composes himself. "Your father would have rather given you to the rebels, who would've seen to it you had a short life rather than one with everything you deserved. I stopped him. For you."

"I don't understand," I whisper, his words sinking in.

"Jewel, you're an anomaly."

I glance at my guys. "Because my dad vaccinated me against vampire venom?"

He remains expressionless. "You weren't vaccinated."

"What do you mean?" Austin asks, speaking up.

Orlando shakes his head. "I can't give away all my secrets now, can I?"

Swinging my hand out, I slap Orlando across the face and push him back. My sudden strength catches him off guard. He doesn't have the chance to move before I land on top of him, grip the front of his shirt, and sucker-punch him in the jaw.

He flips me off him onto the floor and holds me down. Blood drips from his split lip and onto my face, making me freeze. The sweet, tantalizing scent snaps something feral inside me, and I thrash, trying to push him up.

"Stay back!" Orlando yells to my guys.

"You asshole!" I scream, clawing my nails into his wrists. "Don't listen to him," I plead to Kingston. I turn my gaze to Austin and Diego. "Please, get him off. Make him let me go."

None of them moves, fear lining their eyes. But I can't tell if they're afraid of Orlando or me. Maybe the both of us.

Warm droplets of sweet liquid splash on my lips, and my tongue darts to lick them without my permission. I gasp a breath, my whole body reacting to the blood but not in the same way as it does with my guys. Something's different. Things seem clearer. I feel stronger almost.

I ram my hands into Orlando's chest and knock him off me, sending him crashing into a chair. Whipping my head up, I peer around the room in search of the weapon I don't remember Orlando taking from me. It sparkles under the chandelier like my last beacon of hope before the whole world turns into a shit show. Scrambling for it, I scoop it off the ground and launch myself at Orlando.

"Jewel, stop!" Austin flies at me, hooking his arms to my waist. "Please. You need to stop."

"I can't."

Kingston grabs me from Austin and holds me in his arms. "Babe, please. Look."

Spinning me around, he faces me toward the mirror hanging above the dresser. I startle at the sight of my glowing silver eyes, my bared teeth, the blood still spotting my face. I almost look like a shadow vampire but without the fangs. Except my guys aren't scared of them. Everyone is nervous as all get-out.

"What's wrong with me?" I say, my voice coming out as a whimper. "I'm a monster. You guys are scared of me."

Austin and Diego close the space to me, but Orlando stays in his spot across the room.

"We're not scared of you," Diego says first.

"You are."

Austin clutches my face. "No, definitely not. I'll figure this out. If you don't want to stay here, then we'll go."

I groan and cover my eyes with my hands. "I don't know what to do. I've ruined your lives. I've ruined everything."

"Knock that shit off," Kingston says. "You haven't messed up anything."

Diego pulls my hands away and draws his finger under my eyes, smearing my tears. "You've helped us see things we couldn't have without you."

"But now we have nothing."

Kingston sighs. "You're seriously going to make me get all cheesy on you? Because, babe, we have each other. Fuck, I don't know what the hell is different about you, but I love it. And I love you. We can survive on each other. Who cares if you get a little...wild. Austin used to be psycho as hell, and we still kept him around."

I puff out my bottom lip.

Kingston pokes it. "But with saying that, you should know that my capability might only extend to you. As much as I hate it, I can't promise a good life for Dana and

Fallon, not without the assurance of a coven and someone of influence. I'm sorry for being such a disappointment."

"You're not, Kingston. None of you have disappointed me...I just—" I frown. "I'm scared."

"Of what?" Austin asks.

"Orlando," Diego says, answering for me.

I nod. Leaning close to them, I whisper, "What if he's worse than Mitchell? Mitchell said he's the one who nearly destroyed humanity."

The three of them glance to each other and then Kingston whispers, "I don't know if I believe anything Mitchell's said anymore."

Diego nods. "And it could be possible that Orlando is worse, but I doubt it. He could have done a lot of damage already and he hasn't. He's offering us a new life."

"How do you know he'll keep his word?"

He shrugs. "He's not asking us to swear loyalty to him. He's asking us to allow him to show loyalty to us. To you."

"He wants you to share me," I say, shivering. "This doesn't work like that."

"Damn straight it doesn't," Kingston says, squeezing my hand. "And we'd never ask you to do that. Ever."

"But you want to stay." He doesn't have to say so for me to know. I can see it on Diego and Austin's faces too.

"Not if you didn't want to," Austin says, tipping his head toward me.

"I just don't know," I whisper.

"There's only one way to know for sure," Kingston says.

I turn my gaze to him. "How?"

"Orlando can remove the block he put on your mind." Kingston says the words loud enough so that Orlando can hear. "You'll remember things then."

I tighten my jaw, fear sneaking up on me. "I—I don't know. What if things change?"

"They won't," Austin says. "Like we said before, we know you love us and we love you."

"I—" I swallow the burning in my throat.

Orlando risks stepping closer, keeping his hands at his sides. "I'll offer you a deal, Jewel, but this is the only one. Understand?"

I glare at him. "No."

His eyes flash silver. "As stubborn as your father."

"What's the deal?" Kingston asks, speaking up.

I jerk my gaze to him, and he holds up his hands in surrender.

Orlando keeps his attention on me. "I'll allow you to stay under my protection as guests for one month. As a trial."

"What's the catch?" I ask.

"Your matches can help me establish my place among Donor Life Corp," Orlando says.

Kingston covers my mouth with his hand, cutting me off. Spinning me around, he corners me against the farthest wall and blocks me from Orlando's view. Austin and Diego close the space and surround me, all staring at me with expressionless faces.

"That's a good deal. It'll give us time to figure things out," Kingston whispers. "We can get answers."

"He's right, Jewel," Austin says. "It could also leave Donor Life Corp and Mitchell floundering. Anything to weaken their power over us. Because right now, we don't have any. The only reason Mitchell hasn't stormed this place is because Orlando carries the same kind of back-world power. He's ancient. A vampire before the uprising."

I twist my lips. "Are you sure about this?"

Diego nods. "It's a good plan."

I release a breath. "Then okay."

My guys pull away from me and allow me to face Orlando again. "Fine. One month. My guys will help you with Donor Life Corp and we get to stay here."

Orlando tightens his jaw. "That will cover them, Jewel, but not you or your family. Someone must pay their dues."

"What?" I ask.

All three of my guys flash their fangs.

Orlando doesn't back down. "All I ask is for time alone with you and your blood."

"No deal," Kingston says. "Helping you with Donor Life Corp should be enough."

Orlando waves his hand at the door. "Then show yourselves out."

A dozen emotions cross through my guys' faces, and the three of them close the space to me. I knew my dad was right. We sometimes have to do things we don't want to. I should be used to it by now.

Kingston, Diego, and Austin would do anything for me. They gave up their lives as Divines for me. They protect me. They mean the world to me. And I promised that I'd do the same. Because I know they worry about the world outside us. They fear Mitchell and even the shadows. They'd never ask me to do this, to give Orlando time or my blood, but that doesn't mean I shouldn't do it. Because if this is a way to take care of them, to assure their protection, to assure my family's, then it's not even something I need to think about.

I always thought that people do what they have to do to survive. I always thought that was how I lived my life, but I know it's more. It's what I can do for others. For my family. Because without them, I don't even know who I am. I'll do whatever it takes to see to it that we're all okay.

Kingston tries to pull me to the door, but I stop him in his tracks. I look to each of my guys. "I want to take the deal."

"But Jewel, you said—"

"I said I'd always protect you. I promised you forever. Even if that might not be possible, I want to promise you the rest of my life."

Kingston scoops me up in his arms. "If you change

your mind, we'll leave."

I bob my head. "We better."

Austin, Diego, and Kingston all turn toward Orlando. "We accept your deal."

Orlando glances to me, and I stroll forward. "I accept your deal under two conditions."

He raises his eyebrow. "It depends on what."

I take a deep breath. "You can't manipulate my mind."

"Without your permission. I will not make a bargain you'll ask me to break."

Cocky asshole. "Fine. You also have to give me some answers."

"I'll allow you to ask one question right now. The rest will have to wait for our time together."

"Just one?" I can't believe I'm whining, but shit. This friggin' sucks. A dozen thoughts cross my mind. I want to know exactly what's wrong with me and what my dad did. I want to know how my family even got involved with him. And why he chose Brayla.

But then one question comes to my mind, one that I suddenly need to know the answer to right now as I stare at the anticipation crossing Diego, Austin, and Kingston's faces. They have just as many questions as me, maybe more, but there's one that has been bothering them since the moment the venom didn't take and the moment we thought I was immune.

I lick my lips. "Will I ever be able to transform into a

vampire?"

Orlando smirks and reaches out to run his finger over my mouth like he can imagine me with fangs. "Now why would you want that?"

"I promised forever to Diego, Kingston, and Austin. I want to assure it." I turn my gaze to look at each of them, their anticipation in his response as great as mine.

"Right, the Blood Vows."

"Just answer my question," I snap.

"No, you'll never fully transform, Jewel," he says, his voice soft like he's afraid of my reaction.

I sniffle, my heart clenching at the words.

Orlando touches my wet cheek. "But don't worry. You're better than any vampire. Just as strong. Unfazed by sunlight. Regenerative. Dangerous. Immortal."

"Immortal?" Austin asks, taking my hand.

I inhale a small breath, shock and confusion washing over me. "What he said."

Flashing his fangs, Orlando narrows his eyes at me. "If you can manage to survive."

EPILOGUE

COVEN BROTHERS

"YOU CAN'T BE SERIOUS," I say, crossing my arms.

Kingston pops out his bottom lip. "Super serious."

"But it's only for an hour, tops. Getting a meeting with Viorica has proven more difficult than we anticipated, and she demanded that the three of us accompany Orlando," Diego says.

"It's a trap," I say.

Austin shrugs. "Could be."

Kingston nuzzles his face into my neck. "That's why you're staying here."

I pull away and place my hands on his chest. "No, you don't. You can't tell me that I'm staying here to stay safe.

You know the safest place I can be is with you."

Looking at Diego, Kingston says, "Our girl is such a romantic. You guys go. I'm staying. Don't worry, I'll assure to implement the three S-words to assure everything is great. Jewel will be safe, satisfied, and satiated while you're gone."

I smirk at him. "You sure? I'm feeling bitey."

He snaps his teeth. "Me too."

Diego smacks Kingston in the shoulder and pulls him away before I let him sink more into me for all the cuddles. "If anyone is staying, it's me. You're better at negotiations and Austin will assure you don't get ripped apart by a Widow."

I hold my arms out to Diego. "I don't care who stays with me."

He chuckles. "I am the best at satia—"

Austin pulls down the collar of his shirt, making me blush like crazy. "You sure?" he asks, cutting off Diego.

"Fuck, I'm out," Kingston says, poking my chin. "You better take the hour to control that sexy mouth of yours. I want it all over me when I get back."

"Not a chance," Austin says. "Jewel and I have plans."

Kingston tightens his lips. "She might cancel."

I roll my eyes. "Kingston."

"Don't think I'll ever give up."

"You've made that obvious, dude."

Kingston winks at me and opens the door to find Orlando raising his hand to knock on the other side. Orlando smiles at me, and I force myself to return a smirk only to be polite. I don't even want to think about last night and how we spent it sitting in front of the TV without saying much. I couldn't summon the nerve, and he practically tortured me with awkwardness. I don't even know how I'll survive hanging out with him over and over again. But I have to. I promised myself I'd try for my guys.

Orlando pulls out a metal thermos from his jacket pocket. "I have something for you."

I cross the room and take the container, eyeing it without reacting. Giving me his blood is supposedly to ensure that he holds up his end of the bargain not to manipulate my mind without my permission.

"Thank you," I say, setting it on my night table.

"Are you three ready?" Orlando asks, turning his attention away from me.

"One of us needs to stay with Jewel," Kingston says.

"My brother, you know the stipulation. It must be the four of us. But don't worry. Jewel will be safe. Brayla will assure it. Her family is already waiting to share a meal with her," Orlando says.

I crinkle my nose at the fact that he referred to Kingston as brother. I don't know if I'll ever get used to it, but it's all a part of the whole coven thing. Orlando is setting them up to be equals and not above them like Mitchell always assured. It weirds me out, but most vampire customs do.

Austin spins me to him and kisses the frown from my mouth. "It's just one hour. I promise we'll have an amazing night as soon as I get back, okay?"

I bob my head and kiss him again. "I expect dessert."

He chuckles. "Only if I can feed it to you."

"Deal."

Diego hovers close, waiting for me to turn to him, and I fall into his open arms and bury my face in his chest. "Be safe."

"I will be. And so will you. You're a badass, remember. A better fighter than Kingston," he murmurs, kissing me.

Kingston growls. "Not quite, but okay."

Diego turns his head. "Want to bet?"

"Fuck yeah. I'll wrestle Jewel any day."

I giggle. "And let me win."

"If you take your clothes—"

Reaching up, I cover his mouth.

He licks my palm before kissing it. "All right. We gotta go. You better be prepared. You and me in..." He glances at his tablet. "Tenish hours."

Orlando extends his hand to me, and I let him clasp mine and bring it to his lips. "I assure you that we'll return safely. You have my word."

I consider telling him that I only care about Diego, Kingston, and Austin returning, but suppress my sarcasm. "Try not to have too much fun with the Vaduvas."

"You know we won't," Kingston says.

The four of them disappear, leaving me alone in my room. I close my eyes and listen to their footsteps fade before shrugging into my hoodie. Grabbing my folding knife, I hide it in my pocket and head to the door.

My cousins' laughter trickles into the hallway from their shared room, and I smile to myself. I love hearing them. I love being so close, knowing they're safe. It's one of the best things I've gotten out of this weird ass arrangement with Orlando. It's only been days, but I can already see a future with my guys here.

"Jewel."

I startle at the sound of Brayla's voice. I didn't even hear her coming. "Whoa, shit. Don't do that."

She materializes in front of me and smirks. "Sorry. I thought you could hear me coming."

"No, I..." I let my words trail off. That's weird.

"You didn't drink Orlando's blood, did you?" she asks. "When did you last drink from your boy toys?"

I blink at her question. Why would she ask?

"A couple of hours, right? I heard Orlando ask them to have you fast some. He knew you wouldn't drink his blood otherwise. I was counting on it."

Fear cascades over me, and I spin and try to run back to my room. Brayla cuts me off and covers my mouth with her hand to stifle my scream.

"Hayden is heading to your cousins' room. As long as

you don't make a sound, they'll be okay. Don't worry. I'm not going to hurt you, either. You're my best friend."

I gasp a few breaths into her hand, trying to suppress my oncoming scream.

"Just relax and trust me, okay?" she says, loosening her hold on me.

I nod even though there is no friggin' way I'm going to trust her.

She spins me around. "Good. Now, come on. We don't have much time." Extending her hand, she waits for me to link my fingers through hers.

Brayla lifts me off my feet, and the world blurs around us. Streaks of light dance across my vision, and then the warm air cools, and I catch a hint of nature—the freshness of being outside.

The world comes to a halt, and I clutch my head, trying my best to orient myself. I hate moving fast, but especially to unfamiliar places. Glancing around, I take in the dark forest and hear the sound of running water from somewhere. Possibly the river that runs by the estate.

Tugging me forward, Brayla guides me deeper into the night until I can barely see the moon shining above the dense trees. Soft light glows from a cabin window, the structure eerie, almost haunted so far into the forest.

"Where are we?" I ask, swallowing to suppress my fear.

"It's a surprise," Brayla says. "I've been waiting for-friggin'-ever for this, but your guys never leave."

I furrow my brows. "Huh?"

Brayla's eyes flash silver at me, and she smiles, dragging me the rest of the way to the cabin. I pant, trying to catch my breath from the exertion. Sweat prickles on my forehead, and I clutch the knife in my pocket.

Raising her hand, Brayla knocks on the thick wooden door. "It's me," she calls. "I've brought Jewel."

The door swings inward, and I stare in shock at Mr. Diggs. Brayla swore he had gone missing, claiming the exact thing my guys told me in Haven Springs. Donor Life Corp expected him to return to get Mrs. Diggs. I should've known, but I don't even think Orlando knew. "You've come alone?"

Brayla nods. "Just like you told me."

"How's your mother?" he asks, flicking his gaze to mine.

"She's okay, Dad. Dougie, too. We have people watching out for them."

Mr. Diggs nods his head. "Good girl. I'm so happy you could stop by." Turning his attention to me, Mr. Diggs smiles. "You too, Jewel. We've been waiting months for this."

I frown. "What are you talking about?"

A door slams, drawing my attention away from Mr. Diggs. I take an automatic step back toward the door, my heart beating wildly, so frantic that I'm sure it'll crash through my back at any second.

"Jewel. You're safe."

My tongue dries, and I can't force my mouth to work.

"Come here. Let me get a look at you. I need to see you're okay with my own eyes."

I blink, trying to stop the tears from falling. It's been a while since I've cried, and I hate to do so now. "I don't understand."

"You must have a lot of questions."

Rushing forward, I throw my arms around the man I thought I'd never see again, the man who I thought I would never forgive for abandoning me. But seeing him now, standing right before my eyes, none of it matters. None of it seems important.

"Dad, I don't understand," I whisper, letting him embrace me. "You're here."

"Yes, honey. And I'm so proud of how brave you've become."

I squeeze him tighter. "I can't believe it. I can't believe you're alive."

To be continued...

Thank you so much for reading *Blood Feud*! To stay up-to-date on new and future releases, including *Blood Loss,* sign up for Ginna Moran's newsletter or follow her on Amazon. Join her Facebook Group called Paranormal Center for Matches and Mates for sneak peeks, bonus content, giveaways, and fun!

OTHER SERIES BY GINNA MORAN

REVERSE HAREM

The Divine Vampire Heirs Series
The Royale Vampire Heirs Series
Academy of Vampire Heirs Series
The Pack Mates of Lunar Crest Series

PARANORMAL

Call of the Ocean Series
Demon Watcher Series
Demon Within Series
Destined for Dreams Series
Finding Nate Series
Going Ghostly Series
Spark of Life Series
The Merman's Spark Series
When Souls Collide Series

CONTEMPORARY

Falling into Fame Series
Life After Lila

ABOUT GINNA MORAN

GINNA MORAN IS a writer from sunny Southern California. She started writing poetry as a teenager in a spiral notebook that she still has tucked away on her desk today. Her love of writing grew after she graduated high school, and she completed her first unpublished manuscript at age eighteen.

When she realized her love of writing was her life's passion, she studied literature at Mira Costa College in Northern San Diego. Besides writing novels, she was senior editor, content manager, and image coordinator for Crescent House Publishing Inc. for four years.

Aside from Ginna's professional life, she enjoys binge watching TV, playing pretend with her daughter, and cuddling with her dogs. Some of her favorite things include chocolate, anything that glitters, cheesy jokes, and organizing her bookshelf.

Ginna Moran loves to hear from her readers so visit her online at www.GinnaMoran.com. You can also find her on Facebook, Twitter, Instagram, and Snapchat. To stay up-to-date on new releases, sign up to her newsletter. You'll not only get exclusive access to extra stories, but you'll be able to participate in monthly giveaways!

Ginna Moran is currently hard at work on her next novel.